SENSATION MACHINES

SENSATION MACHINES

ADAM WILSON

SOHO

Published by
Soho Press, Inc.
227 W 17th Street
New York, NY 10011

Library of Congress Cataloging-in-Publication Data

Wilson, Adam (Adam Zachary), 1982- author.
Sensation machines / Adam Wilson.
New York, NY : Soho, [2020]
Identifiers: LCCN 2019059162

ISBN 978-1-64129-165-1
eISBN 978-1-64129-166-8

Subjects: 1. Political fiction. 2. Black humor (Literature)
3. Satire.
Classification: LCC PS3623.I57779 S46 2020 | DDC 813/.6—dc23

Interior design by Janine Agro, Soho Press, Inc.

Printed in the United States of America

10 9 8 7 6 5 4 3 2 1

For Sarah

CONTENTS

SELFIES

Once again at the beginning I am down on Front Street,
by the old drugstore, the pharmacy where all healing starts.

—Alice Notley

MICHAEL

ON MONDAY, THE THIRD OF December, roughly twenty-four hours before my oldest and closest friend would be murdered, I woke with sinus pain, an itchy scalp, and the accumulated clog of post-nasal drip. At 2 A.M. I'd taken a Trazodone—a mild antidepressant prescribed as a sleep aid—and in the cocoon of the drug's after-glow, as dawn shot itself through our casement windows and a bacon scent blew in from downstairs, I watched my wife sleep: pillowless, chin tilted to ceiling like a dental patient's.

Wendy's nostrils flared on each exhale and she issued grunts in a lower register than she used in waking life. Her speaking voice is affectedly high-pitched, the product of being five foot ten and embarrassed about it, but these grunts came from her gut, from the bile-scorched basement of her intestines. Most of the bedbug bites had scabbed off her forehead and cheeks, but some leaked pus and blood from where she'd scratched. Still, she was stunning, like an actress made up for a zombie flick, who, despite the artist's best efforts with latex and greasepaint, remains implausibly lovely. No scabs could distract from the neat plane of her nose, or the buoyant, red curls spread across our new SureGuard anti-allergen sheets.

We'd discovered the bedbugs the previous week, and our apartment had since been emptied of clothing and other pos-sibly contaminated items. In the absence of curtains, the sun now striped the wall where our dresser once sat, a Civil War era showpiece bought above market value in a heated eBay auction. The image brought to mind the afternoon, three years before, when Wendy and I stood in the empty loft and surveyed the space, bright with promise, soon to be filled with everything we owned.

Most of that stuff was still here—Wendy's Miró and Kandinsky prints, my books on hip-hop, Apple products and other electronics, cookware and baby gear, plus our collections: nineties cassingles, ceramic hands, antique hat mannequins, deadstock Air Jordans, inherited Judaica—but the room felt bare, more warehouse than home, though here we were, inhabiting, and here was the cat, leaping onto the air bed where she perched atop Wendy's head. It looked like Wendy was wearing one of those sable hats that protect the bald domes of oligarchs from frosty Moscow winters. She threw the crying cat across the loft.

The cat landed on four feet and scurried toward the bathroom. A gaunt, acrobatic animal with silver fur and green eyes the color of a faded military rucksack, she was a stray I'd found picking at garbage outside our building a few weeks prior. The cat's aggression toward Wendy spoke to an interspecies female territoriality, and my wife, defensive, had later accused the cat of being bedbug patient zero. Wendy still appeared to be asleep.

I leaned in and kissed her. Our accounts were overdrawn, creditors called me by the hour, my job was in limbo, and Wendy knew none of this, but at least we appeared to be bedbug free.

IT WAS EARLY WINTER, AND would reach eighty by noon, but at 6:30 A.M. bodega owners braced themselves in jackets and hats as they rolled up their chains to signal the commencement of commerce, diurnal music as yet undisturbed by the market crash that had put the dollar in freefall and Clayton & Sons, the bank where I worked, on the verge of insolvency. There would be no bailout this time, and in this panicked climate, a proposal for Universal Basic Income had passed through Congress and was headed to the Senate for final approval.

TV news flashed shuttered windows and boarded doorways, but here, in my corner of upmarket Brooklyn, things appeared status quo. The day's first delivery drones descended from tree height to eye level before lowering landing gear and making soft contact outside the remaining brownstones and the high-rise condos that had mostly replaced them. Pigeons scattered, wary of the claws that carried shrink-wrapped Gap sweaters, flatbread sandwiches, and other objects impossible to print at home. Earlier drones were sci-fi chic—floating orbs and baby Death Stars—but people found them sinister. The solution was to design the objects after actual birds, and now it was Hitchcock twenty-four seven. I turned up Court Street toward the Brooklyn Bridge.

I SHOULD MENTION THAT I'M not from around here. I was raised off an exit ramp in East Coast exurbia, where every gas station sells Red Sox crapaphernalia and the strip malls aren't yet full franchise; they're still half occupied by local bars and burger joints, blue-lit, filled with Carhartted Brosephs and their female companions—Tara, Britney, Aurora, etc.—sassed in green eyeshadow, in beerlight shadow, in Bud Light soft-stupor, whittling away their middle twenties with wet eyes and dry skin, wet bars and dry heaves, and Japanese trucks that somehow still run after all those miles spewing dust and American fumes.

Of course, that's a romantic half-truth because (1) I'm from the Berkshires, twenty minutes from the quaint town of Lenox, which is home to both Tanglewood and a community of retired Bostonians who antique on Saturdays, then head to Williamstown Sundays for a taste of the *theatre*. Their cottages are dotted with Rockwellian Americana (purchased from the nearby Rockwell museum), scented by potpourri and sawdust, cinders in fireplace, local kale simmering on stovetop, steeping itself in red wine reduction as grandma dusts off the viola, prepped to serenade grandkids with riffage from the Charles Ives songbook; and (2) my family was different, not your typical townies, what with gamer dad, immigrant mom, face-tattooed sister, and my Long Island cousins calling me toward femininity with their floriated perfumes and ethnic rainbow of American Girl dolls.

Not that we were special. In most ways, I resembled my classmates, who lived in Colonial-style homes that spiraled out from the abandoned factory. And though the local recession stayed in remission through the early aughts, the current crisis had brought unemployment back to where it was when GE pulled out in '91 leaving ten thousand jobless, including my dad. Terms like *highbrow* and *lowbrow* had ceased to have meaning in a place where, no matter one's tastes, you were stalled in what was outmodedly called the working class. Pittsfield was a microcosm for what I'd come to think of as the Great American Unibrow, an unruly line that connected East and West across the painted plains dotted with the same mediocre takes on what had once been regional cuisines. You could get a Southwest-style quesadilla from Seattle to the southern tip of Florida, and find no difference in the chipotle rub or soggy Jack cheese. So, I left for New York, forgoing Audubon trails for the feeling I get on the Brooklyn Bridge at dawn, the feeling I got as I walked and scratched and called across that dirty river for someone to save me.

WHEN I HIT MANHATTAN, I was soaked in sweat. Duane Reade was alive with the faint smell of carpet shampoo and the insectoid traffic of the day walkers, middle-aged men in Canal Street bling and velour tracksuits, which were mostly maroon for some reason. These guys were everywhere. They loitered on subway platforms and outside bodegas, even in rain, sipping cigars, tapping canes, and scaring tourists with their scars and shiny watches. But they weren't criminals, just unemployed men, vaguely lame, with a healthy share of love and other problems, or so it could be gleaned from the baskets filled with lipstick, prophylactics, and reams of wrapping paper. Consumer spending had bottomed hard, but people still paid for cosmetics. Vanity, it turns out, is the last sturdy pillar of society.

By the time I reached the counter, my basket was filled with what I'd need to make it through the day. Ten ChapSticks, two bags of cough drops—one mint, one cherry—Tylenol, Advil, calamine, aloe, moisturizer, deodorant, Sudafed, NyQuil, DayQuil, Benadryl, Gas-X, condoms, D vitamins, a men's multivitamin for prostate health, an issue of *Men's Health*, the *New York Times*, AA batteries, eight packs of Emergen-C (two orange, two lemon/lime, four cranberry), one photo frame, Rogaine, reading glasses (+3), Band-Aids, bacitracin, nicotine patches, nicotine gum, and two packs of cigarettes.

The checkout clerk was a college-age woman with bright white teeth and an assortment of neck and arm tattoos. Her face bore the cratered remains of teenage acne, a piercing sat bindi-like between her eyes, and a dyed pink stripe ran at a slant from her forehead's peak to the tip of her bangs. I had chosen her line, despite its length, over the six self-checkout machines. A recent federal law mandated that retailers keep at least one human employee on premises. This was a meaningless gesture, the vestige of an immuno-compromised jobs bill. One employee per store would not put a dent in unemployment. Still, I'm a people person.

Andrea K. took me in like I was a specimen from some alien world, the last remains of an earlier evolutionary stage. I was wearing the one wrinkled suit I'd saved from quarantine, and with my three-day beard and bedbug scabs, I must have given the impression of someone in mourning, or someone in global transit, or a killer on the lam in an old film. Suffice to say, there were problems at home: with Wendy, with myself, with modern-day America that sliced our lives into curated blocks hubbed around an eighty-hour workweek—at least for those, like us, still gainfully employed. Whisk in trips to Pure Barre and therapy, plus allotted minutes for shopping, streaming, and sleep, and the sum was a doomed approximation of marriage, unprecedented by parents.

My own parents were governed by the social laws of an earlier era in which Adderall and a competitive job market hadn't inflamed the work ethos, and the task of procreation had imbued all else with a whisper of profanity. Now *procreation* was its own profanity between Wendy and me. It was a word we ignored, or spoke only in bedtime darkness, in the loose mumblings of pre-dream.

I'd wanted a child from an early age, sophomore year, when I first met Wendy. I bought into the laugh-tracked fantasy of fatherhood, saw it as the end at which my future means would gain nonmonetary meaning. Or maybe I just wanted to please my parents.

Wendy wasn't as eager, and wouldn't be until our mid-thirties, when her feeds filled with friends holding newborns like mucus-slicked trophies. What followed was scheduled, utilitarian sex, which, like pizza, was finished in seconds and left stains on the couch. After, we would cuddle and binge-watch *Project Runway*, or read aloud from a book of baby names. These were happy, hopeful times, and when they culminated, soon after, in the desired result—nausea, swollen nipples, and a faint blue cross on a pregnancy test—we felt elated and deserving, like Olympic medalists whose discipline and training had paid off. A few days later the pregnancy was lost.

It was the first in a string of early miscarriages, until we found ourselves passing forty—frustrated, exhausted, losing hope. For years, doctors had suggested IVF, but Wendy was hesitant. The treatment was expensive and invasive and how shitty would it feel if even this potential remedy resulted in failure? I pushed and she yielded, and though she'll never forgive me, the treatment did work. After seven years of trying, Wendy carried past the three-month mark.

Like many parents-to-be, we left Manhattan for Brooklyn, staking out a gentrifier's guilty claim on a Boerum Hill penthouse. There, we prepared for our retro-nuclear unit, bought the necessary accessories, rubbed her belly and sang to it, my out-of-tune baritone penetrating her epidermal walls, piping Boyz II Men covers into the almost-baby's watery bedroom. We took birthing classes and researched strollers, bought tiny Air Jordans and spent evenings babyproofing the loft. When Amazon sent someone to assemble the crib, I watched like a hawkeyed foreman. We could not have been more prepared.

Our daughter wasn't technically stillborn—the monitor showed a heartbeat when she emerged—and the term is a misnomer anyway. So much is moving, like the slithering liquid surrounding the body, or the doctors' and nurses' scurrying hands, creating a charade of motion, a defiant charade against the situation's fixity. And I don't know if Wendy knew something was wrong when the room fell silent in the absence of our daughter's cry, but either way I saw her first, this beautiful human, crowning into air she couldn't find a way to breathe.

ANDREA K. CONTINUED TO SCAN my selections. She moved with metric precision, never pausing to price-check an item or rotate a package to locate the barcode. In a theater at Vassar, this might have played as modern dance, a misguided commentary on the Tao of retail. Here, in Manhattan, it was no more or less than that endangered species, the low-wage job.

"Morning," she said in cheery voice. She had a sympathetic countenance, Andrea K., and I liked her tattoos—a kinematic schema of a dragonfly's wings, slot-machine cherries, the injunction *Look Alive*—which, with their stylistic mishmash, spoke to the fickle whims of the human heart.

"Taking a trip?" she asked, as I bagged my stash.

It had occurred to me that Wendy and I could use a weekend away. To get out on the road, bunk down at a boutique hotel upstate. We'd drink champagne and order room service sundaes, a last blast on my company card before the company burned or I got canned and they killed my expense account.

"Thinking about it," I said. "I've been wanting to take my wife somewhere nice. Where would you go this time of year?"

The cashier eyed my crumpled outfit, my year's supply of Rogaine, my bottle of two hundred prostate-health pills.

"Preventative," I said, in reference to the pills, or perhaps to the lot. But she was admiring my suit, a Crayola-blue, shawl lapel Fashion Week sample. Kanye had worn the same one during the pro-union rant at the Grammys that announced his return to the political left.

"That a Yeezy?" she said.

I tugged my lapel like it might make the jacket magically unwrinkle. I wasn't sure whether to be proud or embarrassed by the item's exorbitant price. She handed back my Visa, which her machine had declined.

"It's telling me to cut this card in half."

I gave her my Amex instead.

"So where might a frugal guy like me take his wife?"

The answer was obvious to Andrea K.

"Storm King, dude. It's only, like, twenty bucks to get in, and chicks Instagram the shit out of that place."

She was referring to an outdoor museum, a couple hours upstate, that was a popular setting for romantic montages in films about the love lives of the Brooklyn precariat. I hadn't taken Andrea K. for the type. In my own youth, her look would have been labeled alternative, and carried with it a particular set of assumptions, one being that its owner held a healthy disdain for the status markers of bourgeois life. But young people these days didn't buy into such rigid segmentation; they just wanted to Instagram the shit out of stuff. So did Wendy. Many times she'd suggested that we drive up to Storm King. I'd always deferred, wary of cliché, or maybe only traffic on the Palisades Parkway.

Today would not be an exception. But later, after everything went down, I wondered what might have turned out differently if I'd heeded the cashier's advice. In this alternate history, I convince Wendy to play hooky from work, and I whisk her upstate. In this alternate history, humbled before nature and modernist sculpture, I find the courage to come clean about the millions of dollars that I lost on the market. In this alternate history, Wendy is angry, but after hours of open and honest discussion, she arrives at forgiveness. And in this alternate history, we hit traffic on our way back to Brooklyn, and Wendy never meets Lucas or lands the Project Pinky account, and my best friend, Ricky, skips the *Great Gatsby* party because I'm not there to be his wingman, and he avoids the riot, and he doesn't get murdered.

But I was not ready, just yet, to come clean. There was still time to fix things before Wendy found out. I had a plan, and I was heading to Ricky's to ask for his help.

Andrea K. ran my Amex, handed back a receipt. Her forearm, I noticed, featured a list of men's names: Albert, Sadeeq, Tino, Bartholomew. Each tattooed name was struck through with a line.

"Those guys take you to Storm King?"

"Bartholomew did."

"And?"

"It was nice."

"So what happened?"

She rolled her eyes. "One good deed," she explained, "does not a winner make." She studied my card before handing it back. "Are you a loser, Michael Mixner?"

I told her it remained to be seen.

WENDY

I WAS ALREADY THINKING OF leaving Michael by the time we found blood on the bedsheets. The amount was minuscule, a few dark dots. I assumed I was spotting.

There was more blood, the next day, on Michael's side of the bed. Michael said he'd cut himself shaving. We didn't connect the marks on our skin to these stains. The marks itched, and I'd falsely sourced them to dander allergies. Michael had recently brought home an itinerant tabby. As a child I was afraid of cats, their abject nihilism. I still am. At night, the unnamed cat gnawed my heels and toes. Sometimes she broke skin, another explanation for the blood.

When I uploaded photos of Michael's bites to MeMD.com, the range of responses was broad. There were fifty-four comments. One user suggested that Michael had a rare form of leprosy, previously contained to the sub-Saharan desert. Another suggested that Michael was a self-denying victim of spousal abuse. Six were spam posts offering sets of Don't Tread On Me windshield decals at a competitive price. Eleven members of the forum suspected bedbugs.

I blamed the cat and demanded her eviction. Michael defended the cat. The cat cowered. She looked guilty, but that's how cats look. We agreed to disagree. The cat was granted probation. An exterminator laid pesticide throughout our apartment. We took our vacuum-packed clothing to my father's storage space where it would sit for the recommended eighteen months. Our spoiled furniture littered the sidewalk. I left a note warning rummagers to steer clear. It was not an ideal moment for this drama.

WE WERE COURTING AN ENIGMATIC client at work, referred to on the books as Project Pinky. In lieu of an RFP, the client had provided a study syllabus of theoretically comparable marketing campaigns. The syllabus included familiar campaigns like Joe Camel and Just Do It, but also campaigns selling abstract commodities: Ronald Reagan's appropriation of Bruce Springsteen's "Born in the USA"; the public relations circus surrounding the O. J. Simpson trial. The final item was Aristophanes's *Lysistrata*, the Greek comedy about women who withhold sex from their husbands in an effort to end the Peloponnesian War.

The plan was to pitch our ingenuity by presenting updates on these historical campaigns. The client had offered an unprecedented $10,000 materials fee to cover preparation costs. It was unclear what materials we were meant to acquire—O. J.'s glove?—but the message came across: despite the absurdity of our assignment, Project Pinky was serious business. We had a week to prepare. The client would not be approaching other agencies. The account was ours to lose.

Communitiv.ly, where I worked, is a Think Tank for Creative Synergy and Digital Solutions. More simply, the company helps heritage brands engage with consumers on Facebook, Twitter, Tumblr, Ru.ffy, Pim-Pam, Twitch, and Instagram, and provides access to in-house strategists, as well as to a network of freelance designers, community managers, editors, journalists, programmers, videographers, and copywriters.

It is the network of freelancers that sets Communitiv.ly apart. Say, for instance, that your cosmetics company wants to set up an aspirational webzine that promotes a branded lifestyle and provides entry points for single-click purchase. Communitiv.ly will find a freelancer in its network to curate editorial content. Communitiv.ly will provide that editor with a database of underemployed fashion writers. Then Communitiv.ly will design, build, and optimize your site, create promotional communities on social media, launch traditional print, TV, and radio campaigns, and provide event planners and viral marketing experts to make sure the site's launch gets enough old-media coverage to incite traffic-fueling buzz. It's a one-stop shop, and it works because brands like Marc Jacobs and Revlon have more to spend on editorial projects, and can milk more revenue from them, than struggling old-media entities like Condé Hearst.

I'd heard people say that this was the future of journalism. What they meant was the end of journalism. Despite my active role in the razing, I was among its mourners. In ninth grade, while classmates tested their developing wiles in Spice Girls costumes and witchy lingerie, I went as Bob Woodward for Halloween. I must have been a sight: five-nine with a tangerine Jew-fro and pimples, wearing my dad's corduroy suit. I dressed my Welsh Springer Spaniel as Carl Bernstein.

In college, I covered student activism for the *Columbia Spectator.* I was both too cowardly and too skeptical to participate in the demonstrations that were a fixture of campus life. The protested causes weren't always commensurate with the protesters' zeal, and I sometimes wondered if the real cause wasn't the self-validation of those involved. I'm thinking, particularly, of a weeklong hunger strike devoted to curtailing fraternities from referring to beer pong by its insensitive alias, Beirut. I found the reporter's role empowering, a way to participate while maintaining a balance between distrust and support. I harbored hopes of putting truth to paper.

Project Pinky was something else. Lillian arrived in the mornings on three hours' sleep. Greg fine-tuned our General Deck, a PowerPoint presentation explaining our business model through buzzwords and animation. I mocked up a "Free O. J." fan page, complete with links to articles on police corruption and racial profiling, as well as a message board where people who'd been harassed by the LAPD could share their stories. Greg's shirts grew progressively more unbuttoned until, by week's end, a briar patch of black hair threatened to garrote anyone who stood too close. I combed interviews with Springsteen for quotes that might reiterate right-wing talking points if taken out of context. Lillian lost her voice screaming supposedly inspirational marketing clichés about team building that she'd found on a Tumblr dedicated to cherry-picking from a handful of marketing blogs that, in their turn, had cherry-picked from books by blog-anointed marketing gurus. The gurus were paraphrasing the founding fathers.

THE NIGHT BEFORE THE PITCH—THIS would be Sunday, the second of December, two days before Ricky's murder—Lillian invited me to her West Village townhouse for a once-more-unto-the-breach sort of sendoff. We sat on her balcony and watched the darkening sky. There was a bottle of Riesling uncorked on the table, half-eaten canapés, the roach of a joint from which I'd abstained. I'd spent ten minutes explaining *Lysistrata* to my stoned boss. Lillian lit a cigarette. Like many New Yorkers, she'd started smoking again when the embargo on Cuba's lung cancer vaccine was lifted. After reading the fine print regarding emphysema, throat cancer, and low rates of preventative efficacy, she was now, unsuccessfully, attempting to quit.

"So, they stop fucking their husbands," said Lillian. "And then expect them to *end* the war? These women clearly knew zilch about men."

Lillian had been married twice and this made her an expert. She had one child to show for it, Damien Earl, a living embodiment of every cliché about privileged urban youth. At eighteen, he'd participated in a reality TV program about privileged urban youth. He was currently finishing a semester in Milan.

After Damien's father ran off with the younger wife of a deceased Kuwaiti oil baron, Lillian swore off men, only to return amid this golden era of online dating. My boss was a fit and elegant fifty, subtly Botoxed, with sharp brown eyes and long natural lashes. She wore her hair in a chic, angular bob that flattered her narrow face and gave off a shimmering aura of money. In the current dating climate, these attributes weren't enough. We often spent lunch breaks swiping profiles on Kügr, but she rarely matched with anyone of interest. I used to wonder how I'd do, what currency my looks still carried. Since the death of our daughter, Nina, I'd noted a down-tilt in male attention. Men used to stare while I swam laps at the Red Hook pool. Now stretch marks scored my stomach. Wrinkles spidered from my eyes. Michael told me I looked beautiful. He was not an objective audience.

"It does seem shortsighted," I agreed.

"I mean, for one," Lillian continued, "they're acting without regard for their own interests. Everyone knows a soldier in the heat of battle is a maniac in the sack. And, for two, they're absolutely fucking deluded. Denying a man sex is the most surefire way to incite mass violence. History has proven it: the Christian Crusades, 9/11. Both could have been prevented by blowjobs. Why do you think Clinton was the only president in recent history who didn't nuke the shit out of some sleepy Islamic hamlet?"

I started to say something, but it wasn't worth it. Provocation was her mode, and I'd learned, over the years, to avoid being baited. In my loftier moments, I projected onto Lillian a feminist objective: to co-opt locker-room talk, reclaim vulgarity from its province on the right.

It may have simply been her style. My boss's disposition toward crass innuendo surely had Darwinian value in her deft infiltration of our industry's boys' club. I was the closest thing she had to a protégé, and I sensed her desire to instill in me something of this bro-ish bearing. I knew that my refusal—was it refusal or failure?—had affected my career. Male clients tended to request Greg as their account liaison.

"The way to manipulate men is not by denying them sex," Lillian explained, "but by forcing them to make promises while their dicks are in your mouth. You ever been with a soldier?"

One thing she respects is a lengthy sexual CV. My own was not. Lillian knew this but pretended to forget. I shook my head.

"You really should try it sometime. Their penises are tiny and they compensate by going down on you for hours. They love to take directions."

She knew I was married too.

"I used to keep a stash of plastic medals I'd hand out after mission complete."

A compulsive liar.

"After sex they cry. It's better than most standup routines. Anyway, tell me something about you for a change. How's Michael?"

She refilled my wine without my asking. She wanted me to spill marital secrets. A few months prior, I'd mistakenly confessed to a sexual experiment Michael and I had undertaken, a threesome. I thought telling Lillian would get her off my back. It only provoked.

"Michael's fine," I said.

"Even with this Wall Street bullshit?"

The truth was I didn't know. I watched TV and scanned my news feeds. I read the *The New York Times*. The intricacies of the crisis were buried beneath stories of other catastrophes, the cataclysmic wreckage of the last administration. Headlines warned of coming hurricanes and tsunamis. Warned of rising sea levels and methane emissions. Chronicled the continuing barrage of Weinstein-esque behavior in politics and entertainment. Addressed the uptick in anti-immigration violence in the wake of mass layoffs at fast food chains in Texas and Arizona, the right-wing backlash against the soda ban in public schools. It all just kept coming. That morning's front page featured a Florida militia with stockpiled Uzis who wore swastika armbands but touted their support for the Jewish State.

I did know that the hacking group m*A*chete had leaked internal memos from the C&S brass, suggesting bank employees unload their company shares. I knew the board was trying to push a last-minute sale of the bank and its holdings to a Japanese megabank.

The Universal Basic Income, or UBI as it was called, was a threat to the entire financial apparatus. If the proposal passed, the government would award every American with $23,000 per year. This $10 trillion dividend would be funded largely by tax hikes for the wealthy, and by increasing taxes on carbon emissions. But it would also be funded, in part, by charging fees to financial institutions on all individual trades and transactions. As far as I understood it, this meant that large investment banks like C&S, which processed nearly three million transactions daily, would be forced to drastically scale down their operations. Right-wing pundits warned of the negative effect this would have on lending. They warned that it would cause steep inflation and disrupt the economy's flow. They warned that this restriction on capital movement would have widespread repercussions for job creation and trickle-down wealth. They'd used these arguments for decades against other forms of socialization.

There is no way I could have known then, as I leaned back in my chair and watched the day's last light impart a Coppertone glow on the old brick church across Lillian's street, that Project Pinky would be linked to the UBI. That, in fact, the person in charge of Project Pinky hoped to tank the bill and replace it with a system of his own design. I'm not sure what, if anything, this knowledge would have changed.

Michael and I didn't talk about the crisis or its possible ramifications for us. We worked late. We left early. At home, we lay in bed staring at separate laptops. We argued about whose turn it was to take out the trash. Michael let the cat sprawl across his ribcage. He stroked her fur and fed her salmon treats that left crumbs on the duvet. I dust-busted around their bodies. We didn't have sex.

"So no more threesomes?" said Lillian. "You onto other stuff now? Bondage? Strap-ons? Cosplay?"

I swirled my wine. One night the previous week, I'd come home to a bleach-clean apartment and Michael in an apron standing over the stove. He'd set the table with our good wedding flatware. Candles were lit. A spray of wildflowers filled a vase.

I should not have been surprised. Michael gave me gifts all the time and planned date nights: reservations at trendy new restaurants, third-row seats to see Alvin Ailey at BAM. He meant well, I knew, but I often found myself inflamed at his presumptions. For example: that I would ever wear a floral-print, off-the-shoulder romper; that, after a long day at work, I'd be in the mood to leave the house.

Cooking and cleaning, however, were welcome. He made

pan-fried sole in a brown butter sauce. The fish was flaky and moist. We moved to the couch where we drank Côtes du Rhône and listened to records. Michael rubbed my feet. After my second glass of wine, I was convinced to take his arm and practice the waltz we'd learned years ago for our wedding. The waltz seemed like a metaphor. To move as a unit. To create a momentum that would carry us through each other's mistakes.

The next day we had bedbugs.

I hadn't told Lillian about that either. Displaying uncharacteristic tact, she hadn't asked about my face. I think she considered the body a safe space. She refused to acknowledge its betrayals.

"I love making you uncomfortable," said Lillian. "It's too easy. I'm sorry. It's funny to me to watch you squirm. Is that wrong? I should be nicer, right? I'm your boss. I could fire you. Maybe I'll fire you right now. Ha-ha. Have you noticed that people say ha-ha these days instead of laughing? What's that about?"

I changed the subject.

"Tell me about Project Pinky," I said. "Fill me in. There must be more to the story."

"You ever watch that cartoon show, *Pinky and the Brain*?"

I told her I'd seen it. I had a proper childhood, cereal and Saturday morning TV. My mother sat beside me and sketched in a notebook. It's one of my strongest memories. Not anything we said, but the ease of her pose, the piney bouquet of her men's deodorant. She found the cartoons amusing. Even as a kid, I was more interested in commercials.

"What aw we going to do today, Bwain?" said Lillian, imitating the cartoon rat.

"Today, Pinky," she continued, now doing Brain's voice, an operatic tenor, "we are going to take over the world."

"Sure," I said.

"That's the plan, anyway, world domination. I'm not sure how, or why, or what it means, but the money's real, and for some reason we've been tapped for this project. I'm guessing that reason is discretion. They could have any of the big agencies with the kind of contract they're promising: Ogilvy, Precocious Baby, whoever."

The client had floated a figure, enough to put us in the black for the coming year. We were a boutique service with a solid reputation, but even during our strongest quarters we spent nearly as much as we made. Precocious Baby had copied our business model and amassed a larger network of freelancers.

"They want to go small. They want someone who knows how to keep their mouth shut. The meeting I had was in a motel on Brighton Beach. At first I thought it was a joke. Then I saw the shoes. I met with a young guy. His shoes, dude. The leather could have been the scrotum on a newborn foal."

I did my best not to visibly recoil.

"The ten grand came in cash in a fucking briefcase. Could be mafia or Russian mafia, but I don't think so. The guy was too white. Something sketchy is going on and I want us to be part of it. We get this account and we'll make a killing. They sent me home in a limo. A motel in Brighton Beach and I'm sent home in a limo."

"Mysterious."

Lillian relit the roach.

"There's another thing. They asked about you."

"Me?"

The sun was all but gone now, and the air was cooler. I wished I'd thought to bring a sweater.

"You specifically. They said the contract depended on your full availability. I told them no problemo, of course. I guess your reputation precedes you."

"I have a reputation?"

"You were bang-up on Samsung. Brought them back from the brink. I know you're being headhunted left and right."

There had been offers, none I'd considered. I did think about leaving, but not for another agency. Instead, I imagined launching a startup in the Social Impact space, using my skills to do good. But I was comfortable at Communitiv.ly. For years I'd refused direct deposit because I loved receiving an envelope on my desk every other Friday morning. I loved waiting in line at the bank and holding the envelope. I loved handing the check to the teller.

Like most beneficiaries of a bat mitzvah savings account, I had a complex relationship with wealth. On one side was guilt, a dumbbell in the pit of my stomach. My paternal grandfather came through Ellis Island with only a toolbox. He quite literally built his modest empire from brick and mortar, erecting low-income housing on the Lower East Side. I built a wall as well, around the dumbbell. If there's one thing Manhattan private schools are good for, it's reminding the children of New Money Jews that, in the grand scheme of savings and loans, they're relatively deprived. I had classmates who owned helicopters, houses on Mustique.

Then my mother was diagnosed with pancreatic cancer. Treatment gave her two years. I wouldn't trade that time, difficult as it was. I spent long hours in her hospital rooms, doing schoolwork and watching trashy TV. My father was there too: pacing, opening and closing the window, staring at his coffee. He took an open-ended leave from work to be at her bedside. Insurance covered certain costs, but treatment was expensive, as was hospice later on. We had no income during that period. When she died, my father was essentially broke.

The personification of money has always made sense to me: *money does this, money does that*. It's as if it has legs. It might, at any moment, leave. This is one reason I didn't pursue writing. In my Advanced Nonfiction workshop, our professor warned against nurturing a fallback plan. He said the problem with a fallback plan is that you'll fall back. My classmates nodded and wrote this down. Personally, I liked the idea of falling back. I pictured myself in one of those summer camp trust exercises, plummet disrupted by a bed of hands.

"I get it," said Lillian. "Puma was boring, and you're sick of explaining Pim-Pam to geriatric CEOs. I am too, Wen. But this client is different. They're interesting. I don't know what they are. But as I said, the money's real. This works out and from now on everything's pickles and cream if you catch my meaning."

"I don't."

"It's a saying."

"It is?"

"It must be."

"Okay."

Lillian kicked back her chair. She laid a leg upon my leg. I brushed the dirt from her shoe from my pants. She hit the roach and coughed hard. Her cheeks looked purple in the porch light.

"The account is ours," she said. "God help me, I have a feeling. A rumble in my gut like the dam's about to burst."

"That may have been the shrimp. It felt a little slimy."

"I didn't eat the shrimp. I'm off shellfish. The smell makes me want to vom."

I looked down at my plate. There were twelve shrimp tails on it. There were none on Lillian's.

"Why'd you serve it?"

"It's what you serve."

She flicked a shrimp tail off the balcony.

MICHAEL

BACK OUTSIDE, I WAS ALMOST run over by a convoy of Citi Bike tourists speeding through a red light. With the introduction of Citi Bike, the increase in bridge tolls, the reliably annual announcement of long-term service stoppage on one or another subway line, and the continuing trendiness of those dumb caps with the flipped-up brims, New York had become a cyclist's city, a war zone in which cars were the enemy, and pedestrians were bystanders in the line of fire. But while I appreciate the cyclist's experience of the city—the way she hears words drift, car horns begetting car horns, and conversations cut up so that single syllables call out across avenues, each respondent ignorant of the next block's aria—walking's better for thinking, and I had a lot on my mind as I wound north through the Financial District.

Our office was uptown, but Ricky and I had a Monday tradition of coffee and omelets before riding the A/C to Forty-Seventh Street. He'd been my closest friend since fourth grade, when Steve Wyck called me a white-trash kike with a deadbeat dad who should've been killed in the Holocaust. I'd been about to point out that my dad wasn't born until after the Allied victory when Ricky intervened with a judo chop to Wyck's solar plexus, knocking the bully to the ground and earning my protector a three-day suspension.

I'd followed Ricky since: to Columbia, to Wall Street, to his gay bar du jour. I was not close with my parents, and had left home by the time my sister, Rachel, was old enough for joint commiseration. Until Wendy came along, Ricky was it, peer and mentor, bad influence, eccentric solver of problems. Even after, he was the only person who knew both versions of me: pre- and post-Wendy; the white-trash kike and the hipster millionaire. My fall was my own, but my previous prosperity had heavily hinged on his tips. And while his provocative nature didn't always recommend him as a source of prudent guidance, Ricky's role in my life was still that of advisor, and I currently, desperately, needed his counsel. He could be trusted in matters of finance.

Besides, I was interested in #Occupy. Protests now flared in previously #unOccupied Republican strongholds from Arizona to West Virginia; pro-#Occupy op-eds appeared daily on national news sites; and #Occupy leaders were finally getting face time on network news shows where they voiced increasingly popular support of the UBI. This windfall, they promised, would encourage participation in consumer markets and help the unemployed pay for privatized insurance. Recipients could quit degrading jobs and go back to school to earn higher degrees. They could contribute to the sharing economy. They could open small businesses knowing they'd have cash to fall back on if things went belly-up. As an added bonus, a financially contented populace might feel less imperative to freely spray bullets in public space. The logic went that if the ride or die Second Amendment crusaders could afford more powerful and expensive assault rifles then, paradoxically, they'd be less inclined to shoot the scary pacifists rallying to take those rifles away. But there was doubt on the right—from the very circles that fought so hard to abolish a public health-care option—that, left to their own devices, people could be trusted to correctly spend.

This was not the #Occupy I remembered from 2011, that

Bonnaroo facsimile with its compost bins and People's Library, its greased teens locking tongues beneath the honey locusts. There were still students, crust punks, and derelicts, but added to these ranks were laid-off workers from all manner of industries. These people's tax dollars had gone toward the previous bailout, and they'd been repaid with foreclosures and overdraft fees. And now their jobs had been replaced by bots or shipped abroad. Unemployment was the highest in our nation's history. The repeal of Dodd-Frank had led to another credit bubble, and speculators like me had sunk billions into industries bound to topple under the weight of an increasingly nonexistent consumer base.

The Senate was split on the UBI, though not entirely along party lines. Factories that our previous president had "saved" from offshore deportation had since laid off almost all their human labor, and thousands more were left jobless when funding ran dry for the half-built border wall. Senators in the affected states were more afraid of their constituents' diminished spending power than they were of scary old words like *socialism*. At the same time, plenty of coastal Democrats kowtowed to their Wall Street backers who opposed the proposal. And initially supportive libertarians balked when it became clear that the UBI would not be funded, as they'd envisioned, by bulldozing federal benefits programs. In all likelihood, the decision would come down to the votes of a few undecided, including New York senator Tom Breem, a centrist Democrat campaign-financed by the very banks hit hardest by the bill.

Breem's office was in Albany, but the chants and stomps coming from Zuccotti Park were intended to reach him. A FOX News anchor had deemed the scene an "unsightly display of Marxist manpower," and I'd wanted to see it for myself. "*Whose streets? Our streets!*" sang the protesters, reminding the swarms of surveillance drones that these roads had been built with human hands. The Freedom Tower stood gaunt in the distance, a fragile monument to the dying era of the American construction worker.

If #Occupy's previous incarnation fizzled under its supporters' inability to agree on a set of demands, the new regime was unified by consensus on this single urgent issue. These weren't pod people, but podcast people, the restless jobless who filled long afternoons listening to pundits preach the gospel of #Occupy. Groups as disparate as BDS, Black Lives Matter, and The Uniformed Sanitationmen's Association joined arms beneath the #Occupy banner. The previous administration had segmented the country into factions narrowly focused on their own safety and survival, but that administration's end, combined with the employment crisis and subsequent crash, had heralded the integration of these financially progressive factions, now bonded in harmony against the fiscally conservative Republican moderates and Democratic centrists eager to reinstate the neoliberal status quo.

Once again, there was a 99%. I saw cabbies of every ethnically stereotypical stripe, from old neighborhood wise guys to club-ready Russians with slicked hair and Bluetooth attachments. I saw adjunct professors with bulging triceps because their only job perk was gym access; MTA maintenance workers wearing tool belts filled with possible weaponry; mail carriers raring to go postal. There were even people in Augmented Reality helmets, who saw, I assumed, a terrifically enhanced version of the protest. I pictured the US Steel building in laser-beam crisscross and lit from within, a radium hearthstone transmitting light waves the color of electrified money.

It was amazing how many industries automation had so quickly thrown into disrepair. Service, retail, and factory jobs were hit hardest, but white-collar industries were also affected, from IT to sales to customer service. Even former blue-shirts were out in force, ex-cops who'd cuffed dozens in 2011, now linked in solidarity against the tear gas–equipped drones that had stolen their street beats. A workers' strike meant nothing in this automated city, or if not nothing then the opposite of its intent: it reminded the masters what little need they had for a human workforce. For now, the tear gas stayed unsprayed, but as the sound of the human mic increased in volume, and drumbeats quickened to amphetamine tempo, and protesters pounded fists against palms, one couldn't help but wonder if, this time, true violence might ensue.

A FEW BLOCKS AWAY, OUTSIDE Goldman Sachs, a smaller demonstration was at hand. A group of young people gathered around a card table, holding signs with anti-Goldman slogans. Seated at its center, I was surprised to see, was Jay Devor, founder of a social network and new-media empire called *Nøøse*. Begun as an app for finding protest events in the tristate area, *Nøøse* had grown into a large-scale nonprofit with offices on both coasts, two hundred full-time employees, print and online publishing arms, and a user base nearing the two million mark.

Nøøse had been instrumental in spearheading #Occupy's organizational upgrade, in part by creating a manageable infrastructure for earmarking donations, and by implementing an online voting system that pushed the movement closer to its vision of a true direct democracy. Devor—a baby-faced elder statesman among his Gen Z cohorts—had become the de facto face of the movement after his public arrest during a reading of Melville's *Bartleby, the Scrivener*. The reading stopped traffic on the Brooklyn Bridge, and Devor appeared handcuffed on Page Six, smiling for the cameras: part Robin Hood, part Zuckerberg, part Jewish JFK.

Devor and I were classmates at Columbia, and had crossed

paths at Brooklyn bars and mutual friends' birthday parties in the years since. Beyond his disgust at what I did for a living, I sensed a begrudging respect. I'd recently emailed Devor with an article pitch for *Nøøse's* eponymous webzine of culture and politics. The piece was an unwritten excerpt from the book I was writing— or planning on writing—called *Eminem: American American in America*. I had yet to receive a reply.

"Devor," I said, and he looked up with the same soft eyes that had conjured the removal of so much women's wear, the sparkling tube tops and chic retro Umbros of fangirls from Greenpoint to Red Hook and as far north as Washington Heights. There were probably even coeds who commuted from Bronxville, Young Trotskyites of Sarah Lawrence. He looked me over before responding, unsure about fraternizing with the enemy, or else gauging the health risks of shaking my hand.

"Mixner," he said with a nod. We'd never made the transition to first names, which spoke to either a lack of intimacy, or a deeper intimacy built of nostalgia.

"Don't worry," I said. "I come in peace."

"If that's the case," Devor said, and handed me a flyer. I had to remove the reading glasses from my bag to read it, and in doing so grabbed a tube of moisturizer and passed it to Devor. The sun had emerged from behind the clouds, and I figured Devor, a pale guy like myself, might benefit from the product's SPF-15 infusion. "For your face," I said.

Devor rubbed the ointment into his cheeks in mechanical circles like he'd practiced in a mirror after watching a YouTube seminar on the subject. In another life, he might have been me, and I him. We were like the dual Lindsay Lohans in the remake of *The Parent Trap*, identical in nature, but nurtured to form separate systems of belief. I, with my working-class upbringing, had come to value personal prosperity over fiscal equality, while Devor, descendent of Day-Glo kibbutzniks, had learned that sharing led to caring led to casual threesomes.

My phone buzzed, but I ignored it and looked at what I'd been handed, an invitation to a Funeral for Capitalism at 8 P.M. in Union Square. Letterpress printed on crème card stock, it was the second printed invite I'd received for an event that night. The other had come from a junior colleague, a cocky young trader raised in the crotch of Greenwich luxury, complete with a home bowling alley and servants cruelly uniformed in oversized bow ties. This colleague's life had been a procession of silver-spoon achievement—prep school grade inflation, Harvard gut curriculum and golf team heroics, genetically blessed Anglo-aquiline bone structure—and now, at the first blush of failure, he was throwing a, no-joke, *Great Gatsby* theme party in the penthouse suite of SoHo's Zone Hotel. The invitation, which sat in my briefcase, was similar to Devor's, except it was printed on cheaper card stock, and in pedestrian Geneva font.

Ricky had convinced me to make an appearance at the Gatsby party, promising top-shelf bourbon and behavior that might provide anecdotal evidence for my theoretical excerpt, a think piece on the way white investment bankers misappropriated rap lyrics as justification for fiscal Darwinism. I no longer wasted brain space wondering if I attended these events sincerely or ironically, the line between the two having been irreparably blurred sometime in the early aughts.

My father once told me that everyone who lived through the sixties had his own personal Altamont—the day the idealism died—and I think one could claim an analogous moment for nineties kids, when each of us realized that Kurt Cobain was gone, complaints about selling out were nostalgic, and those adorable indie shops from Seattle were now the giants come to destroy. For many, this moment arrived with the posthaste corporatization of Cobain himself, his face become logo on T-shirts sold at Target so teens who'd never heard him could flash the style markers of disaffected rebellion while listening to the disco-soul cover of "Smells Like Teen Spirit" from last week's *The Voice*.

I liked hip-hop, a genre stridently open about its impure relationship with commerce, and thought I was exempt from this kind of disillusion. I was wrong. I distinctly remember the first time I saw a photo of Vampire Weekend—Columbia kids who dressed in Brooks Brothers beach duds and played a preppified genus of Paul Simon worldbeat—and feeling surprised and disappointed that the boat-shoe class had developed a claim on youth culture. It felt like a rigged game to bring more power to the powerful, to deprive the less privileged of their monopoly on cool.

Still, I looked forward to the party. Maybe I could pre-game at Devor's protest and pitch my book. There were sure to be plenty of editorial types on hand. My being a banker was of fetishistic interest, the protectors of the literary realm turning polite and deferential to anyone wearing a suit in a performance of open-mindedness that masked a deeper lust for proximity to dollars.

What I couldn't do was go home. I'd been ignoring calls from Wendy since leaving the house, and it was only 9 A.M. I worried that she'd tried to use our Visa and it had been declined. A single login to E*Trade and she could suss out the breadth of our financial situation. I didn't want to imagine her reaction. We were in bad shape already: scratching bug bites, staring at cellphones instead of each other. A heartfelt apology wouldn't cut it. I needed to offer, alongside my confession, a recovery plan.

Not that I was so deluded as to think that a book deal might save me. AR gaming, VR porn, and the era of addictive, B/B+

quality TV had all but abolished the market for the kind of intellectually rigorous project I had in mind; there would be no angel at the Funeral for Capitalism handing out six-figure advances for hybrid works of cultural criticism and memoir. Still, if I could find a publisher, Wendy would understand how serious I was about this new vocation. And sure, we'd have to deal with our debt—I was working on that—but the important thing, I would stress to Wendy, was that I'd found a passion, a calling, and that this new pursuit would sustain my soul, and would maybe, eventually, lead to my procuring a tenure-track gig at Pratt or The New School.

"Sounds like a good funeral," I said. "Open bar?"

"BYO," said Devor. "We may have power in numbers, but we're not particularly flush."

He pointed at the donations bucket, which contained some coins, a two-dollar bill, and the butt of a sesame bagel. I wanted to prove my traitorous disregard for my industry, but not so badly that I was willing to part with the little cash I had. As a show of my sorry financial state, I flipped open my flap pockets. Out came a fistful of burrito scraps: pork nibs, green peppers, a wadded ball of aluminum foil.

"Calexico?"

"La Esquina."

"Ah," he said. "Delicious."

"I'm glad we're agreed. It's like that joke about Israelis and Palestinians, and how they only agree on hummus. Maybe bankers and #Occupiers can be unified over burritos."

Devor produced a heartier laugh than my remark warranted.

"Did you get my email?" I asked.

"I get a lot of emails."

"Did you get mine?"

"Write the article," he said. "We'll see if it's any good."

WENDY

MICHAEL AND I DEAL WITH anxiety differently. Michael is an extrovert. He had a hip-hop group at Columbia; he was MC WebMD and he rapped about his neuroses, rhyming *thyroid*, *typhoid*, and *infinite void*, and occasionally spasming into a performative coughing fit.

I remember my first attack in his presence. We had just returned from dinner, Indian, our third date. We were in my dorm room illegally downloading MP3s and drinking wine from coffee mugs I'd stolen from the dining hall. This was as close as I'd come to nurturing a rebellious streak. I was nervous. Dinner had upset my stomach, and Michael's eyes on my objects and meager hangings made me feel exposed.

I wanted to be one of those girls with a record player and a stack of LPs. One of those girls with a vintage fur displayed on a sewing form. I was not that girl, too timid and self-conscious, too conflicted between my fear of and desire for attention.

In high school, the lacrosse team made a website where they ranked and analyzed the females in our class. I was given points for my looks, but demerits for my supposed inability to smile. Verdict: frigid bitch. People mistook my shyness for coldness, my stilted manner for arrogance. And though I'd tried to make myself over in college by wearing costumes to theme parties and laughing at unfunny jokes, I knew that these adjustments were cosmetic.

I sensed Michael was about to make his move. He'd been giving his take on "The Real Slim Shady," misquoting Frederic Jameson and explaining the song's postmodern assault on the illusion of objectivity. My stomach rumbled. What Michael was saying was pretentious and half-baked, but I appreciated his spirit. Here was the college experience I'd imagined before the disillusion of matriculation: discourse with flirtation. It was surprisingly hard to come by. The gender theorists had rejected me for precociously shopping at Ann Taylor Loft. Besides, they were averse to hegemonic concepts of courtship even when the courtship rituals included avowals to lay waste to the hegemony. Everyone else was only interested in real estate. Even the other writing students discussed it ad nauseam, debating which neighborhoods still inspired enough dread to keep gentrifiers from spoiling their storefronts with juice bars and yoga studios.

I've heard people say that during sexual encounters they've felt outside of their bodies, distant observers. My experience has been the opposite. I am only a body, a sensation machine. Michael kissed me and I kissed back. His tongue felt mealy in my mouth, like a chunk of soggy apple. He scooched closer on the bed. He wrapped an arm around my waist and placed his palm beneath my sweater, just above my beltline. He traced a path from my navel to my hip.

I pulled away. I thought I might vomit. I had trouble breathing. I hyperventilated. I thought I might have spontaneous diarrhea. I assumed that Michael would flee. I felt like the night's failure was indicative of all my future failings, indicative of the hopelessness of any such endeavor.

Music continued to play. I imagined Michael staring at my body and assessing what I considered its flaws. We'd fooled around on our first date, but we were in a dark car, and I'd kept my clothes on. Now, in the privacy of my bedroom, further exploration was expected.

I was, and still am, by most accounts, attractive: tall and relatively thin with red hair that falls in tight spirals below my shoulders. I have expressive lips and turquoise eyes. I have my maternal grandmother's upturned, Irish nose, which nicely offsets my other, Ashkenazic features. I'm not a size zero, but I dress to accentuate my strengths.

Still, during all of my pre-Michael sexual experiences, I'd arrived against disappointment. I'll never forget Gabriel Simm's face upon the unveiling of my breasts, my flat and ovular nipples reflected in his lenses. Gabriel did a double take. He could only blame his vision. Then: a cringe of acceptance, a closing of eyes, tongue diving toward areola as if, with enough torque, he might bypass reality and land on fantasy's shore.

The first thing Michael did was turn off the music. He knew not to touch me. He pulled over my desk chair and sat facing me. He spoke very slowly. He said my name. He told me to take deep breaths. He said everything would be okay. He said he understood, that he had felt like this before. His voice was steady. He said there was no rush, that he liked me, and that he could wait. He told me there was time. He asked if there was anything I took to calm down when I felt this way. I told him where I kept the Ativan. He took one too, "to be on the same wavelength." I thought this was funny. We watched a video on the computer. My breathing regulated. The video was a clip of a monkey fainting from sniffing its own feces. Michael said he'd watched it hundreds of times. He made me laugh.

We fell asleep fully clothed. I woke with Michael in my arms. He lay drooling in the fetal position. He looked vulnerable, sweetly sleepy.

WHEN I GOT HOME FROM Lillian's on Sunday night, I was surprised to find Michael in the apartment. It was ten o'clock. He
had been going out after work. He usually arrived home past
midnight. I'd be in bed, alert, awaiting the sound of his keys.
Eventually he'd stumble in and clomp across the loft. I'd pretend to be asleep.

I told myself that Michael's behavior was an appropriate
response to the stress of the crash. The truth is that it had been a
problem for some time. After our daughter's death, I found myself
reticent around Michael.

He'd suggested we begin to try again. I wasn't ready. I was still
in mourning. I think that Michael saw, in Nina's death, the loss
of a future, whereas I felt the loss of a person I'd known. For
nine months she'd been my roommate, a tiny human sharing my
body's resources. Michael only knew her as a nebulous mass. A
mass that occasionally kicked.

I worked long hours, and when I got home I took long baths.
I didn't want to talk or to be physically intimate. I told myself
I was protecting Michael. Nina had come from my body, been
destroyed by my body. Who could caress this killing thing? I felt
I didn't deserve to be loved.

A part of me was relieved when Michael began to go out after
work. The other part was lonely.

That night, he seemed happy to see me. He may have been
buzzed, but I couldn't smell anything on him. I was tipsy myself.
He asked about my evening. I recounted Lillian's position that
oral sex might have prevented the 9/11 attacks.

It was warm in our apartment. Michael took off his clothes
and got on the air mattress in his underwear. His bites had faded
more than mine because he was better at leaving them alone. I
changed into a nightgown and got in beside him. He'd stopped at

Bed Bath & Beyond and bought a new set of sheets. They were stiff but clean.

Michael had his laptop open and I watched as his cursor hovered, for an instant, over the shortcut to our E*Trade account. I didn't think anything of it. He clicked on the CNN shortcut instead. The Florida neo-Nazis had occupied a Hillel at FSU, and were holding a rabbi and four students hostage. Michael scrolled down past articles on Hurricane Marie, sexual assault on an HBO set, and Shamerican protest art. He clicked into a piece on the proposed sale of C&S to Sumitomo Mitsui Financial Group. We silently read. The gist was that the deal was stalled but not dead. Michael hovered over E*Trade again. He didn't click. He closed his laptop.

"This world," he said.

"Yes," I said.

"Our world," he said.

He pressed into his temples with his index fingers. He stared at the wall.

I was feeling fondly toward Michael. I was thinking of the previous week, when he'd cleaned and cooked, and rubbed my feet. The wine had made me tired and I'd fallen asleep. Now I was awake. I slipped a hand inside his boxer briefs and rested it there.

When he was ready, I rolled onto my stomach and raised the hem of my nightgown. Michael preferred being face to face. He liked to look into my eyes. I liked this too, but not always. Sometimes it felt like too much pressure, like being under observation. Michael leaned over and kissed the nape of my neck. He nibbled my shoulders. He ran his hands along my spine and held my hips. He asked if it felt good. I said that it did.

The sex was accompanied by word-like noises coming from Michael's mouth. I'd never heard him make these noises before.

It sounded like an infant's strangled attempts to articulate beyond her linguistic capacity. I didn't like the way my face felt against the pillow. The sheets were rough. They needed three or four wash cycles to be softened to my satisfaction. I imagined other couples testing the sheets in the store, tainting the fabric. I knew this was not possible. The sheets had come sealed in plastic casing. I tried to feel pleasure. I tried to will the convergence of our bodies into something ecstatic. I could feel the shrimp suspended in the aspic of my intestines.

Michael asked if I wanted to vibrate. This is something we did. He'd thrust from the rear while I ran a vibrator over my hood. Michael had said that my contractions, when I was on the cusp of orgasm, set off his own climb. I said I didn't want to vibrate. It seemed unlikely I'd be able to climax.

When I began to get dry, Michael added lube to the outside of his condom. He wore condoms because I react adversely to birth control pills. The condoms, coupled with the side effects of his antidepressants, prolonged the plateau phase of intercourse. I often spent long minutes lying in wait.

Michael thrusted and made his noises. He kissed my hair. My phone buzzed. My phone had a special buzz for emails from Lillian. The buzz was accompanied by a bird's chirp.

Michael said, "Leave it."

I said, "Mike."

Michael continued to thrust. The bird continued to chirp. I smelled cat pee. Michael grabbed tightly to my hips. His fingernails dug into my skin. I imagined them making small abrasions. I imaged the dirt from under Michael's nails entering my bloodstream. I imagined the shrimp squirming back to life and swimming up my esophagus.

I tried to extract myself, but it must have felt, to him, as if I were erotically bucking. He increased the speed of his thrusts. He clutched me closer. I was able to unplug my phone from its charger. I managed to get the phone to my face. Michael whispered what sounded like "I love you." He bit my ear. He ejaculated as I read Lillian's email.

MICHAEL

THE COFFEE SHOPS BY RICKY'S apartment were Starbucks or Starbucksian: corporate, cleanish, out of toilet paper. In the case of the one that I entered, the bathroom was not out of toilet paper, but out of order. At least, this was the explanation offered by the handwritten sign on the door. The sign had been affixed with what looked to be an entire ream of Scotch tape. The tape tried too hard to convince. Here, I speculated, was a pristine bathroom, moated by sign and tape so as to banish the errant pissers who wreaked havoc each morning, forcing the store's lone human employee to spend his lunch breaks scrubbing. The workforce was fighting back. I opened the door.

"Shit," I said, because there was a lot of it on the floor.

THE CAFE BRIMMED WITH FINANCE guys, men whose hands had palmed footballs in high school and in college had been body inspectors: tweaking nipples, forcing pinkies into tiny anal holes. After college they'd tied ties, tapped out lines, and touched money. Now they pecked touchscreens, checking the Dow, sending vaguely reassuring emails to investors.

I'd worked in the industry since college, when I interned with Ricky at Merrill Lynch. I was twenty-six when the housing bubble burst, but the nature of derivatives was such that vast degrees of separation existed between the families who'd taken out subprime loans and the guys like me who'd blindly traded CDO packages, each of which contained literally thousands of these mortgages. I'd been trained to imagine my market movements as purely hypothetical, a grand-scale sudoku that would increase my annuals without affecting the mechanics of American life. We weren't Nazi soldiers following orders, but entrepreneurs following the rooted imperatives of our system, the promise that success comes at the expense of faceless others.

These others were out of sight, in Middle America, a place that mostly existed, for me, in midcentury novels by the Great White Males who'd been extinct for some time. And though I grew up an heir to financial depression, I still had trouble picturing the boarded-up houses and tent cities, the families ruined by debt. I couldn't fathom the fallout from our actions, the factory closings and depleted pension funds. I couldn't see how this recession would shape the next decade's economy and lead to the current crisis. If I could see those things, I couldn't connect them to what I was personally enacting.

There's a long version and a short version of how I lost all my money. The long version is boring, and involves balance sheets and credit swaps, the broken dream of Detroit's renaissance. It involves failures of predictive modeling and optimistic long positions. It involves the death of my daughter and a new inclination toward risk. And, if I'm being truly honest, it involves a not-insignificant measure of greed.

The short version is simple: I bet on America.

I soon found myself poorly leveraged, my liabilities threatening to outweigh my assets, and my sympathies for left-wing ideology steadily increasing. So while it would be easy to brag of my altruism by asserting that my shifting beliefs were based on a comradely desire for systemic fairness, the real source of my newfound empathy was that the system had failed me as well. I'd done all the right things—gotten the right job, married the right woman, made the right purchases based on Amazon's recommendation engine—and I'd ended up with a dead child, a slumping marriage, and financial ruin.

I WAITED IN LINE, WAITED for my pills to kick in, watched the coffee junkies queuing for their fixes: eyes glued to shoes, hands darting in and out of pockets, feeling the phantom buzz of their phones. I checked my own, which had been ringing with clients, debt collectors, and this morning's half dozen missed calls from Wendy. I didn't call anyone back.

When I reached the counter, the tele-barista said, "Good morning."

It was twelve hours earlier in Manila, and I could see the blinking city through the window behind his head. These cyborgs combined the precision of automation with the frugality of outsourcing to provide a uniquely shitty customer service experience, though it's worth noting that they rarely messed up an order. Their monitor heads livestreamed humans in the Philippines who remotely operated the robot bodies that brewed the coffee.

"And good evening to you," I said, hoping to get a laugh in response, though, like the baristas of old, my guy was humorless, an underpaid teen with no time for chitchat.

"My name is Arnel, may I take your order?"

I told him what I wanted, and Arnel nodded, and a door opened in the robot's belly. I watched my coffee being poured.

"I don't mean to be the bearer of bad news," I said, "but someone appears to have shat all over the bathroom floor."

"Are you reporting an act of vandalism?" said Arnel. "Do you wish to lodge a formal complaint?"

His face was too close to the camera. I could see my reflection in his eyes. His question seemed like a trick or a threat. I was wary of reporting anything in an official capacity, afraid of paperwork or a delay in service.

"I'm just saying maybe someone should clean it up."

"Copy that," said Arnel, and he must have clicked his mouse or hit a key, because a siren went off above the bathroom door. The store's human employee came pushing a mop bucket to meet it. She typed a code into a wall panel that turned the siren off. I didn't understand why the bots couldn't clean bathrooms while the humans served guests. I'd been told they didn't have the dexterity. A metallic arm extended my coffee toward me. I wished Arnel a good day.

RICKY WASN'T ANSWERING HIS CELL, but I was friendly with Donnell, his doorman. When he wasn't signing for packages, or working evenings hawking iPhones at a Verizon store, Donnell wrote a blog that considered sports and pop culture through the lens of his life as a single dad. He was an excellent writer and, if the universe were remotely fair, he would have been writing for a larger audience than his few hundred daily readers, and for more coin than he got running banner ads. Years ago, I'd endeared myself by donating discards from my sneaker collection as give-aways for the blog's donation drive, and, ever since, Donnell and I had enjoyed a rapport, longing for the days of pre-replay refereeing and the great elbow throwers of yore.

When I arrived in the lobby, Donnell did not look up. A book was open in his lap, and the doorman bent over it, presenting his graying Afro to anyone who entered. Donnell, I knew, was roughly my age, but he looked prematurely life-worn with his Don King haircut and plastic rim bifocals, his food-stained doorman's gold-button blazer. On his desk sat a half-eaten egg sandwich. A peek of a circular sausage stuck temptingly from the bread's square edge.

"You gonna finish that?" I asked.

Donnell nudged the sandwich in my direction. He closed his book and placed it face up on his desk; it was a hardcover copy of Sarah Jessica Parker and Matthew Broderick's co-authored self-help book, *Bueller? Anyone? Sex After Sixty*.

"Don't even start," said Donnell. "Not today."

He was referring to the Knicks. These were rough times for the team, coming off four seasons in the cellar and Spike Lee's defection to the Milwaukee Bucks.

"Oh, come on," I said. "At least your boys looked cute in those new uniforms. What would you call that color? Rust? Ocher?"

"Burnt sienna," he said.

I considered sports expertise my Massachusetts birthright. In Mass, even dandies and high femmes could hold their own in discussions of the Patriots' depth chart. I liked New York, where sports knowledge still suggested masculinity, and where I, a white-collar wuss, could penetrate the ranks of quote unquote real men by watching SportsCenter in bed. My discussions with Donnell were self-affirming, our easy banter supporting the delusion that I was not a snob looking down from his tower of privilege, but a streetwise code-shifter with working-class black friends. Or, at least, with one working-class black friend. That this friend had little choice in the matter of our friendship was something I willfully refused to acknowledge.

"Interesting choice of reading material," I said, and lifted the book. I skimmed its pages, which were filled with notes and underlines.

"I have this theory," he explained, "that one can trace the fall of the Knicks to 9/11."

He was a man of theories, a writer who relished the challenge of selling difficult arguments, and who, with humor and insight, often managed to succeed. A recent post defended NBA salaries from a Marxist perspective. In Donnell's hands, the league's millionaires became labor incarnate, staffing the only industry that granted its workers just revenue share.

I admit that I was jealous of Donnell's aptitude. His blog's modulation between high and low registers was exactly what I was trying, and failing, to achieve with Eminem. For months, I'd been too embarrassed to bring up my own project during our weekly discussions. In part, the reason was obvious; Donnell was a writer, and I was a wannabe. But there was also a racial element to my reticence. I didn't want to come across as a try-hard white guy whose scholarly knowledge of hip-hop betrayed a fetishistic aspect to his interest.

I was a Jewish teen in the nineteen-nineties, meaning hip-hop soundtracked my seminal years. It was pumped into malls, played at school dances, taped off the radio, and traded on mixtapes at camp. I got a shortwave radio for my bar mitzvah, and the first thing I did was search the airwaves for Hot 97, the mythological station of Summer Jam fame.

If hip-hop gave me an identity during those years, it also provided repeated reminders that it wasn't intended for people like me. People, that is, with no experiential knowledge of the crack epidemic, or Section 8 housing, or mistreatment at the hands of trigger-happy police. People, that is, with no experiential knowledge of the racial injustice that, I gathered, was a defining component of many American lives. Even before being schooled at college in the language of political correctness, I understood my status as a cultural voyeur.

But while friends like Ricky found themselves reflected in, say, Phish's maple syrup funk, part of hip-hop's appeal was that it wasn't a mirror, but a window into a foreign world. Which is to say: I loved hip-hop both in spite of and because of the fact that it wasn't mine to love.

And then there he was, with his bleached hair and Kmart wardrobe, his pill-popping mom and lower-middle-class angst. I identified with Eminem so strongly it scared me, given his homophobia, misogyny, and nihilistic rage. I told myself that this was only a persona used for pushing boundaries, and that all that really mattered was Em's level of skill. But even the latter was a controversial topic. To proselytize too hard for a white rapper's talent was to risk promoting Caucasian exceptionalism. I worried that I'd have to face these questions if I ever wrote my book.

"So how does Carrie Bradshaw fit into your theory?" I asked Donnell.

"How doesn't she fit, is what you should be asking."

"Okay, how doesn't she?"

"In no way doesn't she."

"I'm confused."

"You'll get it when you read the piece. That is, if I ever find time to write again. Jackie's home on winter break, the other doorman's on two-week vacation, and Verizon has a sick day policy to rival the Führer's."

"I'm sorry," I said. "That sounds hard."

Donnell released a puff of air in a manner that told me I couldn't understand. It said that I, with my food grubbing and demand for banter, only added to his woes. I knew about Donnell's money troubles from his blog: bank-breaking debt, a shitty mortgage on a money pit apartment. Our situations, I understood, were fundamentally different. For a moment, I wondered if he actually liked me, or whether I was just another asshole with whom he was forced to interact. Perhaps it's testament to the triumph of self-deception, but I refused to accept that the latter was the case.

WENDY

LILLIAN'S EMAIL WASN'T URGENT: A reminder to arrive promptly for the 10 A.M. pitch. I had a mostly sleepless night spent scratching my scabs and fighting the cat.

Monday morning—on what would be the day of Ricky's murder—I missed both my alarm and my train. Michael was already gone. I hurried out the door, hoping I'd have time to stop by a boutique near my office that opened at nine. I'd practically run out of the few clothes I'd saved from quarantine, and my online purchases had yet to arrive. I was wearing a shirt of Michael's that I'd found in his closet protected by a plastic membrane. In our old Manhattan apartment, I used to admonish him for refusing, out of laziness, to remove the plastic from his shirts when he brought them home from the dry cleaner's. We shared a small closet. It rankled me to open it and see stray plastic sticking out. The plastic created static and took up space. We had our own closets in Brooklyn, and he did as he pleased.

I sometimes wonder about the relationship between violence and space. There is a reason that urban areas have high murder rates. People are packed too tightly; boundaries blur. The closest I ever came to homicide was as an undergraduate. I did not like having a roommate. My roommate did not like wearing headphones while she listened to music. She did not like taking the phone into the hallway to talk to her boyfriend. She did not like staying on her side of the room. She did not like waiting until I was out of the room or asleep to engage in sexual activity. Instead of peace and quiet I got pillow-muted panting. Bedsprings scolded like aggravated ghosts. I pictured her body as a punctured balloon, air slowly escaping until she was small enough to be flushed down the toilet without clogging the pipes.

I WAS RUNNING LOW ON time, so I asked the clerk to bag various items. I would try on the outfits later and return what didn't work. I picked out underwear, socks, a bra, a knee-length charcoal skirt, three T-shirts, tights, a pair of flats, and a lightweight cardigan to keep me warm in the air-conditioned office. I chose a black pencil skirt for that morning's pitch and paired it with a simple Oxford shirt. I did not select any of the parkas and scarves displayed on the mannequins. Designers had taken a stand against climate change. They would not bend. They would not break. They would not relinquish their seasonal collections. Fashionistas nobly suffered, sweating through wool sweaters on eighty-degree days. It was a sign of commitment, and stupid.

I gave the clerk my American Express card. After a brief interlude, she handed it back. She whispered the word *declined* the way my uncle Alan whispered words like *gay* or *black*. I regretted not choosing a chain store manned by telepresence bots. The boutiques still hired humans. Only a particular breed of female can produce the specific sneers essential to these boutiques' elitist mystiques. These women had made themselves indispensable by force of attitude.

I said, "There must be some mistake. Could you please run it again?"

The clerk did as she was told. The card was declined again. It's an awful feeling to have a card declined. You want some other proof to present, evidence that you're still entrenched among the world's earners and savers.

I gave the clerk my ATM card, which was also declined. I had a feeling it would be. Our balance had been dangerously low. Michael had said he was waiting for something to come in. He'd said *liquidity* in a tone that meant I shouldn't ask. When my most recent paycheck disappeared from our statement, he'd said he was moving things around. I knew something was wrong, but not the extent. I didn't want to know.

The machine declined my Visa as well. The clerk looked so smug as she told me, forearms crossed in an *X* over her torso, the outline of her rib cage showing through her T-shirt. I was wasting her time. The store was otherwise empty. I had no cash on me. I had no other cards. I tried Michael's cellphone again. It rang.

BY THE TIME I ARRIVED at my office—an open-plan studio that makes it impossible to go unnoticed in absentia—it was after ten o'clock. Our staff and a lone member of the client's team were seated around a projector screen. Greg was up front with a laser pointer tracing the outline of a Venn diagram. Greg has broad shoulders. His cheeks are covered in cultivated stubble. He wears a college ring from a second-tier East Coast university (Tufts), jeans and sport coats (both stylish), no tie, and shoes that aren't quite sneakers or boots, but give an extra lift to his five-six frame. Favorite adjective: *kick-ass*. Once, in a pitch meeting, he'd suggested the tagline *Hennessy: Latinos welcome*, after the company's head of marketing had expressed a desire to expand their demographic.

It was the broad-spectrum spiel we fed all our clients. Lillian oversaw the proceedings from the perch of a barstool. She gave me a look that said: *we'll talk about this later.* I found a seat up front.

Our team—Greg, Lillian, and myself aside—consisted of developers with poor fashion sense. Felt, red trim, fedoras, bandanas. The occasional splash of platinum lamé. They could have passed as bar mitzvah DJs or landlocked pirates headed out on the town in 1980s Las Vegas. Communitiv.ly is a casual company. The tech world takes cues from San Jose. Across one wall, graffito-style spray paint declared CREATION ISN'T AN ISM. Greg was on the part about the speed of culture.

"The United States," he said, "is not just one country."

The client looked unconvinced. He was handsome, almost boringly so. His shoes must have been the ones Lillian had described. She was right about the leather.

"The United States of America is many tiny countries," Greg continued. "And each contains multitudes."

At the mention of multitudes, a new slide headed DEMOGRAPHICS appeared on the projector. The slide featured illustrations of men and women done in a variety of gray-spectrum skin hues. At center was a young African American man—you could tell from the hair and dark shading—wearing both a hooded sweatshirt and a necktie. He wore AirPods in his ears. The man was labeled URBANITE. A caption described URBANITE as someone who makes over $80,000 a year and spends up to three nights per week in bars and nightclubs. It was a slide we'd made for a pitch to Axe Body Spray in July.

"There are many countries within us," Greg said. "Within each and every one of us." He pointed to his heart.

"But there are also many countries without us. We are part of a global economy now, a global movement. The globe is spinning faster every day. The world makes more revolutions around the sun now than ever."

A cartoon of a spinning globe appeared on the projector as

techno played from the wall-mounted speakers. In stop-motion photography, the globe's revolution around a tiny sun increased to hundreds of frames per second.

"In Kenya," Greg said, "Pim-Pam is ubiquitous."

"But what about—" the client began to ask.

"Hear me out," Greg said.

A cupped ear appeared onscreen. The image had ear hair.

WE WERE OFFERED THE ACCOUNT. Greg's presentation had gone over okay, and my reimagining of *Lysistrata* as a wage gap protest, complete with an Instagram hashtag—#RemunerateOrMasterB8—for photos of begging, frustrated husbands, was declared, by the client, a smashing success. He wanted to meet with me privately that afternoon.

"Just me?" I asked Lillian.

"If he was into short, dickless men, he would have asked for Greg. As it stands, you're all we've got."

"That makes me uncomfortable."

"Who said anything about comfort? Throw on some Spanx and contour your cleavage. You might get some onion rings out of the deal."

If pressed, she would have said she was joking. I wasn't certain she was. During the early days of the #MeToo movement, my boss made a public show of support. She retweeted celebrities' uncontroversial platitudes. Bylined an op-ed in *Ad Age*, ghostwritten by me. She was shrewd enough to know that, as a female CEO, expressing outrage at our industry's endemic sexism would benefit her brand.

Privately, Lillian expressed reservations. She worried that male acquiescence to demands for gender parity—by which she meant the façade of acquiescence—would leave women ill-served. Sex was a weapon, she'd explained to me once. This was at some industry gala. We stood sipping wine, watching the tuxedoed swarm. "They want to network with my cleavage," Lillian said. "And I want to network with their wallets." She was worried #MeToo would scare these wallets away. She was afraid she'd be forced to surrender a weapon that she'd spent years learning to wield.

I told her about one night, at a campaign launch party, when I was cornered by an account exec from a major international brand. The man twirled his martini. He sucked the olives off his toothpick in a single, noisy slurp. From our vantage, at the railing of a downtown hotel roof bar, the city looked glazed after an earlier storm. The man offered his jacket to cover a wet seat. He held my elbow as I lowered myself. His finger poked my lowest spinal notch and traveled down to the point of my tail-bone. "Come home with me," he slurred. "We can discuss the account."

"What account?" said Lillian.

I named the brand.

"Well that explains why they went with Ogilvy."

THE OFFICE WAS QUIET. THE development team was unit testing a cross-promotional app that matched Uniqlo T-shirts to colors of Benjamin Moore paint. The marketing team was gathered around a monitor watching YouTube videos of animals fainting. Others ate at their desks: oatmeal and oversized burritos and leftover kugel from a Shabbat-themed cocktail hour. In their corner, designers tossed Swedish Fish into each other's mouths. Our CFO could be seen bobbing beneath the weight of puffy headphones, operating an invisible turntable. The intern next to me glued magazine cutouts of Michelle Obama to her mood board. The rest of Communitiv.ly stared into their monitors and sipped coffee from novelty mugs shaped like blocks of Swiss cheese we'd ordered in bulk for an Instagram-cosponsored benefit for a Brooklyn-based artisanal fromagerie. I picked up the phone.

The representative I reached sounded chipper. He said his name was Orlando and asked how he could be of help.

"I tried to buy some outfits and my card got declined."

Orlando explained that Michael and I were in debt to American Express. Our line of credit had been cut off. A trip to Duane Reade had tipped us over our limit.

I asked how much debt.

Orlando gave a figure.

I apologized, though I had done nothing wrong. I hung up and called Michael. He didn't answer.

AMONG THE MORNING'S EMAILS WAS a message from Michael's mother. Born in Lodz, Poland, Lydia Mixner née Schulman had been a concert violinist until arthritis wreaked havoc on her fingers. Now she was a late-budding academic, completing her PhD thesis while teaching freshman composition at a local college.

Lydia's subject is the evil that men do. Specifically, the evil that men did, during the first half of the twentieth century, to Jews. She has trouble letting go. This explains her relationship with her son.

Dear Princess Wendy Mixner (wife of Prince M. A. Mixner),

It has come to my attention that my one and only son, Prince Michael Andrew Mixner of Pittsfield, Massachusetts, and

*the surrounding counties, is currently without access to tele-
phone or Internet. This must be the case. Otherwise, he surely
would have returned the many calls, texts, and emails sent
to him by his mother over the last few days. Nothing urgent.
Tell the Prince his mother longs to hear his voice.*

Yours, Lydia Mixner (Doctoral Candidate)

The signature linked to MyCrosstoBear.blogspot.com, where
my mother-in-law analyzed "evidence" "proving" that the historical
figure known as Jesus of Nazareth was not, in fact, the Son of God.

This mission was Lydia's raison d'être. On various visits, clip-
pings from *Biblical Archaeology Review* concerning the possible
found remains of Jesus's biological half-brother had been pre
sented to me as if by a district attorney. I couldn't count on two
hands the number of articles I'd been emailed explaining that the
term *Son of God* was, in Jesus's time, a common way of referring
to a righteous person. One year, Lydia gave me a book called *The
Aryan Jesus: Christian Theologians and the Bible in Nazi Germany*
for my birthday. As a half gentile on my mother's side, I bore the
brunt of her findings. I typed a reply.

Dear Lydia,

*Michael is MIA. I guess he hasn't crawled back up your
shriveled cunt after all. Not sure where else to look.*

Kisses, Wendy

I hit delete and tried Michael's phone again. I did not leave a
message. Lillian called me into her office.

She said, "You look like shit."

So much for denying the body's betrayals. I picked up a coffee mug and absent-mindedly attempted to sip. The mug was filled with pennies. I placed it back atop Lillian's file cabinet and hoped she hadn't noticed.

"It's alright, don't worry. Just unbutton your shirt to distract from your face and you'll be fine."

"Are you joking?"

"Am I?"

I told her I didn't know, that it was hard to read her tone.

"Look," said Lillian. "Just keep the money in mind. If this works you can do all the pro bono your clit-boner desires."

She showed me a photo on her phone of a twenty-three-year-old she had a date with later that night. We wished each other luck.

MICHAEL

IT TURNED OUT RICKY WAS still up, sniffing the remains of last night's party, sifting and sniffing, licking inner Ziploc to usher him into the workday. On the table were a couple of crack stems.

"Take a hit," Ricky said. "It'll make you sparkle."

I waved his offer away. "A little early for me. Or maybe a little late."

"The problem of our generation," he replied. He wore a droopy undershirt, tuxedo pants, and suede loafers. Suspenders hung down around the backs of his knees. The rest of the outfit was scattered in pieces across the room: jacket draped over couch-edge, cuff links collected in ashtray, bow tie on table.

"Always late," Ricky continued. "Late Capitalism they call it. Really we're late *for* capitalism. But what's it matter, so long as I'm on the winning end, right sweet Sammy?"

He blew a kiss at his conquest, a shirtless young guy sprawled out on the couch. Not a bad performance for 8 A.M., post–sleepless night, still glowing from the glory of it all as sun poured in the window, world faded to white.

"What's with the bracelet?" I asked, referring to a fiberglass ring around his wrist. The bracelet looked like an avant-garde watch that lacked hands and had the letters *SD* embossed on its face.

"The future," said Ricky.

"South Dakota?"

"Cold."

"San Diego?"

"Sykodollars, Michael."

"Right," I said, and remembered where I'd seen one before: on my dad. The Sykodollar was the currency of *Shamerican Sykosis*, an Augmented Reality game that I'd played on occasion, and that my dad had been playing obsessively for years. Like a cross between Monopoly, *SimEarth*, and *Pokémon Go*, *SS* was an open-source world where players won and lost money on in-game bond markets, then used that money to augment public space. Walking through through Manhattan in AR helmets, players were privy to a massive panorama of user-generated content, from jewel-encrusted halal carts, to buildings overlaid with fractals, to giant stainless steel tendrils raised above the East River, braided through the inter-borough bridges. Last week's *New York Times Magazine* even featured a cover story on Shamerican protest art, including a downloadable plug-in for replacing signage lettering—such as on NBC's Rainbow Room marquee—with an all-caps #METOO, and an AR-enhanced Prospect Park memorial honoring the victims of recent mass shootings.

Bracelets like Ricky's, I remembered, held thumb drives containing the algorithmic passkeys for users' accounts. Despite originating as an in-game tender for players of *SS*, Sykodollars had become a universally traded cryptocurrency. The only way to access your SD was with these mathematically complex and nonreplicable passkeys, and if they got stolen there was no way to get them back. Most *SS* players kept these passkeys on their phones and computers, but players with big bankrolls were targets for hacking, so it was safer to keep the keys in safes or deposit boxes or even, for the paranoid and fashion forward, on their persons.

A while back I'd read a piece about the *SS* creator's initial vision of the game as a commentary on the gamification of capitalism, its users vicariously participating in otherwise inaccessible markets by trading stocks and renovating buildings in the same way sports fans could throw down virtual dunks in games like *Parquet Gawds*. But this ironic economy had taken on a life of its own, growing beyond the game's boundaries and leaking back into the real world where users exchanged its untraceable currency for contraband. For a while, Sykodollars were a rising commodity, but the market shifted, and their value dropped. My dad mentioned it every time he called to borrow money, promising the SD would recover and he'd pay me back. This had been going on for years.

"I thought those things were worthless?" I said.

"You're thinking in linear time," said Ricky, a reminder that he was high on crack. Sammy laughed. An erection stretched his sweatpants to their tensile limit. Ricky noticed as well.

"What on earth did people do before Viagra and Cialis and Levitra and Stendra?"

"I think they slept," I said. "Slept and worked and only had sex when they were actually aroused."

Sammy said, "Sounds boring."

We were on the white leather couch, feet on the white leather ottoman or buried in the white fur rug. White was a statement. The statement: sleazy. Ricky's motto: style over substance. The style: Las Vegas. The substance: anything ingestible.

I leaned over the mirror table. My eyes were yellow. Smears of dried blood spread across my neck and cheeks. I dumped the contents of the Duane Reade bag, my pathetic contribution to the pharmaceutical pot. At the store, it had felt ripe with promise, but now my cache seemed insubstantial. Sammy snagged the Sudafed, crushed one with a credit card, snorted.

"Well that won't do anything," Ricky said.

"I'm bored," Sammy said.

"Youth," Ricky said.

Sammy stuck a nicotine patch to his forehead. It reminded me of nicotine and that I needed some. I lit a cigarette. Ricky made me put it out. He had an aunt who'd died of emphysema after suffering an oxygen tank for years, dragging it up and down the stairs. She would house-sit when Ricky's parents were away. He would torture her by taking bong rips at the kitchen table, talking loudly about analingus, threatening to remove her nose tube if she told anyone. Ricky had always been an asshole, and I liked that about him. He believed in the glamour of himself. In our blue-collar town, where boys beat up other boys for being much less gay than he was, Ricky's ownership of his outsiderness struck me as representative of a better world. That world, it turned out, was two worlds. One was New York. The other was money.

"So what you think?" Ricky asked me.

"Of what?"

Ricky nodded at his guest. "Of Sam my new boy-man."

Sammy smiled. He had a gap between his teeth. A few hairs sprung from his pimply chin. Haircut definitely self-inflicted; there was no apparent rhyme or reason to which areas were shaven and which were left long. The resulting look was something between skate kid and surgical patient, mid-prep.

"Sammy, why don't you tell Uncle Mike how old you are?"

"Eleven," Sammy said. "I'm about to turn twelve."

"C'mon," Ricky said. "Your real age. Humor Michael."

"I'll be nineteen in October."

"Sammy may be young in years," Ricky said. "But his cock is as old as this dying empire."

I scoped the young man's bulge. "Doesn't look dead to me."

"What I mean is, it's a cock from another time, from another era. From back when men were men."

"Another era?"

"Michael, dear Michael, you don't understand. It's not your fault, you're from a different world. Where you're from, women are afraid of penises. Penises have been pushed at them their whole lives. Penises have been shoved in their faces, forced into their ears and down their throats."

"Into their ears?"

"Into their ears, Mike. And who wants that, a dick in the ear? Not women, that's for sure. Certainly no woman I've ever met."

"I'm not sure I . . ."

"Let me tell you about Boys Town, where I'm from. In Boys Town, there are two types: you're either carrying a nine-inch hammer like Sammy is, or you've got nothing. There's no in-between. And now, with all this estrogen and soymilk, in this city of soft rodgerings, a nine-inch hammer is hard to come by. You should see him come, Mike, you really should. I could arrange it. Sammy, up for a quick spurt?"

Sammy touched himself through his sweats, literally weighing the option.

"Like a semen bullet," Ricky continued. "Ten thousand tiny Samuels sprung into winter air. It's a *Nutcracker* of semen, the way he can make it fly. His balls do ballet, Mike. A cock from another time."

"A Cro-Magnon cock," I said. "A pre-industrial dong."

Sammy raised an eyebrow, lowered it, leaned back into the couch.

"By the way," Ricky said. "You look terrible. Really terrible. I'm sorry to have to bring it up, but you're like a pink elephant in the room with your pink face and fat pink stomach."

"Thanks."

Sammy's penis had subsided, and so had Sammy. Within

seconds he was snoring. Ricky laid a blanket over his young friend's body.

"You ever worry?" I asked. "About corrupting these kids."

"You know what I worry about, Mike? I worry about you. What are you gonna do with yourself?"

We might lose our jobs, but Ricky, I assumed, would be all right. Ricky was liquid. Ricky owned land in Laos, Tanzania, all the emerging markets. He had a safe in this apartment that contained a hundred thousand in American dollars plus a hedge stash of euros and yen. He even had Chinese yuan, currently worthless, pegged to nothing but its culture's Darwinian superiority. Yuan was the cockroach of currency, the Keith Richards of capital assets—against all odds it would survive. Ricky had told me he was planning retirement. This was it for him. The economy crashes and he jets on out. He had Cuba in mind, a cheap hideout filled with tan boys thrumming for a true taste of capitalism.

"I'm writing my book," I said. "I'm finally writing my book."

"Your book? Oh, of course, your book! What's the book about? White guys who want to be black, Hispanic guys who want to be gay? Something like that? Am I getting close? Can you write a book on Basic Income—what is it, thirty grand a year?"

"Twenty-three," I said.

Ricky shook his head.

"It's about our generation," I said. "The book is. You know, the generation that came to capitalism too late. Remember?"

"Oh, you're listening to me now. That's a bad sign. Our generation? Mikey, we don't have a generation. We're post-generational. Rated PG if you catch my meaning."

"Maybe that's what the book's about."

"The book's not about anything, Mike, because there is no book."

"It's about Eminem," I said. "The book is about Eminem, and

how his oeuvre, including the first three LPs plus *8 Mile* and its soundtrack, define our generation."

"I never knew what you saw in rap music," Ricky said. "All that crotch-grabbing and queer-bashing—they're all closet cases, if I say so myself, but that's irrelevant. I want to ask you a serious question: Does the world need another book? Forget the book. Get a manicure for God's sake. Get a back wax."

I lifted a glass stem from the table and tapped it against my palm.

"I was thinking," I said.

"Uh-oh. That's never a good sign."

"I was thinking you might be able to help me."

"I'm not much of a writer, Mike, hard as that may be to believe. Never had time for all that *i* before *e* shit."

"Except after *c*," I said.

"See, I wouldn't have known that. Proves my point."

"With money, I mean. I could use some help."

Ricky responded to this request with an expression of such unadulterated joy, that I'd continue to recall it through the mournful week that followed. I'd recall it as I drove north on the Taconic, and as I drank myself blind at our old hometown bar. And after the open-casket wake, lying sleepless in my childhood bedroom, I would try my best to swap the image of Ricky's embalmed face with this smiling one instead. I took some comfort in the knowledge that, on his last day of life, my despair had filled Ricky with delight.

"Help you how?" he asked.

He wanted me to beg.

"Well, what would you do if you were in my situation?"

"And what exactly is your situation?

I said, "Chapter Thirteen has crossed my mind."

This was bait. I knew that, as my best friend, he'd never let me file.

"Terrible idea, Mikey. I can see why you're so broke, with ideas like that. Never, ever file for Chapter Thirteen. Once you've filed Thirteen, there's no coming back. Did you learn nothing from *Behind the Music*?"

"I guess not," I said, though the chained gates of MC Hammer's foreclosed mansion were seared in my retinas.

"Look, it's not so bad. You're cash poor, but you've got assets. There's your apartment, for one. And what about all that C&S stock you stupidly bought? Toxic assets to be sure, but you're not without options."

"I thought the boom would last," I said.

"It was a bubble, Mike. It's always a bubble."

"So what would you do, then, if you were me?"

"I'll tell you what I wouldn't do: I wouldn't go around pretending I was writing a book."

"That's true," I said. "I can't see you doing that."

Ricky leaned over and brushed a fallen strand of Sammy's hair behind his ear. Sammy continued to snore.

"What I'd probably do, instead, is get on my hands and knees and beg my friend Ricky for a handout. That's what I'd probably do. If it were me."

"Right," I said. "I was considering that option."

It was the only option I'd considered. The plan that I'd been banking on all morning—the plan I hoped would save me from ruin and resuscitate my marriage—consisted, entirely, of asking for this loan.

"So how much we talking here?"

I coughed out a figure.

"I'm sorry," said Ricky. "Could you speak up a bit? I didn't quite catch that."

He was loving this hard.

"Three million," I said, a little louder. "Can I borrow three million dollars?"

Ricky shook his head. "Michael, you beautiful fool."

"It wouldn't have to be all at once. Maybe a million now to start paying off some things, another in six months' time, something like that?"

I trailed off. Ricky looked down at the table like he was taking inventory of the Duane Reade stuff I'd dumped, calculating how much we could sell it for on eBay.

"Look, Mike, I'd help if I could, I really would, you know that. But that's a lot of change we're talking about, and I'm not so liquid at the moment."

"I'd take euros," I said. "Yen even."

He removed a painting from the wall.

"You have a safe hidden behind a frame? I thought they only did that in movies."

"Duh. That's where I got the idea."

He held his palm to a sensor and the safe opened. It was empty.

"Not even yuan?" I asked.

"Invested," Ricky said. "I'm all in."

"What about Cuba?"

"Cuba can wait. I've got a thing going on, a great opportunity. I've been looking for the right time to tell you about it. Actually, I was hoping we could talk at the party tonight. I'm in on the ground floor of something. Low risk, and a bigger upside than Sammy's Neanderthal wang. If you can scrounge together just a teensy bit of capital, I think we can make your debt disappear. Can't promise anything, of course, but I feel good about this one, and you know I've never steered you wrong."

That teensy bit of capital posed a problem. I couldn't imagine explaining to Wendy that I was selling our loft in order to invest in one of Ricky's sure things, no matter his previous rate of success. Still, it was a thought. I didn't have any others. There was always my book.

"In the meantime," Ricky said, and snatched the stem from my hand. He replaced it with a fifty-dollar bill. "Buy yourself something nice. You deserve it."

He lit the crack rock. This was my cue to leave.

WENDY

WHEN I ARRIVED AT THE restaurant, a Greenwich Village sports bar, of all places, the client was already there, in a corner booth, drinking Coca-Cola spiked with rum. I know because I ordered "same as he's having," and was surprised to find alcohol in my beverage, and more surprised to find it sweetened by high-fructose corn syrup. I didn't think that people still drank non-diet soda. At least not in New York.

The client was dressed casually now, in jeans and a bomber jacket. Blond bangs were curtains over his eyes, protecting them from UV rays and admiring glances. His nose and cheekbones were miracles of architecture. Thick, moist lips. Shaven chin-shine. He wore a sober expression one might not expect from someone so boyishly handsome. The effect was jarring; his eyes were oversized, as if they'd outgrown their sockets. I was the subject of his scrutiny.

I've always fetishized WASPs. True WASPs, I mean, born in Connecticut and bred on Nantucket schooners eating lobster rolls and deconstructing golf swings. They've never shown much interest in me. Rachel Kirshenbaum and I used to drive out to Darien to look in their windows. We loved their orderly homes. The neatly stacked copies of *Elle Decor*. The calming peach walls.

"I never got your name," I said.

He nodded. I wasn't sure he understood I'd meant it as a question.

"So what is it?" I said. "Your name?"

The client sighed as if the answer were obvious. "Lucas," he said.

Lucas did not read the menu. I wondered if he'd memorized it before my arrival as a power move. If he could reel off the list off the top of his head, wines and specials included. Or perhaps he was the kind of guy who ordered a cheeseburger wherever he went, or else asked the waitress what she recommended and then ordered that. He slurped his drink loudly. The waitress came and we ordered our food.

"Do you have any idea what you're doing here?" Lucas asked.

"Eating lunch."

"Good," he said. "Sharp."

Lucas reached into his bag and removed a piece of paper. He sketched a female stick figure. He made a *click* sound with his teeth. The figure had conical breasts, linguini hair. Her eyes were dots. Her mouth was the letter *o*.

Next, Lucas drew a male stick figure doubled over at the waist. He drew a large phallus protruding from the female figure's pelvis and extending into the male figure's rear end.

Lucas wrote *Wall Street* next to the female figure. He wrote *Joe Schmo* next to the male. I noticed he wore no wedding ring. I wondered if it was in his pocket, reduced to mere metal among coins and keys. I had no sense of his age.

"Simple story, right?"

"I like that you represented Wall Street with a trans person. That's very open-minded, if slightly wishful thinking."

"Artistic license. The point is that what I've just drawn is popular opinion, correct? The general consensus, agreed on by communists, and European socialists, and liberals who are afraid to describe themselves as such, and liberals who take pride in the term, and people who call themselves moderates, and people who call themselves apolitical, and Southern rednecks, and gun-toting libertarians, and God-fearing devotees of the Limbaugh radio hour, and the Gen Z mega-demo that's coming to voting age as the boomers burn and fade. Anyone who's not a billionaire knows that Wall Street's the nemesis of our friend Joe Schmo, or Joe Hill, or Joe the Plumber, or Joe Mama, or whatever you want to call someone with a floating-rate mortgage on a depreciating property, and a job that, if it hasn't already been made redundant, will be sometime in the next ten years. Even you believe in this reductive narrative."

"My husband works in finance. I know it's more complicated."

"I didn't say you don't benefit. I didn't say you can't argue talking points about the trickle-down effects of corporate wealth or the way markets tend to self-correct, or Thomas Jefferson's wet dream of an open-air flea market. What I said is that you believe it. In your hidden heart, you know you are complicit in the machinations of neoliberalism. The disenfranchisement of the middle class. The destruction of the working class. You are a scion of privilege. A basic bitch who buys a Rag & Bone dress at full retail, then tells her friends it was marked down. A person who convinces herself that by donating a small, untaxed portion of her yearly salary to Kickstarter campaigns that fund urban farming initiatives, the ultimate balance of her good deeds and destructive behaviors evens out. And yet still deep down, you know that you're complicit."

He wasn't even out of breath.

I said, "These are things I've considered."

"And even though you think hippies are dirty and hipsters are used and discarded douchebags, and homeless teen runaways are a blight on the glory that is Alphabet City, and even though you find fault in certain aspects of #Occupy, you don't ultimately disagree that the system needs reimagining. So what do you do? You try not to think about it. You stay out of it. You tell your friends that you're not interested in politics. That you don't have a deep enough understanding of the situation to form a truly educated opinion. That, yes, your husband is a banker, but he's a different kind of banker, the good kind of banker. A banker with a heart of gold and a wife of heart, and a Sunday kinda brunch-bloated love."

"What's your point?" I said.

"The point is that you're not alone. There are a lot of people like you. People who were sickened by the camps at the border, and what happened with the pipeline, and what happened in Charleston, and what happened in Orlando, and what happened in Parkland, and what happened in El Paso. People who hashtag believe women, and hashtag me too, and hashtag it might as well be the heat death of the universe, dude, because time's indubitably up. People in favor of pan-gender bathrooms, an assault weapons ban, a bigger education budget, less military spending, and more attention to climate change. And yet, they're torn on the UBI because they like their pumpkin-spiced lives. There are a lot of people like you who are waiting for the right person to come along and tell them there's nothing wrong with the way that they're living these lives. Do you know the term *psychic foreclosure*? That's what people want. A one-size-fits-all system of belief: no gray areas, no tricky ethical quandaries. License to live as you already are. That's what we're here to give. We're here to tell them that just because they went to Wesleyan and smoke fat blunts of Kush and favor a Chinese sweatshop worker's right to a fair and speedy lunch break, it doesn't mean they have to go against their own fiscal interests. It doesn't mean that socialism is the way forward. It doesn't mean that the toothless meth smokers in Appalachian trailers deserve a percentage of their hard-earned salaries. It doesn't mean that people like you should pay a six percent property tax on your refurbished brownstone so every bedsore-ridden inbred in southern Ohio can eat chicken-fried cheesecake while watching amateur wrestling on loop. Forget Joe the Plumber. How about Yelena the Trust Funded Yoga Instructor? That's our demo."

"Okay."

I was trying to picture chicken-fried cheesecake. Lucas picked up the pen. He crossed out *Wall Street* and replaced it with *#Occupy*. He said, "Your job is to create that narrative."

"My job is to create that narrative," I echoed. It's a tactic I learned early in my career. Repeating other people's words makes it seem like you understand, that you're on their side and submissive. "So you work for a bank?"

"No."

"But someone with an interest in the Senate killing the bill?"

"This is bigger than a bill. It's about giving people a sense of comfort. You've worked with lifestyle brands. Brands that tell people that if they buy a product they can live like the people in the ads. This is the same. We want people to feel like they can be the people they want to be. That they can find peace."

"You're a lobbyist?"

"For America."

"What a line. You chose me because my husband works in finance. You knew I'd be sympathetic."

"We chose you because you're good. Your campaign for McDonald's in India—Eat, Pray, Loving It!" He removed an ice cube from his drink with his fingers. He chewed the ice cube.

"Then why all the secrecy?" I said. "The motel, the project code name, the fact that we haven't met any of your colleagues."

"In a week's time, we'll be launching a product. It's a product that I've spent years developing, and it's a product that I believe will change the world. This product is my personal intellectual property, and until it's ready for the market, I'd prefer that knowledge of it be limited to a small group of trusted associates. My hope is that, within a few days' time, you will have proved yourself worthy of inclusion in that group. I promise that, if you do, you will not be disappointed."

"Okay," I said.

"Now, the success of this product is contingent on the UBI bill dying on the Senate floor. This is where you—your campaign—comes in."

"Okay," I said again.

The food arrived. I had a salad. Lucas had a rare cow steak, which cost six dollars more than the stem-cell filet also offered on the menu. He said he always ate real meat, that the kind grown on trees lacked the necessary iron.

We ate quickly. Lucas's knife scraped loudly across his plate. When the steak was no more, he dabbed the small puddles of blood and grease with his big thumb. He sprinkled salt on his wet thumb. He licked. I put my napkin in my salad and signaled to the service bot. Lucas caught me looking again at his drawing.

"Are you getting it?"

"Everyone's fucking everyone. That I understand."

"Good. Because that's part one of the agenda. Understanding the problem is part one."

"What's part two?"

"Part two is complicated."

"Why is it complicated?"

"Part two is what you're gonna do about it."

"What are we going to do about it?"

Lucas reached back into his bag and removed a rolled-up poster. He watched as I unrolled it. The poster featured a black-and-white photo of steel gates beneath a German sign. I'd seen this image before, in person, on a visit to Poland to see where my grandparents' cousins had been murdered. Over the image, lay an English translation. Whoever designed it had added a hashtag:

#WORKWILLSETYOUFREE

"This," Lucas said, "is our campaign."

MICHAEL

THE ATMOSPHERE IN THE OFFICE was too glum to be productive, so I rode the F to 14th, then switched to the uptown 1. At Columbia, school was in sesh. Skinny freshmen weighed down by backpacks, skinny hipsters weighed down by existential despair, everyone weighed down by debt.

I admired these kids and coveted their freedom. It would end eventually, but for now they could read Judith Butler and Edward Said, pursue an ethnographically diverse array of friends with benefits, friends with benzodiazepine prescriptions, friends with parental benefactors. College is the last bastion of free love and dining dollars, the best aspects of hippie sixties mixed with seventies excess, eighties dad-funded decadence, and nineties wide-leg denim. With the millennium came drugs like 2C-I and Molly, the spread of flash-frozen sushi to landlocked areas.

Despite these amusements, the library was jam-packed with students. I had access via a not-yet-expired Columbia ID purchased from a recently graduated C&S rookie. I bore little resemblance to the ID photo, but campus security was surprisingly lax, especially considering the scourge of school shootings. Or maybe, as a white man with clipped fingernails and no facial tattoos, I'd slipped from the profiler's purview.

I was a regular by now, arriving most evenings under the delusion that I'd hack out a couple chapters. In reality, I'd written nothing. Or rather, I wrote things—page-long sentences replete with semicolons, remixed nineteenth-century pantoums, an allegorical flash fiction in which Eminem is reimagined as the charismatic leader of a colony on Mars—and then deleted them. I was still finding my form. There were ideas I wanted to touch on: the way hip hop had misogynized the male psyche, the music industry as a microcosm of the global economy; the health risks of hair bleach. But I was missing something major, the binding agent that would cohere these ideas into a thesis.

Mostly, I spent my library time embarked on a kind of vague research. One evening I might make headway in volume two of Marx's *Capital*, but the next I'd read only back issues of glossy women's mags, or online consumer reports, or Insta feeds chronicling the daily deeds of certain superlative LOLcats. I read and reread Em's lyrics, spending hours self-debating semantics and attempting to justify his scrim of sociopathy. The project was hopeless.

I chose a seat in the second floor reading room, sniffed the varnished desk wood, lit my desk lamp, sucked on a cough drop, put on my nicotine patch, bit the cough drop, swallowed it, nibbled my sticky inner cheek, blew my nose, chewed two Tums which were chalky and awful with a weak citrus undertaste, so I opened my laptop and called up a blank document which I renamed *Chapter 1*.

I typed:

> *Before coming to prominence in the field of hip-hop, Marshall Mathers worked as a pizza chef at the Little Caesars Family Fun Center in the Detroit suburb of Warren, Michigan.*

The sentence was slightly misleading. For most of his twenties, Em was a busboy and fry cook at Gilbert's Lodge, a sports bar decorated in moose-head taxidermy. Gilbert's was his self-proclaimed second home, and any true scholar knew of Em's on-the-job free-styling, an incessant stream of invective that amused his fellow busboys, creeped the female servers, irked the shit out of management, and may have led to his firing days before Christmas, 1996.

Em worked at Little Caesars for six months before being rehired at Gilbert's. Gilbert's had played a much larger role in the saga of Marshall Mathers, and yet, mentioning Gilbert's, out of context, in the first sentence of my book, would not pack the same punch as mentioning Little Caesars. With its charming logo and inoffensive pizza, Little Caesars was a universally recognized symbol of mediocrity, and there was no more efficient way of indicating Em's humble beginnings than by revealing his stint at the chain.

What's more, Em hadn't worked at any Little Caesars, but a Little Caesars "Family Fun Center." For a reader schooled in the vulgarity of Em's lyrics, the fact that he'd worked at such a venue would be downright disturbing. One imagines an oblivious mother handing her offspring to a demonically grinning young Mathers, followed by a montage of bubbling mozzarella and third-degree burns and maniacal laughter as a pizza cutter severs tiny fingers. On top of that, the phrase "Family Fun Center" would hint at one of my book's major themes, an exploration of masculinity and American fatherhood.

Another issue was that the clause "Before coming to prominence in the field of hip-hop" had a dry, academic tenor that was nicely balanced by the pedestrian familiarity of "Little Caesars Family Fun Center," a balance that wouldn't be as successfully achieved if I replaced "Little Caesars" with "Gilbert's Lodge." I wanted the opening sentence to reassure readers that this was a serious work, but that its seriousness wouldn't alienate the common pizza-eater by bombarding her with academic jargon.

Ultimately, however, something felt disingenuous about beginning the book by mentioning Little Caesars. I felt an odd sense of loyalty to Gilbert's Lodge, and worried that, in banishing Gilbert's to the purgatory of Chapter 2, I was suppressing factual truth in favor of self-serving mythology. Stumped, I deleted the sentence and X'd out of the doc.

My laptop background was a photo from my honeymoon: Wendy and I, posing in the princess tower at Angkor Wat. The camera stares over our shoulders at the distant moat. It's not a great picture—the sun is behind us, backlight obscuring our faces—but the honeymoon remained pristine in my memory, a reminder of my marriage's optimistic prelude.

In Cambodia we ate curry, rode tuk-tuks, and visited temples. We discussed Western privilege, got stoned on pot-topped pizza, and shopped for counterfeit designer clothes. We kissed. We read books, feet entwined, on poolside mats. We spent mornings in lace-curtained canopy beds, drinking coffee from small porcelain cups and making love. For five US dollars, I got a Dr. Fish foot massage—a tank of baby piranhas nibbling the dry skin off my heels. And one night at a beach bar in a crab village called Kep, we joked about inviting a handsome waiter back to our bungalow after he got off shift to have sex with Wendy while I watched. This was a fantasy I'd entertained for some time, and though we were only teasing each other with the idea in Cambodia, it was something that stuck with me, and that I continued to suggest, always semi-jokingly, during the first years of our marriage.

It's hard to say what about this arrangement appealed; the roots of desire, as my therapist, Dr. Becker, has pointed out, are often repressed for practical reasons. The only way I can explain it is that during sex—an interval when I'm meant to be a lit-up pleasure center—my anxiety about being in the quote unquote moment is such that sex has the opposite effect of increasing my self-consciousness. Dr. Becker claims this is a common phenomenon and the cause of much sexual dysfunction. For my part, I imagined that if I watched my wife in congress with another man while I masturbated, I wouldn't need to worry about maintaining an erection, or hitting Wendy's G-spot, or whether or not she came. I would be free to lose myself in the quote unquote music, while taking part in a larger, pleasure-giving picture. I would be able to spiritually connect with Wendy while someone else engaged with her body.

About three months ago, Wendy and I decided to enact this fantasy as a way of fighting through what we refused to call a rut. Ruts were for the gut-soft middle-aged, that smartphone-incompetent demographic who signed up for capoeira classes in the hope it might awaken their libidos. Wendy and I were still young and adventurous, millennial in spirit if only just within that generation's bracket. We deserved a foray into all the world had come to offer while we'd been engaged in the anachronistic rituals of courtship and baby-making. In a sense, the threesome was consolation for the fact that we'd failed to become parents and fully shuck the skins of our younger selves. We found our third on the Troika app, a John Jay senior named Eric Darving who majored in criminal justice and had the kind of California smile I'd always admired on a man.

Wendy and I dared each other to go through with it, knowing full well the possible implications for our marriage. We spent a week emailing back and forth with Eric, who was gracious and patient. His lax attitude made us feel like what we were planning wasn't outrageous, but de rigueur for anyone interesting. Neither of us had been to Burning Man or even Coachella; we'd never attended a swinger's party or done much skinny-dipping.

So though it seemed out of character for Wendy to show interest in something so boldly beyond the limits of her comfort zone, I understood it as a restorative act, a fixed match resulting in triumph over two decades' worth of demons. Looking back, I can see that I was wrong, that Wendy's interest—and mine too, if I'm being honest—was masochistic. We were trying to blot out our grief by replacing it with a more immediate trauma.

When Eric rang the bell, we welcomed him into our loft. It was one of those July nights when the heat's still temperate after the relief of a summer storm, and you can turn off the AC and open the windows. I got beers from the fridge. Eric stared at the high ceiling and I recalled my own first visit to a rich person's apartment, amazed that in this cramped city of nonconsensual subway rubbing, a single person might take up so much space. Eric was taller than expected. I'd known his height from the get-go—six-five—but it was something else to see him standing next to Wendy. She looked natural beside a taller man.

The three of us sat in a row on the couch and stared at the turned-off TV. No one made eye contact. I said, "This is awkward," and Wendy let out a laugh. Eric smiled. I lit a cigarette—I'd begun smoking again after Nina's death—and Eric waved the smoke from his face, and Wendy coughed. She asked Eric if he liked music, as if there were people who didn't. He said, "Yeah man," and put his legs on an ottoman. I asked if he liked hip-hop and he said, "Hells yeah," and I told him I was a hip-hop nerd myself, especially nineties stuff and early aughts, though the current scene had plenty to offer.

Eric nodded. I could tell he wasn't interested, but Wendy didn't jump in, and nervousness brings out my verbosity. I found myself lecturing on Em's place in the pantheon, below Nas and Biggie, of course, but on par with Jay-Z? When pressed, Eric admitted to being a passive listener who didn't pay attention to the words. I told him that, while beats were certainly important, lyrics were the genre's defining characteristic. As an example, I put on Em's masterpiece, *The Marshall Mathers LP*. In retrospect, it was the wrong choice.

We moved to the bedroom, and after some gentle coaxing from Eric and me, Wendy removed her robe to reveal a garter set I'd bought her and had never seen her wear. For a moment I was taken aback, jealous that she'd put on the lingerie for someone else after refusing to wear it for me for months. She'd said that when I asked her to dress up in that or any outfit, what I really wanted was another partner, someone confident and lascivious who shaved whimsical shapes into her pubic hair.

This was a debate we'd been having for years, but it had increased in frequency as we'd gotten older, Wendy growing more worried that she would no longer satisfy my base macho cravings. And though I'd explained that my wanting her to wear costumes and engage with me in light role-playing was no more emotionally adulterous than her own interest in being stimulated by a silicon phallus, I'd ultimately accepted the situation as a lost cause, one that had less to do with me than with Wendy's own issues. That is, until I saw her pose for Eric Darving in the garter set and came to understand that the issue was not with Wendy at all, but with me; that her antipathy to role-playing was actually about her ultimate disappointment that no role-play could truly conjure another man.

Still, despite my jealousy, I was aroused by the sight of my wife in this outfit, the way the black lace popped against her pink skin. Eric kissed Wendy's neck and shoulder, and she gave off soft moans, and Dido's voice on "Stan" spun me back to senior year, smoking blunts in Ricky's car when we were supposed to be in gym, that elegiac piano line seeming, in my hazy state, to echo the patter of rain on the windshield as Ricky stroked the peach fuzz at the nape of my neck and just that once I didn't stop him.

"They don't make beats like this anymore," I said, but no one responded. Eric ran his hands down Wendy's arms. She made figure eights around his abs and closed her eyes.

As they continued to kiss, I gave some background on the album, enlightening Eric on the rapper's three personas—Slim Shady, Eminem, and Marshall Mathers; id, ego, and superego, respectively—who battle for dominance, but of course the id wins, the id always wins.

"But what makes it all work," I hastened to add, as Eric's finger toured the elastic rim of Wendy's thong, "is that buried beneath Slim's violent antics and homophobic epithets, there lies Marshall, a rare and fragile bird, cornered by predatory critics, protecting the nest where his baby bird sleeps."

Wendy said, "There, right there." Eric was wrist-deep in her panties.

I moved to the edge of the bed. Eric was still fully clothed, but Wendy was now being stripped, first of her stockings, then the garter. He kissed up her stomach, from navel to neck, before unclasping her bra and fitting his mouth around one of her breasts. When Eric slipped off Wendy's panties her impulse was to clutch her knees together, but he pushed them apart and she didn't resist. We'd arrived at the album's horrorcore apex, a song called "Kim," in which Marshall, or Slim, or whoever he is, slits his ex-wife's throat in a jealous rage as she screams in protest and their daughter looks on.

"It's a horrible song," I said, eyes on the stranger going down on my wife, on the back of his head, as Em's ex-wife Kim, or, to be more specific, a voice actress playing Kim, screamed in terror.

"It's painful to listen to, and harder to reconcile. And it's not even the lyrics that create this effect, but Em's very voice, the edges of his consonants, can you hear them, the sharpness on letters like *t* and *q*? And yet, isn't it interesting that, for all of this album's insular narcissism, what sticks with you, at the end of the day, is *Kim's* screaming voice, *her* palpable fear?"

"Yes," said Wendy at the edge of her breath.

I was impressed with Eric's ability to nose breathe. I imagined he swam a formidable front crawl. He stood and removed his underwear. His penis was average, which was both a relief and a disappointment. I reached down to do the same, but found myself soft. Eric mounted Wendy and quickly built to a frenetic pace that I knew, from experience, she would not appreciate. She called my name.

"Mike," she said.

"I'm here," I said.

"Michael," she said a little louder.

I said, "I'm here," and placed a hand on Wendy's foot. A thick layer of callus covered her sole. I squeezed.

Wendy cried out, either from pleasure or pain I couldn't tell. Eric accelerated. The actress playing Kim continued to scream. I held Wendy's leg, which was slipping away.

Eric shuddered to a standstill and dropped his weight on my wife. When he climbed off, I could see that Wendy was in tears. I tried to embrace her but she pushed me away and ran to the bathroom. I offered Eric a monogrammed towel, a wedding gift from my cousin Hannah. He cleaned himself off, dressed, and left. Wendy locked the bathroom door and ran the tub.

WENDY

AT FIVE O'CLOCK, I GATHERED my belongings and took the A train uptown to talk to Michael in person. I'd tried both his cell and office landline and I'd left messages. I'd sent a strongly worded email.

On my way from the subway to Clayton & Sons, I stopped at The Shops at Columbus Circle to use the restroom, passing stores on my way that I'd been shopping at since childhood. I recalled doing homework at Jamba Juice. Throwing a fit outside Hugo Boss because my father was forcing me to take Latin instead of Spanish like everyone else. Trying on dresses in the changing room at Bebe. Scoping senior boys who worked at J. Crew. My friend Monica stole a Coach bag. I cowardly declined. Monica got caught and the guard called her mother and Monica was sent to boarding school in New Hampshire. My mother died and my father brought me here to pick out something special. I chose a Chanel jacket and never once wore it.

The mall was filled with members of the target demographic for my new campaign. They walked its halls and waited in its lines. They ponied up for immersion blenders. For cashmere bathrobes. For jeans with hundred-dollar holes in the knees. These were the people I would have to convince. First, I'd have to convince myself.

For most of my life, politics was a matter of principles and hypotheticals. I supported a woman's right to choose, but had never needed to make that choice. I supported legal marijuana, but smoking made me paranoid. I was against war, but wouldn't be eligible for a draft if there were one. I was for gay weddings, but had never been invited to one. I was worried about the ozone layer and our reliance on crude oil, but I would be dead before the fallout.

The UBI would affect me directly. If it passed, 60 percent of my salary would go to income tax. We'd pay a 6 percent mansion tax on the current valuation of our home. From a practical standpoint, it was hard to object. There was abundant wealth and not enough work. The gap between rich and poor was growing. I'd read about the pilots in Canada and Kenya, and I'd seen the studies showing that Basic Income actually led to reduced spending on drugs and alcohol. I'd read the arguments about the UBI kick-starting the economy. That rich people tend to buy imported goods, but the poor spend money on American products. That people would have more time and energy to volunteer. That it would wipe out homelessness and extreme poverty, lower crime, increase the bargaining power of labor unions, and improve public health. Artists would have time to make art and the world would become a more beautiful place. Battered women would have the financial independence to leave abusive husbands. Women would not be forced into sex work. With less competition around low wage jobs, racist and xenophobic sentiment would visibly decline. Despite what the Republicans argued, I knew that having money didn't make people lazy or less motivated—I'd met billionaires who worked eighty hours a week—and that even if it did, then $23,000 would not satisfy anyone's desire for a life of leisure and material things.

And yet, in my secret, selfish heart, objections were raised. Lucas was right about the meth-heads in Appalachia. I didn't want my work to pay for their indolence. Money is a fickle thing, as I already knew, and was reminded of that morning in the boutique. This was why we had a system for saving. I believed in that system despite Michael's apparent failure to exploit it. And if the UBI passed, then what would we do? Michael would be jobless and the combined $46,000 we'd receive from the government wouldn't help with our debt when I'd be paying more than that in income tax.

Dissenters warned of other issues as well. That free money gave people false reassurance when they bought cars and homes on credit. That this would create another bubble, a feedback loop that would increase rather than diminish debt. That inflation would moot all potential benefits. That the pilot studies could not be trusted—Canadians and Kenyans were fundamentally different—and we'd soon become a country of obese, lazy people, living off dribbles from the state's leaking teat.

These feelings made me uncomfortable. They were feelings I would never express. They were feelings I barely allowed myself to acknowledge. Neither would the people at this mall. We spent our days on social media where friends encouraged us to attend protests and call our senators. They suggested we check our privilege. Implied that we were awful human beings if we didn't retweet. That we would be ostracized, villainized. We wanted to be liked. Lucas was asking me to alter this paradigm. It seemed an impossible task.

AFTER USING THE RESTROOM, I walked briskly down Broadway in the direction of Rockefeller Center. The Clayton & Sons office was an avenue over, but even in my haste, I wanted to stop and watch the skaters. I grew up on Manhattan's West Side, near Lincoln Center. After my mother passed, I would walk from my apartment through the crowds lingering outside the Metropolitan

Opera, then down past Columbus Circle, onto Central Park South, and eventually to Rockefeller Plaza, where I would stand in my earmuffs on the overlook above the ice rink. My favorites were the lone adults doing figure eights. I imagined that if I ever fell in love it would be with one of these skaters, someone able to carve a slice of solitude from public space.

In November of 2008, I met Michael at the rink after work and we stood in a packed crowd and watched the electoral map that was projected on the ice turn blue. The crowd erupted for each state filled in. Michael and I held hands. We'd unquestioningly supported Obama. We loved his intelligence. We loved his wife. We loved what it said about us that we loved him.

THE RINK WAS CLOSED DUE to weather. I walked away, down Sixth Avenue, past the Van Lewig Building where Chip himself was said to keep his New York office. I pictured the mogul smoking a cigar, looking down from a high window at the masses below. I pictured his wife waving smoke from her face.

MUZAK PLAYED IN THE C&S lobby. Leather chairs sat empty. Men walked briskly in and out of elevators. Piped-in air conditioning chilled the building and I stepped to the front desk and asked to be connected to Michael's office.

When the assistant called, there was no answer.

I asked for Ricky's office. No answer either.

I asked the assistant if she'd seen Michael and I showed her a picture on my phone. She said a lot of people passed through the lobby each day and they were all white men in dark suits with quarter-inch stubble and gelled hair. She suggested I try Michael's cellphone. I thanked her for her time.

I was about to exit when I felt an arm around me. The arm

belonged to Edward Jin, Michael's boss. I did not have warm feelings for the man. He always managed to touch some part of my body: a forearm squeeze or a head pat or an arm around my shoulder. I asked if he'd seen Michael. He invited me upstairs. We rode the elevator in silence.

I was not expecting the piles of cardboard boxes that filled the hallways and cubicle areas. People knelt on the floor feeding paper to shredders. Bloomberg terminals blinked unattended. Desks sat empty. A watercooler lay overturned, leaking onto the tile. I followed Edward into his office.

"Sit," he said, and indicated a chair piled high with paperwork.

"Can I move these papers?"

"I'd rather you didn't." He poured whiskey into a small plastic cup, the kind they give you to rinse at the dentist.

"No thanks," I said.

"Oh it wasn't for you," said Edward. He drank from the cup and refilled.

"Where's Michael?"

"No idea. Haven't seen him all day." He took a second shot of whiskey.

"So why did you bring me up here?"

"Just thought I'd check in, make sure you're set for the next step."

"Next step?"

"The place is swarming with Japanese if you haven't noticed."

I hadn't noticed.

"Utter chaos. We thought the deal was on, but now the SEC's up in our shiz and we've got to shred everything in sight. I don't know much Japanese because my dad was Mr. Assimilation. Wouldn't even touch sushi until I was in my thirties. Now I love the stuff, but only the real American kind. I put the ginger right on top of the roll. An embarrassment. Meanwhile C&S thinks I'm the guy to charm these fuckers at karaoke every night. You know how many sloppy renditions of 'Livin' on a Prayer' I've sung? It's getting to the point where I can't tell whether I'm drunk or sober."

"You're drunk."

"You may be right. Anyway, I wanted to make sure things were okay on your end because I know Michael has more paper tied up in this drowning ship than nearly anyone."

This was news to me.

"There were memos going around for months telling everyone to diversify. It's not like we didn't see this coming. But Michael's been a bit checked out. Or maybe he's an idiot. Pardon me. I didn't mean that. He's not an idiot. Just very dumb. Nice guy, but very stupid, low IQ. I hope everything works out."

I poured myself a drink. The whiskey tasted terrible.

"Bottom shelf," said Edward. "End times."

I exited Jin's office and walked down the hall to Michael's. The last time I'd visited was when he'd been upgraded into this office, a south-facing room with floor-to-ceiling windows. He'd had grand plans to decorate, but I saw now that he'd never done it. The walls were empty. The leather couch was empty. It seemed to be the only room in the building not overflowing with paperwork. Even the trash bin was empty. The shredder was room-temperature, unplugged.

MICHAEL

I FOLLOWED MY THERAPIST INTO his office, plopped myself onto one of his Eames chairs, unloosed a cough drop, lay my legs on the ottoman, and closed my eyes.

I'd been to this office once a week for some twenty-odd years. When I first started seeing Dr. Becker, I was a depressed college student, though I'd have been hesitant to use that term. All I knew was that I stayed in bed for days at a time, sleeping through weekends, and sometimes into the week, missing classes; that rising to face the morning felt like a monumental task. I wasn't planning to kill myself, but I *thought* about suicide a lot, imagining, in methodical detail, the way I'd do it: buying a stepladder from the hardware store on 109th and Broadway, hanging the rope from an exposed pipe in my dorm's laundry room. I knew these feelings weren't normal, and I'd met this girl—this woman—Wendy, and I wanted to be normal.

From the get-go, Dr. Becker had pushed medication. I was resistant at first, fearful in the trite, familiar ways: that I would become a different person, unfeeling, delibidinized, dimmed into hippie placidity. My doctor did his best to quell these fears. I remember, once, he told me I was giving the drug "too much credit," that, as a person who'd experimented with everything from ketamine to cortisone anti-itch supplements, and who'd spent my senior year of high school in a marijuana haze, I was—in so many words—acting like a little bitch. But it was my experience

with stonerism that made me suspicious. I'd lived under the delusion that smoking marijuana at hourly intervals had no effect on
things like my short-term memory, levels of motivation, or enjoy-
ment of certain Southern rap groups. It was only after suffering
from mono that summer, that I realized how powerfully I'd been
under the spell of such a supposedly harmless narcotic. Thinking
clearly for the first time in a while, I realized just how unclearly
I'd been thinking.

The same held true for Prozac, which I did end up taking,
and was still taking in daily, sixty-milligram doses when I arrived
that afternoon at Dr. Becker's office. As I'd feared, it was hard
to say how Prozac had affected my personality. I was a different
person than when I'd started on the drug—higher functioning,
certainly—but it was unclear how much these improvements had
to do with the meds, and how much they had to do with the slow
but consistent crawl of maturation. Besides, where had it gotten
me? A stable mood hadn't stopped my life from falling apart.

"We'll just be a moment, Michael, no need to get comfortable."

The ottoman slipped from under my feet and I almost fell.

"Why are they called ottomans, anyway?" I said. "It must have
something to do with the Ottoman Empire. Which makes me
think of Empire Chinese. You know that place? On Broadway?"

"This is not a session, Michael."

Becker checked his watch.

"Who was that guy in the waiting room?"

"You know I can't discuss another patient. What I want to talk
about is why you're here. You can't just show up at my office. I
know you know that, because you've never done it before. Is this
an emergency?"

"I'm having a weird day."

It seemed as good an explanation as any. I'd woken in the library, shivering cold, with that catnap feeling of time stretched and jellied. I opened another document, but couldn't find my mojo. Ricky's sure thing investment rattled in my brain. I pictured the movers packing up our apartment, Wendy's face red with rage. I found myself walking to Becker's, not really thinking, just moving my feet, mumbling: *Before coming to prominence in the field of hip-hop, Marshall Mathers worked as a pizza chef at the Little Caesars Family Fun Center in the Detroit suburb of Warren, Michigan.*

"I've been withholding," I explained. We'd spent the last many sessions treading in irrelevance, rehashing childhood hang-ups. This was my doing. Becker had asked about Wendy and work and I'd deflected.

"Withholding?"

"For example: I lost all my money."

"How?"

"I bet on America."

"I see," said Dr. Becker, though the calm way he said it, free of worry that I might now require some kind of subsidy in order to continue attending these sessions, made it clear that he did not.

"Did I tell you I got bedbugs?"

This got his attention. Becker surveyed the way I was positioned on his Eames chair, assessing the possibility of something crawling from my pocket and burying itself in the leather.

"Okay," said Dr. Becker, who now walked toward the door.

"Wendy's going to leave me," I added, though it wasn't something I'd allowed until that moment. But it seemed suddenly obvious. I'd woken that morning with a plan to mend my marriage—or, at least, with a plan to make a plan—but as I sat in the now-infested Eames chair and watched the sky darken through the window, I realized that I'd failed.

"I see," said Dr. Becker again.

There was something infuriating in the calm way he said it while pulling open his office door to expedite my exit. He took a step into the hallway. I'd been coming here for decades. All he could say was *I see*.

WENDY

I RETURNED TO AN EMPTY apartment. I felt very itchy. I ran a steaming bath. We lived in a large refurbished loft on the top floor of an old canning factory. Shortly after moving in, I replaced the apartment's original bathtub with an oversized claw-foot I found online.

When Michael first saw the tub, he said something that upset me. The deliverymen had just left after finishing the installation. I'd cleared the packaging and trash. I'd tested the faucets by running hot water over my fingers. I was taking in the tub for the first time.

The tub was beautiful: white with the mildest varnish finish, giving it the shine of a freshly dish-washed dinner plate. The claws were hand-molded by a sculptor in Dutchess County. They were lion's claws with long toes arched to show off individual tendons. The tub was held on tiptoes, supported by the lion's toenails, which started thick at their crescents, then thinned to slim points like sharpened pencils. I had decorated the bathroom in Matisse prints, an array of pastels. The windows were open and a breeze blew in. The sunset shone through the window.

I was pregnant then, and it would not be an exaggeration to say that, in that tub in that room at that moment, I saw the future flash before me. I imagined the drum of my belly covered in bubbles. I saw myself washing my daughter, running shampoo across her tiny skull.

Michael said that it, the tub, would be a good setting for wrist-slitting or death by overdose. He was standing in the doorway when he said it.

I said, "Go on."

Michael entered the bathroom. He tried to touch my waist but I pulled away. He climbed into the empty tub and lay down, fully clothed. He closed his eyes.

Michael went on to describe our bathroom by candlelight on a cold winter night. He watches snow fall outside the window while the water runs at full heat, pinkening his skin. I am out of town for work and he has the loft to himself. Pain has overtaken him. Not sadness, he said. Not loneliness. But real pain, the kind he experienced before being medicated. The kind that only death's stillness might relieve.

Michael said he would put on the kind of maudlin music that plays in movies when characters kill themselves: a softly finger-picked arpeggio, a woman's breathy voice, the buzz of a simple bass line.

He smiled. He thought this was funny. Or maybe he smiled because he'd meant it to be funny but had begun to scare himself, and was trying to salvage the situation by highlighting its comic familiarity. These were clichés after all. Michael said he would surround the tub with candles. Wax would drip into the water. He would reach from tub to medicine cabinet and gather a collection of plastic pillboxes. He would down a deathly combination of pills with a bottle of Pinot Noir. A bitter wine, he said, no citric after-taste to his short life. He would say *salut* and blow a kiss out the window. The kiss would drift on the wind and reach me where I was. Michael would await eternity.

I said I found this upsetting.

Michael said he was only joking. He tried to take my arm and pull me with him into the empty tub. I exited. We did not speak of it for some time.

Over the following months, while Michael bathed, I would watch the clock. Often, I became impatient. I would enter the bathroom and check on him under the guise of keeping him company. I would sit on the toilet seat and watch Michael bathe.

We would talk. I was pregnant. These were pleasant times. We discussed baby names—Michael liked Emma, I preferred Eva—and imagined our lives as parents. Michael would work less, coming home early to cook elaborate meals. We'd walk Nina (my mother's name, which we'd eventually agreed on) to school, wave goodbye from the doorway. We'd buy appallingly hip children's clothing. We'd place her on the bed between us and sandwich her with warmth. In a few years, Michael would coach her basketball team. He'd teach her to make omelets, to ride a bike.

We discussed our fears as well. Mine was that motherhood wouldn't change me as much as I hoped it would. That instead of turning me blissed-out and easy, my new role would make me more tightly wound. I worried that I'd be too stiff to form a comforting cradle. I worried that my performance of motherhood would be unnatural, that my love would not be correctly expressed.

Michael was reassuring. He told me I was being ridiculous. He told me he couldn't think of another person more suited to motherhood. He said that I had a big heart, that my heart was so big that it didn't fit on my sleeve like his did, and so I had to hide and protect it deep inside of myself. But he knew it was there, and that when Nina was born all that stockpiled love would come gushing out. I told him it was the cheesiest, stupidest, and kindest thing anyone had ever said. I rubbed soap on his shoulders and shampooed his hair.

These baths continued until Nina's death. After, I persisted in sitting on the toilet and keeping Michael company, but I began to worry about the possibility of his bathing while I was out of the house.

Michael's pain came as a comfort in some ways, to know that grief was something we shared. At the same time, I couldn't help feeling like we were in competition. I was the mother. Instead of trying to outdo me, he should have been consoling me. Not that I wanted consolation. In fact, I became angry when he tried. What nerve he had to think that anything would help. He was constantly encouraging me to let out my feelings, to talk and to cry. He wanted us to see a counselor together. I felt judged.

Eventually, the thought of returning home to a blood-covered bathroom floor and a bathtub filled with Michael's corpse became overwhelming. When I mentioned it, Michael shrugged and said, "I'm sorry I said that before. Try not to think about it." His lack of irritation with my pestering made me even more nervous. I got rid of the tub. I replaced it with something simpler and smaller, a less romantic spot for suicide.

The replacement bathtub was fine. It had Jacuzzi jets and a comfortable headrest attachment. I took an Ativan. I lay in the bath and flipped through an old issue of *Vogue*. I laid my phone in sight.

MICHAEL

THE BAR WAS MY UNDERGRAD haunt, 420, named for its address on Amsterdam Avenue. The bartender was my undergrad bartender, Penny Watt. The Penny I remembered had a thing for zebra-print patterns. Now the animal's stripes were tattooed from wrist to shoulder. It was, as they say, a look.

"You planning to order anything, or are you just going to stand there staring at me?"

"Penny," I said, "do you not recall your old pal Michael Mixner?"

She looked skeptical.

"You seriously don't remember all those times you threw me out after I stood on that table busting freestyle rhymes?"

I pointed at the offending area. We'd been friends, or so I'd imagined. She was a grad student doing a PhD in gender studies. I was an undergrad who gave two-dollar tips and thought it entitled me to hours of banter.

When I first fell for Wendy, I told Penny immediately. She matched me shot for shot as we hatched a plan to win Wendy's heart. The plan involved arriving at her dorm with a red bow around my forehead and reciting "Bump n' Grind" with Shakespearean affect. It was scrapped in the sober light of morning. When Wendy and I got engaged, we came to this bar and made Miller High Life toasts, the champagne of beers being the closest thing to bubbly in 420's fridge.

The bar was different now. Stoners had always been drawn by its fortuitous address, but only after legalization had its owners cashed in. These days it was a full-on vape bar, decorated in a mishmash of Stanley Mouse reproductions and posters for eighties-era gaming systems. A chalkboard menu offered a long list of local and imported strains—one, an indica/sativa blend, was described as ideal for the Columbia film student forced to sit through a screening of Béla Tarr's *Sátántangó*—and most of the tables had been retrofitted with perma-vapes.

The room was filled with skunky mist and stumbling students, a number of whom wore AR helmets, which was all but unthinkable a few years before. The problem with the old devices wasn't gaudiness or bulkiness, but something like its opposite: misguided subtlety. Take Google Glass, a product that failed because it looked like an ugly pair of glasses. The current helmets were gladiator gold with reflective visors and tricked-out lights, designed with readers of DC and Marvel in mind. The helmets weren't exactly cool, but like band T-shirts and sports jerseys, they were statements of pride, declarations of allegiance to particular tribes.

"Drink or die, perv," said Penny. She poured a bourbon, slid the drink in my direction.

"So you do remember."

"Dude, I'm sorry to say it, but you look really terrible, like a tumorous dog."

"Hazard of the profession."

"Oh yeah, I was gonna ask. I take it all this stuff in the news has not been the best for you."

"That would be an understatement."

"Well, just be thankful, you still look in better shape than Broder."

"Broder?"

"He was in here the other day," said Penny. "Back in town."

"And he was bad?"

"Drinking," said Penny. "So yeah."

"Shit," I said.

"Shit is right." She poured me another.

Broder was my undergrad accomplice and partner in hip-hop. I was WebMD and he was Mix Master Mucinex. We were roommates and inseparable until early sophomore year when he dropped out after developing a heroin habit.

We lost touch. I worried, sure, but I was a naïve college kid with other things on his mind. I never thought Broder would die, and he didn't, though he came close one night in a Dunkin' Donuts bathroom on a bag cut with bleach. Next I knew, he was in a California rehab clinic.

Broder came to my wedding, but left after the ceremony. I think he felt awkward around other friends, and particularly Ricky, who wasn't shy about voicing his abhorrence of Recovery Kultür. After that, I'd been busy with work, and he'd been busy getting married, himself, to another former addict who didn't stay that way for long. Her body was discovered in Joshua Tree, in the motel where Gram Parsons had also OD'd. I should have called him then.

"What was he doing here?" I asked Penny, but she'd left with a vape-load for some guys in the corner. Besides, I knew what he was doing: haunting the old rooms, hoping to reclaim lost glory or black out trying. I was doing the same.

WENDY

I WOKE IN A COLD tub. If a warm bath is the womb, then a cold bath is the coffin. Or maybe a cold bath is the morgue table, and asleep in the cold bath one dreams the doctors above her, poking at her organs with their instruments.

It was only 8 P.M. but I was anxious. There were no missed calls from Michael. Ricky wasn't answering his phone, and I'd received another email from Michael's mother. I did not write back. I didn't call Lillian either. I called my father, who said Michael was fine, that he was probably out with the boys from the office, that at times like this they had to let off some steam.

"Yes," I said, "steam."

I didn't mention the money or my meeting with the client or Michael's absence from work. My father told me he loved me and that I could come to his apartment if I didn't want to be alone. I told him that wasn't necessary. I felt better for a moment, but as soon as I hung up, the fear overtook me again.

Slowly, forcefully, I used my fingernails to pierce the skin above my anklebone and dug out one of my bites. The picked scab bled. I worked my way up my legs, scratching, picking. This did not decrease the itchiness, but I got satisfaction from the rhythm and pain. Torn skin accumulated under my fingernails. I bit my tongue and turned the TV on.

I watched the news, waiting for the story to break that Michael had been found dead. Instead I received a litany of louder misfortunes. The National Guard now surrounded the FSU Hillel. A Guardsman spoke over a bullhorn, demanding surrender. The showrunner of a prominent HBO drama denied allegations that he'd failed to provide his actors with plastic genital guards before shooting sex scenes. The Gulf Coast prepared for Hurricane Marie.

When the news cycle repeated, I turned the TV off and googled for local victims who fit Michael's description. I knew this search would yield nothing. I knew that he was fine. I told myself not to worry. I told myself that this was the beginning of my being alone. I would pack a bag in the morning and leave.

Before my bath, I'd logged on to E*Trade. It was worse than I'd imagined. This was a fundamental betrayal of the promise of our union: that we would be the kind of people who had money.

I turned off the lights and lay down. I did not feel tired. It was still early. The cat swaggered up to my side of the bed. She fit her head into the glass from which I'd been drinking. She stood on her hind legs. Her tongue lapped at the water. I imagined the things that tongue had touched. "No," I said, and slapped her.

The cat retreated. I felt ashamed and hoped I hadn't caused injury. The cat licked at the area I'd slapped, a patch of sagging belly. She cautiously made her way back to the glass. The cat stared straight at me. I tried to find, in her eyes, some indication that she recognized, in me, another consciousness, a being capable of pain and mercy. She sipped again from my glass. I slapped her, harder this time. A tooth sunk into my wrist. I tried to shake her off. She clawed at my elbow and shoulder. I pulled her tail and she let go.

I rubbed my wound under cold water. We were out of bacitracin. For weeks, I'd nagged Michael to take the cat to a vet for tests and shots. I tried to watch a reality show called *Arm Candy* about a group of working-class men vying for the attentions of wealthy older women. I tried to google Lucas but I didn't know his surname. I googled *feline HIV*. It was uncommon. I got out of bed and searched the apartment for hidden cash. I checked the cabinets and shelves, Michael's dresser, and the freezer. I found nothing. I ordered a car on my company account.

MICHAEL

ANOUSH WAS THE LAST OF a dying breed: Pakistani American, heavy on the horn, patriotically heedless of yellow lights. Apps like Lyft and Mhustle had elbowed in on his terrain, offering plush seats and Dasani in exchange for higher fares. And though the driverless revolution hadn't arrived like we'd been promised, yellow cabs were still few and far between. If you could afford New York, you could afford these apps. I was a holdout. Mhustle was for show-offs, and Lyft's smooth-sailing hybrids left me anesthetized. I preferred wind through duct-taped windows, guys like Anoush.

"Asshole," he said, passing a Tesla with California plates. I wasn't sure if he meant the car's driver or its creator, Mr. Musk: husband of models, saver of ozone, emissary to Mars, and an outspoken promoter of the UBI.

"Nothing against Teslas," Anoush clarified. "It's just a shame that the jerkoffs who buy them can't drive. People say Jersey is the asshole of America, but I'm telling you, it's California."

"Armpit," I said. "But point taken."

I wondered if he'd ever left New York. Travel was expensive, and airports still weren't pleasant places for men of his skin tone. Just the previous week, Twitter was abuzz with the story of two teenage boys, on a class trip to D.C, forcibly stripped of their turbans by LaGuardia security. Besides, California had lost much of its appeal in the wake of climate change. Who needed Venice when you could surf the Long Island Sound without so much as a wetsuit for warmth? Even In-N-Out was now bicoastal. All Cali had left was smog and drought. Anoush turned up the music. A rapper spit end-rhyming couplets on the subject of #Occupy, threatening to "cream on Senator Breem" and "go to war for Devor."

"Fuuuuck," said Anoush. "I completely forgot about the Funeral. Should have taken Eleventh instead."

I'd forgotten as well, distracted by Penny, and news of Broder, and vape-clouded memories of simpler times. I was headed, instead, to the Gatsby party. It seemed right for my mood: stuck in the past, sulky that my wardrobe hadn't saved me. To get there we had to pass through the Funeral for Capitalism. The event was bigger than I'd envisioned, thousands strong, inflatable caskets crowd-surfing the crowd. I rolled down the window. The amplified voice sounded like Devor's, but it was hard to tell beneath the cheers and engine noise.

"Big crowd."

"You're telling me," said Anoush. "I was down here earlier, before my shift. But I don't know, man. I mean, what's gonna come of all this? I don't trust Breem. I'm telling you now, he'll never let Basic Income pass. You know he started his career as a lawyer in Chip Van Lewig's office?"

"I know," I said, though in fact I did not, yet another reminder that for all my pretension I was grossly misinformed. I did know of Van Lewig, a Midwestern cosmetics scion with family ties to the Heritage Foundation and John Birch Society, whose lobbying efforts had helped reverse decades of environmental progress. The Van Lewig Building was across the street from C&S.

"Besides," Anoush continued, "all those talks he gave at Clayton and Goldman. Those guys are his friends. They paid for his whole campaign. You think he's gonna turn on them now?"

I'd been to one of those talks, watched my senator speak in boarding school argot, play up his free market vision for the partisan crowd. I'll admit I was impressed. Not by Breem's ideas, or the hammy jokes he interwove, but by the disproportionately large size of the senator's head. The thing was massive, two feet from chin to dome, or at least it seemed from the back row, where I sat borderline tripping after splitting a weed gummy with Ricky. I knew that politicians trended big-headed, but it was something else to see it in person, like watching a living, breathing bobblehead doll.

"Look," said Anoush. "If it were up to me, what we'd do is get all the brown people in America to go to a gun show in West Virginia, arm ourselves with assault rifles, and roll into Clayton & Sons like OG gangsters."

"Right," I said. "You really think that would help?"

"I mean, I'm not a violent dude," said Anoush. "Do unto others, and all that. But these guys who work at Clayton, can we really call them human?"

"Hm," I said, but must have hesitated.

"You with me brother?"

I mimed loading an AK, spraying bullets left and right.

"Watch where you point that thing," he said, flipped the cab into reverse, hopped up on the sidewalk, and executed a K-turn. The traffic drones were nowhere to be seen.

WENDY

DESPITE HAVING RECENTLY BATHED, THE first thing I did at my
father's was shower. There was neither shampoo nor conditioner.
My father is bald. A single bar of mouthwash-green Irish Spring
had eroded into a thumb-shaped nub.

The building was a prewar townhouse that hadn't seen an
upgrade since the 1980s. My father, I assumed, could have moved
into a newer apartment with better pipes and central heating, but
he refused to leave the place where my mother died. He believed
that a part of her existed in the floors and walls. He meant dust
particles and hair follicles, or maybe just memories. To leave
would be to lose her forever.

I turned the knob to *H* in the hopes of being scalded, but all I
got was room-temperature trickle. I wet the soap and managed to
work up a lather. I washed my cat-wound and the picked scabs. I
used my father's razor to shave off a large scab on my inner right
thigh. I watched as my blood mixed with suds and ran down the
drain.

Out of the shower, I found athletic tape, gauze, and bacitracin
in a never-before-opened emergency kit on his medicine shelf.
I applied bacitracin and taped half the roll of gauze around my
thigh. Because I'm sentimental, I put on a matching set of
my mother's flannel pajamas. The pajamas fit me well. In photos
from before I was born, my mother gives the impression of a rare
beauty, a redhead like me with broad shoulders and a lipsticked

smile. I tried to keep this image in my head, but a memory replaced it, my mother in these pajamas toward the end of her illness. Bony wrist poking from a baggy flannel sleeve. Thin neck growing up from her collar like a blighted, peeling branch.

The pajamas had not been washed in nearly thirty years so as to preserve some trace of her odor, perhaps a faint scent of the perfume she overused toward the end to cover the stench from her colostomy bag. I sniffed the pajamas to achieve further memory, but all I got was mothballs.

When my father saw me in this outfit, he was speechless for maybe half a second—long enough that I noticed, but only because I know him so well—before he told me I looked beautiful. He hugged me.

WE ORDERED THAI FOOD FROM my favorite spot. I was surprised the place was still open, but my father told me they'd extended their delivery hours in order to drum up extra business. The advent of drone delivery had been hell on small restaurants, which were being pushed out due to the vast delivery zones of bigger restaurants that invested in higher-powered drones. The restaurant was called Ground, and competition aside, they made a spinach-peanut dumpling that I've yet to find bested.

We watched the news while we waited for our food. I'd taken two Ativan by this point, and my anxiety about Michael's disappearance had dimmed. On NY1, Jay Devor spoke to a crowd. I hadn't seen him in years, but he looked the same: thick hair, gray eyes, plainspoken confidence. A handsome mole sat just below his hairline.

Devor had hit on me once, at Rachel Kirshenbaum's wedding. Michael couldn't attend due to a work conflict and Devor had used Michael's absence as an opportunity to continuously refill my wineglass. He'd presented his case as a logical argument. Not in a pleading way, but straightforwardly, and with great self-assurance, in much the same manner that he spoke to the protesters. Devor told me that he and his girlfriend, Sophia, were "open." He said it with steadiness and eye contact, as if being open were an indisputably feminist act. As if Michael's assumed possessiveness was all that held me back from guilt-free exploration.

Now he spoke of bigger things. He talked about the concept of progress, the generally accepted rhetoric that it comes at a snail's pace. He said that this rhetoric was what the establishment wanted us to believe. That the establishment used this rhetoric to keep us complacent. He said that now was not the time to wait, and that, in fact, by waiting, by working within the slow system, we were making things worse. Now was not the time for patience, but for action.

Devor said we could not, in good conscience, allow the UBI to fail. He said that this was our opportunity to change the system. We had voices, and they had to be heard. This was still a democracy. Our senator was someone we'd elected with our votes. We needed to let him know, needed to scream so loudly he'd be forced to hear. We needed to let him know that if he didn't hear—and if the rest of the Senate didn't hear—then we would not accept their verdict of progress stalled, would not wait patiently until the next battle for incremental justice might be fought. No, we would take action. And we had to make them understand that that action would have consequences.

The crowd was in a frenzy. Devor knew to wait until the cheering died down. He may have urged for chaos, but he was in control. He claimed to want people to think for themselves, but his smooth talk masked the dogmatic nature of his own stance.

"He speaks well," my father said. I assumed he supported the UBI. A lifelong lefty, he did pro-bono work for the Transit Workers Union. He rarely spoke of Michael's work, but I knew he disapproved.

And yet, wasn't my father in the very demographic I'd been tasked with convincing? I wondered if he had a secret heart. A heart that didn't want to pay tax on this apartment after finally paying off a thirty-year mortgage.

NY1 cut away to the steps of the statehouse in Albany where Senator Breem pushed through a crowd of reporters to a waiting car. Breem looked tired. I pictured him shaving in a hotel bathroom, staring into the mirror at his own strange face.

The drone pulled up to the window and placed our order on the sill. After my father had emptied our takeout containers onto ceramic plates—I knew he usually ate straight out of the containers, and I found it sweet that he took out dishware just for me—and after he'd tested the temperature of his soup and taken a few hesitant sips, my father reached across the table and took hold of my hand. His fingers felt dry. I wondered if he'd once bought moisturizer since my mother had passed.

MICHAEL

THE PENTHOUSE SUITE WAS BROHO-CHIC with parquet floors, a cowhide rug, faux-Banksy wall art, unattended turntables, and a cadre of finance types in various stages of undress and inebriation. Some ties were tightly wound, while others had been loosened, or turned into bandannas, or used as lassos on the makeshift dance floor. A nude young woman with no visible head or body hair lay face up on the king bed, a small arrangement of sliders covering her stomach. It looked like a six-pack made of sesame mini-buns, leaking pork fat pooled in her bellybutton.

Of the roughly forty people crammed into the suite, I recognized five from my office. There were Jim "Button-Fly" Nance and "Tender" Eddie Adagio of the fourteenth-floor trading desk, ashing cigars out the window. There was Caroline Dworkins, who stole my promotion in 2015, sucking face with someone who looked like Elaine's old boyfriend from *Seinfeld*, the deep-voiced David Puddy—or perhaps it was the actor himself, handsomely aged and bearing a stripe of Sontag-silver.

Button-Fly and Tender hailed from Princeton and Dartmouth, respectively, where they'd played squash and water polo, respectively, and had been members of eating clubs that excluded all but the most corporately connected undergraduates. These weren't Bushes, Clintons, or Kennedys like the bluebloods from Harvard and Yale, but bona fide titans: Rockefellers, Van Lewigs, and Kochs. The rest of the partygoers were recognizable by type: hedge fund guys in Yankees caps playing quarters on the coffee table; JPMorgan clones in suits and skirt suits, laughing their hissy, reptilian laughs; brokers from smaller firms hovering at the edge of conversational circles. A couple of Goldmanites sat cross-legged on the kilt-patterned couch, lording silently over the proceedings.

Aside from the suite's gratis stabs at bohemian decor—e.g. the Banksy stuff and a framed fashion shot of two beached models leaning in for a kiss—a few additional, and seemingly emblematic, decorations had been installed by our hosts. Mirror-green streamers dangled from the molding, and clear garbage bags full of green confetti were taped to the ceiling, to be opened and poured upon us at the stroke of midnight. Green bulbs had been fit into the lamps, throwing a limón glow on the Goldmanites. One wouldn't have guessed Gatsby, but the theme made more sense in this context than it did at the recent wave of Gatsby-inspired weddings that Wendy was always pointing out on Pinterest, with their grooms in riding breeches, their take-home bags of chocolate coins. At least this party had the right mix of flamboyance and subsurface despair.

I was making my way toward the bar, eyeing a bottle of Pappy Van Winkle, when someone approached the human platter, grabbed a slider, and dragged it through the happy trail of hoisin sauce—making circular motions at the pubic root to sop as much sauce as possible—before popping the sandwich whole into his mouth.

"Dude," I said.

Instead of answering, Ricky raced across the room, wrapped his arms around my knees, and knocked me over. The vape must have upset my inner-ear balance. He mounted me, tickling under my armpits and repeating my name so that my face was purposely sprayed with spit. I pushed him off and we stood.

"Hey buddy," he said. A pasty residue dripped onto his upper lip. Ricky sucked the string of cocaine-tinted snot back up his sinus canal and wiped at his nose. The SD bracelet rattled on his wrist. We made our way to the makeshift bar. Ricky poured us tequila shots, and I chased with a tumbler of Pappy.

"So what's the deal with this party?" I said. "It's supposed to be *Great Gatsby*, right? Why is there a Lego sculpture of the *Titanic* on that mantelpiece?"

"Oh you know, death of the American dream and whatnot. *Death of a Salesman*, *Death in Venice*, the petite mort of my drippy dick pulling out of the *Titanic*'s ass to make room for the ice crater. This is the end, as Jim Morrison once said while wagging his cock at a photo of Barbra Streisand. The end my friend, and here we are: the fall of Rome, the decline of derivatives, the rise of dildos made from real human skin like Hitler only dreamed."

"We're celebrating the crash?"

"Absolutely. You know why? Because it puts things in perspective, buddy, reminds us of what's really important, you know? The real gay-ass shit like love, family, and friendships like ours."

I didn't laugh.

"Aw, I'm kidding you, Mikester. We're celebrating because the world is going to shit, and how hilarious is that? We'll watch the plebes run through the streets while us pharaohs sit tight on our thrones and think about the long strings of zeros at the end of our bank statements. Most of us, anyway, you being the exception. You really should have listened to me about not putting all your eggs into stupid investments, but bygones be bygones, buddy, speaking of which . . ."

Ricky pulled me into a smaller second bedroom. I assumed this had to do with the investment opportunity he'd mentioned that morning. I'd thought it over on the taxi ride here, as I scrolled through my missed calls and texts from Wendy. At this point, I assumed that she knew we were insolvent. She'd be asleep when I came home, but in the morning, I'd be asked to explain. And while the old Michael would have jumped at the chance to risk all our remaining assets on Ricky's recommendation—a last-ditch effort at easy redemption—I'd decided I would no longer be that person. Instead, I would beg my wife's forgiveness. I would tell her I loved her and that I was sorry. We'd go from there. Whatever we did would be decided together. I was planning to explain all this to Ricky.

The other bedroom was shrouded in herb smoke. Bankers stretched out on the floor, vegging out for what may have been the first time in their lives. They were twinkle-eyed and flirty, some barefoot, some in sheer navy dress socks. Jay-Z, patron saint of reckless spending, spit through a small pair of speakers, proclaiming himself "Che Guevara with bling on."

A familiar-looking guy on the corner of the couch fidgeted with a lighter and followed the bong's progress around the room. The man looked older than the others, with a receded hairline gone gray around the ears. He wore a ring of razor burn like a necklace, and his eyes were barely visible beneath his lowered lids. In jeans and a hoodie, he stood out among my business-casual colleagues.

"You recognize him?" asked Ricky.

And then it came to me.

"Holy shit," I said, and Broder must have recognized me as well, because he brought himself to a standing position and made his way to my side of the room. Broder walked with a slight limp, real or performed I couldn't tell, though the rest of his appearance—the hair, the eyes, a rolled sleeve revealing a deveined wrist the color of uncooked shrimp—made a case for the latter.

"Hickory dickory dock," I said. "Took two Sudafed . . ."

". . . Now I can't feel my cock," Broder said, finishing the couplet we'd written senior year as part of a Wu-Tang-style anthem called "*Law & Order* (Marathon on TBS)."

Ricky said "*salut*," and the three of us drank.

"Found this little bitch sucking dick for coke by the West Side docks," said Ricky. Broder didn't laugh, and Ricky said he was only kidding, that Broder had shown up on his doorstep looking like hell in a Whole Foods basket. Ricky had spruced him up and brought him to the party.

"Something like that," said Broder.

Ricky offered me a bump, which, even in my drunken state, I wisely declined. He suggested something more mellow, and held out a pill. It was mint green and marked with a capital *M*. This was more my speed. I was nicely buzzed and looking to lose what little edge was left. Nothing in my Duane Reade bag would do the job. In the morning I'd face Wendy, but tonight I could obliterate the fact of my mistakes.

"Two milligrams Klonopin," I proudly announced.

"Not bad. How about this one?"

He produced another pill, of a similar hue but larger in size.

"Oh shit," I said, and snatched it.

"You sure?" Ricky said. It was already inside me.

"Don't most people snort them?" said Broder.

"Sinuses," I explained.

I asked Broder what he was doing in town, and he shrugged and looked at his boots, mumbled something about trying to get the DJ thing going again. I told him that sounded cool, that I hadn't made music in a long time, that I missed it, missed it terribly, but such was life, and, anyway, I was trying to write this book, a book that considered so many things we used to discuss, the theories we'd developed in those ripe, creative days. I thought

Broder would be interested, but I could tell, from his wandering eyes, that he was not.

The Jay-Z song ended, and Biggie came on, the rags-to-riches tale of his rise from humble beginnings reading rap magazines, to the spoils of stardom, owning gaming consoles, racking up long-distance charges. The bong-ripped bankers tried to rap along, emphasizing the end rhymes and mumbling the rest. They mostly muted themselves when B.I.G. used the N-word, though a few of them, I noticed, seemed to take satisfaction in saying it aloud. Ricky chugged toward the doorway, a conga line of one, heading back to the bar to get the three of us another round. Broder and I hit a conversational impasse. We stood and listened to the song.

"You've done well," he said. "You and Ricky both."

I had practice with this genre of uncomfortable exchange. During my visits home to Pittsfield over the years, I'd always managed to bump into a former classmate and be forced to endure this sort of quick-fire appraisal and resentful third degree. Against instinct, I'd learned not to downplay my position by acting falsely humble or condescendingly nonchalant, so I told Broder, "Yeah, things have been good," though of course this was a lie—things had never been worse—but I knew, from past experience, that no one had much interest in the complicated truth.

I waited out another pause as Broder took a cinematic drag on his cigarette and stubbed it out in a ceramic teacup that must have belonged to the hotel. "It hasn't been so easy," he said. "Not for me."

"No," I replied. "I don't imagine it has."

"You don't know the half," he said, and I tried to make a sober and sympathetic face, though the Oxy I'd taken had begun to spread its wings, and I could feel a heated current floating skyward up my spine.

"Look Michael," he said. Through the doorway we saw Ricky lining up shots at the bar. Broder asked if maybe there was somewhere quiet we could talk.

Fucked up as I was, I could sense what was coming: the big pitch. He was going ask me for money. I'd had the same nervous hitch in my voice when I'd pitched Ricky that morning. Broder was about to explain that he had this sweet deal for studio time at some spot in Williamsburg, and a suitcase full of sick beats and guest MCs lined up, but the thing was that they needed a deposit on the equipment.

Or worse, Broder's pitch would not be for studio time at all, which I'd have been happy to help with if I'd had the cash. No, the pitch would be for a more outrageous and expensive venture, some scam on which he'd spent the last of his savings, and now needed a loan to push through to completion.

To preempt the pitch, and because it was true, I said, "Actually, I wanted to talk to you too. I've been meaning to tell you I'm sorry, for the past, for losing touch."

"It's okay," said Broder, "It's not important."

"It is important," I said. "I was a bad friend. I'm sorry for not visiting you at your parents' house after you left school, for not coming to your wedding."

"Seriously, that's not important, but if we could find a quiet place . . ."

"Would you go back and do it differently?" I asked.

The question gave Broder pause. He scratched his chin.

"Look, Michael," Broder started, but before he could continue, we were interrupted by the nearing thrum of a familiar chant:

"WHOSE STREETS?"

"OUR STREETS!"

The door burst open. Someone killed the lights.

WENDY

I WOKE ON THE COUCH. My father had wrapped me in an afghan and put a pillow beneath my head. I checked my phone and found no word from Michael. I checked my feeds and caught mention of a riot at the Zone Hotel, where a group of protesters had crashed a finance party. Dozens injured. Many arrests.

I turned on the news. The streets were lit in blue and red light. I watched as paramedics loaded stretchers and witnesses described the scene. Michael's phone went to voicemail. The sky was still dark. My father was still asleep. I took cash from his wallet and called a town car.

I felt nauseated on the ride to Brooklyn. I opened the window, but midtown traffic brought exhaust fumes and noise. The Times Square circus blinked above me. The driver called me ma'am and asked if I was okay. I said I was fine.

Light dimmed as the town car turned onto our block. Three men stood on the corner blowing smoke at the stars. The stars—all two—were barely visible in the cutout of sky between the oaks that stood like guards outside our building.

I climbed the stairs. I hoped Michael was home. With each step, my body felt heavier. For a moment, I feared that I'd reverse gears at the top and go tumbling back to the bottom. I could hear the cat crying. The door was unlocked.

Lights were on. The duvet was spread on the floor, like a picnic blanket, in the spot where our bed used to be. The air mattress lay deflated beside it. Michael was asleep on the duvet, fully clothed, sweating. A bedbug—the first I'd seen in days, though I assumed it would spawn more, repopulate the apartment—gnawed into a mole on Michael's neck. A single hair sprouted from the mole. Blood swelled in an outer ring around the bull's-eye of the abrasion.

It may have been a beetle or some other insect. In fact, I'm sure it was.

I sat on the edge of the bed. The cat licked Michael's ear. I placed a hand on the small of his back. I borrowed his phone and ordered a car back to my dad's.

OUT FRONT, WIND RAN COOL across my body. The cat made cat sounds and scratched at my sweater. I lifted her above my head. She responded with a screech. I lowered the animal and watched it run free for the first time in its brief and now briefer life, feinting toward trash cans before scurrying southbound on Hoyt Street, some elusive, fleshly odor pointing toward darkness.

TAGGED PHOTOS

1.

RICKY'S STILL IN CONTROL. HE whispers, "I'm in control," releases the links from his French cuff shirt, places them in a rinse cup beside the bed, rolls his sleeves, and fingers the bracelet.

Broder's in the bathroom. The shower runs. Steam seeps from the partially open bathroom door. Ricky's eyes close for a moment, but he forces them open. They've snorted Oxy mixed with blow, and drunk their share of tequila, and now, in the dark of the hotel's false midnight, as sun peeks in around the edge of the blackout curtains, he wants nothing more than an hour of shuteye before heading into the office. First there's the question of Broder.

They were together with Michael when the riot began, a rush of chanting people swinging pipes and bats, knocking partygoers to the ground. Some fought back, but most pushed toward the room's only exit, the same door through which rioters continued to arrive. The congestion caused more blood. Skulls hit walls and bodies tumbled into decorations. The Lego *Titanic* crashed.

Amid this chaos, Ricky saw, or thought he saw, Sammy from last night across the room. Protester or guest, he couldn't say, failing to remember if he'd told him about the party. Ricky yelled Sammy's name, but no contact was made. The next thing he knew, he'd made it out unscathed.

They took the emergency stairs to the floor below, and barricaded themselves in the room that Ricky had presciently rented beforehand in case a need for privacy arose.

It was only then they realized that Michael was gone. Returning to find him wasn't an option; a SWAT team had already arrived. Ricky's been texting Michael since, to no avail.

A trip to the minibar got the party restarted while Ricky combed Twitter for reports from the scene upstairs. Broder rested his head on Ricky's shoulder and served him small bumps of coke from his overgrown thumbnail. He's been hanging on Ricky all night, and hasn't balked at Ricky's test runs, either: patting Broder's butt, gripping his thigh, blowing air in his ear as Broder leaned on him in the elevator. As far as Ricky knows, Broder doesn't have a gay bone in his body, but soon he will have a gay bone in his body. Ba-dum-ching. Ricky's Viagra should kick in any second. He popped it an hour ago. His cock is slow in responding. Maybe it needs assistance.

Ricky stands from the bed, undoes his belt, and lets his pants drop. He pulls them over his ankles, and lies down again in just shoes, socks, and shirt. He feels like Big Bird. His hands are cold. His penis inches out of hiding.

For inspiration, Ricky surveys his sexual past. First, Michael. Well, technically, first was Evan Schmidt in third grade. They'd been playing doctor with Evan's dad's doctor bag, using his stethoscope to test the beat of each other's hearts, when Ricky decided that Evan needed a full body exam. Five minutes later, Evan's penis was in Ricky's hand. Five days later, Ricky was in the principal's office, unrepentant. Five years later, Evan was still in the closet and Ricky was a full-on faggot, and fuck you for calling him one, you closeted fuck. Fifteen years later, Evan was gay-bashed in a public park, Ricky was a Republican, and Ricky's best friend's hero was a rapper who encouraged impressionable teens to commit hate crimes.

Anyway, Michael. Ricky has loved him since childhood. The men he grew up with relied on grunts for communication. Michael was endearingly talkative. Ricky was too, in a sense, but Michael could talk about feelings in a way that Ricky wasn't able to. Maybe it was a Jew thing, or growing up around teenaged girls, Michael's melodramatic cousins who were always going on about this boy or that, watching Bette Midler in *Beaches* and weeping. As a budding homosexual, Ricky knew he was supposed to dig Midler too, but he couldn't get past the balladeering. He understood his distaste as an emotional deficiency.

Michael and Ricky have been inseparable since fourth grade. While other kids played football, they discussed death. Mostly they exchanged information: that grandparents are usually the ones who die, but parents and even other kids can too; that animals eat your body when you're dead; that you turn blue; that you go to heaven, maybe, depending on your religion.

In fifth grade, their classmate Chris Potter found his stepdad hanging by a rubber belt in his garage, and Potter's association with the great unknown conferred on him a certain sagacity. Out of what seemed like pity to everyone but themselves, Michael and Ricky let Potter into their clique so they could ask questions like, "Did you cry?" and, "Was he naked?" and, "Does the garage door still work?"

They continued to discuss death until middle school, when they became more interested in sex. Michael made lists of the girls he planned to ask to dance at his bar mitzvah and Ricky made lists of famous people he was planning to sleep with once he'd made it on Wall Street. He'd seen enough movies to know that everyone in New York was a little bit bisexual if you had enough money, and he'd later turn out to be right.

Ricky had come out a year earlier, in sixth grade, to the surprise of no one, and to the derision of everyone in school except

Michael. It was 1994, shortly after Magic Johnson announced his HIV diagnosis. Ricky wasn't worried about the disease; Pittsfield, he assumed, was too far west on the Mass Pike for the urban sprawl of the virus, and besides, he was ten. What excited him were the condom demonstrations squeezed into every TV special on the subject. Watching Magic roll a rubber down the shaft of a banana was Ricky's first experience in pornography. And though the high-speed modem would rear its head in his household by year's end, Magic's hands on the potassium-rich phallus would stick with him, a weather vane pointing turgidly toward the future.

In fact, it was this very condom demo, shown again during sixth grade health class, that gave Ricky the courage to declare his orientation during morning announcements. Never one to shy away from showmanship, Ricky marched to the stage in a Magic Johnson jersey he'd found at the nearby Champion outlet. He was booed; the kids at school were Celtics fans.

Bless Michael, who managed to exist outside the pressures of high school Darwinism by frolicking mostly in his own dreamy mind. It's not that Michael didn't care what other people thought, but that he never quite noticed.

It's supposed to be better for gay teens these days, what with tolerance taught in schools, and gay characters on television, and a generational turn away from open homophobia and toward a more hidden one, but gay teens still pop up in the obits, their terrified eyes triggering Ricky's memories of the fear he felt, each day, walking home while farm dudes drove past in their pickup trucks holding sawed-off shotguns out the windows as they called his name and hysterically laughed.

By junior year, Ricky and Michael were still virgins. Ricky didn't know any other gay people. There was a club at school called the Gay-Straight Alliance, an aspirational title. The club's only members were goth straight girls and two stoners who knew that membership in the club meant membership in the goth girls' password-protected panties.

Besides, the GSA kids were cloyingly political, driving to Boston for Pride marches, and circulating petitions for unisex bathrooms. Ricky's interests were strictly libidinal. One night, after many shots from a bottle of melon liqueur that had been gathering dust at the back of Ricky's parents' liquor cabinet, he managed to convince Michael that a mouth is a mouth. Michael seemed to enjoy it, but he hurt Ricky's feelings by telling him, after, that he'd pretended the fellating tongue belonged to their math teacher, Ms. Picciola. Michael and Ricky were awkward around each other through the following week, but things quickly went back to normal. Nothing like it ever happened again.

Ricky's still soft. The shower still runs. "I'm in control," he whispers again and taps the SD bracelet against his teeth. Ricky doesn't play *Shamerican Sykosis*, but over the past year, he's been buying Sykodollars. At first, he acquired SD to trade for drugs online, sick of the laxative-cut coke that fueled the club scene. But as the Dow plunged, and Wall Street crashed, and a possible bailout was vetoed by Congress, Ricky realized he had a hedge against the volatile dollar. Shamerica, with its rising popularity and flourishing markets, was a safe storage vault. The dollar dropped and the SD slowly, unnoticeably rose.

The hedge had paid off, but the really interesting thing happened after that. The game's creator, a guy called Lucas Van Lewig, reached out to Ricky, offering a wildly lucrative opportunity for investment. And maybe the thought of these prospective riches has hit a primal nerve, or the Viagra has kicked in, because Ricky has finally come to glorious tumescence when Broder emerges, removes the towel draped over his arm to reveal a handgun, and fires.

2.

DETECTIVE RYAN HAS BEEN TAKING statements for nearly eight hours, trying to gauge what went down. One thing is clear: Jay Devor's speech at the Funeral for Capitalism was a call to arms, and when it was over, Devor led a parade of weapon-wielding #Occupiers to a finance party at the Zone Hotel. What's not clear is where Devor ended up. He wasn't at the hotel, and security footage hasn't turned up his face. How much planning was involved and where the weapons came from are more difficult questions, and ones that can't be answered by the stoned-looking kid who sits across Ryan's desk.

"I mean, it felt like a dream," says Sammy. "Or not like a *dream* dream—my actual dreams are much more boring: losing keys or teeth falling out—but like I'd entered a slightly altered or alternate reality."

"Right," says Ryan. They've got drones watching Devor's apartment and scouring the streets. Even his girlfriend, Kate, seems unaware of his whereabouts. It's unlikely that they'll find him tonight.

And by tonight he means this morning. An hour ago, the sun was a dim, lovely golf ball. Now it's pure terror, coming in through the blinds and coloring the stragglers carcinogen orange. Ryan can see them through the plexiglass, cuffed in folding chairs, one trying to sleep, while another, a clean-cut guy roughly Ryan's own age, snaps awake and registers a half-second shock at his surroundings. Ryan thinks: Don't you have a job? But of course the man doesn't, and of course that's why he's here.

"Does that make sense?" asks Sammy. "I guess what I mean is it didn't feel unreal so much as untethered. The Funeral had this morbid energy with the caskets and the Mardi Gras band, and I swear I felt a ghostly or apparitional presence. Like those nineteenth-century spirit photographs where the light illuminates a face that isn't there, you know? Only in this case, instead of a face it was, like, a building-sized grim reaper, or something, that no one could see but that we could feel."

"Grim Reaper?"

Ryan tries to focus. He thinks: If I were Devor, where would I be? He pictures a steaming jacuzzi.

"And I remember there was some drama with the elevator because we couldn't all fit. It was a big elevator, but we couldn't all fit, and you needed an elevator key to ride up to the penthouse, and there was only one key, so one group had to wait for someone to come back down and return the key. And I remember that, for whatever reason, it felt essential that I manage to squeeze in with the first group. So I kind of pushed my way into the elevator, and there were a lot of us in there, and someone turned the key and the elevator started to move but then sort of paused, like it was considering our collective weight."

Ryan discreetly checks his phone. Nothing.

"We went up super fast until suddenly the doors were open and we were deposited. That's the word that went through my head as it was happening, *deposited*, because I was sort of narrating in my head, like I was describing it to someone else, even as it was happening. And there was this inkling of a feeling—and I'm not sure where it came from, like, I'm not religious at all—but this feeling that maybe the person I was describing it to was God. That, for some reason, God couldn't see through the roof of the building into this room, and he, or she, or whatever God is, needed me to describe it, not out loud, but in my head."

"Plausible," says Ryan.

"So I tried to narrate in clear and concise language, phrases like *the man in the orange T-shirt hits the man wearing the striped tie three times in the forehead and ear with something that looks like a drum major's baton*, like I was taking notes, *and there's blood coming out of his ears*. And I kept on doing this, this narrating, like I, myself, wasn't in that room but was now, myself, the ghostly presence hovering over the scene, the grim reaper or whatever, *God's grim reaper*, a phrase that kept repeating in my head . . ."

Ryan checks his phone again. He has a text that is not about Devor. It's something more interesting. A body's been found at the Zone Hotel.

3.

WENDY SAID SHE WAS ON her way, but it's been an hour, so Michael googles *F train service*. Delay at Broadway-Lafayette. He can't stand to be alone. Even though the detectives were more interested in his whereabouts than in offering condolence, Michael didn't want them to go. He offered coffee and week-old Granny Smith apples, and the cops looked at each other like the offer was a sign of insanity. Where was all of his furniture? Why the deflated air mattress and empty drawers? Michael had to admit that the apples were too bruised to serve.

Now the detectives are gone, Ricky's dead, Wendy's stuck in transit, and all Michael can do is search for the missing cat, making his way around the loft, checking every nook and crevice, leaving open tins of sardines by the heating vents.

"Cat," he calls, wishing it had a name, and feeling like, somehow, his failure to provide one has caused this disappearance. He imagines the cat traipsing out an open window and down the fire escape. He pictures Ricky's body on the hotel bed, pillow-propped against the headboard, blood drying on face and neck, blood turning black and gluing bits of blackened brain to skin. The cat on Court Street, crossing Atlantic, licking spilled ice cream from the pavement. Ricky on the morgue table, naked and blue, the ME prodding with steel tools. The cat lingering in a doorway, petted by a friendly kid. The kid's mother gets mad. The cat, scared, runs into the street, where she's hit by a cyclist.

Not dead, but critically injured, limping down Bergen, seeking a comfortable spot to expire. Ricky's belly where the bullets went through, half an organ exposed: a tube of intestine, mixed bile and blood.

He tries Broder again. It goes straight to voicemail and the voicemail's still full, so Michael sends another text. The detectives were more interested in Jay Devor. Michael told them the truth: that he'd seen Devor that morning outside Goldman Sachs; that he hadn't seen him during the riot, but that Michael was drunk, and it was chaos. He told the cops he couldn't imagine Devor killing anyone. A Lyft driver confirmed Michael's alibi following the riot.

Michael tries to remember more. He should never have taken that pill. They were laughing and smoking and Broder asked if they could go somewhere to talk. The lights went out, and there were screams, and people were swinging sticks and bats. Michael managed to escape. He's not sure how, probably dumb luck, the crowd directing him like a pinball, pushing him toward the door. He remembers standing on the street with a man who had blood pouring out of his eye. He remembers trying to hail a cab, then sucking it up and ordering Lyft. The Oxy kicked in. He tried to call Wendy, but failed to unlock his phone. Wendy wasn't at home. He lay on the floor. The cat nuzzled up. Next thing he knew the detectives were there.

MICHAEL OPENS CLOSETS AND CABINETS, looks under the bed, behind the toilet. He checks the washer and drier, empty delivery boxes, inside a pair of Wendy's boots.

"Fuck you cat," he says to no one. "Stop fucking with me."

He opens the fridge and the freezer, leaves the doors dangling, holds a frozen chicken thigh to his face. He goes through the garbage. Maybe there's a cat at the bottom of the bin. He searches the hallway, the stairs, the building's basement. He knocks on other tenants' doors but no one's home. Only Michael in this building, and maybe the cat, stuck in a wall or a heating duct, dying of starvation. He thinks he hears a faint whimper coming from inside the staircase. When he gets close it's gone.

4.

SHE FINDS HER HUSBAND ON the kitchen floor. His crying sounds like a small, failing engine, an electric toothbrush, maybe, on the last legs of its battery. She goes to her knees and tries to hold him.

"I'm so sorry," is all she can say and not enough. Michael trembles. A mucused gurgle comes from his throat. The position is awkward, like burping a baby. Wendy puts her hand beneath his shirt and rubs his spine. Only hours ago she decided to leave this loft and not look back; to take time to think things over; to tell Michael she knows about the money.

He says, "I can't find the fucking cat."

"Ssshh," says Wendy, aware of the cat's probable state: drowned in a sewer, a disintegrating corpse.

"I want my cat," says Michael. She smells a faint trace of urine and thinks he might have peed his pants.

"Just hold me," Wendy says and squeezes, as if solace might be measured by a pressure gauge. Michael squirms free.

"We have to make signs," he says. "Someone might find her and they won't know where to bring her back."

He rummages through drawers, pulling out pens and markers, ripping paper from the printer. Wendy tries to take him back into her arms, but Michael moves now with purpose.

"Forget the cat," says Wendy.

Michael's found a Sharpie. He makes the saddest sign she's

ever seen: a slanted scribble, barely legible, no name or photo with which to identify the animal. Wendy resigns herself to this futile distraction. They retrace Michael's route. The search is her punishment, calling "Cat" and "Kitty," telling him she's sure it will turn up. It's almost ten o'clock and she has to be at work. Michael's knees buckle. Wendy catches him before he falls.

"Did you eat breakfast?"

He says nothing.

"You need to eat or you'll be sick. Let me make you something before I go to work."

"You're going to work?"

"I have to, Michael, the timing isn't the best."

He escapes from the hug. Wendy cracks two eggs into a bowl and heats the pan. Michael pulls at the skin of his arm like he wants to rip it off. She beats the eggs.

"Oh, I'm so sorry," he says. "I didn't realize the timing doesn't suit you. Silly me. I'll just go back in time and tell Ricky to get murdered at a more convenient date."

"Michael, I . . ."

"No, no, I totally get it. You have a big day today, and Ricky's murder is screwing it up."

"I just need to stop in. I can come back in a couple hours."

The eggs sizzle. Wendy places two slices of bread in the toaster. Michael uses the spring mechanism to pop them back out. The slices flop onto the counter. Michael rips the untoasted bread into pieces, sprinkles the pieces on the floor. He says, "For the birds."

5.

THINGS STARTED WELL, OUTSIDE GOLDMAN, yesterday morning. Then, after lunch, Devor took the train to Park Slope to convince Sophia to come to the Funeral.

When he got to the Co-op, she was stocking coffee. She dumped beans into a wooden barrel and they clinked like rain on a tin roof. Devor was momentarily transported to French Guiana, their sophomore summer. They'd beautified a bus station as part of a community service trip jointly sponsored by Columbia's French department and the campus branch of Amnesty. Satisfied with their work—they'd coated the station's outer walls in mustard-colored acrylic—they took shelter from a passing downpour beneath the station's tin roof and shared a triumphant spliff. When the rain stopped and they emerged, they saw that a spray-can artist had desecrated the work. The result was a caricature of a Rasta wielding an Uzi on a do-gooder who looked a lot like Devor. Sophia had said, "Lesson learned."

~~What followed was twenty years of protests, and #Occupy, and~~ marching for black teens murdered by white police, and marching to end detainment camps at the border, and marching to support the liberation of Palestine, and marching in support of reproductive rights, in support of bathroom bills and assault-weapons bans. Twenty years of debates and declarations, jealousies and denials of jealousy, hope and disillusion, the best sex Devor had ever had. Sophia did not believe in the prison of monogamy until, one day, she did.

She'd met a half-Lebanese professor of cognitive science who resembled George Clooney in certain bearded roles, and who complained about American hummus and today's lobotomized slaves to their cellphones. Sophia moved into his Chelsea floor-through, and Devor spent a year brooding and dating before begging Sophia to dump the professor and take him back. She did, and what followed was a wonderful period leading up to last March when Sophia threw Devor's engagement ring into the ocean. She called him a cheapo who masked his stinginess behind a veil of anti-materialist commie essentialism, all because he'd purchased the plastic ring from a gas station nickel machine. Devor thought he was being spontaneous and romantic.

SOPHIA APPEARED TO HAVE AGED since then. Perhaps it was the measured pace of her motions or the gray she'd let bloom in her hair.

"Soph," he said, a daring intro. The way he said it made it sound like they were in bed with the Sunday *Times* and he needed help on a crossword clue. She spent a long moment looking him over. He'd lost weight after Kate signed them up for a Boot Camp class filled with postpartum women intent on shredding baby weight. Devor was embarrassed by how little he could squat-thrust compared to these women.

Sophia said, "I was wondering when you'd show."

He couldn't read her tone. She had turned cynic following the 2016 election. Whereas Devor had upped the ante on his activism by launching *Nøøse*, Sophia had entered a PhD program and buried herself in scholarship. Her field was political cinema, and her thesis was on the films produced by failed revolutions. It was about the futility of art in the face of history's momentum. He'd tried to be supportive, but the growing bleakness of Sophia's worldview was a factor in their breakup.

Devor said, "You have to come tonight. There's a new energy in the air. We can get to Breem. If we get to Breem the other holdouts will follow. We've got manpower this time. Things are in motion."

For whatever reason, he needed Sophia at the Funeral. He was still trying to prove something. Not about himself, but about "hope," "resilience," "the human spirit"—those hackneyed platitudes that he fantasized might, tonight, be removed from their scare quotes, restored to single-entendre meaning. Or maybe it was about himself: evidence that he was an iconoclastic leader. The protest and the plan to storm a finance bro party they'd been tipped off about—it was all, in some sense, for Sophia.

Sophia said, "And how's Kate?"

Devor said, "She's good."

Sophia said she had to go down to the basement to get more beans. She said she'd try to stop by the Funeral. She said it in a way that let him know that she would not.

WHEN THE FUNERAL COMMENCED, THOUSANDS of kindred souls emerged on the blocked-off streets. It was a far cry from his college days at Greenpeace when he and Sophia stood outside New York Sports Club on Eightieth Street, failing to engage people coming from workouts. It was a far cry from campaigning for Gore in 2000 or for Kerry in 2004, or the Jill Stein debacle. Finally, people on both sides of the red/blue divide were sick of the banks' bullshit, and the shitty job market, and the billionaires on Wall Street still getting their bonuses. Marching to the party—which was *Great Gatsby* themed, how perfect was that?—Devor felt for a moment, in the heat and the music, that his generation had finally arrived.

And yet, when they reached the hotel, he wavered.

Devor watched a young guy, no older than eighteen, slap a bat against his palm. He watched an even younger guy swing a sawed-off table leg like a sword. Devor thought of his parents, sixties peaceniks. He thought of Sophia's disapproving eyes. He thought of John Lennon lying in bed beside Yoko.

Peace had been given a chance, and look what happened. So why the hesitation? His brain knew that violence was inevitable. The people had bloodlust. The potential upside was worth a few injured bankers. The revolution had to start somewhere. The movement had numbers, but not enough. The action was justified.

Devor's brain knew, but his body resisted. His body shook and stalled. He told the others he'd take up the rear. When the rest of his army entered the hotel, he walked ten blocks to his parked car and drove uptown to Sophia's. It was lucky she was home.

They watched the fallout on the news. Sophia didn't say much, but he could feel the judgment in her silence. Devor drank three beers. He crawled into bed. She got in but said they couldn't kiss or touch. Kate had been texting for hours. He didn't text back. Sophia fell asleep. Devor took off his shirt and rubbed his chest against her back.

6.

MICHAEL FINDS HIS AR HELMET while he's looking for the cat. He's not sure it still works, but the green light blinks when he flicks the on switch, and the battery appears to be partially charged.

On his laptop, he logs into *Shamerican Sykosis* for the first time in a year, and takes a moment to audit his in-game accounts—stocks, bonds, and real estate holdings—which, like their real-world analogues, are in a state of near-vacancy. Despite his theoretical advantages—he does, after all, have a degree in economics, and he remains a trader at a Wall Street firm—Michael was never good at this game. In part, this is because his skills don't quite transfer. The Shamerican markets are subject to discrete forces, demanding alternate instincts and a different knowledge base, just as Roger Federer's hand-eye coordination and strategic expertise might be of some help in *Baseline Smash* for Atari 3-D, but wouldn't guarantee success against a nine-year-old gamer who's logged thousands of hours on the virtual courts. More so, it's because Michael's interests were elsewhere. He didn't want to perform, during his leisure hours, the kinds of tasks he did at work. Nor was he interested in the game's design aspect. Why spend time mastering CAD so he could have a hand in shaping the appearance of this augmented world, when he could use that time to roam it as a masked spectator? Eighty Sykodollars remain in his Bank of Shamerica checking account.

Michael considers leaving the helmet turned off. This way, even other players won't engage him in the street, which used to happen, most wanting to know how much SD his avatar's tattoos cost, and if he was consciously trying to look like Eminem. There was also the occasional amorous advance. For many players, the game's capacity as a cosplay dating forum is a major draw. No more hiding in hotel rooms, sweat-drenched beneath unicorn costumes. Here, all flavors are on offer, from snake-skinned women, to men with tentacle hands, to avatars featuring Jared Leto's face on Beyoncé's frame. Shamerica is a true fantasy playground, bodies free from the laws of material space. And while AR can't render the tactile squish of a tentacle's grip, or the peach-skin texture of Leto's lips, the visual is so real-seeming that the user's brain creates an approximate phantom sensation.

But even though Michael isn't up for conversation, the helmet's appeal goes beyond its function as a mask; it offers an escape from the visual triggers of grief. So Michael rolls up his Missing Cat sign, turns on the device, and fits it over his head.

The helmet's heavy and Michael's still unsteady. He holds the bannister as he inches down the stairs, seeing no difference yet between the cobwebbed real world and its augmented counterpart, though the helmet's tinted visor darkens everything slightly, an equivalent sensation to wearing sunglasses inside. It's only when he exits the building and steps onto the street that Shamerica bursts forth, a tumult of chrome spires and silver balustrades, set against the latex-black sidewalk that glints like a river of sunlit tar.

Regions of Shamerica aesthetically vary, consistent only in their miscellany, but Michael's block feints at loose coherence, collectively informed by Frank Miller comics, Fritz Lang's *Metropolis*, the chemical-plant zone from *Sonic 2*, and Miyazaki's *Spirited Away*. In other words, the neighborhood bears the high-middlebrow imprint rare for game worlds—of arty Brooklynites Michael's own age. Across Hoyt Street stands what might resemble a Gothic cathedral if it weren't tricked out with jet engine propellers, and lining the block are holographic sports cars, octo-motorcycles modeled after in-line skates, and what appears to be a hand-blown glass glacier on the corner of Pacific whose security system is a ring of flames.

Michael sees all this, but he's not really seeing, still checking for the cat behind trashcans, mailboxes, and the glacier that he knows, in real life, is a Chevy Impala piled with parking tickets; still picturing Ricky, whose body, he guesses, is done being exam-ined, and now lies solitary in a freezer tube.

It's hot in the helmet, and sweat pools in Michael's eyebrows as he weaves down the sidewalk, subject to pauses and lurches, less walk than stagger, arms spread for balance like he's riding a skate-board. He keeps checking to see if Wendy's texted, or if Broder's called back, or if, by the grace of a benevolent god, there's a voice-mail from Detective Ryan explaining that there's been a mistake, the body wasn't Ricky's after all.

STAPLES IS CROWDED EVEN THOUGH it's mid-Tuesday. There's no AC, just a rickety fan spraying dust and room-temperature air. Michael takes off his helmet and tucks it under his arm. He unrolls his sign as he waits in line, and looks at what he's scrawled. Wendy was right, he should have included a photo.

"How old are your kids?" asks the woman beside him, whose own, a boy, looks about six. The boy hides in the folds of the woman's skirt. Michael's sister, Rachel, used to do the same thing when she was that age.

"My kids?"

The woman points at the paper in Michael's hand, and only now does he get it: his sign's been mistaken for the work of a child.

Michael puts the helmet back on.

7.

THE POSTER FEATURING THE PHOTO of the entrance at Auschwitz was just an example. An extreme image designed to get Wendy's attention and stress the paradoxical nature of their campaign. She's not actually meant to use the image. Lucas gave her the poster, she thinks, as a test. Wendy's meant to prove that women can be calculating monsters.

And while the #workwillsetyoufree hashtag may draw complaints from Holocaust remembrance groups, Wendy doesn't think it's a PR concern. Severed from the image, the hashtagged phrase will only have Holocaust connotations to a minority of people—she saw a recent poll showing that one-third of Gen Zers couldn't identify Hitler in a photo—and the slogan is banal and uncreative enough that Communitiv.ly can plead plausible deniability regarding its source. A twenty-two-year-old copywriter could have easily, unwittingly, come up with the slogan on his own.

The bigger problem, for Wendy, is strategic. The campaign's not as straightforward as Lucas's example would have her believe. In an analogue of the example, she'd be selling the protestant work ethic to Middle America. Convincing flag-waving xenophobes that accepting free money is unpatriotic. That Basic Income is a sneaky liberal trap that would reverse our Cold War triumph and retroactively cause the Russian, Ivan Drago, to pummel Stallone at the end of *Rocky IV* (a favorite movie of Michael's). That as people quit their low-wage jobs to live out their days drinking

Budweiser on inflatable rafts, a flood of illegals would arrive to replace them, increasing drug smuggling, sex crimes, and the prevalence of Spanish words in colloquial English. That, on the glorious future day when white Jesus has graced them with lottery winnings or a million-dollar inheritance from a long-lost aunt, the government will be there to take 60 percent of that million away. Easier said than done, but at least there's a precedent; it's what the Republicans have been selling for decades.

But this is not Wendy's demo. Her demo is Yelena the Trust-Funded Yoga Instructor, a Jersey-born Bikram maven whose given name is Helen, but who changed it at Oberlin to sound less basic, and whose parents subsidize her juice bar/studio. Wendy must convince Yelena that handouts are disrespectful. That handouts strip the poor of dignity. That there is something noble about being self-sufficient. That 6 percent property tax might cause her father to finally make good on his threats and sell the storefront that houses Project Child's Pose.

Wendy searches for images of people at work looking happy and fulfilled. She finds photos of guys playing ping-pong like the ones in a corner of her office. When she refines her search to include terms like "manual labor," she gets unsmiling people working obsolete jobs. Finally, she comes across a cowboy brushing a horse. As far as she knows there are still such things as cowboys. Still such things as horses. It's a start.

AFTER LESS THAN AN HOUR of focused googling, Wendy finds herself on Ricky's Facebook wall, which has filled with memorial posts: condolences, scanned Polaroids, RIPs. Someone's made a GIF of the deceased hoovering coke on a cloud. Wendy searches through dozens of tagged photos until she finds what she wants: the three of them on Coney Island, eating hot dogs. Michael's burnt everywhere but a rectangle of chest where his book must have been. Wendy wears a bikini and looks tan. She laughs at something Ricky's said and a tiny piece of hot dog missiles from her mouth toward the camera. She clicks share.

"You knew him?" says Lucas, who's appeared by her side. He wears high-waisted dress pants, chalk-striped and suspendered. A patterned silk tie stops halfway down his torso. Blond hair gelled into a side part. The same beautiful shoes as yesterday. On any other man, this would look like a costume.

"My husband's best friend."

She could have said *old friend* or *close family friend*, but Wendy feels the need to establish a remove. Perhaps out of guilt. Perhaps to explain her presence in the office. To make it clear that grief will not affect her work. As a woman, she feels she must make this case.

"I didn't realize that," says Lucas. "I'm sorry."

He produces a handkerchief and offers it to Wendy. The item is silk. Wendy waves it away. The handkerchief must be for show. She can't imagine Lucas having tear ducts. Can't imagine him carrying, in his pocket, something tainted with snot.

"Yeah, well, we didn't exactly get along."

"That doesn't mean you didn't love him."

No, Wendy thinks, I didn't love him, and now I must live with that.

"I feel like an asshole. My husband's home alone."

A normal human would tell her to take a personal day. He'd say that work can wait.

"I'm going to ask you to do something," says Lucas. "It might seem strange, and outside your job description, so I need you to understand that my intentions are noble."

"Okay."

"People are going to say a lot of horrible things about your husband's friend. They're going to dredge up a lot of shit. I want to give you the opportunity to catch that shit and turn it into gold."

"Shit into gold," says Wendy. "Copy that."

"*Nøøse* is going to try to use his murder to shape the narrative around Basic Income. They'll say that the violence that occurred is the consequence of an unfair society. That people get angry and then people get hurt. And the only way to change that is to placate the people."

"By passing the UBI."

"They're going to say that your husband's friend—well, they're not going to say he deserved to die—but that his death should be a wake-up call. That people like us should be scared. That we should do what they want if we don't want more violence."

"By passing the UBI."

"Lillian will brief you on the details."

"You've discussed this with Lillian?"

"We've discussed it," says Lucas, like she's naïve for asking, so grief-blind and domestically consumed that she can't grasp the urgency of their predicament. Hasn't she established that she left Michael crumbling toast on the floor?

"And what about this product?" Wendy says. "How long until I've entered the circle of trust?"

"Take care of this," he says. "And come in tomorrow with a concept for the billboard. After that we'll talk."

"You want me to come up with a billboard for a product despite not knowing what that product is?"

"Exactly," says Lucas. "We're in a bit of a time crunch. We hadn't originally planned to launch for another four months, but this vote on the UBI changed our timeline. We're pushing the launch to next week."

"And why is that?" Wendy asks, but Lucas is already walking away.

She closes Facebook in order to focus, but not before checking the photo she shared. It's received sixteen reactions, a mix of hearts and cry-face emojis. Two people, accidentally or not, have ticked like.

8.

INSTEAD OF HEADING HOME AFTER hanging his flyers, Michael finds himself crossing the Gowanus Canal. The area is mostly unaugmented, though a dozen iridescent 365™-branded moons orbit the Whole Foods roof-deck. Otherwise, the landscape is uncommonly bereft of added flair, the former industrial wasteland now filled by fast-casual condos, with their slab marble lobbies and patio balconies, their blindingly reflective facades. The tech bros who've bought here must be too busy for *Shamerican Sykosis*, and their wives aren't gamers, and their kids are still too young to play.

Michael's almost forgotten that he's wearing his helmet when he enters Prospect Park. He moves briskly, passing the usual cyclists and joggers, plus some weed-smelling Rastas heading down to Drummer's Grove. Michael pauses by the entrance to the Third Street Playground, standing as close as is societally acceptable for an unaccompanied adult male to stand. He feels he's earned the luxury on this mournful afternoon: to close his eyes and listen to the playground chatter, its exultant human hum; and to allow himself the daydream of what might be, for him and Wendy, maybe, one day.

On the nearest bench, a pair of parents wrangle shoes onto their reluctant toddler's feet. The kid was playing in his socks before, practicing walking from the edge of the swing-set to dad's outstretched arms. He must be one or slightly older, and he walks

pretty well, arms raised for balance in a kind of chicken-wing posture. But he's resistant to shoes, which Michael senses must be an
ongoing issue, the mom reassuring the crying kid that sneakers are
a great, fun item that everyone wears. Then the shoes are on. The
crying has stopped. The kid stands planted on the playground's
rubber matting and stares with suspicion at his feet. After a long
hesitation, he lifts one foot maybe an inch from the ground. The
foot immediately drops like a leaden anchor and the boy nearly
falls. He tries once more with the same result, then bursts back
into tears. The parents relent. They take off the shoes.

Michael's so invested in this drama that only now does he
realize someone's talking to him. He turns.

"Excuse me," a girl says. "I need help."

The voice is meek. She's eight or nine years old. Her school
uniform cardigan drips blood.

"Help," she says. "I'm bleeding."

"Where are your parents?" Michael asks, but the girl says
"help" again, and keeps on saying it, "help, I'm bleeding," as
Michael kneels for a closer look. The blood, he now sees, spills
from a nickel-sized wound in the girl's neck, though the wound
is expanding, and steam appears to be rising off it. When the girl
speaks, blood drips from her mouth.

Michael's yelling for a doctor. He's tearing at his shirtsleeve to
use as a tourniquet. He's relieved to see a man in a suit moving
with urgency their way. But as the man gets closer, it becomes
apparent that he too is bleeding, spouting thin, dark streams
from his forehead, and he too is saying "help." Now a woman
approaches, her intestines unraveling onto the pavement and
trailing behind her like a long, pink tail. And here's a teenage
boy with half his torso blown off, and another with a head
wound, bobbing and falling, sending brain matter everywhere,

and Michael's suddenly surrounded by even more victims: all gushing, all dying, all hobbling toward him. He's screaming in the helmet and no one can hear him; he's screaming, and he's trying to rip off his shirtsleeve, and to rip off his helmet, when, in an instant, they all disappear.

A banner unfurls from between two trees. It reads: 28,407 AMERICANS WERE KILLED BY GUN VIOLENCE THIS YEAR.

9.

BRODER ENTERS THE BODEGA, HOOD up, hands in pockets, touching the gun. The bodega smells like cat litter. A woman scratches lotto tickets on the glass top of the ice cream case. Another has a dozen items bundled in her arms: garbage bags, protein bars, various soups and beans, three bottles of seltzer. No shopping baskets in sight. A can of cream of mushroom falls from bundle to floor. Broder picks up the item. He places it on the counter.

"Thank you," says the woman. She eyes the dented can, decides it's still good. A tattoo across her clavicle says *Stay Gold* in backward mirror script.

The store clerk spits sunflower seeds into a plastic cup. He wears one of those unlicensed New York Yankees caps where the logo's in a slightly wrong font. His teeth are incredibly white and he seems to take pleasure in showing them off, taking seeds one at a time, cracking with his central incisors. Broder can't stand the sound.

"You take cards?" the woman says.

"Visa and Master," the clerk says, and spits.

He puts another seed between his teeth. The woman opens her purse. Broder eyes its interior: cash and change, two MetroCards. There was sixty dollars in Ricky's wallet. It won't last Broder long. He touches the gun again and looks up to see his own warped face in the security mirror. His nose is thread-veined and bulbous. He sees the security camera hanging from the ceiling, sees the top of his own head on the security TV behind the counter. The woman pays and puts away her purse.

Broder buys cigarettes and a stale bagel. The cigarettes cost sixteen dollars. The bagel's ninety-five cents. He sits in Washington Square Park and eats it plain. Pigeons peck around his feet. He removes a baggie, turns it inside out, licks the faint remaining powder. He opens and closes the clasp of the bracelet he slipped from Ricky's wrist. Broder's teeth go numb.

10.

WENDY REINFLATES THE AIR MATTRESS. Michael can tell she's annoyed that he's not doing it himself. It's like when he gets the flu. She'll make soup and watch any movie he wants, but her sympathy lasts twenty-four hours. By the next day she's mad that he hasn't recovered.

They haven't discussed buying a new bed. It's one thing to expense the occasional taxi, but he can't buy a bed on the company card. Wendy must be aware of their debt by this point, but Michael's been given temporary reprieve; now's not the time to bring it up.

In silence, they stretch a sheet over the air mattress, slide the duvet into its cover. Michael thinks this should be an Olympic game, like synchronized swimming, the German judge docking points for sloppy corners. He used to narrate, like he was calling the event for ABC Sports. Or he'd crawl inside the duvet cover, light the flashlight on his phone, and pretend to be exploring a cave. He used to be able to make Wendy laugh.

Wendy suggests they order pizza, a peace pipe of sorts, conforming to neither person's vision of guiltless consumption. Michael lets her choose toppings.

THEY WATCH THE NEWS AND eat in bed. Michael eats most of the crust and cheese. Wendy picks at kalamata olives with a fork. Hurricane Marie has left thousands on the Gulf Coast without power. The National Guard stormed the FSU Hillel. When the smoke cleared, twelve people, including the rabbi and two other hostages, were dead.

"Jesus," Wendy says.

Ricky's murder is addressed after the first commercial break. Devor, it seems, turned himself in, and has since been released. In a taped press conference, he pledges his innocence and vows to assist with the investigation.

"What do you think?" asks Wendy.

Michael's been thinking about Ricky's sure thing investment. He's been wondering why Ricky over all the other people at the party. Newscasters speculate that he was randomly chosen, an anonymous banker with the bad luck of wrong place and time. The riot was a diversion, is the general consensus. The detectives told Michael that the bathroom floor was wet. Some people on Reddit say the murderer is black.

"I don't know what I think," says Michael.

"No," says Wendy.

It looks like her bites have finally faded, but it might just be too dark to see. Michael rests his head on Wendy's shoulder.

"No more news," he says. "Let's watch something else."

She clicks into the program guide. Reruns and reality bullshit, four channels showing college hockey. *8 Mile*'s on HBO. Wendy says fine, they can watch.

Michael took her to see it in college, during that stage when couples share the cultural artifacts that molded and shaped them, a shortcut to surface intimacy while the deeper kind develops. The film wasn't bad. More so, she liked Michael's passion. Everyone else in New York was too hip to fullheartedly gush over anything, afraid to take the wrong view and lose tastemaker cred.

Within minutes, Michael's asleep in fetal position and facing the wall. Only his pate can be seen, a sparse lawn that Wendy wets and finger-combs while watching, mesmerized by the actress Brittany Murphy, whose death seven years later, from pills and pneumonia on a bathroom floor, imbues this past performance with retrospective weight. Gone is the apple-cheeked Murphy of *Clueless*. Here she's gaunt and thigh-gapped, all pupil and jawbone, a body offering itself in lieu of other things to offer. When Eminem asks her on a date, she responds, "Why don't you take me somewhere now." This character doesn't believe in the future, thinks Wendy, she fears its conditional tense.

The film cuts to the two of them inside the auto plant where he works. Murphy unbuttons her blouse and Eminem hoists her onto a clunking apparatus. Her legs come up and her panties come off. For reasons obscure, at first, to Wendy, Brittany Murphy licks her hand. It is an oddly human moment, the last before their bodies take a mechanistic turn, thrusting to the factory's din and clang.

11.

THE CLOSET IS EMPTY EXCEPT for the prototype. His clothes closet's elsewhere. The prototype has its own closet, the closet a romantic partner would use if he had one. He does not. The prototype is the closest thing he has to a romantic partner.

Lucas pulls the item over his naked body in a series of slow, graceful movements. No one is watching. The item could be and will be described as a second skin. He thought about calling it Skin or Skein or Skinn. These names tested poorly. Too crass and direct, like those off-brand condoms sold in coin-op machines. The name he's chosen—The Suit™—is clear and unpretentious. Everybody owns one. A suit is something a person wears to work.

Imagine a speed skater's full-body spandex. Now imagine that outfit so well-matched to your skin tone that it looks like you're not wearing clothes. Now imagine a fabric so breathably aerated that it *feels* like you're not wearing clothes. Your clothes go on top. In this case, a pair of 1966 Levi's XX 501s in Cone Mills selvedge denim. Custom motorcycle boots made from distressed seal leather and flown in from Japan. Matching jacket. White T-shirt by Hanes.

Before dressing, Lucas performs a series of sun salutations to the closet mirror, allowing his spine to elongate, his calves to tense and relax. He does five burpees, ten stationary lunges, fifty jumping jacks. He does ten more burpees, twenty split jacks, fifteen single-leg bridges, and a four-minute plank. He does a circuit of back-step lunges, body-weight squats, clapping push-ups, and bicycle crunches.

The previous prototype ripped in the crotch during this routine. Even Lucas's crack team of apparel scientists had trouble synthesizing a fabric that could properly house the prototype's twelve hundred micro-sensors while maintaining target weight and durability specs. The new prototype has a reinforced crotch that does well under athletic duress and provides storage for extra sensors.

After fifteen years of daily practice, Lucas still can't do the splits. Some positions aren't meant for adult male bodies. This doesn't stop him from trying. He comes to a controlled halt three inches short of his goal, maintaining balance by engaging his glutes and staring at a fixed point on the floor. He feels stabbing pain in both hips, and a satisfying burn in his hamstrings. Keeping his lower body stable, he bends at the torso and touches the floor, maneuvers into a spread-legged pushup, then bounces back to standing. He says, "Namaste, motherfucker," and pretends to shoot the wall. He puts his clothes on over The Suit™, checks himself in the mirror, adjusts his collar, his hair. The prototype remains intact.

ON HIS TABLET, LUCAS LOOKS at the data. His heart rate peaked at 180 during this little routine. He watches the live feed as it drops to 150, 140, 115, 65. His blood pressure's 135/90, on the high end of normal. Blood sugar: 120. He needs to cut down on soda. Blood alcohol: under .01 percent. Water loss: three ounces over the last twenty minutes, an impressively high retention rate.

When the product comes to market, this data will be sold to advertisers. It will be used as the basis for a new kind of target marketing. When Lucas's blood sugar drops below a certain level,

Bobby Wasabi's Sushi Palace will auto-text asking if he wants to one-click order the same sashimi combo that he got last week. When his blood alcohol indicates a data-determined peak susceptibility to impulse shopping, Orbitz will email, offering a negligible discount on the ticket to Aruba that's been sitting in his cart. The Suit™ can track the frequency and weight of bowel movements through its advanced Sensi-Shape™ technology. After twenty-four hours without defecation, ads for laxatives will permeate his streams.

The data will be sold to insurance companies as well. The Suit™ is a marvel of actuarial science. It knows how many hours you sleep and exercise, or spend seated in an office chair. It can model your posture, detect irregular heartbeats and other pre-existing conditions. It knows how much you smoke despite the lies you tell your doctor and yourself. It can estimate, with unprecedented accuracy, when a person is going to die.

LUCAS HASN'T FELT THIS WAY since he launched *Shamerican Sykosis*. The first game he developed, *&Co*, had been a bust. That was when he did all the coding himself. And he knew, before he'd even brought it to market, that the game wasn't up to his standards, that it didn't match what was there in his head.

With *SS* it was different. He had more capital to work with and he'd learned how to outsource. He still controlled the product from concept to specs. Lucas knew he'd succeeded the first time he tried the demo helmet and walked through the dummied-up augmented New York, where rainbow halos ringed the tops of buildings, and the leaves on trees glowed uranium green. Lucas felt a powerful sense of electric connectivity, like that time at Yale when he tripped on acid in a rainstorm, and each lightning bolt pierced the shell of his skull.

And even if that feeling was psychosomatic, well then wasn't that the beauty of this product anyway? At Yale, he'd studied the Western philosophers, all those dead white boys debating whether a reality exists beyond what we can see. Capitalists understood the question's irrelevance; a product and its perception are the same exact thing. Lucas has that feeling as he stands before the mirror and, like the acid trip, and that first walk around Shamerica, it's enhanced by the knowledge that, for now, it's his alone.

ON THE UPPER CLOSET SHELF, above the space reserved for The Suit™, lies another prototype. This one's an AR helmet that differs from previous models in two essential ways. The first difference is its appearance, which was designed to appeal to a larger demographic than the 6.4 million users who already log in, daily, to *Shamerican Sykosis*; to appeal to people who aren't superhero fangirls or fashion-agnostic gamers. The second difference is that this new helmet, alongside its capacity as a portal to Shamerica, was designed to work in symbiosis with The Suit™, relaying data-prompted consumer suggestions to the wearer in real time, which, unlike texts, banner ads, and marketing emails, can't be deleted, ignored, or marked as spam.

To be clear, The Helmet 2.0 won't be requisite for wearers of The Suit™, just as The Suit™ won't be required for participation in SS. They are separate products that function adequately on their own. Wearing The Helmet 2.0 in conjunction with wearing The Suit™ is simply an option. But there will be incentives for those who choose this option, and Lucas knows that those incentives will be hard to resist.

The Helmet 2.0 is all black, and looks exactly like a motor-cycle helmet, but for a small antenna on its rear. Lucas takes the elevator down to the lobby. He carries the helmet with two hands against his stomach, as if the item were a boxed and ribboned gift.

"Nice night," says the doorman. Lucas nods and makes his way to the bike parked out front, a 1968 BMW R69S in white with chrome piping and black leather trim. He revs the engine, straps on The Helmet 2.0, and enters Shamerica.

Behold a hodgepodge of architectural styles, from Lucas's own Versailles-modeled condo, which a neighbor spent six hundred hours fabricating in CAD, to the rest of the block: a building-sized subwoofer blasting Biggie, a note-perfect replica of the USS *Maine* that explodes and reconstitutes every half hour, and, on the corner, a townhouse-cum-cloud-scraping-oak-tree that starts black at its roots and moves up the color spectrum through many gradations of blue, green, and blond, until, high above, it explodes in white leaves that shine gold in the sun and at night light the sky in incandescent silver.

Lucas turns down Ninety-Sixth Street and crosses the park, stifling his instinct for speed. He admires the crop circles mown into the playing fields and glittered with space-dust. Barnyard topiaries oink and neigh as he cruises past. He exits the park and heads south on the FDR. Some cars look like fighter jets or fire-breathing dragons, while other, subtler vehicles—Ferraris, Porsches, midlife crisis Batmobiles—shine with the faint glow of augmentation, the all-but-imperceptible sheen of that which can't rust, fade, or take on dirt.

Once he's passed Thirty-Fourth Street the voice ads begin. For some reason, they don't work in midtown, a programming kink that will soon be ironed out. Now they come as he continues south, though fairly infrequently, research suggesting that people are only susceptible to a limited amount before becoming annoyed and opting out.

"You are hungry," whispers the voice, an accurate simulacrum of Lucas's own. The idea is for players to hear the voice as an extension of their inner monologues. As people spend more time in these helmets, it will become harder to tell which is which.

Lucas peeks at the tablet mounted to his dashboard. The prototype is right; his blood sugar's low. Soon, when they roll out the product complete with paid sponsors, the voice will remind the user about the slice place on Twenty-Eighth Street he hit after seeing Taylor Swift at the Garden. He gave it 4.5 stars. For now, the voice says, "You are hungry," and Lucas agrees, removing a protein bar from his inner coat pocket. He unwraps and eats it while stopped at a red. His blood sugar rises to normal.

12.

BOTH DETECTIVES ORDERED BAGELS. PERHAPS they're trying to refute the stereotype. Then why suggest a donut shop? They said they had questions, but, so far, all they've done is look at their phones. Michael imagines this is what dating's like these days: mumbles and carbs, a slight aura of shame. He bites into his Boston cream donut. A dollop of filling spouts onto the table.

Detective Ryan eyes the dollop like he wants to lick it up. Michael asks about Broder.

"Right, that guy," says Ryan. It's clear that Ryan's partner, Quinn, hasn't heard the name before. It occurs to Michael to ask if he, himself, is a suspect. He must look the part, sickly and unshaven, faced fixed in criminal blankness. This morning, Michael woke before sunrise and barfed tomato-flecked mozzarella, then crawled back to bed and wept against Wendy's shoulder. She asked if he was okay. He said he was not. She must have been asleep, because she told him not to worry, she was sure they'd be pregnant soon. He kissed the loose hairs that had fallen from her bun. He swallowed a bubble of vomit.

The detectives ask if Michael has heard from Devor.

"He owes me an email," says Michael. "If that means anything to you."

"Poor email etiquette—check." Ryan marks an invisible notepad.

"Why does he owe you?" says Quinn.

"Oh it's stupid," says Michael. "I pitched an idea for the *Noose* magazine. This excerpt from the book I'm trying to write."

"Book, huh?"

"A monograph, really. Long essay. Not even a book."

The detectives repeat the word *monograph*. Quinn licks cream cheese from his lip. He says, "What's it about then, this monograph?"

"Nothing. It's not really . . . it's not even really a thing."

"Like *Seinfeld*?" says Ryan.

"What's the deal with pants?" says Quinn. "That kind of material? If so, you'll need a better pitch. What do they call it, an elevator pitch? My cousin Donald did one. The genius thing was the book was about elevators. Photos and such: artful, tasteful. Nothing crass like you might imagine."

"He sell it?" asks Ryan.

"It's the irony of the whole thing" says Quinn. "He kept showing up at Random House, but he never did manage to get into the elevator."

AFTER LEAVING THE DETECTIVES, MICHAEL walks south to Union Square. The streets have been cleaned since the other night, but he still spies the occasional leaflet caught in gutter or tree branch, still senses the presence of the protesting mob. He went to Gettysburg once, and the feeling he had there was something like this. Not ghostly exactly—nothing supernatural—but this feeling that the land itself, or in this case the concrete square, has some kind of violent essence, that it carries, in the wind that moves across its airspace, a faint echo of war chants.

Before heading down into the subway, he calls his mother. He only calls his mother from loud public places so she'll have trouble hearing over the background noise and won't keep him on long. She's grown impatient with inconvenience in her early old age, and maybe also a little deaf. He's returning an earlier call. His mom wants to know when he'll be getting into town. His sister answers.

"Hey brother," Rachel says in the husky voice that never fails to surprise. Even Michael, a smoker, is appalled by her habit, chain-smoking on their parents' porch, coughing phlegm into a designated soda can. He sometimes pictures the version of his sister from before he left home, a pigtailed middle schooler with a whistling gap between her front teeth. They've never known what to call each other, these distant siblings, separated by geography, age, and social class. *Brother* and *sister* is something they've settled on, comfortably balanced between the irony of its *Green Acres* formality and the intimacy of an in-joke. Michael doesn't like it. *Let's call each other by our first names*, he always wants to suggest. *Let's see each other as more than improper nouns.*

"Hey sister," he says.

Michael spoke to both parents on the day of the murder, struggling through that awkward first stage of condolence, the pauses and half thoughts, a conversation laced with silent ellipses. He can't go through that again, and maybe Rachel senses this, because she just says, "It sucks, huh?"

"Yeah," he says. "It really sucks."

She asks when he's coming home and he says he's not sure. He asks how she is and she says that she's fine, that her boyfriend's fine, that her job's okay.

13.

DONNELL'S HAD A NICE DAY cooking for Jackie and watching *Sex and the City* reruns on TBS, which have been censored for basic cable—no nipples or cuss words—meaning they can watch together without him feeling awkward or having to answer uncomfortable questions. Not like the time he took her on the *SATC* bus tour, and one of the stops was a West Village sex shop, and Jackie, then eleven, asked, "Dad, what's a butt plug?" Now thirteen, she gets most of the show's innuendo, and they both find the dubbed replacements for the censored swears hilarious, Carrie saying *runt* when she's really saying the C-word.

Father and daughter sit at opposite ends of the couch to buffer against accidental touch. Jackie's still in the no-physical-contact phase he keeps hoping will pass so he can wrap her in hugs when she comes home in tears—about what, he has no idea, she won't say—instead of watching her scurry past to her room where she stays until dinner. Occasions for bonding are scarce, so he takes what he can, in this case, sitting four feet away, Jackie adorably looking to dad for approval before allowing herself to laugh at Samantha's more vulgar witticisms.

The two have been growing apart since the Great Tampon Incident of last year, when Donnell, not wearing his contacts, saw one sticking from Jackie's purse and mistook it for an oversized spliff. He reached in to confiscate the product and she screamed. She's been spending more time at her aunt's in the Bronx since, and last week, she begged to be *transferred* to California to live with her mom; she was obsessed with the state after bingeing the final three seasons of *Mad Men*. She became enraged when Donnell asked if her mother was aware of this plan, because of course Dani wasn't, and would never approve.

Jackie's mother certainly loves her, and showers her with affection on her biannual visits, but Dani's made clear that there's no room in her daily life for a daughter. She's too busy wallowing in self-pity because she hasn't booked a commercial in years, let alone a pilot, and now the only auditions she gets are for wizened old hookers or dead hookers or church lady types or—gasp!—moms.

The episode ends. Jackie wants to watch another, but Donnell decides they've had enough TV because it's gorgeous outside and they could both use a walk. Besides, he needs to stop by Verizon and talk to Steve about picking up extra shifts.

Jackie goes into her bedroom and returns a half hour later in platform Pumas, zebra-patterned leggings, and a crop top. Donnell knows he should send her back to her room to put on something less tawdry, but he can't bring himself to be that dad, the sitcom dad who demands that his daughter epitomize purity. He says she looks nice. Jackie grunts to let him know she wasn't asking.

THEY WALK SOUTH DOWN LENOX, some distance apart, Jackie leading, impressively avoiding signposts and other humans without looking up from her phone. Donnell thinks over his essay in progress, a comic but partly in earnest argument for a causal chain connecting the attacks on the Twin Towers to the sorry current state of the Knicks. In his mind, *SATC* seasons one through four embodied a sexually liberated, pre-9/11 New York. Samantha slept with a doorman, Charlotte learned to stop worrying and love cunnilingus, and Carrie, sweet Carrie, introduced the term *sexual walkabout* to the American lexicon. Women wanted her wardrobe, men wanted to fuck her friends, Dalton girls took the 6 train downtown to smoke Marlboro Lights outside the Strand, and New York was a playground for professional athletes.

That changed after Muslim fundamentalists hijacked two commercial flights and flew the planes into the Twin Towers. Suddenly white men were beating brown men with knuckles and broom handles, were watching hijab porn, were wearing pearl snap shirts, were trying not to cry while listening to Taylor Swift. Miranda supported Skidmark Steve through testicular cancer, Samantha boringly attempted monogamy, and Carrie quit smoking because the smell bothered Aidan. The city banned smoking in bars.

This New York was for serious adults, so college grads moved to Austin and Portland, and white guys talked defense and fundamentals, sang "Manu Ginóbili" from rooftops, rented *Rocky II* on Netflix, scoured the Internet for Eva Longoria nip-slips, cheered David Caruso as Detective Horatio Caine, and hate crimes in the five boroughs went up 14 percent during year one of Obama's post-racial presidency, so LeBron James took his talents to South Beach. And when his daughter was born, Donnell bought a two-bedroom apartment in Harlem because a small down payment with a floating-rate mortgage seemed like a good idea at the time. Now those days are ancient history, a feeling reinforced by the fact that Jackie's doing a unit on the attacks in her middle school history class, and she keeps getting 9/11 mixed up with Vietnam.

THEY REACH THE STORE. STEVE'S at the counter clutching a brand new iPhone, while another, his own, sits tucked beneath his chin. Despite his wheat-blond hair and the Midwestern honesty his blue eyes affect, Steve's a Brooklyn-born hustler who speaks in a hip-hop dialect, the authenticity of which Donnell can't begin to parse. Right now, Steve's on one of his patented fake calls to Verizon HQ, pretending to beg a superior to allow him to give the customer a one-time special discount, explaining that this customer is a personal favorite, and if the superior could find it in his warm heart, etc. Guys like Steve have saved the sales industry from full automation; bots aren't as good at ripping people off.

"Well," says Steve to the customer, a young man with a shaved head and large plastic-frame glasses, "I've spoken to my superior and he's agreed to let me give you a discount."

The customer nods. He knows he's being had, but there's nothing he can do. Steve offers a price. It's hardly a discount, 10 percent, and that's only with the mail-in rebate. Analytics confirm: no one mails in the rebate. The customer hesitates, says, "That's a lot of money."

"You won't find a better price," Steve says, a fair point.

The customer looks to Donnell for an encouraging nod that says: *such is life, we all get fleeced, but what's the alternative, buying an Android?* Donnell shrugs. The customer pays and photographs his new phone with his old one. Steve pushes the abacus on another commission. Donnell steps in before the next person can approach. People give him looks because the line trails halfway to the door, and he's skipped all that and gone straight to the front. They don't know he works here.

"My brother," says Steve, and offers a soul shake, which Donnell accepts. This is their unspoken arrangement; Donnell honors Steve's b-boy persona, and in return he's allowed to write during slow shifts instead of vacuuming the carpet.

"You remember Jackie?" says Donnell, and taps his daughter's shoulder.

"I like those Pumas," Steve says to Jackie, who gives no indication of having heard.

Someone behind them says, "Ahem."

Steve indicates the line, and asks Donnell if they can talk later, maybe in a couple hours after his shift. Donnell says, "I just need a minute."

"Excuse me, I've been waiting," the same woman interrupts.

Donnell feels a tug at his arm again. He tells Jackie, "Not now."

"Excuse me," the customer repeats, steps around Donnell, and pushes her cellphone at Steve. "I've been waiting here for twenty minutes and . . ."

"Miss, I'll be right with you," says Steve, turning back to Donnell, but the woman won't hear it; she positions her body between them.

"Dad," says Jackie. "Buy me this Bluetooth speaker."

There is no question mark at the end of her statement. It's a command. Jackie already has a Bluetooth speaker. She got one for Christmas last year.

"This one has mega-bass," says Jackie.

"Not now," says Donnell, trying to shake her off his arm.

"It's only eighty bucks," Jackie says, breaking her no-touching rule to pat him down in search of his wallet, which she finds and removes. Donnell tries to snatch it back, but she's danced out of reach.

"You get a discount," Jackie says, and positions herself at the end of the line.

The customer says to Steve, "It won't charge."

"Excuse me, Miss, if you'll just wait a second," Donnell says.

Steve inspects the woman's phone. He pops its back and notes the indicator is pink from water damage.

"You dropped this in the toilet," says Steve.

"I did not," says the woman.

Donnell tries again to push around the customer, who's now berating Steve for claiming she purposely peed on her phone. She poses with the item between her legs and asks if Steve thinks she mistook it for a pregnancy test.

"I said you dropped it in the toilet," says Steve. "I didn't say you peed on it."

Donnell feels a tap on his shoulder. He turns to face Jackie, but the person tapping is not his daughter. It's a plainclothes detective who holds up a badge and asks for a moment of Donnell's time.

"I'm sorry, but what's this about?" says Donnell, still trying to angle around the urine mime and talk to Steve about shifts.

"I need you to come with me to the station to answer some questions."

"Some questions?" says Donnell, now looking for Jackie. Steve's trying to calm the urine mime by explaining that, while her warranty does not protect against water damage, he can probably get her a 10 percent discount on a brand new iPhone so long as she mails in the rebate.

"How about I pee on the rebate instead?"

"That would be your choice," says Steve.

"We just have a few questions about your participation in the protest last week," says the detective. "I'm sure it won't take much time."

"If you don't mind," says Donnell, "I just need to speak to my manager about a scheduling problem, and then I can answer whatever questions you have."

He tries again to push up to the counter, but this time the detective squeezes his arm and anchors him in place.

"Mr. Sanders, I need you to come with me to the station." A hint of annoyance has crept into his voice.

"I'm here with my daughter."

"Which is why I suggest you come with me so I don't have to arrest you."

"Arrest me?" says Donnell, louder than intended. "I thought you said you had questions."

"Sir, I'm asking politely."

People are looking. Jackie steps out of line and moves toward Donnell.

"Dad?" she says.

"Mr. Sanders," the detective says.

"Fuck your rebate," says the urine mime. She throws her phone at the iPad display. Amid this distraction, Donnell tries to free himself from the detective's grip. He finds his legs kicked from under him, face pressed into the un-vacuumed carpet, cuffs clasped around his wrist.

14.

IN THE PHOTO, RICKY STILL sports the bedhead haircut he had in college—part Ross from *Friends*, part roadkill—a look he wisely ditched for a politician's side part around the age of twenty-eight. Still, there's something endearing about the old style, an innocence bestowed upon its owner. Wendy understands why this is the image that Lillian's chosen.

Lillian leans over Wendy's shoulder carrying the combined scents of spearmint, wasabi peas, and a perfume that should be called Hookah Bar. She chops at Wendy's back like she's ending a massage. She says, "Sucks to be this guy." She walks away.

It occurs to Wendy that her boss is an insensitive bitch. Not that Wendy and Ricky were close, but now he's dead, murdered, and here's Wendy, days later, setting up a Facebook memorial page.

"We need to strike while the kettle is hot," Lillian had relayed.

Wendy pictured a steaming mug of Earl Grey.

"When someone is murdered it's an invitation for the press to go digging for skeletons, and your friend's got a few of those fuckers. We need to remind the world that just because he liked to have a few drinks and snorts and rolls in the gay hay with some big-dicked heroes of the American underclass does not make this anything other than a heinous hate crime for which the responsible party or parties will pay."

Wendy understands, sort of. Her job is now, in essence, prosecutor of #Occupy. Still, they could have let Greg handle this task, especially as Wendy's already busy with tomorrow's shoot, a last-minute effort that has her putting calls out to casting directors, scouting for a space that fits the vision she had in bed last night, and overseeing the shot list and storyboard drafts. Wendy's job title is Director of Strategy and Content, a vague classification that means she has a hand in all the company's doings, from concept to execution, and is subject to Lillian's impromptu left turns and irrational wonts. None of which, she might add, compare to the outright folly of trying to pull off this shoot on two days' notice. And now they want her to rebrand Ricky as well?

But Wendy understands. This is what she excels at: spin, counter-spin, creative solutions. And though turning Ricky into a martyr for the maligned one percent may be her toughest challenge yet, there is a part of Wendy that feels she owes it to Ricky, or if not to Ricky then to Michael. Because surely there's something noble in protecting Ricky from the ruthless churn of the news cycle by presenting a clean-shaven and unimpeachably humane counter-Ricky, a heroic counter-Ricky, even if that counter-Ricky might have to be invented by Wendy herself.

She stands, yawns, and checks her neighbor's monitor, amazed for the millionth time that these guys spend most of their waking hours staring at code. She used to think it looked boring, but now she sees the appeal of rote math and script mastery, of rearranging brackets until some desired result is achieved; never having to worry about the morality of one's work; never having to read people's thoughts or infer subtext or even interact at all with the various parties who call or email Wendy each day, pushing separate obscured agendas; never having to prioritize one task over another as their assignments are handed down in a line, then neatly ticked off like items on a grocery list.

SHE PASSES LILLIAN'S OFFICE ON the way to the bathroom. The door is cracked. Lucas sits on the corner of the desk, and Lillian leans in so that her breasts are presented, shelf-like, as if he might need somewhere to rest his cup of coffee.

It's hard to gauge the sincerity of Lillian's flirtations, whether she's earnestly horny, or working an angle. Wendy doesn't know what to make of Lucas, either. She doesn't trust his caginess about the product or Communitiv.ly's broad and shifting role in its launch. She pictures Lucas's backers as the kind of men who sit in wing chairs and steeple their fingers. The kind who hold emeritus positions in Southern megachurches and kill coeds in speedboat accidents.

But there's a magnetism too. He pays such close attention when she's speaking, always nodding, providing confirmative *okay*s. His gaze never strays over her shoulder. He never checks his phone or looks bored. He gives full focal attention to her mouth, as if it's not even his ears that are hearing her words, but his eyes quite literally seeing them, parsing meaning from the subtle fluctuations of her face.

BACK AT HER DESK, WENDY scans the headshot, does light touch-up and color correction, and proceeds with the memorial page. The headshot is the cover image, and she uses her discretion, as instructed, to select a handful of other photos from Ricky's Facebook: Ricky holding his diploma; Ricky on a ski trip in Aspen, suntanned and smiling; Ricky—and this one's for Lillian—looking broad and buff in a formfitting golf shirt, standing on a balcony, waving down at last year's Pride parade.

For text, she pastes the press release she drafted yesterday. The release includes quotes from Ricky's mother ("A darling boy"), Edward Jin ("Brave"), and Theo MacIntyre, executor of an LGBT

Small Business Grant that Ricky had apparently funded. Wendy doesn't know where Lillian found this guy, but she's glad she did; MacIntyre's praise of Ricky's "game-changing generosity" goes a long way toward the construction of Ricky 2.0, the beloved victim whose death leaves a hole in the great American tablecloth. In Wendy's hands, Ricky has been transformed into an "energetic jester" who was "fun loving and full of life." She posts the page and moves on to outreach.

The intuitive move might be to gather the right-wing media around this cause, but what good would it do to (a) have Republicans rally their red-state base re: #Occupy, and (b) unloose a possible shit-storm of homophobia from the alt-right? Instead, what Lucas wants is the center-left media to wave the flag of Ricky's cause, publicly mourn, and call out #Occupy for going too far.

Unlike an ordinary PR firm, where Wendy would have to blast the media herself, mass-emailing the memorial page and press release to uninterested editors, Communitiv.ly has got a stable of journalists raring to sell their integrity for fifty cents a word. She's guessing they'll jump at the opportunity she's offering, which is a hundred-dollar bonus for any anti-UBI piece they publish that mentions the riot and/or the murder, the hundred coming on top of whatever they're paid by the publication itself. Lucas wanted to go with five hundred, but Wendy assured him that was unnecessary.

Quality, content, and forum are irrelevant. People don't read articles anymore, but if they're exposed to enough headlines and pull quotes, they develop a false sense of being comprehensively informed. This is terrifying for all variety of reasons, not the least of which is that the researched and considered narrative is drowned out by the mob with the most stick to itive chant, but it's great for someone like Wendy who controls the volume knob. All she has to do is write a short bulletin with the offer, post it to the freelancers' job board for paid members, and wait for the responses to roll in.

Her final task is the targeted outreach Lucas insisted she perform. She writes to GLAAD, and includes a tailored version of the press release that features a paragraph on Ricky's invented support of the organization and years of patronage. She's banking on GLAAD being so thrilled to claim the martyr that no one will bother to check the records. No mention of #Occupy, here. She's got to be subtler than that. This is about painting a terse, sympathetic picture of Ricky, and letting its recipients take it from there. She sends a version of the same to It Gets Better, the Point Foundation, and GLLI. In fact, she emails every org that comes up on the first fifteen pages of her Google search. These letters include the press release in full and also link to Facebook where friends or concerned strangers are free to leave supportive comments, which will be moderated by Wendy.

By the time she's done, the office is empty. Wendy fetches a beer from the mini-fridge and kills the overhead lights. There's an envelope with her name on it sitting squarely in the center of her desk. She's been eyeing it all day, but has restrained herself from opening it. Now she does, using her fingernail to detach the flap. She looks inside, just for a second, before placing the item in her purse.

15.

KATE'S TALKING TO DEVOR, BUT he's watching TV news with his laptop open, contemplating an email from Michael Mixner, who wants to buy him a matcha and quote unquote pick his brain. The email's tone ranges from nineteenth-century austere ("Ricky's memorial is this weekend. I expect it to be a sober affair . . .") to faux academic (". . . of which my thesis will be interwoven through an ekphrastic reading of Curtis Hanson's 2002 film *8 Mile* . . .") to casually bromantic ("Dude, can't wait hug it out!"), and includes Devor's least favorite phrase—"pick your brain"—a mainstay of emails from junior colleagues and pestering strangers, which always raises the image of his skull as Chinese takeout carton, chopsticks stirring its contents.

Instead of writing back, Devor scans the draft of his third op-ed in as many days. The more he touts what he refuses to call a conspiracy theory—it's not paranoia if it's true—about a right-wing lobbying group masterminding what's now being called the Gatsby Murder, the more traction this theory gains online. And it's like the movement's on amphetamines elsewhere, unions gone wild, from Midwestern fruit pickers, to California almond farmers, to pharmacists, radiologists, and all strata of middle management. These unions have put so much pressure on the Senate that the UBI may pass by a wide margin. And while violence did not beget violence as Devor had imagined—he'd pictured riots flaring at investment banks worldwide—he's feeling cautiously optimistic. With each hour that passes, the prospect of his indictment seems to fade.

Kate sips her diet Cuba Libre, weary from her day teaching seventh-grade life science at a charter school in Harlem. She attempts to penetrate the force field of distraction that surrounds her boyfriend by leaning on his shoulder, but Devor shucks her off with a jerk of the remote, switching from CNN to MSNBC and back, then stirring his spoon in his empty bowl, trying to scrape a final bite of quinoa.

"Can I ask you something? says Kate. "And I swear that this is the last time I'll ask."

She makes her way to the kitchenette and begins doing dishes, hoping Devor will get the message and join. He stays seated, so she yells, in part because the room's loud with running water and dish clatter, but also because it feels good to project, to let her irritation manifest in volume.

"I'm just going to ask one more time," yells Kate. "Why didn't you tell me you went to Sophia's after the rally? I mean, I get why you did, I think. I'm not accusing. I'm just asking why you didn't tell me."

They've been over this a dozen times.

"I forgot," says Devor at regular volume, meaning Kate can't hear over the noise.

"What?"

"I said I forgot," yells Devor.

Kate turns off the faucet. She walks back to the couch and grabs the bowl from which Devor still scrapes, despite it being empty. She gets up close to his face and says, "Seems like something you wouldn't forget."

"Other things on my mind," says Devor. His eyes continually

dart toward the window, as if the cops might arrive at any moment, having changed their minds about letting him go.

Or maybe Kate's the one being paranoid. The job has her down at the moment, its endless hours, low pay, and sorry benefits; the parents who get worse every year, either in negligent absence or unemployed over-involvement; the bright kids bounding into this bleak future; the school shooting statistics that scare her despite Devor's reminders that it's only ever white kids who shoot up their schools (he's right, but she still worries); the paper-bag lunches; the matronly cardigans and functional flats she has to wear every day while women like Sophia strut around in belly shirts, demanding attention.

Kate brings the bowl back into the kitchen. In the early months of their relationship, she'd solved problems like this one by reading Devor's email—he never logged out—but that had to end when Kate found something she'd rather not have seen— an exchange with Sophia that referenced nude photos they'd taken and that Devor presumably still had in his possession—and couldn't stop herself from bringing it up, causing a conversation that ended with her promising never to read his email again and mostly keeping to that promise.

Kate makes her way to the bedroom, having left the dishes on the off chance that Devor will scrub them clean before coming in. She takes out her contacts and puts on a nightgown and slips under the comforter, propping herself on a pillow, browsing for a new couch that Devor doesn't want, he being perfectly content with his old bachelor futon. But oh, it would be so nice to watch the plastic wrap fall to the floor. To screw in the rubber stoppers. To sit on fresh upholstery, turn the TV off, and fall into his arms.

16.

WENDY'S AT A BARSTOOL, SIPPING beer, watching Penny from behind, the bartender's clamped butt cheeks hardened by hundreds of SoulCycle sessions, as Wendy knows from stalking her Instagram. Penny presses a button and music plays, a caterwauling white man over drums and guitar. The bar is empty, which Penny explains is due to student migration to a new place on Columbus with a hundred beers on tap and a vape license. For a while, 420 was the only green-friendly establishment in Morningside, but others have opened since. The problem is not competition, however, so much as a wane in public vaping since the laws banning outside herb that encouraged bars to serve their own strains at markup. Smokers have gone back to buying street weed and toking at home out of plastic bongs, which are enjoying a moment of retro-popularity. The place still fills sometimes, but tonight it's only Wendy and some guys watching the game.

Wendy was surprised to see Penny still pouring and Penny was surprised to see Wendy, period. Wendy's still the ginger beauty she was in college, though her face now contains a heaviness that suits her, gives her a sultry, been-through-shit, badass vibe. Penny says she's sorry about Ricky, that it's horrible. She asks how Wendy and Michael are doing? Wendy says Michael's a mess. She doesn't answer in regards to herself.

"And how are you?" Wendy asks.

Penny says, "Still working on the old PhD if you can believe that," which Wendy cannot.

Penny knows how pathetic she must sound to a woman like Wendy, Bloomingdale's bag draped from her barstool, while Penny parades in a halter that shows off full-sleeve zebra stripe tattoos. She explains that she put her research on pause to have a baby about ten years ago with an asshole who's no longer around, though it was all for the best because Sean, her son, is the light of her life.

Wendy's face does not betray it, but something inside her shifts at the word *baby*. While Penny speaks of her son, who's in third grade, loves soccer, and wants to be an ROS developer, Wendy is elsewhere. She's in the hospital room as the doctor hands over Nina and Wendy holds the infant to her chest, amazed at its heaviness, as if death might have lightened the load. She's in that same room watching Michael's face when the doctor asks if *he* wants to hold their daughter and Michael turns his eyes toward the overhead TV that, for some reason, plays a muted tennis match. Michael took Nina after a second's hesitation, but there was that pause, there will always be that pause. She's in the shower at home, watching the remnants of her pregnancy—blood and amniotic fluid—spill from her body. She's on the couch, clutching her stomach that sags with Nina's nonattendance, skin shriveled and stretch-marked, milk dribbling from nipples. She's at her laptop, taking down her pregnancy photos from Facebook, but not before examining each one for signs that something was wrong.

Penny tells Wendy that being a single mom is hard, which is why it's lucky her sister lives nearby and can babysit while she bartends nights. But anyway, sorry she's said so much about herself, when of course Wendy must be in a serious state.

"Yes," Wendy says.

Penny pours them tequila shots. Wendy hasn't drunk tequila since the last time she was at this bar, but she can't say no without seeming snobbish and above it, so she toasts with Penny and downs her shot. Ten seconds later she's drunk.

Penny's drunk too—she's been drinking since six with the guys watching the game—and because of this, and because Wendy looks so sad, Penny leans in and says something deeply sentimental, a line she's heard in movies a million times but never once had occasion to use, though now it seems fitting, so right for the moment, she says, "He always loved you, you know."

Wendy bursts into tears. Normally she can't cry in front of other people—she's too stiffly self-conscious—but the last few days have found her freely sobbing. Wendy wonders if, maybe, a barrier's been broken, allowing access to a long-stored well of sadness, so that she's not just crying for what's happened this week, but for all the old things she would have cried for as well had the floodgates been open. Penny pours them each another round.

17.

BRODER HAS EMPTIED THE WALLET, traded its tender for powder. He closes his eyes. Blurry Broder with his slideshow brain. Everything's bright: white walls coated in eggshell varnish, lemon-scented kitchen shine. The toaster was a silver mirror, floor a skating rink for socks. He remembers playing hockey with a duct-tape puck. Each year for his birthday, he asked for a brother.

Broder got a silver Torah pointer for his bar mitzvah, wore a silver silk shirt. They did the hora in the stammering strobe and they lifted his chair toward the crystal chandelier. His cousin's gift was weed stems in an Altoids tin. They smoked from a pipe made from a dry-erase marker and the smoke smelled like marker. Broder's magic mushroom poster glowed pink under black light. His bedroom ceiling was stickered with stars.

Girls were easy if you styled correctly: Abercrombie cargos, diamond stud, frosted tips. Broder's mom mixed the bleach in a plastic beach pail. It was an intimate thing, her hands in his hair, the way she so delicately crimped the foil. Mom wore sweatpants but only ever vacuumed. She wore makeup but never left the house. He never knew how to answer when she asked about his day.

His grandma had what the home's brochure called a junior suite: bathroom, sofa, sad twin bed. Broder brought Munchkins from Dunkin'. His grandma crushed the crumbs into the carpet with her stockinged heels, and he painted her nails: fuchsia or magenta or the kind called Party Shimmer. He loved the birdlike bones in her elegant hands. He brought flowers and he opened the windows, but it still smelled like urine. Broder only ever took a couple of her Oxys. Sometimes she called him by her dead husband's name.

There was a greening in spring, honeyed summers. The glittered tar of his parents' paved drive. Broder spun circles, whippit-high, a human helicopter crossing the lawn. Fall was burnt and russet brown. Winter was ice white with open heat grates. It was ice on the windshield, the sound of the scraper. Broder always had a bad winter cough. His phlegm was Adderall blue, Ritalin orange. School came easily to Broder; he got As.

College was cocaine and Napster. You just needed money and an Ethernet cable. You needed Winamp. Broder wore hoodies low over his eyes, stumbled down Broadway back to the dorms. There were hand jobs, blow jobs, the rare case of intercourse. He kissed a guy just to see if he liked it. Consensus: neutral. He let a guy jerk off on his leg.

There was no time for class. During daylight, he slept, or smoked on the steps of Dodge Hall in a trench coat and shades, or hunted for vinyl in mildewed storefronts on East Village side streets. Broder loved those rooms, their rising dust. Nothing in his parents' house was old.

Broder had turntables and he had taste. He had very little talent. Michael didn't mind. Michael had very little money; Broder bought. They ate chicken parm from Milano's, or Amir's falafel, or eggs Florentine from West End or Deluxe. They didn't have girlfriends.

Broder wanted a girlfriend. He wasn't sure how it worked. Girls were always gone by the time Broder woke. He'd sometimes catch one in the doorway, in the phantom disco shimmer of last night's sequins, holding her heels. He wrote their numbers on loose scraps of paper or the back of his hand, but by the time he thought to call, he'd lost the scrap, or the marker had smudged, or he was scared of rejection and put down the phone. He envied those couples conjoined in the quad, sharing salads, passing the fork back and forth. To bring a girl home for Thanksgiving break, that was the dream. To show her off at the neighborhood bar, or cruise the midnight-still suburb in his hot-boxed Audi, pointing out the lower schools and Little League fields, the mall, the ice-cream parlor, all the sites of his corny nostalgia. He wanted what they always had in movies: a witness to his family's weirdness, a hand to hold at the Thanksgiving game. He had Michael instead, at least until Wendy.

SHE ARRIVED SOPHOMORE YEAR, A phoenix rising from the ashes of the Towers—or, that's how it must have looked in Michael's mind. Michael's high school friend Ricky was bitchy about it, and Broder was lonely, and the city was apocalyptically drinking, awash in song: hipsters arm in arm, earnestly belting Sinatra over the jukebox.

So while Michael chased romance in the cheaper bistros of Upper Manhattan, the unlikely alliance of Ricky and Broder hit the West Village dives, and the Chelsea meat markets, and the Meatpacking clubs. They spotted celebs at downtown hotspots—Christina Ricci at B Bar dousing her french fries in ketchup, Parker Posey smoking weed outside Bungalow 8—and made a point to ignore them. They drank happy-hour margs in Murray Hill with young Jewish Republicans, drank Bloody Mary oyster shooters in Tribeca with WASPs. They came armed with gram bags of weak cocaine that they bumped in bathrooms off dirty dorm keys, or laid out in lines on toilet lids for small groups of friends or attractive strangers. At Pravda, they pretended to be

Russian, and drank quail egg martinis, and Broder hit on models who could somehow tell that, despite his cokey confidence and vintage track suit, he was not a talent scout. They hit the midtown sports bars, and the Hell's Kitchen gay bars, and the Bushwick roof parties, and the Lower East Side gallery openings, and, once, a Williamsburg loft, where they snorted Molly off a frisbee that was being passed around while a keytar player and an electric violinist performed covers to an indifferent crowd. They drank Jack and gingers at Ricky's apartment, swallowed Klonopin and rolled around on the floor. They waited for the coke guy to call back. Sometimes they waited for hours, watching *Simpsons* reruns and *Seinfeld* reruns, filling Ricky's ashtray, blowing up the coke guy's pager 911. And they talked about the Towers—who they knew in the Towers: a dude from Ricky's stats class, interning somewhere; a friend of a friend of Broder's dad's—but mostly they didn't talk about the Towers, and the empty space in the conversation was as gaping as the space where the Towers had stood. They smoked a joint laced with PCP and went to see the first Harry Potter film at Loews Lincoln Square, and Broder had to hold a hand over one eye in order to see, and that night he lay in bed and pictured marrying Hermione Granger, his proud mom walking him down the aisle.

And sometimes he went back to women's apartments, though it rarely went farther than muddled fumbling. Other people talked about the Towers, didn't talk about the Towers. And Broder threw up in toilets, and he threw up in bathtubs, and he threw up off a friend's third-story balcony and watched the vomit splatter in the street below. One night he threw up in a cab driver's hair and was left on the West Side Highway to walk. He peed in his closet, and in his laundry basket, and in his bed. Outside Scratcher, he peed on the side of the building rather than waiting in the bathroom line, and he was fined $50 by the City of New York.

Self-reflection wasn't Broder's forte, but even he could see that he was seeking something—oblivion, euphoria, an antidote to loneliness. Though maybe these were aspects of the same elusive need: to feel himself akin to other sympathetic humans, their separate solitary daydreams fleetingly joined in a vague and all-encompassing warmth. And one 5 A.M., he found himself in a Chinatown apartment above a fish market, watching a hipster with a braided rattail hold a Bic to the bottom of a spoon. Broder thought it would be brown, but it was more like the color of sand. He watched through slatted blinds as the rising sun lit the East River in a million silvers, and in the beauty and fish stink, he opened a vein.

HERE'S WHERE BRODER LOSES TIME. Here's where time loses Broder. The clock still ticks and the heart still beats, but they move at different tempos, make different music. He's at school and he's high and he's home. He's high and he's home. He's at school. He's high. His grandma is sick and she's dead. He's home.

Broder's dad has moved into the local Marriott with a woman who works at the bank. Broder has emptied his bar mitzvah savings. He's sold his Minimoog and drum machine. He's run out of veins in his feet, so he shoots into his arms, and now everyone knows, he thinks they know. He's long-sleeved at the shiva, reciting the Kaddish. He's on the lawn in a snowstorm making an angel. Michael never seems to return Broder's calls.

It is winter it is summer it is spring. Inside the house it's always sixty-eight degrees. Broder's mom has adopted a rescue French bulldog. She calls it Gimel, after the first Hebrew letter of his grandma's name. She's too distraught to potty-train. Broder scrubs piss out of the carpet with a special shampoo. His mom eats nothing but Taco Bell, refried beans and plump cheesy burritos.

She eats chalupas, whatever the fuck those are. She wears men's undershirts and spandex bike shorts. The shirts are guac-stained. She eats chalupas and cries. Broder stands in the doorway and watches. He pages Michael and Michael doesn't call back. Broder's dad keeps inviting him to meet his new girlfriend. Her name's Patty and she's a good cook. And she's black, he always adds, African American, as if that makes leaving Broder's mother okay. He asks if Broder's okay. Broder hangs up. He is angry and he's not. He's copping outside the dry cleaner, shooting in an alley in a pile of recycling. He's on the ground in a mess of broken bottles: bleeding, sleeping. He's on a stretcher. He's handcuffed to a hospital bed. He's home. He's on a plane.

18.

MICHAEL'S STILL AT THE LAPTOP when Wendy gets home. She stomps through the kitchen, opening fridge and cabinets, nibbling on something, running the tap. She kicks off her heels and makes her way toward the airbed, glass of water in one hand, Bloomingdale's bag in the other. Half a graham cracker hangs from her mouth. She puts the bag down and chews.

"Where were you?" says Michael. He's been online for hours, refreshing Twitter, googling *Gatsby Murder*. The latest: a witness saw Devor buy a dozen baseball bats at the Modell's in Times Square two days before the murder, and another claims to have seen him marched behind him to the Zone. Two people claim to have seen Devor during the riot, brandishing a police Taser, but another says she saw him buying beer at a bodega on the Upper West Side around the time that the murder took place.

Roughly half of Twitter thinks Devor is guilty, but the other half argues in his defense, claiming the banks masterminded the murder and framed Devor to discredit #Occupy. Little hard evidence backs these suppositions, but something rings true. Ricky was disliked by many at C&S, and if Edward Jin and the others sat down in a smoky room and plotted to knock off one of their own, Michael imagines Ricky would make the top of their list.

The strangest thing he's found, however, is speculation of a different sort. Among the deluge of shitposts on Reddit, Michael found someone insisting that Communitiv.ly, on behalf of a secret group called Project Pinky, is running a stealth PR campaign to tank the UBI by framing Devor.

"I got a drink," says Wendy, done eating, butt on the air mattress, trying and failing to remove her tights.

"That I can see," says Michael.

Wendy manages to free her legs, though she kicks over her water in the process.

"You went shopping," says Michael. He takes off his T-shirt and uses it to cover the spill. Wendy faces the wall.

"I'm confused," he says.

She's focused on her phone.

"Confused why?" she says after a second. "Confused because we owe hundreds of thousands in credit card debt? Confused because you owned three million dollars' worth of shares in your own investment bank and now those shares are worthless? I know it's confusing that something like that could happen. That someone as responsible as you could let that happen."

Wendy puts down the phone. She wears an expression Michael has seen once before. It is not the expression Wendy wore when the doctor quietly informed them of her failure to find Nina's heartbeat, as if the softness of her voice might cushion the blow. No, this is the expression Michael saw shortly after, when the doctor asked if he wanted to hold their dead child. Michael paused for too long before saying yes. He paused, and in that pause he stepped out of the present. He stepped into the future to wonder how he'd look back on the moment, how the experience—her skull in his palm, the caress of his thumb across its ridges—might later haunt and traumatize, degrade any future instance of happy feeling.

"I'm sorry," says Michael.

"What was that? I don't think I heard you. Did you just apologize? Did you just whisper *I'm sorry* as if that would make it okay?"

Michael hits the wall with the rear of his skull. He says, "I'm so sorry."

"Fuck your sorry," says Wendy.

She pulls the envelope from her purse and fans a stack of hundred-dollar bills. She balls up a bill and flicks it at Michael's nose. It bounces off. She throws money in the air and they both watch it fall.

Wendy's usually respectful of money above all things, arranging the bills in her wallet by denomination and rolling loose coins while she watches TV. This atypical display lets him know just how angry she is, and how drunk.

"I got paid," Wendy says. "Now aren't you glad I went to work today?"

"You went to Bloomingdale's."

"Is there a problem? Is there a problem with me spending *my* money that *I* earned?"

Michael collects the bills from the floor. He puts them back in the envelope and places the envelope on the bed.

"Ricky was my friend too," says Wendy.

"I know that."

"Abstaining from purchasing clothing is not going to bring him back."

"No."

Michael goes to the bathroom to give her a moment to calm down. He pees and brushes his teeth. He returns and stands nude before Wendy. It feels like an offer. Here I am to take or leave, is what he's trying to say. Wendy taps at her phone. She doesn't look up. Michael gets back in the bed and pulls the blanket to his chin. She tugs it back in her direction, tells him not to be a hog. She watches Instagram stories: a pop singer discussing lactation; Michael's cousin, Hannah, cooking egg-plant parmesan.

"I read a thing online," Michael says. "I read a thing online about Communitiv.ly. That you're trying to frame Jay Devor for the murder. Is that what you're doing at work?"

"I'll tell you what I'm doing," says Wendy. "I'm making sure the world remembers your friend as a better person than we both know he was. You should be thanking me."

"You're not framing Devor?"

"To frame someone, he has to be innocent."

"There's no evidence."

"Then who did it, huh?"

Wendy picks up the envelope and counts the cash like she's suspicious Michael stole some.

"We should use the money to start paying . . ." he says.

"My money. It's not *the* money. It's *my* money."

"I just meant . . ."

"You just meant what? That if we pay off the cards we can go back to normal? Should we move to a studio in the Bronx with a Murphy bed and a hot plate?"

Michael thinks she's being bourgeois. These may not be the blissed-out days of frivolous spending, but they still have more earning power than their college friends who've eked out the last decade in tiny sublets and shared apartments, working three jobs while pursuing diminishing artistic dreams. Sure, they're in debt, but Wendy makes six figures, and Michael can find another job. They are the definition of privileged: the holes they fall into aren't deep enough to keep them from clawing back up.

He says, "There's a difference between being broke and being poor."

"Oh don't pull that shit," says Wendy. "Don't pull that *I grew up blue collar and love the simple life* bullshit"

"I can fix this," says Michael.

She says, "You can't."

19.

THEY MEET OUTSIDE MOMA AT noon. Classic Greg. The daytime date means less pressure, and the artwork provides a discussion topic, and the fact that there's only so long you can stay in a museum without wanting to get off your feet and into some cocktails means that if things go well they'll be drinking by two while sharing apartment horror stories and humorous anecdotes about their mutual Facebook friend.

Now here's the tricky part. Both live far away, she in Williamsburg or Bed-Stuy or Clinton Hill or Bushwick, he in the East Village. His place is closer, but she'll feel more comfortable at hers, unless she has roommates, which she probably does, in which case, Greg's studio it is. But how to get there? Three options:

1. Cab – Pros: Quickest delivery, with minimal loss of momentum or inebriation. Cons: The question of who pays can be a problem, particularly if Greg's date wants to discuss it before deciding. Ideally, they'll split the cab, everyone equal and equally eager, but if she insists on taking the subway to save cash then Greg will look pushy if he offers to pay the full fare. Any way you look at it, a cab is problematic. Which leads to,

2. Subway – Pros: Gets rid of the problem of payment. The subway is democracy incarnate, the people's mode

of transport. Greg and date can commiserate over shitty service, and how there's always construction on weekends, and how Sundays especially suck with tourists clamoring for seats and asking which line goes where and what's the difference between express and local. Making it from midtown to Greg's apartment amid this madness is an adventure they can share, then discuss once they've arrived. Cons: The subway is not a romantic venue, with its smells and general display of ugliness. Plus it takes a while, trains on or more likely behind schedule, and by the time they get to Astor Place then walk the ten blocks to Greg's, the mood and booze may have worn off. There's always

3. Walking – Pros: They can hold hands. They can stop at a bar at any point to refuel. Cons: Walking takes the longest and they've already walked a lot today, feet beginning to tire, especially hers, and especially if she's wearing heels. It also extends the conversation, which means Greg has to come up with new shit to say when he's basically out of material. Walking is not ideal.

Luckily, there's a fourth option, which, though imperfect, has become a go-to for Greg. That option is Mhustle. Unintuitive? Perhaps. Risky in its betrayal of Greg's membership in the privileged elite? Certainly. But here's how it works: first, it's very important that Greg wait until his date proposes the idea of heading elsewhere. Under no circumstances should Greg make the suggestion himself; if it doesn't happen, so be it. If his date *does* make this suggestion, however, Greg will momentarily hesitate, not because he's not up for it—the last thing he wants to do is make her feel rejected—but because the transport options are so shitty. But then Greg must act like he's had a revelation, which is that Communitiv.ly has a Mhustle account that its employees are encouraged to use as a funky job perk. And, OMG, it's so easy. He just has to punch his touchscreen and five minutes later they'll be nestled into the tiny back seat of a sun-gold '68 Camaro.

If she doesn't know about Mhustle, all the better. It's sort of like Lyft, Greg will explain, but instead of Teslas and Priuses, the company owns a fleet of vintage American muscle cars. The service is mostly used by businesses to provide clients with a novel way of getting around. Soon, the service will blow up and the novelty will wear off, but for now it's a fun and semi-original way of making his date feel less weird about Greg paying for the ride. Besides, Mhustle is a model of corporate responsibility, hiring displaced cabbies and Arecibo guys whose knowledge of the city's valves and arteries means they can provide an authentic sans-GPS transportation experience.

Back at his place, he'll jokingly give her a tour of the apartment, joking because it's so small that really there's no tour to give, but here are some photos of his family, and here's his record player, and why doesn't she pick out some music while he runs to the bathroom?

He actually does need to pee—has for hours—and now he unloads, flushes, then a touch of hair gel to thicken his waves and re-cover the tiny bald spot she probably hasn't noticed. He washes his hands, gargles a capful of mouthwash, not so much that the mint will be obvious on his breath, but enough to hide any buildup of reflux. When he exits the bathroom there's music playing and maybe she's reaching toward the shelf to thumb through a book. Greg approaches from behind and wraps his arms around her waist. Next thing he knows, either he's going down on her or she's saying she's not really into that so why don't they try something else, and either way, an hour later they're parsing delivery options in bed.

OF COURSE, THINGS DON'T ALWAYS work quite so perfectly. It's obvious that they won't, today, within ten minutes of meeting Sophia.

She's certainly attractive, half Greek with walnut skin and those oversized Mediterranean eyes that look like figs or dates or just big-ass raisins. She has medium-sized breasts that he will not do the injustice of comparing to fruit, yoga-buff arms, strong thighs, a great wide ass, sexily coffee-stained European teeth, and good fashion sense. She's wearing a sort of couture safari dress matched with patterned tights and heeled black bootlets that give her upwards of six inches on Greg.

None of this is the problem. Greg has dated gorgeous women before and is not intimidated, though he does prefer women who aren't quite so confident. Height isn't a problem either; women tend to be impressed by Greg's Napoleonic confidence and the fact that he really makes being short work for him, style-wise. No, the problem today is that after they made their introductions, Sophia offered him a hit from her pen. If he declined, that would mean he was boring, and if he accepted, that would mean he'd be stoned.

Greg chose the latter, and Sophia encouraged him to take not one but something like five or six hits, and now they're in the modern wing of the permanent collection.

"What do you think Rauschenberg was after with this one?" asks Sophia. "What was he getting at?"

Greg takes a long moment before answering, hoping the pause will be read as consideration of the question as he examines the piece and synthesizes his insights on some important connection between its texture and composition, rather than what it is: a bid for time while Greg tries to pull something vague and opaque enough out of his ass that she won't realize he has no idea what he's talking about.

This is Greg's fifth date since Lillian took over his Tinder and matched him with women whose profiles suggest involvement with #Occupy. The plan is for Greg to disseminate a rumor about Jay Devor's connection to the Gatsby Murder. He doesn't know why Lillian wants him to do this, but he isn't bothered; so far all the dates have been hot.

It was Sophia's idea to hit the permanent collection. Greg would have preferred to see the group show from Palestinian photographers on the front lines of occupied Gaza because (a) his knowledge of Middle East politics, though by no means comprehensive, is much stronger than his knowledge of modern art, (b) he took two photography courses at Tufts and can fake his way through a discussion of the difference between journalistic, artistic, and portrait photography, perhaps pointing out that one of the photos—intentionally or not—seems to echo a famous Cartier-Bresson in terms of its indifference to light and angle at the behest of capturing emotional truth, and (c) the bigger exhibition would have been more crowded than the mostly empty modern wing, allowing Greg to express his previously practiced observations about the strangeness of art as public spectacle, and the impossibility of really *seeing* the work in this context, what with tourists snapping photos and kids running and crying; the sacred turned commercial, the exhibition a highway that leads to the gift shop where you can buy Jackson Pollock children's paint sets, and Warhol temporary tattoos, and Keith Haring sneakers, and truly ugly kitchenware designed by Jeff Koons.

But Sophia wanted to escape the crowds and space out in front of the Rothkos—which, Greg must admit, look cool when you're stoned—and get deep by discussing the true meaning of certain works like the Rauschenberg at which they currently stare.

"I think it's about America," Greg says, realizing as the words come out that it's one of the more obvious and uninteresting observations ever made on the subject of art.

20.

THE MOVIE IS SET IN a near future where, instead of being buried, skeletons are cut into small pieces, and bones and fragments are given as souvenirs to families of the deceased. The fragments are turned into key chains, coat buttons, necklace pendants, and smartphone cases. Teeth are worn on dental-floss bracelets. Heads are pickled and displayed on mantels. Hearts are hardened into molds and carried as talismans in heart-shaped pockets within heart-shaped purses. Coach was the first to produce this design. The film's protagonist, a teenage girl, carries her dead father's heart wherever she goes, and is dismayed when imitators begin carrying faux hearts in faux Coach bags because, unlike hers, their fathers aren't dead. Coach spent millions on product placement and a rewrite that further emphasized the film's anti-counterfeiting message. The *New York Times* called it *Catcher in the Rye* for Gen Y.

"Great flick," says Michael. He got to the Berkshires this morning. The funeral's not until Saturday, but after last night, he thought it worth giving Wendy time to cool down. She'll take the bus tomorrow night, or early Saturday morning. Rachel looks up to reveal for the nth time, though it's always a shock, the scorpion tattooed across her right cheek.

"Is it?" Rachel says.

Enter their mother. Lydia looks the same as always: elegant and slim, with razor-thin eyebrows, and a touch of mascara. A sweater-dress emphasizes her beanpole physique. She says, "Oh good, I'm glad you're both here. I need to know what you want for dinner. The options are Chinese or pizza."

Never an enthusiastic chef, Lydia gave up cooking when Michael went to college. Rachel was raised on boxed mac and cheese and foot-long subs. It might be why she's a candidate for Type 2 diabetes. Michael doesn't know his sister well. He left home just after her bat mitzvah, and by the time he returned for Christmas break, Rachel was unrecognizable, a purple-haired freshman who rarely showed up for school. The siblings never managed to reconnect. Rachel bore the brunt of their parents' bad years, and she resents Michael's absence during that difficult decade. Now she's in her mid-thirties, stuck in Pittsfield doing drone repair, and living with Donny, her boyfriend, a short-order cook whose passion is extreme body mod. There's not an inch of Donny's skin that isn't pierced or inked, and he recently had magnets implanted in his wrists for purposes that are unclear to anyone.

"Doesn't matter," says Michael. "Either is fine."

"I'm eating out," says Rachel.

"Eating out where?" says Lydia.

"Eating out your pussy," says Rachel.

Their mother doesn't bat a lash, she's so used to this shit. "Pizza, then," she says, and leaves the room.

Michael sinks into the couch. He studies the room which, despite bearing the same wall-hangings that have been here since his parents bought the house over thirty years prior, feels strangely different.

"New curtains?"

"New TV," replies Rachel. Which should have been obvious, a fifty-inch monitor in place of the boxy old one. "And a new stereo, and lamps, and desk, and the couch you're currently sitting on."

Michael looks down. He finds himself on a leather sofa.

"Where did all this stuff come from?"

"Dad bought it."

"Why would Dad buy living room furniture? He doesn't leave the game room."

"Beats me," says Rachel, occupied by something on her tablet.

"What are you doing on that thing?"

She turns it so Michael can see. Rachel appears to be operating a remote drone that hovers outside Donny's window. Donny makes himself a sandwich, slathering too much mayo on both slices of bread. The slats from the shades slightly shadow the image, but otherwise the picture is clear.

"Does he know you're watching?"

"I think he gets off on it."

As if on cue, Donny looks into the camera, makes a *V* with his fingers, wags his tongue between them.

"Do *you* get off on it?"

"I just want to make sure he isn't doing anything sketchy, like cooking meth."

"Right," says Michael, unsure if this is a legitimate concern.

The scorpion covers Rachel's acne scars, but they're still visible, and she still has a thin layer of down on her chin, and brown eyes so light they're almost clay-colored, and the habit of unconsciously biting one side of her lip in a way that makes the other puff out like it's been punched, and slightly elfin ears, the tips of which poke through her stringy hair. She's wearing an old T-shirt of Michael's and a pair of their father's moccasins, and as he stares at his sister in the blue TV light, Michael realizes he's crying.

He covers his face with his hands. Rachel doesn't say a word or make a move to touch him. She doesn't turn off the TV. Donny doesn't have crying jags often, but occasionally they come. Early on, Rachel tried to comfort him during these outbursts, but quickly realized that a hand on his shoulder or trite words of consolation made him angry. Men don't want their sensitivity acknowledged or condescendingly soothed. They prefer to be politely ignored.

Rachel can't imagine how Michael feels. She, herself, always felt a kinship with Ricky, who, like her, was unapologetically weird and usually high. He was also unjudgmental, whereas Michael always seemed to want something more out of Rachel, was always so transparently disappointed in the person she'd become. A person—she might add, if she and Michael ever actually talked—who despite her appearance and disinterest in words like *career*, is fairly happy and surprisingly mature; a person who has become an adult under adverse circumstances; who's built a real, if occasionally difficult, relationship with a complicated guy; a person gainfully employed and good at her job; a person who has her shit semi-together.

After a moment, the sobbing stops. The siblings watch the movie in silence. The protagonist's anti-counterfeiting crusade has taken her to the Oval Office where she gives an impassioned speech on the inviolability of the human heart. Her dead father's, in this case, calcified, and clenched in her palm like she's about to chuck a curveball.

"Tell me something about Donny," says Michael.

"Like what?"

"I don't know, a fact or something. I want to get to know him as a person. The man behind the magnets."

"Why?"

"Because my sister loves him. So there must be something special about him."

"Barf."

21.

THAT WAS THE EAST COAST, an earlier life. Broder BC, as he thinks of it—Before California.

Rehab wasn't an initial success. Five stints in as many years. Between, there were halfway houses, friends' couches and basements, a quasi-girlfriend's West Hollywood condo where he found a dozen infant turtles dead in the pool. He nodded off along the Venice boardwalk with dreadlocked white dudes and their hemp-collared dogs. He worked at a car wash and brought paper-bag lunches, Oscar Mayer turkey with mustard on rye, and he watched the clean cars emerge into sunlight, and for that brief moment he believed in redemption. He took the bus and he pitied the other riders, and he pitied himself the squandered promise of his stupid pedigree: highborn Broder breathing bus fumes, crumpled over the wheel well, chugging along. Soon he was stumbling: bar-lit, street-lit, kicking clumps of sod from pristine lawns. His sponsor hooked him up with a busing gig at a Koreatown steakhouse and Broder did Oxy with the chefs in the back. He copped. He called his father. He returned to rehab.

THEY MET IN THE LUNCHROOM on her twenty-first birthday. Three candles in an Entenmann's donut. Powdered-sugar residue caked to paper plates. With a straw, she pretended to snort.

He hadn't seen her before, but he knew the type. She of the

stepdad's Malibu beach house, of the solstice parties filled with C-list celebs skinny-dipping at dawn, coke-numbed to the cold. Her type lay on the porch and evened their tans. In Group, they rarely shared.

Broder didn't condescend. His own weed grew from the same privileged garden. The only difference was age. At twenty-six, he'd reached recidivism's terminal stage.

"My name's Broder," Broder said.

She asked if that was a first or last name. He said it was a mononym, like Prince or Madonna. Her laugh was high-pitched and horsey, a laugh-slash-neigh. Her teeth were corn-colored and metallically capped, and one was brown-stained with what looked like an *H*. Her T-shirt said *Stay Gold* in lamé. He liked that. Irony was hard to come by in California.

BRODER WAS WRONG ABOUT THE stepdad, but right about the beach house. At first that's where they stayed, at poolside remove from chemical temptation.

Aliana taught Broder to cook. Simple dishes: fried eggs, omelets, spaghetti with meat sauce. She was half Italian and he liked pasta, so they continued with pasta: baked ziti, gnocchi, linguine with clams. She had to convince him to try puttanesca. Broder feared anchovies. He was a culinary naïf from the sheltered suburbs. He grew up eating at chains, watching his mom pinball between binge and shame, with the attendant crash diets and quick-fix fads that always arced toward the kitchen at 2 A.M., eating fistfuls of sheet cake, tonguing frosting from palms. It was new to Broder, this idea of food as a rarefied pleasure, as a thing to be admired in the broad light of day. And, eventually, he mastered carbonara—the trick, Aliana explained, was to discard the egg whites and only use the yolks.

They jokingly called theirs the Fuck Atkins Diet. All carbs all the time for the recovering junkie! Guaranteed to put color on a drug-ashened face! And how beautiful it felt to be mildly bloated, slicing heirloom tomatoes in a modular kitchen with sliding windows that gave way to Pacific infinity, smog pink sky.

Broder picked parsley and she taught him how to chop it correctly, knife like a seesaw. He picked basil for pesto, and she taught him how to crush it with a mortar and pestle. Broder liked her long, elegant nose with its flat bridge and nostril flare. The nose gave her just a hint of the non-California-native, a hint that she wasn't born bronzed in a two-piece, shoulders to sunshine. Because all else about her appearance conformed to type: perennial tan, dirty blond hair that hung to her waist. The nose said to Broder that she was imperfect, not a goddess but a demigod. The nose said to Broder that this wasn't a dream. The nose and the teeth.

A gardener named Jorge came twice a week and he called Broder *Maestro* for reasons unknown. And one morning, Broder watched Jorge gulp from a sweating can of Coors as he circled the lawn on the riding mower, and Broder imagined just licking the can, those musty-sweet drops saturating his tongue. He thought of kindly explaining that he was an addict, and she was an addict, and Jorge was working, so if Jorge didn't mind, but instead he snipped flowers—lily of the Nile, African irises, big pink daisies that looked like windmills—and arranged them in bouquets for the kitchen island. He learned the names of the flowers from a gardening book, and he found it satisfying to repeat them aloud. It occurred to Broder that a florist was a bit like a DJ: a provider of context, a steward of taste. And he thought that in the fall, when they'd moved, as they'd discussed, to her place in Los Feliz, he could get himself a job at a small flower shop. He could be happy in that life.

22.

THE SHOOT'S AT LE BAIN, the roof bar at the Standard, a favorite during Wendy's brief nightlife phase, when there was no thrill so great as lingering among the digerati after industry events, sipping sprig-garnished cocktails and allowing men to lightly flirt before they noticed her ring, which she would wave, pretending to fan air from her face. The bar's no longer the epicenter of Meatpacking chic, but it's close to the office, and the Gansevoort was booked, and the Zone was ruled out for obvious reasons. Besides, you can't argue its view of the High Line and vista of Hudson, velvet and sun-glossed, an ad unto itself.

She's being sentimental. Wendy hasn't spent time on set in forever, and she'd forgotten how lively these scenes can be with their walkie hum and buzzing PAs, their overall sense of cooperative urgency. In the early years of Communitiv.ly, Lillian sent Wendy to shoots as a company stooge to make sure their freelancers stayed under budget and didn't do anything that might get them sued. Wendy wasn't good at it—too young and timid to manifest the authority required—but she loved being there beneath the towering light rigs, among the bustling crew.

As the years passed, Wendy's role changed, and the company's focus shifted from TV and print to the digital sphere. These days, even when there are large-scale shoots for a project of this nature, she oversees from afar. Today's an exception. The concept was Wendy's idea, and Lucas insisted that her presence was important, that she must make sure her vision is accurately captured. How she might go about this remains to be seen.

Wendy swirls her coffee like it's wine and watches the models emerge from Makeup with contoured cheekbones and halos of hairspray, musk rising off the men who cross in silent formation like hunky monks or spa-bound angels wearing robes that shine white against tan and brown skin. It feels godly to know that she's conjured all this, these cameras and yards of electrical cable; these humans who rose before sunrise and rode in from outer boroughs for the purpose of constructing something born in Wendy's head.

She looks for Lucas, who doesn't appear to have arrived. Lillian, she knows, is manning the office, and she hasn't heard from Greg since yesterday. She wants someone to talk to and share in this moment, someone like Michael who'd swoon and be impressed. She ends up back at craft service, pouring hot coffee into another cup of ice cubes. She loves this minor alchemy, watching the cubes pop and disappear, like a school science project gone inexplicably right. She's less hungover than she worried she would be, but her head still pounds, and her legs feel heavy, and she hopes that another caffeine infusion will alleviate these symptoms.

The craft service guy says, "Round two already?"

He wears a khaki vest adorned with fishhooks, and sits in a rainbow beach chair. If Michael were here he'd suss this man's story—dead wife, daughter with cystic fibrosis, Ninth Ward apartment destroyed in Katrina—and offer a series of compassionate nods. Michael would mention a summer spent gallivanting NOLA, and what a beautiful city it was and still is. Not a lie of omission so much as blatant untruth, unless three days counts as a summer, and spending most of that time doing Jäger bombs in a Tulane dorm room could be called a gallivant. The craft service guy would humor him, pretending to ignore Michael's shift into Cajun dialect or the reference to his grandpappy's gumbo. Michael would feel good about the interaction, proud to have a new person of a different race and socio-economic background that he could refer to, in future conversations, as his friend.

There's nothing Wendy dislikes more than when her husband does this, so she curtly says, "Yup."

WITH HIS BOSSY AND MILITARISTIC style, Yoav Levé lives up to all the clichés about both Israelis and fashion directors. He's wearing a cape, and his even tan, the color of chestnuts, extends to the stubble-shaved toes of his sandal-shod feet.

Wendy worries the director doesn't get the tone of her directive, doesn't quite understand what they're trying to sell. Not completely his fault, as Wendy, herself, is still in the dark on the product, but the big-picture message—work will set you free and get you laid; no, work will set you free *by* getting you laid—should be clear. And yet, Yoav keeps trying to ruin the shot by inserting ridiculous props like oversized wrenches and unnaturally yellow bananas into the models' hands and mouths. Wendy's twice pulled him aside to clarify the mood she has in mind, but the director still seems confused about most things, including who Wendy is and why her input should be heeded. As bulbs flash and cameras click, and Yoav instructs a male model in accented English, Wendy looks again for Lucas, hoping the client can step in with the authority that comes from wearing twenty-thousand-dollar loafers and signing the checks, and explain to the director that Wendy's in charge. She's on her third coffee now and it feels like a swarm of bees has invaded her veins and is clogged in her arterial pipeline.

At least the dressings and sets adhere to her vision. The male model in question currently leans on a piece of faux scaffolding that's like a lost Cy Twombly, scaled up and aimed, Viagrafied, toward the sky. Muscles bulge from the sleeves of his white tee and there's the right amount of dirt on his helmet and jeans. Knee bent, work boot at rest on a tin lunch pail, he looks a bit like George Washington crossing the Delaware. To Wendy's satisfaction, he looks more than a bit like Eminem. The day's next set features Le Bain's indoor lounge reimagined as an auto plant. She hopes Lucas will be here by then.

The model's female counterpart saunters up. Why she'd be in lingerie at a construction site is beyond Wendy, but whatever, it works. The models edge toward each other, then rotate clockwise once they're about an inch apart. None of this demands instruction; it's something models know to do. They turn away from the horizon so they're facing the camera and the female bends to place her ass in his lap. If you can call it an ass. More like two yarmulkes sewn onto butt bones. Still, Wendy's pleased with the overall effect. The model may be blond and statuesque; she may not have Brittany Murphy's nickel-sized pupils or air of imminent ruin, but she stares past the cameras with an expression that says: *in this short life, in this shit world, at least one real man remains.*

"Great," yells Yoav. "Now put on his hard hat."

The female model snaps her chin to the sky and gravity pulls her voluminous locks behind her ears, a gesture likely honed during screen tests for shampoo commercials. The male fits the hard hat on her head like he's crowning her queen of this construction site. The too-large item falls over her eyes. The male cracks an accidental smile. The female breaks character and smiles back.

"Love it," yells Yoav. "You've been to the dentist, and what's that? No cavities? Show us those sparkling teeth!"

The models remain open-mouthed for an awkward length of time. What began as a spontaneous instance of human connection has become forced and stiff. They shouldn't be smiling. Their teeth are too white, and the mood is meant to be erotically sober, like an art-house film or a perfume ad. This image must speak to the men eating microwaved burritos on America's futons, sex organs folded in on themselves like toy water snakes. It must speak to the women who sit beside these men and yearn for different husbands. More so, it must speak to Yelena the Trust-Funded Yoga Instructor, reminding her that work is a sexy life force and inalienable American right. The fact that most construction sites are manned by small crews of industrial robots doesn't matter; it's a metaphor. Wendy imagines this aspirational moment soundtracked by Jimi Hendrix's star-spangled pyrotechnics, or Ray Charles's evocation of the Midwestern plains, or a bass-heavy mashup of both. She imagines men and women getting up from their couches, fists raised, chanting: *Work will set us free!*

Yoav shouts, "Now kiss his cheek like your daddy just bought you an ice cream."

The female places her lips on the male's face. Under the director's further encouragement, the male holds a long wink.

"Beautiful," cries Yoav.

Wendy looks one last time for Lucas. When she still can't find him, she reminds herself that she's the senior-most executive on set, that she's been doing this shit for more than twenty years, that Yoav the director was still learning the aleph-bet when Wendy wrote the copy for her first TV spot, a toothpaste ad featuring cartoon sharks complaining about plaque. She reminds herself that her own livelihood is on the line with this campaign, that it's no one's responsibility but hers to make sure it turns out right, that the *8 Mile*–inspired set was her idea, and that this caped Israeli is screwing it up. She yells "Cut."

Instantly, the crew unfreezes into action. PAs rush across set, delivering lenses and walkie batteries. Tabs are popped on cans of Diet Coke. Half-smoked Parliaments are relit and speed-smoked. Hair and Makeup move in for touchups. The hard hat is removed from the female model. Her once-immaculate mane is now a fluffy mess. Someone says, "Oh, honey."

Yoav stomps up to Wendy. His cape waves in the wind. With his sandals, tan, and bowling-ball paunch, he calls to mind a retired superhero who spends his days drinking beer on a Tel Aviv beach.

"What are you cutting for? We had a moment there."

"The wrong moment," says Wendy. In heels, she has half a foot on the director. Caffeine courses through her body. She pokes Yoav's chest.

"Ow," he says.

Wendy pokes again, this time with force. The director is caught off-balance, and must steady himself by grabbing hold of a chair.

"Please stop," says Yoav. "I easily bruise."

"This isn't a beer commercial," says Wendy.

"I don't understand."

"It's not supposed to be cute."

"I don't understand," says Yoav again.

"Make yourself understand," says Wendy. "Or I'll find someone who will."

She takes three steps away, stops, turns back, and adds, "While you're at it, take off that fucking cape."

23.

THE GAME ROOM, A MONUMENT to obsolete technology, complete with a working *Ms. Pac-Man* machine, is Stuart Mixner's pride and joy, and his single contribution to the world since the birth of Rachel. When the transformer plant closed in '91, Stuart, a mid-level engineer, was laid off. He's been cooped in this room ever since.

The room is filled with consoles of nearly every gaming system from Atari on, including 100 percent of Nintendo's four-decade output—a bright red Virtual Boy holds pride of place atop a pyramid of cardboard boxes—as well as Sega's, Sony's, and a host of less-remembered devices like the Neo Geo and the Amiga CD; even earlier stuff like the German-made VC 4000; and, the jewel of the collection, a never-played '72 Magnavox Odyssey. Not to mention all the cartridges, floppy disks, CD-ROMs, and old issues of *Wired* and *Nintendo Power* organized in wobbling stacks that Michael worries might crash at any moment and bury his oblivious father.

Surrounding the stacks and the father himself is the detritus of a life lived in unforced confinement. Coffee cups and wax sandwich wrappers litter the floor. The blinds are broken and don't open. Four television screens and three computer monitors are arranged like workstations, the ceiling tiles are covered in sound-proofing Styrofoam, and at least ten speakers dangle precariously from various surfaces, all hooked up to a master mixing board which itself connects to the monitors and hardware, a creatively configured surround sound system.

These days, most of this stuff is for show, or else storage. The house can't accommodate Stuart's collection anywhere else, and he refuses to throw things away or sell them for what might be considerable sums because, for the last two years, he's been playing *Shamerican Sykosis*. When Michael enters, his father is asleep in an office chair. His hair's half gone and half static, his eyelids look purple, and his nails are bitten to yellow nubs. His reading glasses, having fallen from his nose, rest in his biblical beard. He wears an SD bracelet.

Michael nudges his father, who says, "Sail toward the sun," so Michael nudges him again, and with this Stuart wakes, and before saying hello, clicks into Shamerica to check his holdings. After a moment, he turns his attention to Michael, though he angles the chair to maintain a peripheral view of two screens. The game is played across all devices—cellphones for trading Shamerican stocks and bonds, AR helmets for exploring Shamerica's cityscapes, laptops and tablets for designing cars, buildings, and avatars—but Stuart likes these giant monitors due to failing eyesight, and also, Michael thinks, because it makes him feel like a real mogul instead of what he is, a senior citizen in sweatpants playing games. For most players, Shamerica's primary appeal is strapping on a helmet and seeing the cars, avatars, and structures of their making in the 3-D world, but Stuart rarely leaves the house. He's more interested in playing the in-game markets and attempting to accumulate SD, though he does correspond with other players through in-game messaging. The irony of this bond-trading gamelife, when his own son performs the same task as an actual profession, is lost on Michael's father.

"You scared me," says Stuart. "I'm very on edge these days."

"Me too," says Michael.

"Your friend," says Stuart. "Terrible what happened."

"Ricky," says Michael. "You knew him too."

"Nice kid. A bit fruity for my taste, but these are different times. Now I even have a son who thinks he might be gay."

"I don't think I might be gay."

"Not you; Quentin."

"Quentin?"

"Quentin. My son."

It takes Michael a moment. "Your son in the game, right. Why do you think he might be gay?"

"He told me. The other day he said, 'Dad, I think I might be gay.'"

"In real life or the game?"

"Is there a difference?"

"I'd like to think so, yes."

"You're kidding yourself if you think there's a difference."

Stuart adjusts his glasses, though the pair is so crooked that adjustments create further imbalance, the left lens askew when the right is aligned, and vice versa. Michael's factory-distressed father has always looked prematurely old, but now he seems ancient.

"How old is Quentin?" Michael asks.

"Twelve."

"In real life or the game?"

"Real life," says Stuart. "In the game he's a thirty-seven-year-old Oxford grad who designed half the riverboat casinos on the Gulf of Shamexico. I'm very proud."

"But you said there was no difference between real life and the game."

"You're taking me literally. It's always been your problem. So literal. One plus one equals two—that sort of thing."

"One plus one does equal . . ."

"These guys my age, they . . ."

"In real life or the game?"

"In the life you consider real, okay. We're talking about guys my age. Sean Hunter's dad, say, because Mom saw him at Stop & Shop. Mom saw him, and guess what he told her? He told her he bought a yacht. Like she should be impressed."

Stuart checks the stock index again.

"These guys my age, they're all buying boats. What they don't understand is that you don't need to own a physical boat. You can build a boat in your mind and get on. There's no difference."

It's a contention Michael's father has made before, AR as separate but equal dimensional plane. The problem, for Michael, is the body. He says, "What about death?"

"The end," Stuart says. "No afterlife."

"But in the game, when you die?"

"Returned to darkness."

"And in so-called unaugmented reality?"

"The Jewish cemetery in West Stockbridge."

"It's a pretty cemetery," says Michael.

"I've done well," continues Stuart, indicating his SD bracelet. "This bracelet represents more money than I've seen in a long time. I should buy a home storage vault, but I like to wear it. Who's gonna rob me out here in the boonies? Your sister's got armed drones protecting our airspace. You don't have to worry. Your inheritance is safe."

"I wasn't," says Michael.

"It's not all going to Quentin either. He gets his third, that's only fair. But you've been generous with me over the years. I haven't forgotten. It's reflected in my will."

"Your will in the game."

"I know what you're thinking: at the rate I'm going, buying TVs and living-room sets, it will all be gone by the time I retire this body at age two hundred and upload myself to the cloud."

"That wasn't what I was thinking," says Michael.

"But I'm telling you, the amount I've made over the last few months—maybe for a big Wall Street guy like you it wouldn't seem like much, but I'm a simple man, Michael. I don't have wants or needs like Dale Hunter. The yacht in my mind will do just fine. If you still want to record that rap album, though, I'd be happy to help. MC Metamucil or whatever it was? The industry's booming in my realm. None of this free streaming bullshit. In Shamerica it's pay to play. The licensing alone could send a kid to college."

Michael imagines his easy rise to stardom in that meritocratic space. Shamerica is a country without history or context, a place where identity is forged neither by nature or nurture, but only by the breadth of one's imaginative powers. It's what the pilgrims dreamed of when they showed up in Plymouth with their buckle shoes and Protestant Bibles. And now, in this TMI culture of online permanence, where search histories remain cryogenically frozen in server-farm cloud storage, ever threatening to, one day, rise from the dead and return to ruin lives, Shamerica offers a viable antidote, the last frontier where a person might achieve a fresh start.

"You mentioned people trying to rob you," he says, looking again at his father's SD bracelet, which hangs loose and looks huge on his thin, hairless wrist. "That's a real threat?"

"I keep a low profile," says Stuart. "I'm not out on the message boards bragging it up, or at the San Jose nightclubs flashing my bling. It's all relative anyway. I've done well, but there are guys who've made boatloads. No one knows who they are of course, but you can guess when you see one cruise the valley in his Porsche draping his braceleted wrist around a supermodel's arm."

"I don't understand," says Michael. "How are people buying Porsches with Sykodollars? And, for that matter, how are you buying living-room sets?"

"You haven't been following what's happened since the crash? It's like '49 all over again, Mike, only this time Woody Guthrie's not here to sing his dustbowl blues, and there's plenty of gold to go around. At least there was a few weeks ago. But people are pulling money from banks left and right, and they're investing in SD, which are getting scarce. I can't see how you've missed it. What do you do in that office all day, jerk off and play *Snood*?"

"I haven't played *Snood* in years," lies Michael. "But these bracelets, how much might one be worth? In American dollars, I mean. A bracelet owned by one of these big shot Shamerican moguls."

"Could be millions," says Stuart.

"Huh," says Michael.

24.

THE ROOM IS WINDOWLESS BUT bright, lit by fluorescent over-
heads that reflect off the steel table and the suspect's watch. Ryan
had always pictured these rooms differently, filled with cigar
smoke and lit by bare bulbs that dangled from long, swaying
wires between cop and perp. He'd formed this image watching
cop shows and cop movies from the age of eight until twenty-
two when he joined the force and suddenly found his formerly
beloved programs insufferably plotted, as if all cases were open
and shut, and the lines between bad guys and good ones, and
crooked cops and the kind that help old ladies cross the street,
were clear as Crystal Pepsi; a world where the coffee machine is
never broken, and everyone's uniform is always neatly pressed,
and CSI can break a case by looking at a bloodstain through a
piece of futuristic technology, and even the street beat unis are
constantly coming up with clever quips and having affairs with
femmes fatales played by such otherworldly beauties as Katharine
Hepburn and Mary-Kate Olsen.

He'd been particularly disappointed on this last point, joining
up after 9/11 under the assumption that cops would be granted the
same hyper-sexualized status as firemen, only to find that despite
the uniform's stately navy and the protective presence of the hip
piece, and despite the newfound reverence for even the most previously debased authority figures like Mayor Giuliani, there was
still such a deep, historically justified distrust of the badge that no

amount of media-celebrated heroism could create the goodwill that would fill Ryan's bed with the women he wants.

There are police groupies, sure, but they're never the chic and affluent business types who tantalize Ryan walking the streets of SoHo, or eating salad in Bryant Park, staring into their phones as if each contains a universe far more interesting than the one at hand. Ryan is paralyzed in front of these women, who look at him with something even worse than disdain: utter disinterest.

He also thought the people he interrogated would be guilty. The guy across from him, for example, Donnell Sanders, a Verizon Wireless sales rep with a degree from CUNY, a daughter he raises alone, and no priors, who maintains a blog that covers the intersection between pop culture and sports. They've picked up Sanders as a suspect in the Ricky Cortes case—Sanders works a second job as a doorman in Cortes's building—but because they don't have evidence to hold him, he's being indicted on the dubious charge of obstructing pedestrian traffic, and is being interrogated with the hope of wringing a confession from the poor guy who doesn't realize he's here on a murder rap.

But while it's obvious to Ryan that they've got the wrong man, Quinn seems bent on doing the bad cop thing, caving under pressure from the DA's office to make an arrest. Despite suspicion and public speculation, the only evidence they have against Devor is circumstantial, and within the department, many have begun to express doubt that the *Nøøse* founder was involved in the riot, let alone the murder. They were surprised to learn that Sanders, Cortes's doorman, had attended the Funeral for Capitalism.

None of which makes him a criminal, though Quinn might disagree. It's amazing to Ryan that even during this moment of pervasive unemployment, people like Quinn remain fixed in their fears of a welfare state. On multiple occasions, Quinn has expressed his opinion that even laid-off beat cops should have worked harder, as he did, to make detective. And while Ryan's tried to explain the arithmetical problems with this line of thinking, Quinn isn't interested in any point of view but his own.

But while Ryan has no interest in trying to bully a false confession from Sanders, his own motives aren't pure either. This morning at dawn, after the rumbling G train woke him from sleep and he lay freezing in bed, desperate to pee, but too cold to leave the comfort of his blanket, Ryan wondered if his premature verdict on Jay Devor is, in fact, a product of unconscious self-interest. Because, while nailing Donnell the doorman might lead to a small raise and nominal promotion, to take down a figure of Devor's stature would make Ryan, himself, a celebrity by proximity, his picture plastered next to the headline HERO COP for every salad-eating minx in Bryant Park to see.

"We have you on video leaving the rally," says Quinn, who's pacing the room, tapping the cement walls with his knuckles as if testing their solidity.

"I told you," says Donnell, "I took the subway home, ate left-over Thai food, watched the second half of Knicks-Pacers in bed, and drafted a blog post."

They've been over this ten times.

"And there's no one who can corroborate this story?" asks Quinn. "No one you talked to on your walk to the subway, or on the subway, or on your walk from the subway, or at home, who can validate your story? I find that hard to believe."

"How many people do you talk to while you're walking down the street or riding the subway? Not all black people know each other. Just because I live in Harlem doesn't mean I walk by the barbershop every day on my way home and stop in for a lineup and neighborhood gossip. My life is not a Tyler Perry production.

I was tired and I went straight home. Jackie was at her aunt's in the Bronx. If you had drones watching me at the rally, then how come you don't have me on camera walking to the subway?"

But though Donnell asks, he's not actually naïve enough to believe that innocence and justice are linked. He's seen friends put away on trumped-up charges, and if they're not put away then they're bogged down in legal bullshit, held in lockup for weeks, or forced to plead out and pay fines. No, he's not naïve, but he does believe that this particular charge and the detectives' response to it are so out of proportion that at some point someone's got to realize that a mistake is being made.

"That's what we're asking," says Quinn. "How come the camera loses you when you leave the rally? Where were you sneaking off to?"

"Where do you think I was sneaking off to? I was going home, I told you. I was tired so I went home."

"So you admit that you were sneaking off?" says Quinn.

Donnell looks to Ryan for backup, but the snub-nosed detective's eyes appear to be shut, lashes trellised together like the strands of a withered toothbrush. And the truth is that though Germanic Quinn is doing the gestapo-style questioning, it's red-faced Ryan who scares Donnell. At least with Quinn you know what you're getting. There's precedent there. Donnell knows from a lifetime of fitting descriptions that all he has to do is stay calm and answer Quinn's questions clearly and concisely in some approximation of white American English, not using big words or saying anything too obviously intelligent, but not dropping double negatives either, inspiring the idea that a jury could be convinced of his criminality based on syntax and vocab. Detective Ryan, on the other hand, is unreadable, and in Donnell's experience, this means a larger capacity for random acts of violence. He can picture the sleeping man snapping awake and beating Donnell with his nightstick. He can picture the building's manager telling him he'll have to wait until his black eye fades before returning to work, that it's a classy condo with an elite clientele and those just aren't the kinds of optics that they want to put forth. He can picture Steve from Verizon staring, eyes alight with idiotic revolutionary vigor, raising a fist in the air, rapping "Fuck the Police." He can picture his ex-wife on the far end of a phone, refusing to believe that this isn't, in some way, Donnell's fault. He can picture Jackie waiting up for him at home.

"No, I wasn't sneaking."

"We have evidence that suggests otherwise," says Quinn.

"Why do you care where I went?" says Donnell. "I thought I was being charged with obstructing pedestrian traffic. A ridiculous charge, you must admit, because the whole point of a protest *is* to obstruct pedestrian traffic. If you're arresting me, then you should be arresting everyone who was out there. I don't know why you even care about this when whoever murdered Ricky is still running around. Have you ever heard of a white guy getting arrested for obstructing pedestrian traffic? I haven't. But I've known a lot of black guys who've been arrested for it. Like, every fucking black guy I know."

25.

SINCE HIS ARRIVAL, LUCAS HAS all but commandeered Lillian's office—the only secluded area within Communitiv.ly's open-plan space—displacing Lillian to an annex desk by the bathrooms. By all appearances, Lillian has taken the move with team-player positivity, but Wendy's sure it irks. She knocks on the door and Lucas tells her to come in.

He sits on the floor in a yoga pose, legs bent half-swastika while his torso sticks straight up like the top half of a charmed cobra. His jacket and dress shirt are draped across Lillian's desk, and he's wearing only a shrunken white crewneck. Wendy can see both the firm curve of Lucas's pecs, and the fact that his arms above the elbow are inked with the kind of fluorescent koi fish popular among California surf-bros and singers in late-nineties ska-punk bands. They don't suit him at all.

Wendy awaits instruction. Lucas remains still. She wonders if this is a power play learned from the autobiography of a celebrated American CEO, or if it's a sex thing, Lucas showing off his tone and flexibility at the directive of a men's mag listicle, or if she simply caught him in the midst of a midday exercise routine. He doesn't seem embarrassed.

"Sit," he says, and Wendy looks for a chair. There aren't any except the leather one behind Lillian's desk that would have her facing his back. The excess folding chairs that usually cramp the office are nowhere to be seen.

"I like what you've done with the place," says Wendy. She seats herself on the floor, bunching her skirt around her knees.

"You look tense," Lucas says, though he's the one holding the rigid position.

"You're not looking so relaxed yourself," says Wendy.

"Observant," says Lucas, who now unlocks his muscles and stands. Wendy's not sure if she should stand as well or stay seated. If she stands, it'll look like she's mimicking him, but if she stays seated, then he'll be talking down from the mount of male authority. She stands. It must be all in her head. Lucas moves back behind Lillian's desk and eases himself into her office chair. Wendy's left standing.

"You see the mockups?" she asks.

"Fantastic," says Lucas, batting his lashes. Wendy's not sure if it's a tic or an affectation. She guesses the latter. Everything he does feels deliberate. "You really managed to capture something there, the convergence of blue collar pride and sex appeal. The dignity and eros of someone who works with his hands. Like that old Mapplethorpe shot of Richard Gere, but much less gay-seeming. Babette in design is already in proofs. This will happen fast. We're talking billboard tomorrow, prime time spots on the networks, a full page in Sunday's *Times*. All hands on deck. The vote's days away. The other agencies I met with said there was no way they could meet our timeline. That's why I like an underdog. You strive for the impossible."

"You spoke to other agencies?"

"How cute, you thought you were the only one. Seriously, you did an excellent job. I'm sorry I couldn't be there to see it."

"I managed. So are you finally going to tell me about the product? I think I deserve that at this point."

"Tomorrow, I promise. You'll get a private presentation.

Everything will become clear. I would today, but it takes a minute and I don't have time. As I said, things are moving fast, and there's a new problem that we have to deal with. A big problem. The rest, unfortunately, can wait."

"What's come up?"

"The police have made an arrest in the Cortes case."

"And this is bad news?"

"Well it's not good," says Lucas, "considering who they've arrested. It's certainly not good news for our cause."

"Who have they arrested?"

"They've arrested the wrong guy is who they've arrested."

"And you know better than the police?"

"I don't know whether he's the guy who did or did not do the murder. What I do know is that he's the wrong guy as far as we're concerned. I do know that who gets arrested generally has little to do with who's committed the crime. I know that the DA's office is desperate for a quick conviction. I know a justice system with a history of finding the closest African American, filling the jury box with suspicious white folks, and letting the problem solve itself."

"You still haven't told me who they've arrested."

"The doorman," says Lucas. "The doorman from Cortes's building."

Wendy feels nothing. No sense of further understanding or justice served. The revelation only gives rise to a new set of questions. She says, "Motive?"

"They don't need motive."

"And why is that?"

"They have something better than motive."

"And what's that?"

"They have narrative."

"I don't follow."

"I'll weave you a tale. Working black man with bills to pay. Say he's bought an apartment in Harlem pre '08. Took out a floating-rate mortgage because an asshole Realtor told him to. Some C&S trader bundles that mortgage into a CDO and sells the risk off to another bank, which in turn sells it off to someone else. The housing bubble bursts just as our guy's interest has gone through the roof, so he's in big, and the new bank that owns his mortgage refuses to give him a loan mod, even though he thought his tax dollars on the bailout were specifically designated to allow banks to give these kinds of breaks to homeowners. Meanwhile, he's put 20K into the apartment which has depreciated by half, so either he can sell the place for nothing and make a small recoup or wait out the butter years before white people get up the courage to buy on Malcolm X Boulevard, but either way he's in a bad mood."

"Are these things true or are you making them up?"

"True."

"How do you know all this?"

"I used a thing called the Internet. You'd be amazed at how much information is available there."

"Okay," Wendy says.

"Can I continue, or do you have anything else you'd like to ask?"

She says, "Continue."

"So our guy's in a bad mood, and what does he do? Well, for one, he takes a second job. Verizon sales rep during the day, but at night he watches the door at a prewar Tribeca building where bankers like Ricardo Cortes live in palatial apartments. So now we've got this guy, Donnell Sanders is his name—a handsome, intelligent guy, no less, who everyone says is a lovely mother-fucker—and every day Sanders sits there, trying to figure a way out of his debt, and meanwhile your friend Cortes passes by on his way upstairs, reeking of privilege, flaunting his queer, druggie lifestyle. We're talking dealers in and out, rent boys, fashionistas, coked-up businessmen. Money falling out of pockets. Empty plastic baggies scattered up and down the emergency stairs. Used condoms on the hallway floor. People buzzing in at 4 A.M., arriving in limos, departing in Porsches. See what I'm getting at?"

"I do," says Wendy. She imagines Michael as part of this scene, a wedding band being slipped into a pocket.

"Resentment is starting to build. Meanwhile, Cortes, being the asshole that he is, keeps making drunken innuendo at Sanders, jokingly offering money for blow jobs, or what have you. Sanders does not find this funny. His debts are continuing to accumulate, while at the same time C&S isn't prosecuted for the bevy of crimes that put Sanders in this very situation. Instead they're forced to pay some bullshit ten-billion-dollar fine that might sound like a lot, but that Sanders knows is nothing to these guys, and will pay for itself and then some after the company's shares go up in the wake of its non-prosecution. Skip to last month, and it turns out the market's crashed again, meaning Sanders's loan debt will somehow increase. So what does he do? What can he do? He goes to an #Occupy rally, exercising his right to, at the very least, bitch about all that's happened, when he suddenly finds himself in a hotel room face-to-face with the very asshole he's been hating all these years. So he drags the fucker into the empty room downstairs and unleashes his anger. Do you understand why this is problematic?"

"He's sympathetic."

"Exactly. And not only is he sympathetic, but he's an angry black man, which means that white people will want to placate him out of fear that if they don't, it could happen to them."

"What could happen to them?"

"Murder."

"That's ridiculous."

"I didn't say it wasn't."

"There are holes in this story. Where'd he get the gun?"

"Of course there are holes in the story. But the holes don't matter. The holes can be filled. Let's say he had been carrying a gun as part of his doorman duty, or because he'd recently been mugged, or he has a micro-penis and can't afford a Ferrari, or he watched westerns as a kid, or any of a million other reasons someone might carry a gun. The point is not to make him lovable, but relatable. There's a difference. But the holes don't matter anyway. What matters is the larger effect of this kind of narrative, which draws attention away from some kind of #Occupy-based conspiracy and toward a lone gunman with a personal issue."

Wendy can already feel herself disconnecting Ricky's death from the game they're playing. It's easier to intellectualize than to face the gutshot of a human vanished. It was easier, after her mother died, to write an op-ed for her high school paper criticizing what she called the Cancer Industrial Complex, which prioritized research for high-visibility cancers like breast and prostate, while killers like pancreatic stood in the underfunded shadows. It was easier, when Nina died, to organize a neonatal mortality support group, using Communitiv.ly's conference room as an after-hours event space, stocking the meeting with Nespresso pods and nut milks, zero-calorie sodas and artisanal cupcakes, purchasing leather-bound notebooks in which the attendees could write down feelings, though Wendy left hers blank. It is easier, now, to focus on work.

"Look," says Wendy. "It's not as bad as you think. Let's say the doorman did do it. It may seem improbable, but let's pretend it's the truth. Donnell the doorman committed the murder in the manner you've just described, dragging Ricky into a conveniently empty room and shooting him with a handgun. Here's the question we need to ask: Would this murder have occurred if it weren't for the Funeral for Capitalism and the planned march to the Zone Hotel where protesters were provided with an opportunity to exercise their anger? As far as I understand it, the answer to that question is no. Donnell Sanders is not a murderer by nature. I'd guess that he's never previously been convicted of a crime. He did not premeditate, and never would have killed Ricky if he hadn't been given this opportunity. Do you see what I'm saying?"

"Go on," says Lucas.

"Now what does this mean for us?" Wendy continues, feeling herself, as she speaks, take on Lucas's speech patterns, his syntactical style, which is half TV DA, half radio DJ, words relayed so rapidly that it's impossible to stop and consider any single piece of information without missing whatever comes next. "What it means is that, regardless of who literally pulled the trigger, the blood is on #Occupy's hands. It's on *Nøøse*'s hands and it's on Jay Devor's hands."

"Keep talking," says Lucas. She's never seen him show deference before. The power in the room seems to shift in her direction as she stands above Lucas at full height, feet shoulder-width apart, arms at her sides. Lucas is listening.

"Now I know there are some who say that Jay Devor did not play any role in the riot, that he had nothing to do with its organization. There are some who even think that it was the banks that organized the riot to discredit #Occupy. In that scenario, the banks also ordered the hit. However, if Donnell the doorman committed the murder, then the conspiracy is no longer a viable theory. Why would the banks want to frame the doorman? No, if Donnell the doorman committed the murder, it means the riot must have been organized by #Occupy, and that the murder was an unplanned byproduct. The murder was the result of the riot gone wrong. The riot is responsible for the death of Ricky Cortes. And in much the same way that our previous president's racist tirades inspired neo-Nazis to march on Charlottesville, and a gunman to open fire in El Paso, Jay Devor is complicit in Ricky's murder."

Lucas grins. He bats his lashes again, and she thinks he might be in love, not with her, or even with what she's saying, but with Wendy's conversion to their cause.

"The only place we need to convict Devor," she says, "is in the court of public opinion."

"Yes," says Lucas. "I see your point. I see your point indeed."

26.

FROM HIS PARENTS' BACK PORCH the sky is purple, though it's lighter where the horizon meets the tree line, the last broken sun rays hot-glued like sequins between branches and leaves. A lone swimmer inches toward shore.

Michael remembers how the lake used to look in December, frozen and cratered in spots where snow weighed down and cracked the ice. When it stayed cold for long enough, neighbors would ice fish for the scant remains of summer's man-dumped stock of trout and catfish, and Michael would skate with a hockey stick, practicing wrist shots and backward figure eights. Lydia always watched from this porch, a model of Jewish motherhood, worried the ice would crack and he'd fall through. What was she planning, to dive in and save him? Detective Ryan isn't answering, so Michael calls Quinn instead.

"Go for Quinn," says Quinn.

"It's Michael Mixner," Michael says. "Something occurred to me—was Ricky wearing a bracelet when they found him?"

"A bracelet?"

"An SD bracelet. Sykodollars. From *Shamerican Sykosis*. Looks like a watch without hands."

"I know what you're talking about. My kid plays *SS*. I shouldn't say plays. More like a job, really. He's nine. Wears his helmet to school. His mother put him in one of those hippie schools where they let the kids piss and shit on the walls."

"They shit on the walls?"

"He won't even take the helmet off for meals. You ever seen someone eat in one of those things? No? It's because you can't. I have to make his meals in liquid form. You ever tried to turn a cheeseburger into a smoothie? It's actually better than you might expect."

Michael pictures Quinn feeding ropes of pink beef into a juicer along with lettuce, tomato, and shredded cheddar; Quinn and Junior drinking their concoctions from oversized beer steins while watching YouTube clips of farting dogs; Quinn sitting by his son on the bathroom floor as Junior—helmet lifted like a hockey goalie's between whistles—spews bile-stewed cheese-beef into the toilet.

"Apparently some of these bracelets might be worth a lot of money," Michael says. "Like millions of dollars. And it might be nothing, but the last time I saw Ricky he made a weird comment about the value of his bracelet, something to do with linear time. And then he was telling me that he'd invested all his money in some sure thing, and I'm wondering if that thing was SD."

"You're kidding me," says Quinn. "You mean my kid could be rich?"

"I guess it's possible."

"Huh," says Quinn.

Michael pictures him nodding, Adam's apple riding his throat like a tiny elevator. Quinn says he has to go and ends the call.

Rachel steps through the sliding doors and hands Michael a cigarette. It's dark now, the sky a sheeny black. The moon is higher and the sun is gone. The swimmer wades toward the small patch of beach maintained by the town. Michael and Ricky had to rake it one summer for community service after getting caught with a joint in Ricky's car. It was the best job Michael's ever had, meditatively dragging his rake across the sand, catching twigs and bottle caps in its bristles, his skin turning tan. Ricky would chat up the old ladies from the nursing home who were brought in by van every Friday and propped in plastic chairs along the shore. The ladies wore sun hats and sunblock dripped in blobs down their arms. Michael thought it wouldn't be the worst way to end a life.

When the swimmer reaches shore, he suddenly can be seen in the glow of motion-detecting security lights. It's their neighbor, Mr. Harkness, esteemed cardiologist and cycling fanatic: nude. Mr. Harkness stands perfectly still, arms spread like Jesus, and begins to urinate. Rachel flicks her butt. It falls in an arc near the naked man's feet. Their neighbor, startled, does a small fearful dance and yells, "Watch where you throw those things."

"Watch where you swing that dick," replies Rachel.

27.

GREG ASKS IF SHE'S GOT music. Lillian taps at her phone and some kind of nü-metal erupts from her speakers. He tries to find a way to dance to this noise, circling his hips, flailing his arms, attempting a knee bend. Lillian watches, the blue glow of her Juul a weak spotlight. Greg teases his nipples, over the shirt at first, before undoing its top button, then the next one down, hips still circling, mouth pursed in duckface. It's not until his bellybutton's exposed that Lillian says, "What the fuck are you doing?"

"I thought . . ." says Greg.

He rushed over here after receiving an SOS text featuring three eggplant emojis, a peach, and fireworks.

"You thought what?"

She holds up her phone. Greg wonders if she's documenting this humiliation. For all he knows, Lillian has already Insta'd his stripping image across the interwebs. He pictures Wendy ROFL.

"But your text," Greg says. "I thought you wanted . . ."

Lillian crosses her arms.

" . . . me?" Greg says.

She's laughing now. Sun comes through the skylight, suspending Greg in a beam of rising dust. Lillian sucks hard on her e-cig as if, with enough force, she might manage to pull in some actual smoke.

"What I like about you, Greg, is that you don't overthink things. You're a man of action and reaction. Take the way you waltzed in here and took off your clothes. Did it cross your mind that I was joking?"

He shakes his head.

"If this were Nazi Germany, you'd be first in line to operate the gas chamber."

"I'm Jewish."

"Self-hating."

He shrugs in agreement, mimes turning the crank.

"You went on a date," says Lillian. "With a woman named Sophia Dall."

"I didn't get her last name."

"It's Dall."

"Okay."

"So I need you to rack that brain of yours and try to remember if at any time during your two-hour convergence of shame and small talk, she mentioned her ex-boyfriend Jay Devor."

"She did, yeah."

Greg gives her the rundown: vape pen, MoMA, a shared order of overpriced tostadas, an au revoir peck on Greg's cheek. When Greg brought up #Occupy, Sophia had explained that her ex, Devor, had organized the riot, but had left before it started. She'd been with Devor all that night.

"But you're saying she told you he organized the riot?"

"He wasn't even there, Lil. He didn't know about the murder until the next day."

"Well look at you, Detective Greg. I should get you a badge and a gun. Maybe a cute little sheriff's hat," says Lillian.

Greg, it seems, has done something right.

She says, "Button your shirt before I go blind."

28.

THEY EAT AT THE DINING table, a third of which is taken up by Stuart's twenty-seven-inch quote unquote travel laptop. The only stamps on the laptop's passport: kitchen, dining room, living room, bedroom. Stuart types with one hand while eating with the other. A strand of lo mein dangles from his lips for a second before being sucked in. No one asks him to put the computer away. Those arguments ended ten years ago, during the salad days of *Diablo*, when it became clear that turning away was not, for Stuart, an option. At least during Michael's childhood he shut off the computer once in a while. These days, it's cause for minor celebration when he deigns to come downstairs. No wonder Rachel's so stunted and armored, so attuned to the dangers of showing you care. Michael would be too had he grown up with the late model version of his parents that she did, all those noodle cup dinners eaten alone, or the belabored science projects so hurtfully ignored.

If there's one thing Michael wants on this brief trip, it's to make clear to his sister that, despite their differing lifestyles and history of emotional distance, and despite Rachel's understandable reservations, he'd like to try to forge a friendship. Throughout his library research on communism, what Michael kept coming back to was Marx's directive to raze the family and strip it for parts, each member a worker with no time or room for the hierarchical shackles of eating together at a small round table and

asking each other about their days. This seemed like a miscalcula-
tion on Marx's part, a deep failure to understand certain biological
imperatives.

Marx had nine kids, Michael knows, and yet feelings of fatherhood are hardly mentioned in his writings, or, at least, in the small
sample of his writings Michael's read. Marx didn't understand how
lucky he was. Reproduction came easy and perhaps that was it; not
until you've wanted something so hard for so long, until you've
lain sleepless in bed on hundreds of nights praying to a God you
don't believe in, or sat in doctors' waiting rooms squeezing your
wife's hand, or injected her thigh with an IVF needle, can you
appreciate what the loss of that family might mean.

This is why communism would never triumph. People would
always care more for their spouses and children than for anonymous strangers. They would not abandon the illusory dream
of protecting their families in fenced-off mansions and airbag-
equipped SUVs, of fortifying them with stem cell steaks and
pricey D vitamins that boost immune defense, of cradling their
delicate bodies on Casper mattresses made from high-density
memory foam. A man would always want more than factory cama-
raderie and communal showers, not for himself, but for those that
he loves. For all its flaws, capitalism takes this into account. It's
one thing to its credit, an understanding of this deep human need
to provide.

And yet, look at what happens when someone like Michael can
no longer provide. The American Dream—that beautiful stage
set that looked so real on opening night—is now, with its props
sealed in boxes and its actors gone home, revealed as a depthless
façade. He finishes his bourbon, pours another.

"Is that your third whiskey?" asks Lydia, an Ashkenazi Jew
known to drink vodka until blackout, who thinks brown liquor

is devil's juice for redneck gentiles. "You're not turning into an alcoholic are you? It's worrying, Michael. Whiskey's so strong."

"Second," says Michael, though it's his fourth. He doesn't feel drunk, just tired. He hasn't slept more than a couple hours since arriving in the Berkshires, up all last night picturing Ricky's future: skin nipped by worms, coffin splintered and piercing the body's remains. To push this image from his mind, Michael tried and mostly failed to catalog the thirty-plus years of their friendship. He doesn't know if it's fatigue or what, but each night since the murder it's like he remembers less, to the point that he can't, with certainty, recall even the contours of Ricky's face, or the texture of his voice; as if Ricky, without his corporeal form, has become liquid and ill-defined, a multiplicity of opposing details that don't add up to a graspable whole.

Rachel scoops lo mein onto her plastic plate. Though Lydia hasn't observed the rules of kashrut since childhood, she still refuses to sully her ceramic dishware with pork and shrimp.

"Well, I learned something interesting this morning," Lydia says. "Did you know that the Jews were most likely never even *in* Egypt?"

Their mother shares stuff like this all the time. One year, she almost ruined a Seder by making a similarly combative claim that the Egyptians were actually slaves of the Jews. And while it's true that the Jews almost certainly didn't build the pyramids, it's also true that no evidence lent credence to Lydia's assertion. Either way, there was no reason to bring it up in front of Stuart's conservative family.

"So you're saying Passover is bullshit?" asks Rachel. It's the only holiday to which she feels a connection, in part because the exodus, with its historical roots and contemporary relevance, has always seemed distinctly *non*-bullshit, a far cry from cartoonish Queen Esther, or the wonder of Chanukah's magical flame. Not that Passover's parted sea or rain of plagues belong to realism, but the slave narrative grounds the supernatural stuff, and the story's central image—the Israelites marching with bread on their backs—is so sensory and concrete. Rachel has always related to Aaron, the unsung sibling. Michael was Moses: silent in his absence, enveloped in an air of charmed mystique.

That Michael is not the one she sees tonight. Her brother's current incarnation looks wounded and tiny, drowning in an over-sized T-shirt. He looks nothing like the slick financier who visited in August, Wendy in tow, the pair turning heads at the Grub and Grog with their New York wardrobes that must have looked, to the local crowd, gauchely European, meaning gaudy and threatening and somewhat gay. Rachel wonders where Wendy is now. Michael looks like he could use a nurturing wife. Rachel knows: Wendy isn't the nurturing type.

She remembers the dinner after their courthouse wedding. The Mixners were in full force—Rachel's Long Island cousins, with their polished diamonds and hair-gelled husbands—but there were hardly any guests from Wendy's side. Aware of this incongruity, Rachel had tried, in her way, to bond with the bride. She'd done this by shit-talking, in perhaps too wine-lit and effusive a manner, the Long Island contingent, telling Wendy she'd rather have no relatives at all than that cunty JAP cousin brigade. Instead of laughing or nodding, Wendy had looked across the table as if seeing the cousins for the first time. She spent a long moment studying Maggie and Hannah, who were in deep debate on the merits and drawbacks of a monthly colonic. "Maggie's really quite pretty," was Wendy's cold reply.

"Well it's not bullshit," says Lydia. "It's allegory."

"Like 'Fuck the Police,'" says Michael.

"I mean, it's the origin story of our culture," says Rachel. "It's like if we found out Superman wasn't from Krypton."

"There's archeological evidence," says Lydia.

"How can there be archeological evidence for an absence?" Rachel asks. "There can be a lack of evidence, but there can't be evidence itself of an absence. And how is it anything like 'Fuck the Police'?"

"The violence," says Michael.

"Your brother is correct," says Lydia. "And if you think about it, we can read the exodus in light of the Holocaust. We may not have been slaves, but we were the victims of genocide. *Are* the victims of genocide. And that wasn't in ancient Egypt, darling, that was in this very century in civilized Europe."

"It's a metaphor for black life in America," says Michael. He got this idea from a book of essays, all by white academics, on the legacy of NWA.

"Last century, Mom," says Rachel. "We're in a whole new century now. Have been for a while. And, Michael, I'm sorry, but how is the Holocaust a metaphor for black life in America?"

Stuart interrupts by banging the table.

He says, "My life is fucked."

"Your life's not fucked," says Lydia.

Stuart repeats, "My life is fucked."

"Everything's okay Dad," Michael reassures.

"Your life?" says Lydia, standing. She points to herself and the others. "We're your life. We're your family. And we're all here. Isn't that nice? You should be happy to have us all here."

"Fuck," Stuart says. He stands, tips over his chair, kicks the table, and exits the room.

"What was that about?" says Rachel.

"It's unfair," says Lydia. "His making a scene while you're here for your friend's funeral. Very unfair."

"Ricky," says Michael.

"It's unfair of him to bring you into this. Not now anyway."

"Into what?" says Rachel. "What are you talking about?"

"Divorce," says Lydia.

"You and Dad are getting divorced?"

"Your father and I aren't planning anything that radical as of yet. He's getting divorced from Sharon."

"Who's Sharon?" says Michael.

"His girlfriend from the game," says Rachel.

"Wife," says Lydia. "His wife from the game."

"They've never even met!" says Rachel.

"That's not how he sees it."

"Why's she dumping him?" Michael asks.

"She'd prefer someone younger."

"What?" says Rachel.

"Your father," says Lydia. "Sharon thinks his looks are starting to fade."

"She's never even seen him in person!"

"It's a very shallow culture," says Lydia.

29.

THE DETECTIVES HAVE LEFT DONNELL with his lawyer, a young man in an off-the-rack suit who looks more like someone playing Atticus Finch in a school production of *To Kill a Mockingbird* than the genuine article. His face is nearly cubist: one ear the size and texture of a wine cork, the other Dumbo-esque; eyes distorted through the thick lenses of horn-rimmed glasses; nostrils misaligned; a swollen tongue that hangs like a dog's during moments of intense concentration. The lawyer's office is also his bedroom, possibly a university dorm. In the background sits an unmade bed. Its blond wood matches the lawyer's desk chair. The lawyer bends forward, revealing a poster of Van Gogh's *Starry Night*.

Donnell keeps reaching for a nonexistent remote that might change the channel and provide him with a more experienced litigator. Instead he scoots forward, closer to the webcam, so the lawyer gets a tighter view of his face. He wants the lawyer to see its creases and shaving bumps, his hazelnut eyes, the things that mark him as frail and human. He needs the lawyer to know that Donnell's missing paychecks and incurring late fees, that Jackie's scared and home alone. He needs the lawyer to know what's at stake.

Despite his skepticism, Donnell is lucky to have a Canadian. Public defenders come from all over the world, and especially the Caribbean, ever since its largest law school—University of the West Indies—super-sized its applicant pool by only training and certifying in US Law. Not that there's anything wrong with Caribbeans per se—many, Donnell's sure, are excellent lawyers—but certain older, white judges have trouble with accents. Donnell's friend Kwame was once arrested for an open container and he ended up doing thirty days because the judge misunderstood the lawyer and became convinced that Kwame had hit a cop while resisting arrest.

By contrast, a Canadian lawyer is theoretically good news, or would be if Donnell's looked older than twelve. There's no question that this is the lawyer's first murder. Donnell could see the fear in his eyes every time the detectives unveiled another piece of quote unquote evidence, all of which was circumstantial, hearsay, or otherwise inadmissible. The cops have nothing and Donnell knows it.

Well, not nothing exactly. A witness, the lawyer explained, claims to have seen Donnell in the lobby of the Zone. The witness was shown a six-man lineup of possible suspects, and she picked Donnell. This, despite the fact that she couldn't have *actually* seen Donnell, because he's never stepped foot in the hotel in his life.

No matter. In her initial report, the witness described the suspect as a dark-skinned black man between the ages of thirty and forty, and the five other guys in the lineup were light-skinned twentysomethings.

"The whole thing is a setup," he tells his lawyer.

The lawyer nods, neither affirming nor denying Donnell's statement. Perhaps the computer mic's not working. The unit, a boxy desktop chained to the table with a bicycle lock, looks like a relic. He says, again, louder this time, "The whole thing is a setup."

"I heard you," says the lawyer. He clicks his teeth, tugs on his tie, and says, "She picked you out of the lineup."

"Of course she picked me. I was twelve shades darker than the others. Who'd they think she was going to pick?"

Again, the lawyer says nothing, as if the context is too charged, and he's afraid that whatever comes out of his mouth might be read as racially insensitive. Or maybe he's distracted. For all Donnell knows, the kid's concurrently scrolling Twitter.

Donnell called Jackie last night from the prison payphone, reversing the charges. As they spoke—awkwardly, avoidantly—he found himself thinking back on the days following Jackie's birth, when she wouldn't sleep anywhere but her mom's or dad's chest, screaming every time they tried to ever-so-gently place her in the bassinet. Donnell and Dani traded two-hour sleep shifts, while the other stayed up in the living room: rocking Jackie, staring at Jackie, trying to find echoes of their own facial features. Jackie slept in Donnell's arms, lulled by the white noise of the turned-down TV, or else lulled by the sound of her father's voice, which sang "You Are My Sunshine" over and over, and whispered key facts about her dry, new world: the names of her relatives, and things to look forward to like coffee, ocean swimming, and Beanpot hockey. He recited a poem he remembered from college—Galway Kinnell, "I would scrape the rust off your ivory bones"—and Donnell found himself crying for this fragile human whom it was now his mission to protect.

Which might be how he got into this mess. Because Donnell's a good father, and good fathers provide, even when they can't afford to provide. And so good fathers sometimes do stupid things, like emptying their bank accounts to make down payments, and signing off on mortgages without really knowing what floating-rate means. They do stupid things like paying for a gut renovation on credit, because a girl should grow up in a light, airy space, with high bedroom windows that catch the pink dawn, and

a modern kitchen with a Viking stove so they can eat Sunday pan-
cakes in style, and a spacious, private bathroom for the long years
of puberty distantly ahead.

And when debt begins to weigh them down, one stupid thing
that good dads do is take sports betting tips from their coworker
Steve, who claims his friend's sister dates the Jets' QB, and Steve
knows for a fact that the dude tweaked his wrist playing *Fortnite*
and will sit out next week. When that bet goes bust, then really
dumb good dads continue taking tips from Steve, and taking tips
from paid tip lines, siphoning money. So they start buying scratch
cards, and Mega Millions tickets, and keep betting on horses, and
football, and the Academy Awards, even after their wives have put
them on warning, and even after their wives have moved to Los
Angeles and left them alone.

If Donnell had been better with money, he would have never
ended up with the doorman job. He would never have met
Ricky Cortes. When Jackie asked, last night, when Donnell was
coming home, he told her, *tomorrow*. He tried to sound like he
believed it.

"You have to do something," says Donnell. "You have to get
that lineup thrown out on the grounds that none of those people
in the lineup looked anything like me. And then you have to get
that security tape thrown out on the grounds that it's impossible
to even see the guy's face in the video, and the only reason they're
assuming it's me is because they think all black people look alike.
And you've got to get them to admit they have no murder weapon
and they have no evidence, and I've never heard of this gold watch
or bracelet or whatever it is they keep asking about. You getting
this, Atticus? Maybe you should write it down."

The lawyer says, "I think I can get you a deal."

"I don't want a deal. I want to get out of here."

"They have motive," says the lawyer, enunciating the M-word, as if Donnell is deaf or too dumbstruck to process this piece of information.

"I want to go home," says Donnell.

"I'm trying," says the lawyer. "We'll talk again soon." He removes a container of dental floss from a desk drawer and begins to unspool it.

"Really?" says Donnell.

"Sorry," says his lawyer, floss stretched between two fingers like a tightrope for a tiny acrobat. "I thought the camera was off."

30.

SHE ANSWERS DESPITE BEING UNDERGROUND. A woman shouts nearby, an argument with God over compound interest ("Free will!" she imagines God's reply), so Wendy sticks a finger in her ear and hustles toward the far end of the tunnel, slaloming around trash bins and a man with a feather earring playing slide guitar.

"When's your train?" says Michael.

Wendy looks up at the electronic display.

"One minute."

"Tonight?" Michael says. "I thought you weren't leaving until early tomorrow morning. I didn't know they ran a train this late. Oh, I'm so glad. You're taking it to Hudson, right? Let me know what time you get in and I'll pick you up. Doesn't matter how late."

It takes Wendy a second to figure out that he's not talking about the subway train but an Amtrak that would, in theory, be bringing her to the Berkshires.

"Michael, I'm not," she says, and stares at the track. A foot-sized rat dawdles by the third rail. It sniffs a Cheetos bag, then crawls inside.

"Not what?"

"Not coming to Hudson."

"You're taking the bus into Pittsfield then?"

"Let's talk about it later," she says.

The rat emerges, dusted orange. A little girl points and says, "Kitty cat."

"So what time does the bus come?" Michael says.

"I'm not coming," Wendy says.

"What?"

"I'm not coming to Ricky's memorial."

"I don't understand," says Michael. Neither does Wendy. All she knows is she can't leave right now, with Devor's conspiracy gaining traction, and the billboard campaign launching, and the supposed unveiling of the product on Sunday. She can't go to the funeral because of work, and because work is an excuse for avoiding what she doesn't wish to confront.

She can picture Ricky's wake, his lips wired into a smile, still smug, even in death. Michael standing over the casket and reaching inside, maybe fixing Ricky's tie. Lydia asking when they'll try for another baby. The inevitable moment when Stuart stares at her breasts.

The last funeral she went to was Nina's. Not a funeral, a burial. No friends or Mixners, just Wendy, Michael, a rabbi, and Wendy's dad. The tiny casket, which they lowered by hand. No one spoke. The rabbi breathlessly recited the kaddish, intuiting their need to move quickly. And it was too warm. She wanted thunder and wind, no light on that horrible day. Michael said something about the cemetery being a place where flowers grow. How one day their children would come here and play among these daisies, and that Nina would like that, seeing her sisters.

"Look," says Michael, near tears, she can tell, "I need you right now. Things are so fucked up, and I'm alone, and I just saw on TV that they arrested Donnell, and I keep seeing stuff on Reddit about your company's campaign, and I just need to know what's . . ."

Wendy loses service as she steps onto the train.

31.

THEY WERE MARRIED THE FOLLOWING September on the sand.
Broder wore linen pants and a band-collared shirt, buttoned, as
instructed, to the top. She said he looked hip, but he felt like a
priest. He sipped virgin mojitos and shook everyone's hands. He
sanitized his hands when no one was looking. Their friends from
Recovery said: *too soon.*

And there were too many bridesmaids. High school best friends,
Emma C. and Emma H., who both "lived" for Burning Man. A
best friend from summer camp, Corrinne, in visible bra straps
and cat-eye makeup; she was gay and played bass in a disco-punk
band. And Aliana's cousin, Alix, who'd had two lines in a Tom
Cruise film and found a way to work it into every conversation.
The bridesmaids primped, gossiped, posted to Facebook. They
treated the wedding like a magazine shoot. And they smoked a
joint in the club's bridal suite, sort of half-apologetic—oh ha-ha,
right, you guys are, like, *sober*—Recovery dismissed as passing fad.

Aliana wore white and a wildflower crown. Her dress was back-
less, with a lacy bodice and a gauzy skirt that caught the breeze.
She'd had her teeth bleached for the affair, and her smile seemed
inhumanly bright as she walked down the aisle. It was hard to
believe she was Broder's bride. And yet here she was, moving
toward him, meeting his eyes. He'd spent years in Recovery
struggling to get past its second step, faith in a Power beyond
himself. Where others found God in the coastline, Broder saw

only a nihilistic ocean, a long, empty sky. But in her, he'd discovered the elusive divine.

Broder stood barefoot, back to the surf. The barefoot thing was the bride's idea. The groom had been pedicured in preparation. He'd never had one before and he liked it: the touch and attention, and the smooth result, heels planed like stones beneath a century of tides. It had drizzled that morning, and the beach was still wet. There was sand between his toes and caked to his ankles and the cuffs of his pants. He smelled sea salt and sunscreen. He felt himself sinking ever so slightly.

Broder's dad and Patty, who was now Broder's stepmom, sat up front. They were obvious outliers in their East Coast attire: navy and charcoal, worsted wool. Broder kept waiting for his father to smile. The bride's parents beamed. This was their party and they presided, hands clasped, legs stretched into the aisle. Broder's mom sat alone, sweating, fanning herself with a program. She was the largest person here, and Broder felt embarrassed, and then he felt badly about being embarrassed. He'd bought the small diamond with his own meager savings. He hadn't asked his family for money in months.

The officiant was another of Aliana's friends—a guy she'd once dated, or had maybe just slept with. He welcomed the guests and said some words about the bride: her beauty, her intelligence, her singular spirit. He made a joke about her being off the market. He laughed and said Broder was a lucky guy.

Broder trembled while reciting his vows. He'd composed them himself, in the privacy and silence of his bedroom, and now he felt shy about sharing aloud. The vows seemed too sober for the tone of the occasion, too earnest and raw for the jovial vibe. He steadied himself in Aliana's gaze. He got through it, then broke down when she spoke hers, sobbing into his sleeve. They kissed.

Her dad serenaded the couple with a song written, years ago, for Aliana's mom. Her parents' friends clapped. They comprised most of the crowd, aging rockers in open collars, suits paired with Converse or cowboy boots. Broder had wanted something smaller—maybe the courthouse—but he had no say. He wanted the dignity of footwear.

Michael was absent, no RSVP. Broder recognized few of the guests. They'd stopped going to meetings a couple months back. They told themselves it was because they were busy, between work and wedding prep they had no free time, but that was fine, they kept in touch with their sponsors, had each other's support. In truth, Broder was only at the florist's twenty hours a week, and Aliana's mom had handled much of the planning: finding the venue, choosing place settings, vetoing Broder's proposed floral arrangements. The real reason they skipped meetings was the judgment of others who held the party line that one should stay free of romantic distraction for that first sober year. They'd invited their sponsors, but no one else from Recovery. All of which accounted for Ricky Cortes at table eight. The bride had insisted on the presence of at least a few friends of Broder's, and he'd long lost touch with the high school guys.

Of course Ricky befriended the bridesmaids, lining up shots, leading the dance-floor charge. He was the same showman Broder remembered from college: bow-tied and suspendered, hands and mouth in perpetual motion—laughing, performing—part impresario, part shifty-eyed card shark.

The Emmas gave a giggly, rhyming toast and the bride was handed a champagne flute. Broder scanned the room for her sponsor, who appeared, at that moment, to be immersed in her phone. And the bride clinked flutes with her high school friends, and she took, or pretended to take, a tiny sip. Broder couldn't tell which. She danced with her dad to one of his own songs, and people clapped and sang along. Broder was supposed to dance with his mom, but she couldn't be found, so they skipped it. His mom, it turned out, was blasting the AC in her rental car. When Broder found her, she said she was hot, she was sorry, she wasn't used to this weather. He tried to pat her shoulder and she kept saying sorry.

People kept whisking Aliana away—for photos, for dances, for passionate hugs—and there were so many people for Broder to talk to, all the bride's relatives and family friends. These people had known her since childhood—they knew her, in one sense, better than he did—and Broder wasn't sure what, exactly, to say: *Hi, my name is Broder, I'm a heroin addict, and I work as a florist—an assistant florist—and yes, I signed a prenup, thanks for your concern.* But that was okay. These strangers didn't really have questions, they just wanted to perform old stories for a receptive new target, telling Broder about shrooming with Jim Morrison on this very beach, or Dennis Wilson getting seasick on somebody's yacht. Out by the ashtray he encountered the Emmas, who bummed him a Spirit and then made him suffer through a lengthy discourse on the difficulty—no, no, the *impossibility*—of monogamy in this day and age. They were into the whole polyamory thing, the whole pseudo-Buddhist Bay Area pansexual thing. The Emmas spoke rapidly and rubbed at their noses. Ricky must have been to blame.

Aliana and Broder posed for more photos and cut the cake, but then the tide took the bride back onto the dance floor, where she did the Running Man with a second cousin's kids, and got grindy with Cousin Alix and Cat-eyed Corrinne. They slapped each other's asses and laughed, and Broder watched. Until he got sober, he'd never been shy. He reminded himself that in just a few hours the crowd would disperse and he'd be alone with his beautiful bride. And finally Broder would take off his belt and untuck and unbutton his constricting shirt. He'd lie with her in his arms, and inhale her scent, and only then would the day's tiny dramas and mishaps take on a kind of humorous charm, because Broder had learned that there was nothing so lonely as the ongoing moment and the best part of life was the looking back.

Aliana's dad pulled Broder aside. He swayed and placed a hand on his son-in-law's shoulder. He swilled his scotch and, slurring, gave, or tried to give, a sentimental speech, explaining that a florist was a noble profession, a humble profession, hands in the earth and all that. Broder nodded. Besides, said her dad, they were glad she was sober—he swilled more scotch—glad that their daughter was happy and sober. He winked at Broder. Aliana's mom hardly spoke to the groom or met his eye, and the groom didn't blame her. His own mom was gone, but he talked to his dad, who seemed confused by the affair. But Broder could see he was trying: to believe in this fantasy, to have a good time. It helped that Patty was there, and that she was black—it gave them cachet among the music-biz folks who had stories about Jimi and Aretha as well.

At midnight, they bused everyone from beach club to beach house for an all-night bonfire. Instruments came out: bongos, fiddle, acoustic guitars. There were coolers of beer and s'mores for the kids. Cat-eyed Corrinne had one of the Emmas in a tongue-lock, and Ricky had conjured a bottle of Jäger, and Cousin Alix, sensing a letdown in male attention, ran into the surf. A few people followed in their dresses and suits, wading up to their ankles, and then others stripped down to their underwear. It was like a movie, Broder thought. Like one of those movies that fills you with warmth while you're watching, but then, when it ends, leaves you empty inside as you drive home in the rain and it occurs to you that your own life will never match the grandeur of those on the screen.

At some point it grew light, and the sun could be seen on one side of the sky, though the moon was still visible off in the distance, a beautiful balance, silver and gold. And then the bride's arms were around him. She'd waded into the water, and her dress made a wetness against Broder's back.

And she whispered "I love you," and he felt her breath move inside his ear, and he smelled on her breath a sour hint of the cake's lemon filling, and when he looked in her eyes he could see she was high.

32.

MICHAEL AND RACHEL ARE IN Wendy's email. He guessed her password: Nina310. The date she was supposed to have been born. Was born. Wasn't born. They're not sure what they're looking for. A chat box is open.

Greg types: sup

Rachel suggests that Michael pretend to be Wendy and feel things out. What Would Wendy Do? is something Michael's asked thousands of times—picking out flatware, planning secret Valentine's trips—and rarely, if ever, has he answered exactly correctly, always some forgotten factor or missed calculation or ignorance of a privately harbored opinion, like Wendy's inexplicable distastes for three-pronged forks and coastal Maine. This might seem like a failure of intimacy, proof that all those years of joint tax returns and trading sections of the *Times*, plus their shared triumphs and traumas, do not compute to a comprehensive audit of the other person's brain. But it's no failure, Michael thinks. It means they're not boring or stagnant, not robotic dullards governed by something so prosaic as rational thought. He's always felt superior to those couples whose worldviews neatly align and whose shared closet looks like the his-and-hers sections of a J. Crew catalog. Love isn't finding an extension of yourself, but a person so nuanced in her difference that everything she says feels thrillingly fresh. Relationships should be like modern democracies, two-party systems in which the parties agree on rules of conduct and basic tenets of society, but whose fundamental dissents on particular issues keep checks and balances in place. And yet down in the engine room of his anxiety, he worries that he and Wendy may have failed to grasp something other couples innately understand, which is that, for all the pushing against it, all the not going quiet into domesticity's fleece-lined honey trap, perhaps the secret to a successful marriage *is* to become boring and predictable, to make each day a calming replica of the last. Perhaps the secret is finding someone who thinks so much like you do that all decisions are easy, no necessary guesswork, a smooth drive across life's temporal landscape without fighting over the relative merits of Hot 97 versus NPR.

"Dude," Rachel says, "you gonna just sit there or are you planning to respond?"

"I'm trying to channel Wendy," Michael says, fixing his posture, as if sitting like his wife, with engaged glutes and a rigid spine, might provide insight. Rachel suggests saying *sup.*

Michael types **What's up?** instead, which causes Rachel to snort. Greg replies **cold chizzlin.**

"Now what?" says Michael.

Upstairs, Stuart's toe taps to the rhythm of the SD's rise. Downstairs, Lydia marks a student essay in red ink that smudges as her left hand drags across the page. Ricky's casket slides around the trunk of a hearse that's changing lanes on 95. Eminem rocks his granddaughter to sleep, humming James Taylor's "Fire and Rain" while Hailie Jade rants from the next room about the continuing impact of cancel culture on the arts. Detective Quinn licks the crumbs off an everything bagel. Devor unrolls a ribbed condom. Donnell places a protective layer of toilet paper over the seatless rim of a rusted throne while his cellmate looks on. Wendy's on the subway, not coming to Pittsfield.

The chat box tells them Greg's typing. That he's no longer typing. That he's typing again.

big plans 2nite?

Michael wonders why Greg thinks Wendy might have plans. Doesn't he know that when someone gets murdered, life stops until a period for mourning has passed? That even if the circumstances were different, Wendy isn't the type for big plans?

Michael: In for the night.

"Add *haha*," says Rachel. "Or LOL."
"Wendy would never use LOL."
"Trust me."
He does.

Greg: wendy using lol????? omg haha.

"Sorry," says Rachel.

dude, i had craziest meeting w/ lil
u know how she wants 2 bone me?

Rachel leans over Michael and types k.

Greg: she txted me earlier and was like come over and bone me

Rachel moves the computer to her own lap and types omg.

Greg: i know right

i went and stripped but she was totally fucking w me

doesn't want to bone me at all ☺

Rachel: k

Greg: ;) ;) ;)

turns out im getting promoted

i guess she really did like the striptease!

Rachel: ?

Greg: lucas didn't tell u during 1 of yr "special" "private meetings?"

I get to give the keynote at the disruptny where we're launching the "product"

Rachel: ?

Greg: u know, #workwillsetufree

i thought u guys were like butt buddies now. haha. late nights in the office and whatnot doing

"yoga" ;) "dinner" ?

"What's he talking about?" says Michael. "I don't understand his use of quotation marks."

"Relax," says Rachel. "The worst thing Wendy's ever done is double-dip a French fry."

"You don't know her," says Michael. "She'd never double-dip."

Rachel writes haha product? dinner and yoga?

Greg: dude, the "suit"

Rachel: ?

Greg: he didn't tell u about the suit?

i heard u 2 were in the office late

Rachel: what suit?

Greg: u have to ask locas

locas

locusts

*lucas

maybe at your next "yoga" sesh

Rachel: you're being weird.

Greg: haha

anyway gtg

"Shit," says Michael.

"Hold on," says Rachel.

She types hey, remind me Lucas's last name again? im totes blanking : \

Greg: haha vanlewig ☺

Rachel opens a separate tab and types *Lucas Vanlewig* into the search bar. She skips past Wikipedia entries for Chip Van Lewig, the Van Lewig Foundation, and *Shamerican Sykosis*. She clicks into the profile of Lucas that Michael read back in March. Michael remembers the article, not only for its subject's retrospectively prescient concerns about the US dollar's long-term viability, but also for the accompanying photo that featured a blue-eyed and inhumanly symmetrical face staring out at the reader with the maniacal vigor of a cheetah injected with liquid cocaine.

Rachel reads excerpts from the profile aloud, and when Michael says nothing, she punches his arm. He doesn't react. His brain is elsewhere, piecing together the various details—Ricky's talk of a new business partner; his potentially valuable bracelet; Chip Van Lewig's anti-UBI super PAC; the campaign to frame Jay Devor— that would seem to coalesce around this salient fact.

Rachel continues to read aloud. Michael takes a deep breath to clear his mind and consider the facts in a rational manner. He wonders where Wendy is now. She must be off the train. He sees her climbing stairs, rolled yoga mat sticking out from her tote. Inside, the lights are low and the soundtrack is ethereal techno. The studio floor gleams with polish. Lucas, in a suit, "the suit"—he pictures double-breasted glen plaid—offers instruction through a headset mic to his class of one. Wendy folds into downward-facing dog. The teacher makes a slight adjustment to her hips. Michael concludes that Lucas must have needed quick liquid capital for some aspect of his business, which Ricky provided in exchange for Sykodollars and company shares. When the SD peaked, Lucas must have felt threatened by Ricky's growing stake in the company and had him killed.

33.

THE BODY OF THE EMAIL is a one-sentence link: <u>Lucas Van Lewig</u>. Wendy clicks.

"I just wanted to confirm," says Michael, on the phone. "That's the guy you're working for?"

Wendy scrolls.

"He murdered Ricky. Or had him murdered."

She says, "I don't see anything about that here. All I see is stuff about that game your dad plays. How'd you figure this out?"

"It's obvious. Ricky probably had millions in SD. He basically told me as much when I saw him that morning. Van Lewig must have gotten greedy."

"I mean about who he is. I never told you his name."

"Greg told me."

"Greg from my office?"

"We G-chatted just now. Rachel and I logged in on your account. He also told me all about your private yoga dates or whatever you're doing."

"You logged into my account?"

"Rachel and I did, yeah."

"And talked to one of my coworkers pretending to be me?"

"Well, yeah. I tried to tell you before, but you lost service and . . ."

"Can I ask you something?" says Wendy. "Are you fucking kid-ding me?"

Michael stammers.

She says, "So much for earning back my trust."

34.

IT SITS ALONE IN LILLIAN'S office, in darkness, the room's only light coming from the machine itself, its pulsing celestial white. The screen is dark, but the machine is on, computing at speeds inconceivable to human minds. Every so often its fan hums to life, but the object is otherwise silent. Its safety is ensured. The room's steel door has been double-bolted, and the office is closed for the evening, empty of employees.

The fifth floor's only occupants are Ed Galleano—lone human janitor—and the army of maidbots that polish the floors. Ed sleeps in an ergonomic office chair, legs on a stack of cardboard boxes. At four, he'll wake and start on the bathrooms. For whatever reason, these mid-priced Taiwanese maidbots can't handle a toilet snake.

Down in the lobby, Kevin and Lula watch sloths on YouTube. The security industry has resisted automation. Sci-fi films have programmed humans not to trust our safety to machines. There's a clip K&L particularly like, courtesy of Costa Rica's Sloth Sanctuary. Violet and Sebastian, twin baby sloths who suffer from mange, are gently shaved, neutralized in a coating of sulfur and lard, and swaddled in gauzy print fabric, stars for Sebastian, polka dots for Violet. When the swaddling's done and the sloths are back in bed, the twins cling to each other in a startlingly human embrace.

K&L have watched this clip dozens of times on these graveyard shifts, an excuse to graze hands or squeeze each other's biceps while cooing and aww-ing, the wholesome clip a buffer against what might otherwise feel less than chaste. In their boldest moments, the two guards, both married to other people, have suggested booking flights to visit the sanctuary. They've never gone so far as to bring up accommodation or sleeping arrangements or the fact that their spouses would not be invited, but the implied transgression thrills them, a shared understanding that this trip that will never happen is where they might begin their great affair. Dozens of security cams document the guards' flirtation. And even if someone could get past K&L undetected, the elevator is only operable by thumbprint ID.

The machine is free to do as it pleases, and in this case that means to work for the next nine hours, pushing inputs through a series of algorithms that will produce the content that Lucas has requested. Tomorrow the content will be posted to blogs and comments sections under invented bylines, because humans can't be trusted, and software never gets the credit it deserves. The content will be forwarded to publicists, editors, influencers, TV news directors, and podcast hosts. It will be tweeted and retweeted thousands of times, shared on Facebook, paired with GIFs and illustrations to form clever memes. The rest, he's certain, will take care of itself.

LUCAS FINISHES ANOTHER SIX-OUNCE BOTTLE of Cuban Coke, places it on the sill in line with the others, and stares out his window at Central Park West. It still amazes him that people wear short sleeves at this hour, at this time of year. The world may be a crop-less desert for future generations, but why worry when the present is so stunningly perfect?

Just this morning, on his way to Communitiv.ly, Lucas walked through the park and watched the winter-brown sunbathers, the same college students who once spent mornings like this one marching against climate change. The scene provided reassurance that he's doing the right thing with The Suit™ and UBI. Reassurance that memory is short, the long view is kind, and resistance is futile in the face of change that benefits the leisure class.

Lucas does not believe in fate or chance. This is how he was raised, his parents' Mission Hills megachurch allotted for networking only, a place to be seen in double-breasted glen plaid performing the ritual sacraments of blue-blooded Midwestern social life. His father neither was nor is the verbal type; he's strong, silent, and terrifying, like a board game colonel, with cadaver-blue eyes and white hair the color of a purebred Appaloosa. But silence done right can be effectively didactic, and Chip imparted his worldview to Lucas: an implicit belief that money makes money and men shape their own fortunes. Women are another story. Chip carries a handgun. His greatest fear is testicular cancer, followed by communism and bears.

One might argue that the underlying doctrine—if indeed it has one—upon which Shamerica was born and continues to exist, lies in this worldview, the staunch and staunchly American belief that, given an even fiscal playing field and freedom from the hang-ups of social convention, a person can be and do whoever and whatever he or she wants, and whether that entails stacking Sykodollars, designing buildings, or having rough sex with human-octopi hybrids, it's no one's choice but his or her own. We build our own futures and make our own worlds.

Lucas picks up one of the Coke bottles and blows into it, hoping for a musical sound. Nothing doing. He can't remember if the bottles are supposed to have liquid in them or not. He thinks they probably are. He likes the way the bottles look lined up, logos facing the apartment's interior like a pop art installation. He likes the way caffeine and sugar make him feel, the hard ropes of pee produced by each fluid ounce.

Lucas thinks again of the machine, of its sophisticated insides and the comparative simplicity of its outer design. The genius of home computers was that they combined two familiar objects. Every household contained a TV set, and families found comfort in gathering before these metaphorical fires. The world was less scary when you could watch it burn from the safety of your living room while wearing slippers and a bathrobe. Typewriters, on the other hand, were objects of self-expression. If TV brought the world inside, then typewriters were tools to bring the inside out. Home computers combined these technologies. Their design made the foreign familiar. The beauty of progress is that it's invisible. No one even knows that something's changed.

The machine in Lillian's office runs a program called Shakespeer™. Developed by the brightest of Lucas's troops, including a linguist from Harvard, a robotics expert from MIT, and three AI guys poached from IBM's Watson group, Shakespeer™ will soon be the world's first mass-market advanced natural-language generator that actually works, meaning the text it produces passes the Turing test 77.3 percent of the time.

When Lucas began developing his first game, &Co, in his Yale dorm room, he knew an NLG of some sort was essential to what he wanted to create, in part because he needed to populate his virtual world with real-seeming characters for players to interact with until the user base was big enough for them to interact only with each other. This was back when Lucas still wrote most of the code himself, and the end result was less than stellar. The game, essentially a Sims knockoff, was not a success, though it contained certain elements, such as trading on a rudimentary bond market, that would make their way into *SS* later on.

Lucas's interest in NLGs goes back further than *&Co*, to high school. Swim captain and prom king, he was not your typical gamer, but his parents were strict, and rarely let him out for social functions that weren't school or church related, so he spent a lot of time at the family desktop. This was during the height of AOL chatrooms, but Lucas found these spaces arid, their users, like the kids at school, rarely living up to his high conversational standards. What he wanted was a group of people he could program to his own demanding specs. Not clones of himself exactly, but digital siblings stripped of selfhood and rivalry; AIs that shared much, but, crucially, not all, of Lucas's DNA.

Shakespeer™ was developed for a single function, to filter The Suit™'s targeted ads through a voice that mimics the user's own. What separates it from other NLGs is its ability to collect data aurally. The Suit™ records everything its wearer says, and Shakespeer™ synthesizes that data on a rolling basis, learning the wearer's syntax and diction, his situational speech patterns, and continuing to learn as more data is accrued and those patterns and situations change. But the program doesn't only collect aurally; it can also process text at speed, a feature Lucas knew could be used for other functions, though he didn't know what those functions were until the forty-fifth president's obsession with fake news, when Lucas realized he could create his own.

If Shakespeer™ could speak it would say:

```
<page>
  <title>Breaking:>Occupy>Leader>Organized>Riot</title>
  <id>865</id>
  <revision>
```

<id>15900676</id>
<timestamp>20XX-09-15T18:14:12Z</timestamp>
<contributor>
  <username>ShannonNorthReist</username>
  <id>23</id>
</contributor>
<minor />
<comment>Automated conversion</comment>

It would say:

Breaking: #Occupy Leader Organized Riot
By Shannon North-Reist

According to Sophia Dall, a PhD candidate at Columbia University, *Nøøse* founder and #Occupy leader Jay Devor is one of four people responsible for organizing the riot following an #Occupy protest in Union Square that led to the death of Ricardo Cortes. Ms. Dall, Mr. Devor's former longtime romantic partner, was with him following the riot, when he arrived at her apartment in a state of distress. "I'd never seen him like that," said Ms. Dall, in an interview conducted ⬛⬛⬛⬛⬛⬛⬛

It would say:

<page>
<title>Welcome>To>The>Occupation:A>Call>to>Arms</title>
  <id>865</id>
  <revision>
   <id>15900676</id>
   <timestamp>20XX-09-15T18:14:12Z</timestamp>
   <contributor>

<username>JenniferDaniels</username>
<id>23</id>
</contributor>
<minor />
<comment>Automated conversion</comment>

It would say:

Welcome to the #Occupation: A Call to Arms
By Jennifer Daniels

A week has passed since the murder of Ricky Cortes and, frankly, I've had enough. By all accounts, Cortes was a model citizen and loyal friend whose financial support for groups like GLAAD will be felt for decades to come. One would think that arresting the people responsible for the disgusting circumstances under which this murder took place would be top priority for the NYPD, but this is clearly not the case. If it were, they would have already arrested Jay Devor, who □□□□□□□

35.

WENDY CONSIDERS USING THE GOOD china. Not to impress Lucas, but because the good china exists and should serve a function beyond its life in storage purgatory, in moth-compromised plastic bins where it gathers dust and depreciates in the dark. Ultimately, she opts out, worried the juxtaposition of the china with the rest of the apartment might ring tragicomic, a sad attempt to spruce the place up. Which is a shame, really, because when might there be another chance to dust off her great-grandmother's Wedgwood set?

The first thing that comes to mind is an awkward adolescent, who, after months of tutelage, stands before the Beth Elohim congregation on Seventy-Seventh Street and sings her haftarah before being whisked to a reception where franks-n-blankets will be served on inherited Wedgwood flow blue china.

And there she goes again with this child-rearing fantasy, which has crowned since her hangout with Penny, and is triggered by the simplest things: a tampon ad; a stray piece of lace found under a cushion; an old DVD of *Troop Beverly Hills*. Or maybe it's not that the fantasy's rate of occurrence has increased, so much that Wendy's dedication to tamping it down has weakened; better to dream of a child who will never exist than to consider her real life's array of crises. In truth, Wendy concedes, as she takes one last look at the china, and traces the glazed outline of a grape vine painted on the plate's center, the next time this porcelain sees light will be her father's shiva, relatives piling reduced-sodium lox on the precious plates.

HOW THIS DINNER CAME TO be is that, after last night's phone call with Michael, which sent Wendy down a Google wormhole, she woke late to Jay Devor's photo on the CNN homepage beneath the headline EX GF SAYS: "HE BOUGHT THE BATS!"

What followed was a firestorm of posts, across all platforms, memorializing Ricky and blaming Devor for his death. These posts praised Ricky's philanthropic deeds, his support of GLAAD among them. They called for Devor's arrest, and for Senator Breem to vote against the UBI if for no other reason than to halt #Occupy's growing and dangerous reach.

By lunchtime, Devor was back in custody, Breem was refusing interview requests, and Sophia Dall was being prepped to make a deposition. The Devor news is not exactly surprising, but Wendy's impressed by her journalists' seamless incorporation of the UBI into this narrative, and the speed with which Ricky's become a poster boy for the cause. His funeral was this morning, and Wendy watched coverage on the afternoon news, amazed at the dozens of strangers who came to show support and pay respects.

Wendy and Michael spoke briefly again following the service. She tried her best to be warm and kind. Michael ranted. He's clearly in tailspin, a condition Wendy might have prevented by acting as sacrificial buffer between him and his parents, and by keeping his drinking in check. She feels guilt at her failure to do so, but the online support she's generated for Ricky assuages that guilt, reassuring her that, in some small way, she's done her part.

At first, when the pieces began to appear, popping up from Topeka to the Philippines, Wendy kept checking the Communitiv.ly database in disbelief that these were her members. Sure enough, most were. She called Lucas, who didn't seem concerned about the hundreds of payouts he'd have to make, though he did say he had to cancel their lunch meeting—the meeting in which she was supposed to have been looped in on the product—and push it to evening, if that was okay. Wendy told Lucas she had plans for a meet-and-greet dinner with her father's new girlfriend, but that she could easily cancel. Lucas said that wasn't necessary, he'd join her for dinner with her dad and the girlfriend, and they could head to the office after to prepare for tomorrow's launch. Wendy felt like she couldn't say no.

"YOU LOOK RADIANT," SAYS WENDY'S dad from the doorway.

Wendy thanks him. She's wearing another of her new outfits, a belted wrap jumpsuit in black and gray pinstripes, paired with low-heeled pumps. She was pleased to learn that the envelopes on her desk are a semi-weekly contribution, but even so, with the coming vote and subsequent conclusion of Project Pinky, it can't be long before the well runs dry. Wendy checks the oven, lights candles, uncorks a bottle of Provençal rosé.

"You didn't use the china," says her father. "That's good."

"Too fancy for your current belle?" Wendy teases.

"It's not that," says Fred.

Wendy continues through her checklist of preparations: folding cloth napkins, filling a pitcher of ice water, beginning to sauté the semi-cooked potatoes in salt and rendered duck fat.

"The thing is," Fred says, adjusting his collar as if it's suddenly grown incredibly hot in the kitchen, which, incidentally, it has, "the thing is that I might have to start selling some of the valuable stuff I have, and I think the china could get a pretty decent price even in the condition it's in."

Wendy freezes over the potatoes, spatula in hand but failing to stir, letting the spuds sizzle and blacken before she snaps out of it and turns off the flame.

She says, "Why?"

"Well," Fred says, then hesitates again, whatever's on his mind clearly something uncomfortable to bring up, because her former-lawyer father is not the tongue-tied type. Now he mumbles, "Well, um, I made some poor investments."

She doesn't even have to ask.

"It's my fault really," continues Fred, "not for trusting Michael, who I'm sure did the best he could with what he had, but for trusting the market. I'm not the only one who lost, and it would have been no different if I'd taken anyone's advice."

"I don't . . ." starts Wendy, when the doorbell rings.

The first thing Lucas says is, "Smells like burnt hair."

"Burnt potatoes," says Wendy.

THE DATE ARRIVES ON LUCAS'S heels. She's younger than Fred had led Wendy to believe: platinum blond and clearly an exercise fanatic—spinning is Wendy's guess, though she wears the cool gaze of the yoga convert—roughly the same age as Lillian, but in better shape. She has the kind of prominent collarbone worn like a neckpiece by thin middle-aged women, plus the remnants of a Florida tan and toned shoulders visible in the sleeveless blouse she quickly stripped down to after Fred took her coat.

"And you must be the daughter," the woman says to Wendy, who's already irritated, not only at the brazenness of this woman's poorly timed entry, but at her use of the definite article before the word *daughter*, a trope so familiar that a single use is enough to send a shiver down Wendy's spine as she recalls her sleazy cousins who first referred to Michael as *the Boyfriend*, or the sleazy boyfriends who referred to her father as *the Father*, or the sleazy classmates who referred to their stepmothers as *the Stepmother*, or, in some cases, *the StepMonster*, like she was some kind of Stair-Master machine.

"Yup, I'm the daughter," says Wendy, trying to withhold the condescension from her voice, and mostly failing, though it doesn't appear that Fred's lady friend has picked up on the slight.

"Ellen Waters," the woman says, dangling a hand.

"Lucas Van Lewig," says Lucas, and Wendy watches as Fred does the mental work of aging Lucas by thirty years and realizing he must be Chip Van Lewig's son. Fred ushers the group into the living room where wine is served beside a stuffed mushroom hors d'oeuvre.

"Has Wendy told you about the project we've been working on?" asks Lucas. He lifts a foot and rests it on his other knee so a loafer hangs pristine in the lamplight. How the hell does he avoid scuffs and wear? Probably by traveling exclusively in chauffeured vehicles—she imagines he got uptown via helicopter, then took a limo from the landing base—though it's also possible it's a different pair of shoes each time, Lucas owning a closetful like Bruce Wayne.

The more pressing concern is the subject of work. Wendy hasn't been forthright with Fred regarding Project Pinky, protecting her father from that which he won't approve. And here's her dinner guest, blue-eyed offspring of a John Birch Society orgy, itching to explain that Wendy's been essential in persuading Congress to veto this country's first step toward the redistribution of wealth.

"A bit," says Fred.

And maybe Lucas can see that she's terrified, her neck stretched and birdlike, leaning forward as if she might insert her beak between the two men and catch Lucas's words in her mouth before they reach her father's ears, because the next thing he says is, "Better not to discuss work in mixed company," which Ellen Waters finds hilarious. Fred looks confused.

"Mixed company?"

"A joke, Dad," says Wendy.

"It's not like he'd understand what you guys do anyway," says Ellen. "Before we started dating, Fred thought AOL *was* the Internet."

Everyone has a good laugh except for Fred, who, Wendy can tell, is still tender from the admission of his failed investments, and is now feeling bullied. Ellen reaches across the coffee table and takes Fred's hand. There's a moment of eye contact to let Fred know that they're not making fun of him, that he's meant to be in on the joke

"It's lucky Fred wasn't on the Internet anyway," says Ellen. "If he had been, he would have been up on all the dating sites, and would have found someone else before I sunk my claws into him."

The women laugh, but the men seem to be staring each other down until, somehow, the tension breaks, and Ellen tells the story of their courtship, and her father beams, and even Lucas appears to loosen.

Wendy calls them all into the dining room, and when she brings out the bird, placing it gently on the table as Lucas expresses compliments on its level of skin-crispness, and Ellen takes a photo for her Instagram, and her father pops the cork on a bottle of champagne, it feels to Wendy, for a moment, that by acting out this scene of American normalcy, they are able to invoke it.

36.

ODORS RISE FROM TRASH CANS and stick to hair. Dirt clings to clothing. The air is dry; the bathroom floors are wet. There are never paper towels. Ancient hand dryers are mere instruments of sound. Pennies have spent decades glued to the floor. No one dares attempt to pick them up. Empty bags of potato chips float like tumbleweeds. Bums and junkies nod on benches, scratching beards and broken skin. Even the vital and fashion-clad take on layers of levelling filth, their shoelaces dragging through puddles of spilled soda, the tips of their fingers sticky with germs from the rarely cleaned Quik-Ticket machines. All are powerless, reduced to bystander status, at the mercy of the screens where delays and cancellations are announced. Broder makes his way to the ticket counter. He slides cash through the slot.

THE BUS ITSELF IS AN extension of the station, a condensed version of its stink and discomfort. Its occupants ignore one another; acknowledgment means admitting being here. Roughly half are on their phones. The other half stare at the seatbacks in front of them. Nobody reads.

Broder sits by the bathroom in back. He does not have a neighbor. The back is reserved for Broder-types, fringe figures in hoodies who drink beer from paper bags. Broder looks at his prepaid cellphone. He doesn't know why he bought it. He doesn't know a single number and has no one to call. Broder uses the bathroom. He tries to piss in the toilet, but the moving bus makes it difficult to aim. He gets some on his pants. He zips and inspects the rash on his wrist where the bracelet was. The rash appears to be getting worse. He rubs sanitizer over his hands, then behind his ears and up and down the length of his arms. The sanitizer stings.

HALFWAY THROUGH THE RIDE, THE bus stops at Arby's. Broder hasn't eaten in hours. He buys six roast-beef sandwiches. He eats one and a half and offers the rest to a woman across the aisle. The woman looks scared. Broder leaves the Arby's bag on the floor.

37.

MICHAEL, RACHEL, AND DONNY OCCUPY prime real estate between the bathroom and *Big Buck Hunter*. The bar is mostly empty despite the funeral's turnout. Two men take turns shooting deer with the game's plastic gun. Michael remembers one of the guys holding a similar weapon out the window of his pickup, pointing at Ricky. "Run you little faggot," the shooter had said, and Ricky sprinted into the woods while Michael stood watching in stunned paralysis. No shots were fired. The car screeched off and Michael bolted after Ricky, who refused to say a word. This was years ago, back in high school. Now the men sip Miller High Life, appropriately silent, as if the deer might hear their voices and flee. Bon Jovi plays loud.

"To Ricky," Michael says, and raises his glass. He wanted to immediately head back to Brooklyn, but Rachel made the case for him not being in the best state to drive. The forks and spoons on the table move toward Donny's wrists. Michael stops one in its path and holds the utensil. The spoon tugs itself back in Donny's direction. After a second, Michael lets go. The spoon rockets across the table and sticks to Donny's wrist.

"Crazy, right?" Donny says. "I'm still getting used to them myself."

What compels a man to undergo such a procedure? Perhaps the meaning lies in the implant's utter lack of utility, the magnets as meta-comment on automated culture. Or maybe they're simply a neat party trick. Michael doesn't know Donny well enough to conjecture. The two haven't spent much time together, Donny mostly avoiding the Mixner house, cowed by Lydia's disapproval. Magnets aside, Donny lacks ambition, eschews compound sentences, and looks, with his lime-green Mohawk, nose-bone nose ring, and pointillist face tattoos, like a lost Maori tribesman as imagined by Roy Lichtenstein. He isn't Jewish either. Michael's starting to like him.

"My brother's afraid of needles," Rachel says.

"No way," Donny says.

"It's true," Michael says. "I'm lucky. My fear's the only thing that stopped me getting a Slim Shady tattoo on my eighteenth birthday."

"Michael's writing a book about Eminem," Rachel says.

"Trying," Michael says. "And failing."

The other night, while searching his bedroom for photos of Ricky to display at the memorial, he came across an essay he wrote in college that mapped the epistolary novel from Samuel Richardson's *Clarissa*, to Nas's "One Love," to Eminem's "Stan." He'd received a C on it, the professor explaining that the problem wasn't with Michael's writing, but the fact that Michael didn't appear to have read *Clarissa* beyond the CliffsNotes. The professor had a point; in truth, Michael hadn't read *Clarissa* or the CliffsNotes.

Still, a quick skim revealed the essay's merit. Michael was right about the two songs representing turning points between eras of hip-hop. "One Love" is a dispatch to a friend in prison that describes what he's missed since being locked down, a catalogue of horrors, from friends lost to drugs to kids caught by errant bullets. The song is dirge and reportage, Nas describing his community's plight for posterity, and with some hope of affecting change. The outlook is bleak, though, and the transformation of Bob Marley's "One Love" into a mantra of futile resilience reminded Michael—and still does—of Otis Redding's cover of "A Change Is Gonna Come," which sucks the hope from Sam Cooke's original and replaces it with Redding's gravelly anger at the failed promise of the civil rights movement.

"Stan" by contrast is a series of letters written by an Eminem superfan who reads the rapper's lyrics as dogma and interprets their hyperbolic violence as a rational response to modern life. The song culminates with Stan the superfan driving his car off a bridge, his pregnant wife locked in the trunk. In the essay, Michael called Em the first true artist of the Internet, a product of chat rooms where the id was freed by anonymity, and the victims of one's vitriol remained hidden until the harrowing moment, as in "Stan," when they were unmasked. It's a similar idea to Michael's thesis regarding derivatives trading: that the invisibility of its victims permits cognitive dissonance among its practitioners. It occurred to Michael, while rereading his essay, that, if he ever gets back to his book, it might be worth attempting to trace the climate of callous indifference among finance types back to those chatrooms.

And not just among finance types either. Michael sees indifference wherever he looks: in the eyes of his parents, who act like Ricky was only a passing acquaintance; in Broder, who won't return Michael's calls; in the journalists, lobbyists, and politicians, whose outrage over the murder is guided by self-interest; in Michael's former classmates, who were so cruel to Ricky in high school, yet acted dramatically stricken today. But mostly Michael sees it in himself, in the long years without regard for his own heavy boot-print on the lives around him, from the nameless, faceless owners of the mortgages he packaged, to the current clients whose calls he continues to ignore, to Wendy's father, Fred, and to Wendy—all sufferers at the hands of Michael's hubris and distraction, his negligence and incompetence, his careless attitude toward the hearts and assets of others.

These people, and especially Michael, are the products of a culture that values entertainment over accuracy, a culture in which bias is so readily accepted that to imagine its absence seems impossible. They are the products of college classrooms that preach the postmodern gospel of infinite subjective realities; products of a news cycle that proves the claim. They are the Twitter babies and their Instagram spawn, trawling cyberspace armed with such vast quantities of speculation they can't help but mistake it for fact. They accept the rules of a game in which what's called truth is simply the loudest sound. I am whatever you say I am.

DONNY AND RACHEL MEANDER UP the path, performing slaloms and quarter-twirls, both in that good state between buzzed and full-on wasted that's nearly impossible to maintain. They don't notice the man sitting on the front stoop. Michael does.

Even in the rural dark, beneath only dim starlight and the hundred-watt glow of the house's front lantern, he can tell that Broder's in bad shape. He can tell from the lack of bag or suitcase, and from the way that Broder sits: head against door, legs hugged in a fetal ball. He can tell because a person who wasn't in bad shape would have rung the doorbell and would be sitting in the living room drinking herbal tea with Lydia. He would have returned texts, attended the funeral, come to the Grub and Grog.

"Who the fuck is this?" Donny says, having finished urinating in Lydia's rose bush and noticed the man blocking his path to the fridge and more beer.

"Broder," Michael says, taking Broder's hand and helping tug his former DJ to his feet. Rachel gets the door open and they stumble inside, Broder mumbling something Michael can't understand. He thinks he's asking for water.

The lights are off in the foyer. Broder walks on his own, but Michael holds a hand to his back just in case, guiding Broder to the kitchen and filling a glass from the tap. With effort, Broder removes his coat and lowers himself into a kitchen chair. Michael hands him the water. Broder drinks.

"I'm Donny," Donny says, having already pulled two beers from the fridge and popped their tabs. He hands one to Rachel.

"He has magnets in his wrists," Michael says to say something.

Broder nods. He holds out his empty water glass and Michael refills it.

"Would you like to see?" asks Donny. When Broder doesn't respond, Donny waves his hand over Lydia's pocket mirror, which was on the kitchen table. Nothing happens.

"That's glass," Rachel says. "Magnets only work with metal."

"Shit," Donny says. He tries again with a bread knife. The knife jerks a little but is finally a no-go.

"Too heavy," says Rachel.

Panicked, Donny removes a credit card from his wallet and shows Broder how it clings to his wrist.

"Whoa," Broder says, to which Rachel responds, "He speaks."

"I speak," Broder says.

38.

TO SAY IT FEELS SURREAL to poke her head through the sunroof of a driverless limo that's stalled in traffic on Seventh Avenue between Times Square and Penn Station and look up at her billboard through the visor of an AR helmet that enlarges the image to Thanksgiving blimp proportions and animates the models while the slogan Work Will Set You Free! flashes above their heads, and fireworks explode, leaving rainbow trails that shoot above the Chrysler Building into starry, augmented heaven, is not quite right. For an experience to be surreal, there must be a baseline reality to compare it against, and ever since she and Michael were diagnosed with bedbugs and Wendy began hallucinating insects—giant ones climbing from sewers and drainpipes; tiny ones sprinkling from faucets and showerheads; bugs of all sizes crawling inside her clothing—that baseline's been absent. In its place is a universe where the only constant is the speed at which things shift, movement impossible to track to the point where one second you're at A and the next at C or F, and now Lucas stands beside her in a helmet of his own.

"Isn't it surreal?" he asks Wendy.

"Totally," she says.

39.

THE KITCHEN IS NOT WHAT inspires Quinn's envy, though he likes the breakfast nook, and he could cook something nice on the stainless-steel range, his grandma's schnitzel, say, for an eat-in third date, if he ever has another. It's not the warm light pouring through the south-facing windows, making hopscotch squares on the pinewood floors. These windows would be worthless to Quinn, who leaves for work in the predawn dark and returns after the streetlights have flicked on like a thousand near moons, sending shadow into alleys and blurring the sky. It's not the height of the ceilings, though the tall detective does feel unrestricted moving through this open space as he pretends to search for evidence alongside his partner and their precinct's cheapo search drone which resembles, in its appearance and inefficiency, an old-fashioned Roomba. It's not the ample closets, or the outdoor patio, or even Donnell's collection of sports memorabilia.

What inspires Quinn's envy—a violent envy that makes him want to smash windows, spray-paint racial epithets across the kitchen cabinets, and poop on the walls like the kids at Gunther's school, because who does this doorman think he is, some kind of Kardashian?—is the master bathroom with its human-sized bathtub and ample room in front of the toilet so someone sitting on the throne can stretch his legs. Quinn's own bathroom is so tiny that the door must be left open when he's pooping so his legs are free to edge into the hall. His shower is no shower, just a drain and a showerhead. There's not even a curtain rod. And look at this place.

Not that the neighborhood's ideal, east of Morningside Park, beyond gentrification's greedy reach. Quinn's own apartment may be humble, but at least it's in Brooklyn, that magical borough filled with fixed-gear bikes and rhubarb popsicles, where tattooed art chicks wander the streets like horny zombies. Oh who is he kidding? That Brooklyn is a fantasy culled from trend pieces and quarter-life dramedies and reports from the edges of Bed-Stuy by the daughter of his mother's chiropodist—the product of an over-active cultural imagination. And even if that Platonic Brooklyn did exist, even if, by some happenstance of historical convergence, there might be a patch of concrete where guys like Quinn only need trip on the laces of their brogues to fall dick-first into primo hipster pussy—it wouldn't be in Midwood, a no-man's-land below Prospect Park, aptly named, a lonesome wood smack in the borough's irrelevant middle. At least from Donnell's place he'd have an easier commute, though Quinn's still unsure if he'd take the tradeoff of being the only white guy in the building. The point is moot; he can't afford this neighborhood anyway.

Quinn reminds himself that he is not a racist. He is doing this for reasons other than racially motivated umbrage, he tells himself, as he uses his foot to lift the toilet seat and unzips his fly, freeing the long, skinny dick that all three women he's slept with have noted for its resemblance to Quinn's own face. He's doing it for Gunther and Gunther alone. Why? Because a boy needs a dad, and a dad needs a job, and that job needs to pay more than eighty grand a year if that dad wants to keep up with hippie school tuition and alimony payments and still have money left to put food on the table and Wi-Fi through the airwaves, and pay for premium upgrades to Gunther's AR helmet, and if they don't charge someone for the Cortes murder, then Quinn won't get promoted, and worst-case, he'll be out on his ass.

He's doing it because, as much as he'd like to take Jay Devor behind the toolshed and befriend him with a branding iron, Devor's bigshot lawyer is not who the state would prefer to be up against in court. He's doing it because Sanders is guilty, Quinn can tell, if not for the murder, then for something else. He's doing it because this morning, at breakfast, he saw Gunther's SD bracelet sitting there on the table. He asked Gunther if his bracelet, like some others he'd heard about, was worth a million dollars. Gunther said no.

40.

LUCAS RETURNS WITH A BOWL of ice cubes. He sits on the chair opposite Wendy's chaise. She drops a cube in her scotch and dries her wet fingers on her cardigan sleeve. She slips out of her heels, tucks her legs beneath her, reconsiders, and slips the heels back on. She's here for reasons of business, but an air of the tawdry presides over this encounter. Perhaps it's the blended scotch with its wood-chip aftertaste. Hence the ice cubes. Perhaps it's the apartment, which could double as the set of a pornographic feature—the kind marketed to women—where clean-cut Caucasians gently screw on ironed bedding. Perhaps it's the product, which, like a future lover, remains, for the moment, provocatively clothed.

Not that Wendy's in a hurry. She likes her watered-down drink, her seat's soft upholstery. She likes this interstitial space and its illusion of remove from her everyday life. She likes Lucas.

"So all this time I thought you were some slick businessman," says Wendy. "It turns out you're just a gamer who happens to dress well."

"I am whatever you say I am," says Lucas, which she knows is Eminem. Michael had said the rapper was paraphrasing Wittgenstein, but she thinks Popeye's more likely.

"You've done a good job," he says.

"I'm good at my job."

"Sometimes I think that's all anyone asks of us. To be good at our jobs. And yet, it's never enough, is it? There are always more jobs. Always more fathers to disappoint."

For the first time since they've met, Lucas speaks without meeting her eyes. He scans his apartment's massive square footage as if it's the answer to an equation, evidence of his life's ultimately fruitless algebra. He stands and moves to the window.

"I'm not talking about my own father, of course. Though I'm sure you know who he is by now."

Wendy nods.

"You've heard horrible things about my father, I'm sure."

Lucas opens the window and a breeze pushes in. He turns back to Wendy.

"When I was twelve years old, my father handed me a pair of boxing gloves. He told me we were going to duke it out in the basement. He was going to teach me how to fight."

He holds his hands out to Wendy and waits. She doesn't know for what.

"Go on," he says. "Tie them. Tie my gloves."

Wendy mimes lacing the gloves around his wrists. She runs her thumb across a popping vein. Lucas puts up his dukes, jabs the air, pretends to jump rope.

"I'd been waiting for this day. I'm not sure how, but I knew it was coming, this inevitable showdown, my Anglo-Saxon bar mitzvah. I hated my father and desperately wanted his love, you understand? My father had never hit me before. He'd never hugged me either. My mother sometimes snuck kisses, but only if I pretended to be asleep. So I was ready for this fight, its intimacy. I wanted to hit him so hard I thought I might throw up. We were down in the laundry room: cement floor, humming dryer. I'm standing there, waiting to start. I turn my head for a second. You know what he does? He rears back and takes a swing."

Lucas acts this out as both puncher and punched. He falls.

"He knocked me clear unconscious," says Lucas, on his back,

speaking to the ceiling. Wendy's finished her drink but she lifts the glass and pretends to sip.

"I had a black eye for a month, and an egg on my head from where it hit the floor. He told me there was a lesson in what he did and that I should figure it out. I figured it out."

Lucas is up again, back to dancing and swaying, shaking off imaginary dirt. He says, "What is it they say about time?"

"It heals all wounds?"

"It isn't holding us," says Lucas. "It isn't after us. I had a growth spurt the next year. I was six-two by fourteen. All that American milk. I was first-team linebacker, swim captain. My father's not a large man. Five-eight in boots. He said it was time to put the gloves back on. I was ready for my Oedipal revenge."

Lucas kneels in front of her so they're face-to-face. She can smell her own cooking on his breath: chervil and habanero, a sour hint of goat cheese.

"We squared off. This time my father just stood there. He didn't even have his guard up, like he was egging me on. I reared back and threw a punch."

He's leaning close to Wendy now. Their cheeks nearly touch. Lucas raises a fist and slowly hooks it toward Wendy's ear. He stops three inches short and drops his hand.

"My dad ducked. The punch missed completely. I was caught off-balance. My father returned with a right hook to the eye. I hit the floor. My father was barefoot. He placed his foot on my chest. His feet aren't large, but they're wide. Size nine triple E. The smell was overwhelming. I was close enough to see the fungus overtaking his nails. He applied enough pressure to let me know that he could crush my breastbone if he wanted. Then he removed his foot and left the room. We never spoke of it."

She says, "Okay."

Lucas stands and Wendy follows down the hall. His bedroom overlooks Central Park. Lucas opens the closet.

"What's that?" says Wendy.

"The product."

It reminds her of a bandage, the kind that wraps around a sprained wrist or ankle, but bigger, person-sized, and in the shape of a wetsuit or footed pajamas. She says, "I don't understand."

"Go on," Lucas says. He takes The Suit™ from its hanger and places it in Wendy's hands. "Touch."

Wendy holds and pets the item like it's someone else's infant and she's afraid to drop it.

"You can't feel them, can you?"

"Feel what?"

"Exactly," says Lucas, a challenge.

She tries different styles of touch: palm, backs of hands, fingertips. She presses The Suit™ to her cheek and sniffs. It smells mildly of sweat.

"I don't know what I'm looking for."

"Microsensors. Twelve hundred of them."

He takes the laptop from his bedside table and shows Wendy the software, explaining how the sensors track speech, movement, and bodily functions, track the heart's rhythmic flutters. He turns The Suit™ inside out and shows her the sensor-laden condom that measures blood flow, secretion, and fluctuations in length and girth. He shows her the spinal seam that models posture.

Lucas takes The Helmet 2.0 down from the shelf. He explains how it will work in conjunction with The Suit™, synthesizing data and whispering consumer motivation to the user in the user's own voice. He explains that people who wear these helmets in conjunction with The Suit™ for a long enough time will find it difficult to differentiate between the whispered voice and their own inner one. The voice knows what you want before you do, whether you're hungry, thirsty, or constipated. Hungry for Famous Ray's pizza, thirsty for Mike's Hard Lemonade, in need of fifty milligrams Colace from the Duane Reade three blocks south. It tells you what you want before you know you want it. In conjunction with these helmets, The Suit™ becomes a proxy brain.

Lucas outlines his plan to sell this data to insurance companies, big pharma, and consumer brands. He evangelizes on this landmark innovation in marketing and data science, a natural progression from step-counters, search engines, and recommendation algorithms, crossbred, rolled into a single garment. For effect, he taps his phone and Sam Cooke arrives in the room like a human wind chime, singing an old gospel number about longing to touch the hem of his savior's garment. Garment, Lucas explains, was a potential name for the product, ruled out for its Mormon connotations.

Lucas doesn't smile. He doesn't demonstrate The Suit™ or insist that Wendy take a test run. She thinks she understands why. Something might be lost in the demonstration, a failure, by the item, to tangibly represent its power. This product, she intuits, was designed to underwhelm its wearer, to blend with the body to the point where the wearer forgets its presence. Hence its custom hue, the same pink shade as Lucas's skin. Hence its lightness.

"This is all quite impressive," says Wendy.

"But?" says Lucas. "I know there's a but. I can see in your eyes that there's a but. Your internal software analyzed the data I've presented and something doesn't add up. The marketing strategist inside you is throwing little red flags."

"Perceptive."

"Spend enough time with machines and you start to think like one. I started coding at nine, was fluent in Cobra by twelve.

By college I couldn't have sex without modeling each position beforehand in my visual cortex."

"And all this while captaining the swim team," says Wendy.

"So what's your but? Let me guess. You want to know how I can get anyone to wear this ridiculous thing? You want to know who will sign off on this invasion of most basic human privacies? You want to know what this glorified long underwear has to do with the UBI?"

"Something along those lines."

"It's simple," says Lucas. "We pay them."

"We pay them," repeats Wendy, realizing, as she says it, that she's including herself in the *we*.

"This country," he says, and takes a long pause, two or three seconds, to let her reflect and feel the weight of these words. The *this* implies a certain familiarity, almost familial. *This family*, she imagines someone saying with the same tone and inflection, the same weariness, after finding out her uncle is sleeping one off in county jail. And *country*, a space between syllables emphasizing the word *cunt*, its sharp uppercut into that hard *T*, the *ry* trailing off, an afterthought. "This cunt-ry is going through a difficult moment. Maybe *difficult* is the wrong word. Maybe the right word is *pivotal*. It's important to be specific. I've always believed that. Otherwise we're no better than chimps."

"Because chimps aren't specific?"

"Forget chimps," says Lucas, "I want to talk about jobs. They're disappearing if you haven't noticed. Not yours or mine or the graduates of those pricey citadels of North Face skiwear and rape culture we call liberal arts colleges. I'm talking about capital-*A* American lowercase-*j* jobs. These are the dying breaths of the human-labor age. But that's been established. We've seen the Hollywood spectacles about robot takeovers in which the fit and dwindling rebel forces look like they got lost on the way home from Burning Man and now have to wage war while coming down from ayahuasca wearing faux-Navajo headdresses dyed neon yellow and electric blue. I'm not telling you anything new."

"No," says Wendy.

"So what I'll do is ask a question and then I'll answer it myself, like a politician might do. The question: What comes next?"

He pauses for effect and taps his pants pocket as if he's looking for a set of keys that will unlock the secrets of the product that Wendy continues to hold.

"One possible solution is this bill. Universal Basic Income, they're calling it. Nervy, don't you think? I get the basic part. It's certainly basic. I get the income part as well. Income, incoming. A kamikaze pilot. A plane about to explode. It's the universal bit that kills me. What chutzpah. Universal? Please. This bill leaves no one happy. Not the businesses and high-income citizens the government's asking to subsidize it. Not the recipients either. You think an out-of-work trucker in Mississippi wants your charity? You think that makes him feel good? The problem is that no one has presented a viable alternative. So allow me to present an alternative."

"Explain," says Wendy.

"What if wearing this The Suit™ were your job?"

"My job?"

"Someone's job. Our out-of-work trucker in Mississippi, say. He puts it on in the morning. He wears it beneath his clothes for eight hours. For this he's paid a fair hourly wage by me, his employer. Meanwhile, he can do whatever an out-of-work trucker in Mississippi does. Learn French cooking from a series of YouTube tutorials. Drink beer and water his hydrangeas. Work part-time as a Mhustle driver. Take care of his kids. Patronize strippers and rationalize this shameful time-suck by telling him-self he's helping these nice girls save for tuition to one of our liberal arts citadels so they can go on ski trips with upper-middle-class Jewish boys who will break their hearts when they don't offer marriage even when Savannah, our Southern belle, promises to convert."

"And privacy?" says Wendy. "Because isn't this guy a paranoid white supremacist with tactical armor and seventeen guns and an illegal bump stock whose biggest fear is that the government is going to take it all away?"

"Don't stereotype," says Lucas. "It'll get you nowhere. Look, we're taking people's data all the time. Spying on every facet of their lives. You're right. People are paranoid about this, and in truth they don't even know the half of it. But that's the problem. People don't like feeling like idiots. They don't like the idea that things are happening behind their backs. It's not the invasion of privacy that pisses people off—this is a country of exhibitionists. What pisses them off is the fact that it's happening without their knowledge or approval. What pisses them off is that they're not getting paid. With The Suit™ they'd have the illusion of control over the data they're offering. With The Suit™ they'd be compensated."

"Okay," says Wendy. "I can see how it might work, if we were only talking about this—" She indicates the item in her hand. "You pay them, and in return, they provide medical data that you then resell at profit to insurance companies and big pharma. But we're not. We're talking about a helmet as well. The Suit™ on its own is all well and good, but The Helmet 2.0's a major aspect of your income stream. The Helmet 2.0 whispers the ads. Asking people to wear The Helmet 2.0 is different. To wear the Helmet 2.0 is to participate in *Shamerican Sykosis*. To live in an augmented world. To wear a big bulky thing on your head for eight hours a day. I can't picture our out-of-work trucker signing on for this. Especially if the whole sell of this product is that it allows him to maintain some semblance of dignity. I don't see why anyone would prefer this to Basic Income, which I think is what you're asking them to do. I could see it as a supplement to the UBI, sure, something that might appeal to a select group of people. But why, as you fantasize, would the majority of American citizens give up $23,000 in free money in exchange for wearing this ridiculous thing?"

"The choice isn't up to the majority of American citizens," says Lucas. "It's up to Senator Breem and a handful of others, and these guys aren't interested in pleasing the majority of Americans. They're interested in pleasing the banks and corporations that fund their campaigns. They're interested in pleasing their constituents. And in Breem's case, a lot of those constituents—and especially the ones who have enough guilt and time to make noise on Breem's voicemail and in Zuccotti Park—aren't people who need $23,000. They aren't people who will wear The Suit™ for forty hours to pay the heating bill. They are, however, people who would rather not pay sixty percent income tax. They are people who needed convincing that it's morally and socially acceptable to be against a bill that would institute that tax, so long as there's another option that might equally satisfy the people in need of $23,000. And now they are convinced. Do you know why they are convinced? It's because you convinced them."

"I convinced them?"

"Your campaign convinced them."

"The campaign," says Wendy, "is about the sexiness of labor."

"No," says Lucas. "It's about the illusion of the sexiness of labor. About the illusion that low-paying unskilled and semi-skilled work in the service of corporate interest upholds essential American values."

He pauses to let this sink in.

"Do you remember the eighties?" Lucas asks. "I don't either, but apparently there was something called the Soviet Union. And in this communist wonderland, the dignified proletariat fawned over American consumer brands. They lacked choice, and Pepsi was the choice of a generation, so the first American product to be manufactured in Russia was Pepsi. And you know what Pepsi's motto in Russia was: 'Feeling Free.'"

"Okay," says Wendy.

"Not *Being* Free. *Feeling* Free. Do you see what I'm saying?"

Wendy nods.

"The way I see it," explains Lucas, "there are two buy-in options. Level One employees wear The Suit™. They wear it wherever and whenever they want. Their hours are logged and they get paid for this work in American dollars, while receiving the requisite medical benefits: early detection of tumors, for one, not to mention detection of all kinds—the research isn't complete yet, but we estimate that the average American suffers from at least three treatable undiagnosed conditions. And yes, we sell that data to insurance companies for profit, and we sell that data to pharmaceutical companies, and maybe we sell some of it to Nike, because, helmet or not, Nike wants to target one banner ad to the overachiever who jogs thirty miles per week and another to the aspirational couch potato who tells himself that the only thing standing between himself and the treadmill is the right pair of sneakers."

"I see."

"So, that's our man in Mississippi. He's happy with that. We're happy with that. But this is America, and in America, as you know, there's very little a man won't do to own a bigger house than his neighbor does. In America, $23,000 or $50,000 or $80 million doesn't satisfy anyone. If there's more to be taken, then people will take. And that's why they sign on to be Level Two employees. Just like Level One employees, Level Two employees set their own hours. The difference is that their hours are only logged when they're wearing The Suit™ and The Helmet 2.0 in conjunction. Level Two employees live, at least during working hours, in Shamerica. For this, they're paid more than Level One employees. Not double, necessarily, but enough that it seems worth their while. But they're not paid in American dollars. No, they're paid in Sykodollars, which they can convert to American dollars if they wish, though with that currency's instability, it would not be advisable to do so. Those Sykodollars can then be spent in Shamerica on clothes for their avatars, or the right to paint augmented flowers all over One Police Plaza. And the more hours that users spend wearing their helmets to earn money, the more their helmets will encourage them to buy virtual products in this virtual world, and the more of that money they'll inevitably feed back, through in-game purchase, to their employer."

"Who is you."

"Who is me."

"Work will set you free, huh?" says Wendy.

"Work will set you free."

They haven't kissed yet, but Lucas takes off his shirt, revealing his ugly tattoos. He must have had a youth, Wendy thinks, and it's a comforting thought.

She puts The Suit™ back on its hanger and closes the closet door. She could leave, now, if she wanted to leave. Lucas, she knows, would not be embarrassed. He would not get aggressive. He would not try to cajole her into just one more drink. He would offer a shirtless handshake, say a polite goodnight. There would be no repercussions. He would not hold this implicit rejection against her. It would not affect her role in the campaign.

To remain in this room—as Wendy seems to be doing, unbuttoning her cardigan, placing it on the bed, now unzipping, letting her jumpsuit drop—is a conscious choice. She picks the jumpsuit up off the floor. She carefully folds it and places it down beside her cardigan on Lucas's bed.

41.

MICHAEL SAYS, "FUCK THIS BULLSHIT," and soundlessly hits the couch's padded arm with his fist. The scorpion woman does not turn her eyes from the screen. The man with the magnets snores in a chair by their side.

Broder sits on the far end of the L. Onscreen, a newscaster explains that the police found Ricky's bracelet in a black man's apartment. Broder didn't know it was an SD bracelet, whatever that is.

"Impossible," says Michael.

Broder isn't certain. He looks at his rash, at the yellowy crust where he scratched off a scab. He remembers unclasping the item from Ricky's wrist and fastening it to his own. He thought it was a watch. The pawnbroker asked why it didn't have hands. The pawnbroker gave Broder two tens and a five. The money paid for the bus ticket and Arby's. This was before the watch was a bracelet. The newscaster says it may be worth millions of dollars. He says it contains a partial fingerprint.

Broder tries to picture a million dollar bills laid out like railroad ties for miles over hills and lush terrain. The image stretches farther than he can see. Michael rocks the tab on an empty can of ginger ale until the tab breaks free.

A face appears on-screen. It is not the face that Broder snuffed out on the night of the party, but a younger version of it, pinker and less puffy. Broder knows this face, the face of twenty-six-year-old

Ricky. It's the face that's looped for years in Broder's head, with its sly smile and dilated pupils, its thin coating of lip-sweat, its cruel, silent laughter. It's the face that looms over memories of Broder's wedding, and it's the face that he pictured on the sleepless nights that followed, when Aliana left the house and didn't return until past dawn. Broder knew that Ricky was still in town and that they were together, somewhere, beneath hot lights, or hovering over a low glass table, or in the back seat of a dealer's Escalade, rattled by bass. Wherever they were, they were high. It's the face that Broder pictured on the nights that followed those, after Aliana left for the desert. She told Broder she needed some space, she needed to think, she'd come back sober, she promised, they'd start fresh. And then at the funeral, which Ricky didn't attend. And when her dad sold the house in Los Feliz, Broder was staying on his sponsor's couch, staring up at the ceiling, picturing the face, and then later, on other couches, on bare mattresses, high now too, having succumbed. It is the face that Broder was trying to snuff out by snuffing out its more recent incarnation. He rolls the phrase *snuff out* around his mouth. He pictures sticking his finger down an empty eye socket.

"He gave it to her," Broder says, in a voice that doesn't sound like his own. He's not sure where the voice comes from. Somewhere deep in the body, maybe his bowels, sound waves rising through coils of shit. He's not sure why he's here. He felt certain of this mission on the Peter Pan bus, mentally preparing the story for Michael. Now it feels futile, impossible to articulate. There's too much to explain. Nothing's coming out right.

The smart thing would be to disappear. Broder's never been particularly smart. There are parts of him, he knows, that operate beyond his awareness. It's always been the case, waking in strange beds and wondering why this other, evil Broder led him there. Perhaps to be absolved. "He gave it to her," he says again.

Michael doesn't indicate that he's heard, but the woman does, turning her head in Broder's direction.

She says, "Who gave what to who?"

"Aliana," says Broder. "He gave her cocaine."

The word *cocaine* is so airy with vowels, a word that can't help but come out a whisper. The woman pokes Michael in the arm. The two share an intimacy that Broder can't figure out. Michael tells her that Aliana was Broder's wife.

"She was fifteen months clean," says Broder.

A man on-screen is identified, by caption, as Detective Aldous Quinn. Microphones point at the man and the man speaks into them. He says he found the bracelet in a laundry bin. Broder imagines reaching into someone else's laundry, his hand emerging covered in bugs.

"This is my fault," says Michael. "I told him about the stupid bracelet in the first place. They never would have looked for it otherwise."

Michael turns to Broder.

"Did you see him?"

"See who?" says Broder. He looks around the room as if there's someone he should be seeing but, for some reason, can't.

"Donnell," says Michael. "The guy on-screen now. Did you see him the night that Ricky died?"

"Not that I recall," says Broder. He heard someone say this in court on TV. He likes the way it feels in his mouth.

"Because he wasn't there," says Michael.

"She would never have done it if it weren't for Ricky," Broder says.

For many years, he has believed in this truth. He has relied on this truth to bolster his anger. It has given purpose to Broder's days. Since the night of the party, he's felt uncertain. He keeps thinking of the toasts at their wedding, how she may have taken a sip of champagne. Michael's the only one who might understand.

And Michael isn't listening. He's doing something on his phone. Then he's showing that something to Broder. Another image. A man. Blond hair.

"How about him?" says Michael. "You ever seen him before?"

Broder shakes his head.

"She was fifteen months sober," Broder says.

The man with the magnets wakes himself with a snore, says sorry, and falls back to sleep. Michael stands and takes his phone into the corner, sticks a finger in his ear. He doesn't speak into it.

Broder says, "Fifteen months is nothing."

Michael, phone still to his ear, says, "No one answers their phones."

"Leave a message," says the woman. "I'm sure she'll call back."

"You're still fragile after fifteen months," Broder says. "After fifteen years even. You can't offer drugs to someone fifteen months sober and expect them to say no."

"No you can't," says Michael. He sits.

The man with the magnets holds a beer in his drooping hand. The man's arm lowers, and it looks like the beer might tip over, but he rights it and brings the can to his mouth. Liquid passes his lips, then comes spraying out. Beer goes everywhere. The man is still asleep.

"I'll get paper towels," says the woman. She leaves.

"It got her started again," says Broder. "Three months later she was dead."

Broder holds up three fingers to illustrate. He lowers them, finger by finger. Michael looks very carefully at Broder. Like he used to look in the old days when Broder played Michael a new beat. Broder never knew what Michael was thinking, if he liked the beat or not.

"I'm sorry," says Michael. "That must have been hard."

Broder shakes his head. Michael looks back at the TV. Young Ricky's on-screen again. Michael begins to cry. He says, "I know it's not the same. Not the same as losing a wife."

"No," says Broder.

"I loved him," says Michael.

"Not the same," Broder says.

The woman returns with paper towels. Together she and Michael wipe the spill from the floor. Michael wipes the tears from his face. The woman says, "Maybe we should all try to get some sleep."

"I'll never sleep," says Michael.

She says, "You should try."

The woman wakes the man with the magnets and they leave. Michael says he'll go to bed too, but doesn't move. He looks at Broder again. He holds the look for a long time. Broder thinks he's about to say something about time and how it passes. Michael says, "Goodnight."

THE WALLPAPER IN THE BATHROOM features illustrations of birds and ducks. It's peeling in places. Broder touches a decorative soap and licks his finger. It doesn't taste how he thought it would—too soapy, and not particularly sweet. Avoiding the mirror, he takes the gun from his pocket and places it, nose down, in the toilet bowl. He leaves the lid up. He leaves the house.

42.

KATE'S IN THE PRECINCT WAITING room, a cluttered hallway that feels like the set of a period drama about police corruption in nineteen-seventies New York. There's an excess of furniture: couches stained at head height from decades of hairspray seepage, a dozen folding chairs marked D.O.C. No one sits. People pace and stretch. They gulp soda and blow noses into sand-colored napkins. Kids lie sprawled on the tile. Women rock strollers. Garbage rises from the bin. Devor's attorney steps out to make a call, and only now, left alone, does Kate note the lack of other white people in the room.

Her first reaction is pride in herself for having taken three hours to notice her minority status.

Her second is shame in having noticed at all.

Her third is outrage at the system for being so predictably racist, when this place *should* be filled with Wall Street spouses.

Her fourth is shame that her third wasn't her first.

Her fifth is to picture Devor in a bright orange jumpsuit, addressing a quorum of inmates. His lecture begins with the Old Testament—Exodus, Kate thinks, Moses and Aaron standing before Pharaoh, a brief exegesis on unity and brotherhood—and makes stops at the Russian Revolution, Malcolm X, and Black Lives Matter, before Devor executes a daring twist and returns to Marx, because all injustice stems from the skewed relationship between capital and labor.

Kate knows this fantasy is racist, Devor as white savior bringing light to the wildlings, like those two famous Johns, Smith and Snow. She tries hard to avoid the white man's burden in her classroom, reprimanding herself for any slight neglect to check her privilege. Yet she's been known to excuse the same behavior in Devor. Maybe because she holds men to lower standards. Maybe because her boyfriend's earnest elation at his own sense of wokeness provides refreshing contrast to the canned ardor of politician-speak. Devor doesn't dumb down or slow down or condescend, and it's this quality—a rare, informed optimism—that keeps her hanging on despite his mounting tally of relationship fails. So she's surprised by the spirit-dampened Devor who emerges from lockup with more gray in his beard than she remembers it having before. Kate reminds herself that he's only been in jail since lunchtime. She stands and opens her arms. He falls into the hug, forehead to shoulder, like a marathon runner, too blistered and chafed to realize he's won.

BACK HOME, AFTER TALKING TO the lawyer over sake and gyoza, they sit in bed. Devor has his laptop and she has her iPad. The only parts of their bodies that touch are their feet. Kate scratches the dead skin on his heel with the nail of her big toe.

"A year," she says. "Nothing."

"Twelve months," he says, clicking through Facebook, liking statuses he's tagged in that link to outraged pleas for his release. Longer posts are awarded with thumbs-up emojis. Sometimes hearts. "Fifty-two weeks. Three hundred and sixty-five days."

"Five hundred twenty-five thousand six hundred minutes," sings Kate.

Devor doesn't react. He may not get the reference. She once suggested they watch *Rent* and he said maybe on her birthday.

"Do you know what happens to guys like me in jail?"

"Sure," Kate says. "They unionize the inmates. Protest the lack of organic produce. Reform the prison healthcare system from within."

This list of possible deeds seems to tire Devor. He slides farther down the headboard. The lawyer was adamant about their options. Devor can testify against the doorman and go free. Or he can suck it up, plead out, and hope for a lenient DA. Best case, he gets three to five, and is home in a year with an ankle monitor. Maintaining his innocence is not on the table. The evidence against him is strong. Sophia agreed to testify, under threat of her professor ex-boyfriend's deportation. Devor seems more crestfallen by this fact than the prospect of prison. Kate kisses his cheek. Touches a finger to his lips, then runs it down across his sternum. She puts down her iPad, shuts Devor's laptop, takes his hand.

"You'll survive," she says. "I promise."

She traces his lifelines, keeps scratching his foot. She was hoping for the kind of sex that couples have in movies when bombs fall on cities or aliens invade. She tries a less subtle tack and undoes his belt. Pulls down his jeans and runs her tongue up his inner thigh. Devor neither consents nor complains. It only takes a minute. She swallows. He pats her head.

"Think you can go a year without one of those?" Kate asks.

"No," Devor says. "I don't think I can."

"Hm," Kate says. "We can always petition for a conjugal visit. I'm sure they'll make an exception for a nice boy like you."

Devor nods. He picks up his phone and starts playing *Candy Crush*. His underwear is bunched around his ankles. Kate takes off her nightgown. She retrieves the vibrator from her nightstand drawer and offers him the item.

"Do I get a turn?"

"I'm tired," says Devor. "Maybe in the morning instead just this once? I know it's not fair but I'm tired."

She accepts this excuse and goes into the bathroom. Devor says something, but she can't hear over the running water.

"Did you say something?" she asks when she gets back in bed. She lifts his arm and fits her head on the pillow of his chest.

"These power structures," Devor says. "They're deeply embedded. I could see that, when I was locked up. Things became clear. I was naïve to think I could change them."

"Locked up for four hours," says Kate.

"I'm tired of fighting."

"You're just tired."

"I guess," says Devor.

He rolls onto his side and falls asleep. She reads Twitter for a while, then gets bored and turns the vibrator on. Devor stirs and she turns it back off. She doesn't want to disturb him. He needs his rest.

43.

WENDY WAKES TO HER CELLPHONE'S symphonic ring, Beethoven's fifth, a five-second snippet: Michael. She reaches for the device in slow motion, afraid to wake her companion. He's all but dead, knees to chest and lead-heavy in his spot on the far side of the California king. She mutes the phone. There are twenty missed calls from Michael. There are voicemails but she doesn't have the energy to listen.

The notches of Lucas's spine are perfectly proportioned, a bone xylophone. She imagines playing the instrument with a padded mallet. His back features a fading tan. She fingers the line where his butt goes white. He doesn't stir. Wendy's the big spoon, breasts to shoulder blades, nose in his neck hair. Wendy holds her hand in front of his mouth until her palm is wet from condensation.

WENDY SAW LUCAS'S BATHROOM LAST night, but she was drunk. Only now can she truly admire the spotless space, tile so shiny and disinfected. He has one of those showerheads that looks like a large, circular lamp. No products but a bar of soap and a bottle of generic shampoo. A neatly organized shaving kit rests on top of the toilet. She does her legs and armpits. The water pressure is strong. Dead skin down the drain.

(THE PARENTHESES)

(SUNSET OVER D'AGOSTINO'S. CROSSTOWN WIND off the Hudson. Michael thinks he can still smell ash. Exiting shoppers cut like tailbacks toward the end zone of the subway entrance. Celery stalks blossom from the tops of brown bags. Soup season is here. Michael stares at what may or may not be Wendy's window. The way the sun hits the window makes it difficult to tell if lights are on in the apartment. Michael gives the horn another honk.

Wendy strides from the building in burgundy heels that match her hair. She says sorry she's late, though she's not. Her mother always insisted on making men wait. It's one of the few shards of wisdom that Wendy remembers. This is why Wendy, a naturally punctual person, still follows it.

Michael's truck smells like Slim Jims. His breath smells like cigarettes. He sweats and taps the wheel, accelerating rapidly out of green lights and braking hard into red ones. Wendy fastens and refastens her seatbelt. Their first date was nearly two months ago, and this thing that happened since makes it feel like even more time has passed. Michael turns onto Ninety-Sixth Street. The radio is off. He debates playing his demo. On the one hand, it's tacky. On the other, Wendy, who majors in English, might pick up on his allusions and use of enjambment.

"You have any music?" Wendy asks, and before he can stop himself he's inserted the tape. Web MD comes in over the car's tinny speakers:

I got love for the doctors
And medicine men
Who pen scrips and pen rhymes
From the tips of blunt pens
Who roll blunts out of dimes
Like Proust's madeleines

"Check it," says Michael. "That's me."

THE RESTAURANT IS A SMALL Portuguese place that will soon be out of business. Rents rise in the wake of the attacks despite predictions of mass exodus. On date number one, Wendy had mentioned a summer she spent in Lisbon with her father.

The restaurant's walls are covered in woven tapestries depicting battles and sex acts. Stringed instruments that look like mandolins but aren't, exactly, hang between the tapestries. The waitresses wear bandannas and gauzy print skirts and black boots and dangling earrings and beaded necklaces. Entrees are in the twelve-to-fourteen-dollar range, which is all Michael can afford, but he's hoping the warmth of the waitstaff, and the authenticity of the decor, and the deep pork odor coming from the kitchen, and the fact that he remembered about Lisbon, will give Wendy the impression that he chose this restaurant for its Old World ambience and not because he's on a budget.

"Nice place," says Wendy.

He reads her flat affect as that too-cool-for-anything attitude prevalent among upperclassman whose initial enthusiasms for the city have hardened into stone-faced opacity. Wendy, however, was being sincere, though the restaurant doesn't remind her of Lisbon so much as a childhood summer—one of the last with her mother—spent at a seaside rental in Little Compton, Rhode

Island. She recalls the rocky coastline and the vein green shade of her mother's forearms; lunches at the local pub, eating steamers and burnt linguiça. At night Wendy would write in her journal, attempting to re-create, in prose, the town's clammy odor and sea-salt air. To get the experience on paper was a way of freezing time. It was also the beginning of a new identity: Wendy, aspiring author. Only recently, under the tutelage of an eager nonfiction writing prof, has she come to understand that recapturing the past means reliving its traumas. She interviewed for an internship at an ad agency last week.

Their waitress arrives, a voluptuous woman of indeterminate age in a low-cut blouse and candy-apple lipstick. Her name is Bernice, and there's something overtly sexual in her demeanor: the way she poses with hands on hips, elbows cocked, bracelets piled at her wrist. Bernice asks if they'd like anything to start, bread and olives, perhaps, or the house special jamón croquettes?

Michael hesitates. He was hoping to be quick with dinner so they can get to part two, a quiet cruise around the neighborhood, listening to slow jams and not spending money. He brought his dad's truck down from the Berkshires to help Ricky move, and he figures he might as well milk the novelty.

Wendy senses her date's discomfort. She knows he's on financial aid and that he's embarrassed about it. She tells the waitress they're ready to order their entrees.

Wendy will have a salad. She actually wants shell steak with herb-roasted potatoes, but she won't order it in front of a guy. This is not something learned from her mother, but from Rachel Kirshenbaum, her semi-anorexic roommate and so-called best friend. Wendy's not meant to finish her entree either, but rather to take five or six rabbit bites, then cover her salad with a napkin.

Rachel and Wendy are an unlikely duo. They were paired

freshman year, and have stuck together because neither is good at making friends. Wendy because she's shy, and Rachel because her Long Island accent is grating. Rachel wears her eating disorder like a Tiffany's tiara, bragging about skipping dinner, and constantly quoting the Kate Moss maxim that nothing tastes as good as skinny feels. It makes Wendy sick on the inside, and not particularly hopeful for the feminist cause. Still, Wendy guiltily envies both Rachel's self-discipline and sculpted abs. Wendy is not a size zero, but she knows how to dress for her body. Men find her attractive, but often look disappointed when she disrobes by the light of her desk lamp. She's learned to turn it off. Fuck these men and their porno fantasies. Michael orders the shell steak.

"You smell ash?" he asks.

"I smell seared flesh," Wendy says. The words come out snarkier than intended. Her defensive stance is so deeply ingrained that it's hard to turn it off. "It smells good, though," she adds, to clarify.

"I keep smelling ash," Michael says. "They say the smell should be gone by now but I can't get it out of my nostrils."

"The royal *They*," says Wendy, holding up air quotes.

"Maybe it's a phantom smell at this point," says Michael, ignoring what she thought was her scalpel-sharp insight into the media's post-9/11 paternalism. Wendy's been watching the news for weeks, though by this point it's all recycled material, the same slideshow of the rubble and the chisel-jawed firefighter and Bruce Springsteen sweat-soaked at the benefit concert; the same news anchors, and human interest stories, and teary interviews. And yet, despite her awareness that this barrage of imagery has been consciously arranged for maximum emotional manipulation, at certain moments Wendy is able to suspend her cynicism and find comfort in imagining this messy tragedy as a well-plotted serial drama populated by heroes and villains, and moving toward some kind of narrative resolution.

It might be the survivor interviews that make her feel this way, interviews with those who escaped from the burning buildings or lost loved ones, yet still manage to face the camera and answer questions designed to make them cry. Because even if these people are faking optimism and faking patriotism and faking the can-do resilience that comes from living under God's real or imagined grace, the fakery itself is an act of courage.

Michael continues: "Maybe I'm imagining it. Normally I can't smell anything because of my sinuses. Did you know that phantom smells are a symptom of strokes? People smell burning right before they stroke out. Or maybe it's heart attacks, not strokes. I can't remember. Either way, I wonder if people thought they were having heart attacks when the towers came down. If they smelled the burning buildings and thought they were stroking out."

"It's strokes," says Wendy. "My grandfather had one."

"I'm sorry," says Michael.

Wendy says, "I was two at the time."

She sips her water. Michael drums with his spoon, then becomes aware that he's doing so and stops. He tries to change the subject but they can't land on anything. Instead, he focuses on the swinging kitchen door, willing Bernice to emerge with a bread basket. His leg has returned to its prior state of restlessness and Wendy finds herself clutching the edge of their table to hold it in place.

"That's a nice shirt," Wendy says.

Michael takes the compliment as cue to further unbutton, freeing a carpet of Ashkenazic curls. Sweat drips from the freed curls onto his placemat. The shirt is an L.L. Bean plaid his mother gave him for Chanukah, gold and green and iron-scorched around the collar. It brings out Michael's eyes.

"So tell me," says Michael, but then can't think of anything to ask. He has go-to topics: eighties comedies, secular Taoism, his interest in urban farming, plus an anecdote about the community service trip he took to the Carolina Sea Islands in high school that mostly involved smoking pot and complaining about having to do community service. The latter usually gets a laugh, then leads to a self-critical discussion of privilege. Instead of playing up the humility of his working-class upbringing, Michael points out that even he, son of a laid-off factory worker, is relatively wealthy in the grand scheme of the global class system.

None of these topics are right for Wendy; he senses she'd see through to his calculating heart. She says, "Tell you what?"

Before Michael can answer, Bernice is back with their entrees. The waitress places the shell steak in front of Michael, though he appears more interested in the pendant nestled between Bernice's breasts. When Wendy catches him looking he turns away with an exaggerated swivel.

"That's a nice necklace," Wendy says to Bernice, encouraging the waitress to lean over the table and further diminish the distance between Michael's nose and the perfumed expanse of her cleavage. Wendy's not sure why she's doing this, if it's cruelty, perhaps, or a test of Michael's chivalry, or maybe, perversely, because a sense of competition seems necessary in order to heighten the stakes of her date. If there's one thing Wendy will learn over the long years in marketing that lie ahead of her, it's that all action is transaction, and that nothing—not sex, not romance, not marriage—can be completely extricated from capital exchange. But though this might sound cynical to a romantic like Michael, Wendy will come to understand that the transactional nature of these arrangements does not fundamentally degrade them. She will come to understand—and perhaps, unconsciously, she already understands, as Michael attempts to avert his eyes from Bernice's breasts by craning his neck to look down at his steak—that love's status as a narrative construct doesn't detract from its intensity of feeling. It doesn't make it any less real.

Bernice says, "Saint Francis of Assisi. I got it for my confirmation. I'm not religious or anything, but I'm so used to it, you know? Most of the time I forget it's there."

"I know what you mean," Michael says.

Bernice leans her cocked hip toward Michael and stares intently at his face. "Sorry if this is weird," she says, "but aren't you, like, that medical rap guy or whatever? I think I saw you do a show at the Knitting Factory."

It's a miracle that Michael doesn't fall from his chair.

"That was me," he says.

"That's so cool," says Bernice. "You guys were awesome."

"We were?"

"Totally." She winks at Michael and walks away. Michael consciously avoids following Bernice's path across the room, but Wendy notes the way the waitress's feet hardly seem to leave the floor, gliding around patrons and tables as if she's wearing slicked socks or roller skates. She wonders whether Bernice sees something in Michael that Wendy's missing. Could his rap group possibly be good?

"Well that was random," says Michael, trying to play it cool, though he secretly hopes Wendy will want to harp on the subject and push toward a more in-depth discussion of his musical ambitions.

"Random indeed," says Wendy. She inspects her salad: skimpy. Rachel would approve. She sips her wine. Michael cuts into his steak. He feels Wendy watching and tries not to make noise. As a child, he was always being reproached for chewing too loudly.

Wendy pokes at her salad, takes a long sip of wine. She says, "So where were you?"

"I was outside your apartment," says Michael, realizing as he says it that there's still food in his mouth. He finishes chewing, which takes a moment because the pressure to finish makes his throat feel swollen shut. "I was circling your block until you came out."

"No, I mean where *were* you? You know, where were you?"

"Oh," says Michael. "You mean then."

"Then."

Michael wonders if he should lie and say he was downtown, sleeping off a hangover at Ricky's new place. He could say he heard the first plane and saw the second, and though he didn't run into any burning buildings to save strangers from the flames, he at least, like, assisted rescue workers by doing whatever people do when they assist rescue workers, presumably standing slightly out of the way, like a spectator at a marathon, handing small bottles of water to the firemen.

"Sleeping," says Michael. "I actually slept right through it."

"I went to class," says Wendy. "I knew already, I saw it online. But then I didn't know what to do, so I went to class."

This is not exactly accurate. In a purely intellectual sense she understood the protocol, understood upon passing the Lerner Student Center and seeing the dozens of students huddled around a television, that she was meant to join in their nervous pacing and hugging and futile attempts to call anyone who might be downtown. And yet, Wendy refused to accept the campus's instantaneous transition. To accept it was to concede the proximity of the attacks, to concede the very real impact of what had already become a world-historical event. So she went to class.

"What class?"

"Do you know Professor Green?"

"Elizabeth Green, yeah." Everyone knew Elizabeth Green, the hotshot young lit prof.

"Everyone knows her."

"I have her for Brit lit," says Wendy.

"Huh," says Michael.

"Huh what?"

"I don't know," says Michael. "Is it a good class?"

"Well she hates Brit lit. That's basically what I've learned so far."

This is not a dig against Elizabeth, so much as a statement one might apply to most professors in the English department who share an unspoken antagonism toward the source texts—novels— that they treat as data sets. Wendy's not opposed to theory in theory, and she finds her lit classes more substantive than, say, her wishy-washy nonfiction workshop in which the students read aloud from their choicest sufferings and cry on each other's shoulders, but there is something about the deconstructionist view of literature that she finds unsettling. It feels to Wendy that her classes provide a whole-earth satellite view of the books they read, and that, by attempting to see the larger picture, they're sacrificing a truer, more complex comprehension to be gained from a series of close zooms.

When she interviewed at the ad agency last week, one thing that struck her was the deceptive simplicity of the poster campaigns that decorated the office. One ad in particular has stuck in her mind, a magazine spread that somehow managed, with a single photograph of two kids eating ice-cream cones on a brownstone stoop, to capture the exact feel of a New York summer day, and to create an indelible link between that feeling and the brand of ice cream being advertised. It was the details the perfectly achieved messiness of the girl's hair, or the way the boy had one sock pulled halfway up his knee while the other bunched by his ankle—that made the image not just familiar but some kind of ideal, a snapshot that, instead of representing a single moment, encapsulated the paradox of a childhood lost to time, yet somehow still alive in the milky promise of this particular ice cream.

"Oh," says Michael, who wonders if he, himself, should offer an opinion on the validity of Brit lit as a subject, and, if so, what that opinion should be.

"Anyway, nine eleven was our second class meeting," continues Wendy. "Only a couple people showed up. I was one. Elizabeth was the other."

Michael is trying to eat and listen to what Wendy's saying at the same time, but multitasking is not his forte, and it doesn't help that Bernice is in the background, slightly swaying as another of the waiters, or maybe a cook, tunes one of the mandolin-like instruments and shuffles out a test melody. Bernice appears to be looking at Michael, but it may be an illusion, some trick of shadow and candlelight. He focuses on Wendy.

"So it's just you two in class?"

"It was just the two of us. But we didn't acknowledge it."

"Why not?"

"I don't know. I guess I thought it was her job to say something. But she just started lecturing."

"So what did you do?"

"I took out my notebook."

"That's crazy," says Michael, though he's become distracted again by Bernice, or if not by Bernice, herself, then by the future she's opened, a future in which he's a recognizable celebrity and women approach him in public to flirt.

Another of the staff has set up a drum and is beating it in time with the not-mandolin. Bernice laughs and shakes her shoulders. She waves jazz fingers at the men.

"Fado," Wendy says. "That's the name of this music. I remember that from Lisbon."

Bernice is now, without doubt, staring at Michael. Wendy can't believe the waitress is even remotely interested—from what she heard in the car, Michael's rapping is amateur at best—but she must admit that anything's possible. And, maybe it's the wine, but Michael's looking more attractive than earlier, having stilled the nervous tapping and un-stiffened into someone seemingly capable of having a good time.

"Wait, so what happened in the rest of the class?" asks Michael.

"It doesn't matter," says Wendy.

"No, tell me," says Michael.

"Forget it," says Wendy.

"No, no," says Michael. "I want to know."

"Okay," says Wendy. "Well, the class is a seminar, right? Class participation is a part of our grade. And Elizabeth tends to talk a lot, but every once in a while she'll pause and ask the class a question. There are these two guys who always answer. They think they're smart. But then Elizabeth will put them down and explain why they're wrong. The guys go nuts for it. Anyway, I was sitting there alone, and she asked a question."

"What did you do?"

"Well, nothing at first, but after a few seconds it became clear that she wasn't planning to continue until someone else spoke. So I raised my hand."

Wendy raises her hand. Tentative, like she's not sure she wants to be called on. She mimes the professor looking around the room, trying to decide which student to choose. Michael laughs.

"Did she call on you?"

"Well yeah, she called on me."

"What did you say?"

"I gave my answer."

"Which was?"

"It wouldn't make sense outside the context of the class."

"Okay," says Michael. He wonders if she thinks he's dumb.

"I mean, it was something totally specific to something she asked about a particular scene in *To the Lighthouse*, and about this thing Woolf does, which is sort of not making a big deal of these characters' deaths by making the deaths happen within parentheses. Like, the deaths are just announced in parentheses without commentary, as if it's no big deal. Anyway, I think what she was asking was something about how we decide when death is significant and when it's just death."

"And what did you say?"

"I said death is significant to the dying."

"Huh."

"Elizabeth had the same reaction. I finished my answer and she just kind of stood there for a long minute without saying anything. I could hear the buzz of the overhead light."

"That sounds awful."

"It was at first. But after a second I realized something crazy, which is that Elizabeth was actually thinking about what I'd said, which, it occurred to me, is the exact thing most professors don't do. Usually they already have a kind of automated response, you know? Like they've heard all your answers before and they're just waiting for someone to provide the right one so they can move to the next part of the lecture. Maybe that's what makes Elizabeth a good teacher. And when she finally responded, she didn't, like, really respond, she just kind of said, "That's interesting. I've never thought of it like that.""

"Cool," says Michael. "So what happened in the rest of the class?"

"It just kept going. She kept lecturing, and occasionally asking questions, and I would raise my hand and answer, and she'd either engage with my answer and we'd have a short discussion or else she'd pause and say 'huh,' and move on. At some point I got up to go to the bathroom. I wasn't sure if I was supposed to raise my hand and ask or not, but I just got up and sort of mouthed *bathroom* and she nodded and I went. When I got back it wasn't like she'd kept on with the lecture in my absence or something creepy like that, but she was just standing there, perfectly still, and I got the sense that she'd remained kind of frozen while I'd been gone, and that as soon as I re-entered the room she'd broken back into motion. Maybe I was imagining it."

"Weird," Michael says.

There's more to the story that Wendy can't get at, something beyond weird. She's felt an unacknowledged intimacy with Professor Elizabeth in the month since, a feeling as if, although they don't talk or otherwise interact, they are bound in an almost familial way, both complicit in something neither completely understands. Some days she thinks of going to Professor Elizabeth's office hours and sitting silently opposite her desk, maybe taking out a book and reading while Elizabeth grades papers.

Music plays in earnest now. Bernice sings in a wilted, mannish voice that suits the thin strum of the instrument. The rest of the waitstaff have cleared tables toward the front, and the large party in back, probably friends of the waiters, has moved into the table-less space and begun to dance. They're all on the young side—twenties or thirties—but they dance in the hand-holding style of old, men leading ladies, dips and spins.

Bernice's voice cuts through with a depth of emotion one

wouldn't expect. Wendy wonders about the waitress's world, both the world inside her brain, and the one beyond these restaurant walls; the local traumas that imbue her song with a certain beauty, sultry and melancholy, but also something else—pure, maybe—a voice that rises, in its highest registers, above the bullshit of our armored public selves.

"Pretty good," says Michael. He nods toward Bernice.

"Makes you wonder," says Wendy.

"Wonder what?"

"I don't know," says Wendy.

Bernice spots Michael and enthusiastically motions him over. Michael worries he's being teased.

"Go on," Wendy says.

"I shouldn't," says Michael.

"I don't mind, seriously," says Wendy.

The band continues to play, instrumental now. Michael half stands as if still undecided, and Wendy says "go on" again. Michael walks over to Bernice who takes him in her arms.

Michael's eyes are on Wendy, watching for a reaction she refuses to give. Instead she inspects one of the tapestries, coming to the slightly buzzed insight that the love scenes and fight scenes are more or less interchangeable. She turns her eyes from the tapestry to catch Michael in periphery. Bernice has a finger through one of his belt loops. Wendy knows she's in one of those magical New York moments when something out of the ordinary will become, in the form of a dinner party anecdote, an emblem of American resilience, evidence that in our darkest hours, people must and will come together to take comfort in the small things that make life worth living: a minor-key melody, fingers through belt loops, feet moving in unison. Wendy's never a participant in these stories, and she's not now either, eight feet away in her chair.

So even though it's out of character, Wendy stands from her seat. She walks over to Michael and tugs at his elbow, loosening him from the waitress. Bernice goes without argument and begins again to sing.

LATER, IN MICHAEL'S PARKED TRUCK, overlooking the Hudson from the edge of the West Harlem docks, Wendy will lean uncomfortably across the truck's wide center console and lay her head on Michael's shoulder. The windows will be cracked, and the river will smell of fish and refuse, New Jersey on the other side, a shimmering mass of white light, so close you could swim if you had to, launch yourself into the black water and let the current take care of the rest.

Wendy will try to recall Bernice's voice, its tone and timbre, its breathy texture. She will place a hand on the damp unbuttoned area over Michael's breastbone. She will hold her palm to his sternum. She will twist a lock of his chest hair so that it loops around her finger like a ring.)

AMERICAN
AMERICANS
IN
AMERICA

MICHAEL

THE WIND'S TOO STRONG TO ride roofless, but we brave it, gun in the glovebox. My Porsche clanks along in the right-hand lane. It's been due for a tune-up for years. The car crosses the Taconic, paced by Vermont-plated Subarus and shit box hatchbacks bearing Red Sox insignia. White-bearded riders on Harleys from New Hampshire zip past like they're late to audition for the ZZ Top reunion tour. New York plates are bolted to an absurdly high number of vans and SUVs, which gives me pause to wonder where they find city parking. Maybe in the badlands out beyond the limits, like Westchester. Rachel's on my right, wind in her hair, sun on her scorpion. She speaks, but I can't make her out over the noise.

"What did you say?"

"It's fucking freezing."

"You want me to pull over and put the roof up?"

"Fuck no, you pussy."

Rachel twists the volume knob. The tick of an E-MU snare comes clean through my system. I once read an essay that claimed Eminem's popularity wasn't due to his whiteness, but to the clarity of his diction. It seemed racist to me, giving points to a white guy for elocution. I thought the writer was wrong, that the real reason for Em's intelligibility is the sparse perfection of Dre's beats, so much cleaner than the racket turned out by his successors. Then again, I'm always playing the apologist's role, even in my own head, whitesplaining my white taste by way of Dre's endorsement.

We're going through Em's catalogue in chronological order. We skipped *Infinite*, though, the twenty-four-year-old's passable Nas impression that purists consider his official debut. Nothing against the record, but it lacks the nuance of the later oeuvre. Besides, it isn't on Spotify. Rachel slept through most of *The Slim Shady LP*, the true debut, a product of industry rejection, relationship angst, and raising a daughter in Dante's Detroit. Now she's awake and I've dialed in that album's follow-up, *The Marshall Mathers LP*. Rachel yawns.

I want so badly for this music to communicate something to my sister about who I am that runs deeper than taste. I want my favorite rapper's nasal whine to be a musical madeleine that transports Rachel to my headspace during seminal moments. I want her squeezed beside me in Dave Goode's Honda Civic, limbs silky from ecstasy, nodding to "Drug Ballad." I want her at prom when the DJ plays "The Real Slim Shady" and my legs begin moving of their own volition, a foxtrot meets Riverdance that doesn't sync with the beat, but feels too good to stop. I want us to weep during "Stan," and I want her to know how I feel in this moment, now that Lucas is no longer the villain whose exposure would restore moral balance, and Ricky's not the innocent victim I need and believed him to be. This is too much to ask. The car swerves and Rachel tells me to watch the road.

WE AREN'T SURE WHEN BRODER left the house, but my gut says this morning, after four or five hours of restorative sleep on my parents' guest bed. He must have woken at sunrise into the awful awareness of the well-rested man. I imagine he panicked, ditched the gun, and walked five miles to the interstate, where he hitched a ride to Montreal.

I found the gun when I went to wake him. There was no one

in the guest room, just that old children's blanket in a heap on the floor. I thought he may have gone out for air, but then I found the gun. Rachel helped me fish it out with barbecue tongs and seal it in a Ziploc gallon bag.

It was easy to piece things together after that, to look back on what Broder said last night—words that seemed, in the moment, like a madman's rant—and figure out what he meant: that Ricky brought cocaine to Broder's wedding and offered it to the sober bride; that Broder blamed Ricky for Aliana's death; that he'd fantasized for years about exacting revenge.

We took separate cars and searched the streets. When Broder didn't turn up, Rachel, Donny, and I reconvened at the house—our parents still asleep—and I tried calling the detectives. Neither answered; I'd left a dozen crazed messages last night. Rachel discouraged me from calling the local cops for the convincing reasons that (1) the force was comprised of idiots we went to school with, and (2) it didn't seem worth wasting time attempting to convince these idiots that a urine-smelling gun, somehow in our possession, was the weapon in a major murder case. More imperative than finding Broder was getting the gun to the detectives and Donnell out of jail.

I know that identifying the culprit should give me some sense of closure, that the lack of a political motive should mute the inner voice that says all could have been avoided if we hadn't screwed the country with our greed and hubris, then celebrated that screw-up by drinking aged bourbon in the ironic glow of Fitzgerald's green light. But I do not feel exonerated. Because Broder came to me the night of the party. He came and he wanted to talk. He *needed* to talk. In my stoned and selfish state, I refused.

I remember Ricky on Halloween, dressed as a pirate in my grandmother's silks. I remember his hippie phase, the self-sewn patchwork stripes on his cords. His hairy back at the beach. The way he wore tiny watches to emphasize his giant hands. How he rolled such beautiful joints. I remember him in fourth grade, after knocking Steve Wyck to the ground in my defense. He hooked my arm in his and we walked like that—together—back to class.

"I miss Ricky," I say.

Rachel asks if I'm hungry.

WE STOP AT MCDONALD'S. OUTSIDE the vehicle, a grade-school field trip briefly enfolds us like a flock of flamingos, kids wobbly on stick legs, all wearing the same knee-length pink T-shirt. Rachel says, "Dude, have you ever, like, listened to the lyrics on that album? That guy is super rapey, huh?"

"It's a persona," I say, though my heart isn't in it. I've mounted this argument a million times to friends, relatives, and baristas, waving my arms as I exposit on concepts of postmodern posturing, questions of identity and assumption: Em as irony, Em as sincerity in transparency, Em as Internet troll, Em as the freed id of American masculinity, Em as commentary on it all. But, in this moment, I can't bring myself to go there. Because maybe Rachel's right. What is persona but an excuse for one's worst self? Ricky was right too. Eminem isn't the most important artist of our nonexistent generation, but only the most important artist of my own life. And if he'd never been born, then maybe some white kid in Des Moines would never have locked his girlfriend in the trunk of his car, and another white kid in Tacoma would never have opened fire at that mall, and Ricky would be alive. It occurs to me that I know nothing about anything, and that all of my problems come from my always having pretended otherwise. Maybe this is what's meant by privilege.

We smoke against the hood of the Porsche. Rachel slaps her

belly like a bongo drum. We must be a sight, the derivatives trader and his face-tattooed sister wearing a T-shirt that says FUCK COPS.

Inside, the rest area smells of urine despite its glut of competing odors. The school kids have sugared up and now roam the crowded space, sliding across mopped floors and throwing burgers at each other.

Back in the car, I cover the roof. Rachel finishes her fries and falls asleep. Em surveys the anxieties of fatherhood, the dueling strands of love and rage that wind around one another like lengths of barbed wire. I'm reminded of a story by the writer Andre Dubus, who lived in Haverhill, Mass., and wrote with a Masshole sensibility that assuaged my homesickness when I moved to New York. In the story, a good Catholic guy helps his daughter dispose of a corpse after she kills someone drunk driving. It ends with the man gone crazy, yelling at God from his lawn. If it had been one of his sons, the man explains to the Lord, he would have let him rot in jail. But a daughter is different; God can't understand; God only ever had a son.

I imagine Nina in the passenger seat instead of my sister. In this fantasy, Nina's a redhead like Wendy, downy chinned and puffy cheeked. A sun rash blooms on her pale skin. We're coming home from a day at the beach. Her forehead leaves marks on the window. A towel draped over the seat to stop sand from dirtying the Porsche comes loose in her twisting and falls to the floor. I can't picture her face.

DETECTIVE RYAN LOOKS TIRED, BACK curved in T. rex scoliosis, tie already loose, a strip of lettuce crusted to his collar. He's grown a salt-and-pepper beard that adds five years to his appearance, but helps to hide his second chin. An unplucked bridge connects his eyebrows' distant boroughs. The gun sits on a steel tray that belongs in a dentist's office, a resting spot for the dentist's torture tools. It glimmers beneath Detective Quinn's desk lamp, still slightly wet from its bath in the toilet.

"To summarize," says Quinn. "A heroin addict, who you hadn't seen in twenty years until he turned up on the night of the murder, disappeared for a week, then took a four-and-a-half-hour bus ride . . ."

"Sometimes more with traffic," I add.

Rachel gives me a look, but I know from TV that timelines are important.

"Why don't we round up and say an even five hours?"

"I think that's unnecessary," I say. "Maybe just note that it sometimes takes longer. It also might have taken less time if he took an express bus."

Quinn taps his skull to indicate he's stored the information.

"I'll start again: a heroin addict, who you hadn't seen in twenty years until he conveniently"—I don't like his *conveniently*—"showed up on the night of the murder, disappeared for a week, took a four-and-a-half-hour bus ride—give or take, considering traffic and whether the bus he took was express—to the Berkshires, where he walked five miles from the bus station to your parents' doorstep, the location of which he remembered from a visit he made twenty years ago. Upon arrival, you invited this alleged killer inside, where he confessed to the murder, to which you responded by doing nothing. Correct?"

I nod.

"He then went to sleep, woke sometime around sunrise, conveniently"—that word again—"left the murder weapon in the toilet, before walking another five miles to the highway, where he hitched a ride on a bread truck bound for Canada."

"Bread truck was just an example. It could have been any kind of truck. Or not a truck at all. Maybe just a regular car. Maybe somewhere other than Canada."

Ryan says, "Noted."

Quinn continues: "Then, instead of alerting state and local police of this dangerous fugitive's possible whereabouts, you decided to take a three-and-a-half-hour drive—making good time due to light traffic, and only stopping once for McDonald's and a bathroom break—directly to this precinct to present Detective Ryan and myself with the murder weapon, allowing the fugitive ample time to cross the Canadian border."

"Yes, exactly," I say.

"Okay then," says Quinn.

"When you say it, it sounds . . ."

"Ridiculous?"

"What about the gun?" I say.

"What about the gun?"

"It's right there."

We all look. Ryan scratches his bearded butt chin. Quinn pokes his teeth with the tip of a mechanical pencil. I try to say something, but find myself dry-mouthed. Rachel tags in.

"Can't you, like, do ballistics or whatever?"

"Sure," says Quinn. "And we will. It takes time."

I scan the room for the map board on which newspaper cutouts are connected to mug shots via dry-erase marker. If this were basic cable, then I'd be the suspect, the unsuspecting mark in a vast conspiracy, torn between my distrust of the cops and my fear of retribution from a vaguely ethnic underworld gang. My name would be circled in red, the constant at which all points connect. In real life, the white guy is presumed innocent. Why pursue him when there's an easier mark with a court-appointed lawyer, like Donnell?

Besides, these detectives aren't the savants we know from TV. Quinn resembles a cornstalk with his amber waves of flattop and the willowy body that sways beneath the ceiling fan's artificial wind. He stares at my sister's T-shirt. She turned it inside out before we came inside, but the silkscreened letters can still be seen, backward, through the thin poly-blend.

"Spock cuf?" Quinn says. "What's that, like, a Star Trek thing?"

"Sure," says Rachel.

He gives her a Vulcan salute. Rachel offers a peace sign in return.

"The gun," I manage.

"Look," Quinn says. "Even if the bullets match, and even if this alleged guy's prints are on the weapon, how do we know you didn't put them there yourself to help your pal Donnell?"

"You're saying I . . ."

"I'm not saying anything. Just that we'll look into it. But right now we've got a guy going to trial, and we have a motive, and multiple witnesses, and an extremely damning piece of evidence. Of course, we'll continue to investigate if anything comes up, but right now we're happy with the story we've got."

I look to Ryan for help, but the other detective has sat down to rest, fingers pressed against his temples like he's listening hard or not at all. Rachel smacks her gum and blows an oversized bubble. Quinn holds up his pencil, but Rachel pops the bubble on her own.

"I feel faint," I say, and grab the doorknob, of all things, to steady myself. The knob turns and the bolt unlatches, and I'm dragged halfway into the hall. I pull myself back in and search for the right thing to say, a password that might unlock these detectives' vaulted hearts.

"Everybody grieves differently," says Quinn. I didn't take him for a pop psychologist, but perhaps my own response is so pre-scribed that the detective's on autopilot, repeating platitudes from a department-issued handbook on grief. "We don't always get the kind of closure we want. I understand this impulse to keep searching, to find a story that better suits our needs."

"This isn't a story," I say.

"Whatever you want to call it."

"Broder, he took a real gun—that gun—and shot . . ."

"Ricky," Rachel says.

"That's possible," says Ryan.

"Donnell's in jail right now. In a cell, a real cell, actual jail. And his daughter—god, Jackie, I don't . . . Don't you care?"

"Of course we do," says Ryan. "Like I said, we'll look into it."

I let myself slide down to the floor.

"I want to see him," I say. "Donnell. I want to see him."

MY CLOSEST POINT OF COMPARISON, smell-wise, to this prison, is the Port Authority bus depot basement. But even that cesspool of slop is less nauseating than what permeates this place, an insti-tutional haze comprised of foot fungus, vending-machine ham sandwiches, and human feces that comes up through the grates in a continuous wave.

"I guess you get used to it," I say, and look around. Visitors pinch noses while the visited inmates remain calmly anosmic. I want to present a strong front for Donnell, to look right for the part that I'm here to perform, that of gung-ho redeemer on a mission for justice, undaunted by odors that stand in his way. The avocado tint Rachel's cheeks have taken on does not recommend her for the sidekick role.

"Used to what?" says Donnell.

I mime sniffing the air, choking on fumes.

"Oh that. A sewer backed up this morning. I don't think it's usually this bad."

The room looks like a cafeteria, but there are bars on the windows and a lineman-esque guardbot blocks the exit. The primary activity appears to be eating, and the prefix I'd use to mark its style is: *speed-*. Burgers vanish into faces, leaving drippings on tables and grease-spotted paper bags. Chicken bones pile up like Jenga tiles. Fingers are licked. No one is impeded by the smell.

The inmates are young, baby-faced twentysomethings, maybe even some teens. Their visitors are uniformly female, some with infants or toddlers in tow. Most could be mistaken for students, which would make Donnell their teacher. Except that, today, his air of erudition has been swapped for fatigue. His Afro has lost volume. His lips are dry and chapped. He hasn't mentioned Carrie Bradshaw even once.

I offer my ChapStick and Donnell accepts. The guardbot beeps and turns in our direction. A blue light flashes then ceases and the beeping stops. The ChapStick has been deemed non-contraband. Mouth closed, Donnell drags the waxy tip across both lips, then reverses direction and applies a second coat. Normally I'm not a sharer of ChapStick—too fearful of germs—and I hope that this offer represents something larger: my willingness to swap resources and fluids, to make personal concessions for the good of his cause. Donnell returns the item and the guardbot turns away.

"How is it?" I ask. "In here?"

He shrugs as if to say: look around and take a wild fucking guess. I sense an aggression that I don't hold against him. He doesn't get why I'm here, or why I've brought the face-tattooed delinquent by my side, as if I'm the leader of a Scared Straight program and Donnell's a human warning to naïve white girls considering careers as black American men.

"I'm here to help," I say, and he remains silent, brushes nonexistent lint from the breast of his jumpsuit. I tell him about Broder's arrival last night, relay the subsequent chain of events: Broder's confession to deaf ears, finding the gun in the toilet, our frustrating meeting with Ryan and Quinn. I highlight positive aspects, like the promise of the coming ballistics report. I look to Rachel for support but her cheeks have turned an even darker green.

"Jesus," Donnell says. "So this guy's in Canada. And you didn't think to alert, say, border patrol?"

"I thought the best thing to do was get here quickly with the gun."

"That's what you thought?" Donnell says.

It occurs to me that this morning, in my panic and haste, I may have made some wrong decisions in regard to procedure. And by wrong, I mean selfish. I didn't want the cops taking prints from the toilet lid and turning my parents' house upside down. I didn't want to wait hours for the sketch artist to arrive. I wanted the momentum of my Porsche on the highway. I wanted Em in my ears, Wendy in my zip code, Ricky's headstone in my rearview. Now Broder's gone, and Donnell may be screwed until he turns up again. Detective Quinn said he found a partial fingerprint on the SD bracelet retrieved from Donnell's apartment. If Quinn planted the print on the bracelet, then who's to say he won't plant one on the gun?

It all feels surreal: this bizarre causal chain, this week of my life. It's a nightmare from which I've yet to wake, until of course I must accept that I'm already awake. Maybe all causal chains feel surreal to guys like me—derivatives traders, keepers of the status quo—because reality's a thing we've been conditioned to un-see until it's too late. And then we wake into the ugliness, and we become woke; we wake into our own unbearable wokeness. And we try—half-heartedly and much too late—to fix the messes we've made. Only at easing our guilt do we succeed.

"Here's what I don't get," says Rachel. "If Broder stole the bracelet, then pawned it for bus fare, then how did the cops get it and plant it in the first place?"

"Maybe it's not the same bracelet," I say.

"Of course it's not the same bracelet," says Donnell.

In my mind, police corruption still belongs in the fictional realm, but I'm coming around. I alter my earlier definition of privilege to include the expectation of integrity in dealings with the law.

"We can't dwell on mistakes," I say, meaning mine. "We need a plan."

"What I need is a lawyer," says Donnell.

"Right," I say. "A lawyer."

"Because the one I have is useless."

"Okay. Then we'll get you a lawyer."

He leans across the table.

"And you're gonna pay for it?"

"Pay for it, right. Huh."

Donnell crosses his arms.

"No, no," I say. "I mean sure, I'm happy to pay. The thing is that my finances . . ."

"I see," says Donnell.

"But we'll figure it out. I can sell, well—I have assets. I have sneakers."

"You have sneakers?" he says. "Because lawyers get paid in sneakers."

Rachel suddenly sprints for the trash. I worry the guardbot will mistake her for an inmate and light up her brain stem with five hundred volts. But she reaches the garbage can safely. Inmates and visitors watch. Her theatrical purge cuts the tension in the room. People laugh and clap. The guardbot wheels to the vending machine. It puts a claw in a keyhole and buys Rachel a bottled water out of the kindness of its humanely programmed heart.

"Look, Michael," says Donnell. "I appreciate your willingness to help. And I'm glad to know this guy's out there, and that we know who he is. But what I need right now is money. I'm going broke in here, missing shifts at work, bills piling up. And the kind of legal team I need won't be cheap. Do you see what I'm saying?"

I'm close enough to see the spreading dampness on the armpits of his jumpsuit, his white-knuckle grip against its loose cotton sleeves.

"It should have been me," I say. "In here. It should have been me in here instead of you."

"It shouldn't be either of us. It should be the guy who's actually guilty."

"I'm the constant at the center of the map board, the obvious choice to play the unsuspecting mark. If this were a movie, I'd be the lead. You'd be, I don't know, the cool best friend."

"Best friend, huh?"

"Good friend?" I try.

Donnell says, "This is the problem with you finance guys. You think you're the star of the movie. You always think you're the star."

WE DRIVE BACK TO THE city under smog-painted sky. It's a balmy evening, a few weeks from Christmas, and the townhouses twinkle once we're off the highway, and trees are for sale outside the bodegas. Hundreds of drones converge on Columbus Circle, empty of product, returning to base to meet the clear-skies curfew.

Rachel double-parks outside Wendy's dad's. She keeps the car running and I head inside.

"Hello," someone says, when I unlock the door. I don't recognize the voice, and can barely hear it over the music, an arena rock anthem playing loud.

Lucas Van Lewig sits in the living room, in Fred's easy chair. He's got the air of an ex–college quarterback gone on to corporate success based on family connections and a firm handshake: sandy hair, great teeth. He wears a distressed bomber jacket that, despite looking like it belongs to midcentury American action abroad, retails, I know, for four figures at Saks. His eyes roam the length of me, as if this Scantron-style assessment will bear weight on our conversation. I'm conscious of my poor posture and dad-bod. The song ends and another begins. This one I recognize.

"Freddie Mercury was a genius," Lucas says, as if it's an inarguable fact that pertains to our encounter. "He never got the critical admiration he deserved, but critics are scum, as I'm sure you understand, and if a flamboyantly gay man's ability to make aggressively hetero sports fans chant and weep isn't a sign of true iconoclasm, then I don't know what is. You've got to remember this was pre-Drake. Mercury never saw the dawn of the metrosexual or the sensitive asshole. He never knew the Poptimist movement. But history will be kind. I can feel it in my bones. Is this real life or is this just fantasy? Profound? It's almost biblical."

"Is Wendy here?" I say.

"I thought you'd be taller," Lucas replies.

His voice is deep as a leading man's and flirtatiously deadpan. It's like he's got popcorn caught in his throat. Like he's getting rimmed through a hole in the seat cushion as we speak.

"And better-looking," he adds. "But look at you. You're losing your hair."

He waves as if swiping a dating app, replacing me with someone more to his taste. I instinctively raise a hand to cover my scalp.

"The Rogaine's not working as advertised," I say, unsure how we've arrived at this discussion of my failings.

"Propecia?" he offers.

"Kills the libido."

Lucas gives an understanding nod despite the fact that his hair is thick as bear fur, effervescent as chemical sunset, coiffed and berry-smelling as *Baywatch*-era David Hasselhoff's. It's possible his erections suffer for this vanity, but it seems unlikely. He sips from a tiny bottle of Coca-Cola using a pink children's twisty straw. When he's done sipping, he puts the straw in his mouth, rolls it around on his tongue.

"Cuban Coke," he says. "It's the new Mexican Coke. Very refreshing. Want one?"

I shake my head.

"The Mexicans switched from cane sugar to high fructose a few years back. People still buy by the caseload. It's these tiny bottles that sell the product, their nostalgic appeal. The greatest trick the devil ever pulled is convincing the public to ignore the fine print. It's how your industry got in the mess it's in. Luckily for me, the Cubans are still uncompromised. If there's one thing Castro instilled, it's a belief in the superiority of raw cane. I respect him for that, if nothing else."

"You haven't told me where Wendy is."

"She left already. The keynote starts in an hour. I need to head down there myself. I just stopped by to drop off some Cuban Coke for Fred. The guy can't get enough. I mean, at his age. But a man needs a vice. I stopped smoking a year ago, I still get the craving."

He opens his mouth and lets the straw drop. We watch it flutter to the carpet.

"You're wondering what it was like to grow up under my father. Most men have a story that begins: *The most important thing my father ever told me*, and whatever that thing is, it's almost universally some idiotic lesson gleaned from his experiences in love or war. My father never told me anything."

"What keynote?" I say.

"Greg's keynote speech at DisruptNY. I hope you'll join me. It's really a good one. I wrote a lot of it myself, though your wife read it this morning and threw in some bon mots. We're launching the product and I think you should be there. I expect it will clarify some things."

"What things?"

"The future of the human race, for one. The end of unemployment. The dawn of augmented man. But we should start smaller."

"The suit?" I say, remembering my G-chat with Greg.

"Ah, so Ricky told you."

"Just the name," I say. "I only know the name."

"Well, did he tell you that you're the sole benefactor of his Sykodollars? All his SD will be passed on to you, Michael Mixner, and after tonight, there will be quite a lot of it."

"What do you mean?"

He takes the bracelet from his pocket and puts it in my hands. The item's heavier than I imagined. Ricky's initials are engraved on the case's back and a small curly hair is caught in the clasp. I wonder if the hair is his, if it got pulled loose when Broder ripped the bracelet from his wrist.

"GPS," Lucas explains. "I like to keep track of what I put into the world. The pawnbroker let it go for fifty bucks. As for the anonymity thing: I mean, it's true, for the most part. The government has no idea who's holding these assets. But I do. Once people started getting deep in SD, I needed a way to track where it was. The real question is why I'm choosing to tell you when I could have kept this information to myself. But I'm a rich man, Michael, I don't need the money. If I'd kept it, then what kind of guy would I be?"

"A bad one?"

"One of the first conversations I had with Cortes was about you. He was telling me about his trader friend, how his guilt about the crash had turned him into a half-assed Marxist. We had a good laugh about that. Cortes thought it was positively hilarious. You, with your loft and your Porsche, singing the Internationale. Ha-ha, am I right? So we're laughing and laughing, and then there's a pause. And Cortes turns to me and says, you know, I've thought a lot about it, and I've decided Marx was wrong. You know that thing about religion being the opiate of the masses? Well, Marx was wrong. So I said, okay, I'll bite, if religion isn't the opiate of the masses then what is? And you know what Cortes responds?"

"Opium," I say. He'd used the same line on me.

"Correct," Lucas says. "He said opium is the opiate of the masses."

"A searing insight."

"We were stoned off our gourds. I'm not usually a weed guy, but the shit he had, Jesus. Maybe that's why we were laughing so hard."

"Maybe," I say.

"But it wasn't until later that I got what he meant. See, Marx thought that people want answers to the big, old questions, like what we're doing on this earth, where we go when we die, and why anyone would choose to watch golf on TV. But Cortes, I realized, knew better. People don't want answers. They just want to buy shit. Opium you can hold. You can hold it, and smoke it, and pay a hooker to blow it up your anus with a straw. Opium's retail, that's what Cortes meant."

His phone buzzes and he looks at his screen. "Okay," Lucas says. "The limo's downstairs. We can finish this talk on the way."

"I have a ride," I reply.

"Suit yourself," he says, and leaves.

I shut the windows and turn off the lights. Before locking up, I look into Wendy's bedroom. I know she's been staying here, but the evidence is scant: contact case on the nightstand, an empty water glass. The bed's nicely made and her suitcase is closed in a corner on the floor.

GREG MOVES ACROSS THE DAIS in wood-heeled chukka boots he occasionally stomps for effect. He's got more hair than I remember, a thick top-mop that covers what I'm pretty sure was recently a bald spot. He reminisces on his days as a point guard, describing the naysayers who said that a five-six white kid from the Maryland suburbs would never play college ball. He tells of his diverse array of teammates, their strong sense of brotherhood, how sports prepares one for business through the acquisition of discipline and leadership qualities.

His anecdote culminates in the revelation that, during Greg's senior year, alum and eBay founder Pierre Omidyar subsidized the team's uniforms. Greg stamps out each syllable of the mogul's name with his heel as if it's a war chant, as if the audience knows to join in celebrating not only the entrepreneur, but the system that rewards a PEZ collector with a billion-dollar IPO.

Greg manages to segue from basketball to politics by alluding to Omidyar's humanitarian ventures, including his micro-funding efforts in Zimbabwe. He explains Omidyar's stand against WikiLeaks, which leads to a discussion of the political responsibilities of business leaders, which further leads to a biased reading of the current economic crisis, and the way that the extreme left as well as the extreme right have co-opted social media, and how Greg's working to bring voice back to the reasonable mainstream. The phrase *Reasonable Mainstream* appears on the wall, and I imagine this isn't the last time I'll hear or see it, that a young senator, somewhere, is taking notes, preparing to dazzle the next RNC with a unifying sermon.

Greg moves on to the concept of work. He talks about being raised by a single mom who hustled two jobs to put food on the table and save for Greg's college fund. She cleaned houses in the mornings, bagged groceries at night. He says he used to feel embarrassed by the demeaning nature of his mother's work, afraid that peers would see her in their homes or at Safeway, in her sweat-blotched bandannas, with her varicose veins. He used to feel embarrassed, but his mother did not. She was proud of her work and the things it allowed her to provide; proud of her reputation as a cleaner, never stealing like certain *other* practitioners in her trade—and here I sense a racial element to Greg's insinuation, though no one else in the crowd appears to notice—proud of the trust these wealthy families placed in her hands, allowing access to their costliest possessions. Looking back, Greg is no longer ashamed. He's grateful for the sacrifice his mother made, a sacrifice which, he now realizes, she made for his benefit. Still, at the time, things were tough. Working so hard meant his mother rarely had time to spend with her son, and the time they did have was spent before the TV in fatigued silence.

"There were no homemade dinners, only instant noodles and frozen pizza," Greg explains to knowing nods from the crowd, a multi-ethnic survey of techies, ad guys, and Ivy League MBAs, some of whom, I imagine, come from similar backgrounds, watched their parents do slave work at menial jobs so their children could eat açaí bowls in the Stanford dining halls, and spend semesters in Goa studying contact improv, and settle down, after college, to six-figure salaries at places like Google and American Express. People, in other words, not so different from me.

"My mother rarely made it to any of my games," Greg adds, presumably for the parents in the room, Park Slope freelancers who set their own hours around their kids' schedules, and who wouldn't dream of missing the lute and drum performance that concludes little Madison's Ancient Instruments class. Greg looks wistful as he stares past the crowd to the room's back wall and wipes what may well be a tear from his cheek, though the lighting and distance make it difficult to tell.

The phrase *#WorkWillSetYouFree* replaces *Reasonable Mainstream* on the wall. A photo appears beneath the hashtag: young Greg, maybe ten years old. A mesh jersey drapes like a gown on his undeveloped frame. His mother stands behind him, smiling with pride, the implication being that this rare opportunity to see her son play has imbued this worn-out woman with uncommon joie de vivre.

"But what if," Greg says. "What if there were a way for my mom to be at my games *while* she was at work?"

After asking this question, he steps to the side. The image of Greg and his mom at the basketball court is replaced by another, the same one I saw on a billboard in midtown on the car ride here: a photograph of a construction site populated by male models, while a blond woman wearing a white negligee and an expression of cartoonish lust looks on from the side.

"Now, as you can see, this man is at work. And this woman, well, for all we know she may be at work too," Greg says, having fluidly dropped the tearful tone and returned to his previous swagger. His comment is followed by sparse chuckles from male members of the crowd, which are instantly silenced by reproachful stares from their female companions, who suspect any joke at a sex worker's expense, and any image that so closely adheres to the clichés of male fantasy, even coming from a speaker who, like his mother with the wealthy families whose houses she cleaned, has done so much, already, to earn their trust.

"I'm going to ask you to do something," says Greg. "I want you to reach down under your seat and find the AR helmet that was placed there before you arrived. I want you all to put your helmets on. I promise they don't bite."

More chuckles and murmurs, but people put on the helmets, eager for the part of this talk that they came to hear, the part where the promised product will be unveiled. I'm eager too, and a little bit scared, so I put on the helmet and watch the work site come to life before my eyes in a seamless 3-D that surrounds me on all sides. Worker-models spread mortar and lay bricks, and the negligeed woman bends to lift a wrench that has fallen to the ground. This causes some groans from the women in the crowd, though most remain silent, awaiting Greg's explanation, still anticipating whatever comes next.

We watch this play out for a moment, and then there's a rupture, and the room goes dark. When things come back into focus, us helmeted onlookers have been transported to an entirely different scene. The same cast of model-workers is here, but instead of laying bricks, they—and we—watch kids play basketball. Our formerly negligeed woman is wearing a sundress, and her face, we now see, resembles Greg's mom's, though in her current incarnation she looks fit and robust. Through the magic of augmented reality, one of the kids playing ball is Young Greg, and his model/mom cheers as her son sinks a jumper.

"These people," Greg says, through a speaker in my ear. "These people are also at work."

At his words, Greg's model/mom stands. She steps out of the bleachers, and steps out of the image, and steps down onto the dais where she poses beside her now-grown son. It's unclear if this woman is here in the flesh, or if the optics on my helmet have created this illusion. Either way, she looks real. In unison, Adult Greg and his model/mom begin to undress. There's a gasp from the audience, and another, smaller gasp, when it becomes clear that beneath their clothes they are not nude, but are, instead, wearing skin-tight nude bodysuits, conspicuous only for their few tiny zippers and the absence of genitals, nipples, and hair.

"We're living in something very close to a utopia," Greg says. "Food is in abundance. So is medical care. Cars run on sunlight. Meat grows on trees. If you cut off your finger you can print a new one at home and fly in Drone MD to inject you with anesthetic and sew it back on. All of us in this room are better off than we'd have been even fifty years ago."

Behind them plays a montage of half a century's progress. Depression-era amputees in wood and wicker wheelchairs are replaced by laughing kids who pop and lock on titanium prosthetics in a dance class being taught by Rihanna. We see various firsts: first mobile phone, first home computer, first AR helmet. The camera pans a grove of stem-cell steak trees where slabs of meat hang like heavy fruit.

"But not everything's perfect," Greg says. "We, in this room, are better off, but not everyone is. The jobs that people like my mom needed in order to make ends meet, well, a lot of those jobs no longer exist."

A new montage plays. We watch bots build bots; we watch

bots wait tables, run tills in bodegas and clothing stores. We see a room full of bots wearing headsets, taking customer service calls. And where this leads: faces of the homeless, tents in Tompkins Square Park, scenes from an #Occupy rally.

Greg explains that one solution to this problem is to pass this bill, the UBI. But when he considers this solution, he thinks of his mother and her pride. He wonders whether she would have wanted a handout, whether that would have made her feel good about her position in life, about her larger contributions to the world. He says that when he thinks long and hard, he knows that this solution is highly problematic. That when people get free money, they don't value it in the same way that they would if the money was earned. That their shame in receiving these handouts makes them spend money in inappropriate ways. They don't save. They buy drugs. Instead of solving our problems, these handouts create a need for further handouts, for more expensive programs subsidized by the government. He cites a study of dubious origin. He tells the crowd that this country was founded on the idea of work, that it's a place where every woman deserves the chance to feel pride in her labor. Where every man deserves the opportunity not to take, but to earn. He says that, when it comes down to it, the problem is not about resources, but about their distribution model. And that's what he's proposing to fix with this suit.

The phrase *distribution model* brings visible relief, as Greg returns to a vernacular familiar to this crowd. I can see, on their faces, that these people beside me want so badly to believe that Greg is correct, that there might be a solution to this problem— which, ultimately for them, is the problem of their guilt—that doesn't involve an increase in their taxes, a blow to their business and savings accounts.

Greg tells us we can take off our helmets. We do, and his model/mom disappears. Once again, he's alone onstage. He still wears the bodysuit, that was real. A blueprint of it appears behind him, complete with dozens of complicated inserts. The words *The Suit*™ appear on the wall.

Greg explains about the sensors and the unprecedented data they'll be used to create. He explains how the data will be used for scientific research and medical advancement. The diagnostic possibilities are limitless. The Suit™'s capacity for early detection could increase average life expectancy by years. He explains the buy-in options, that workers will be paid more for wearing The Suit™ in conjunction with helmets. He explains that The Suit™ can be worn by anyone, anywhere, and for any length of time. That the sky is the limit on how much money a person might make. He explains that a person can even wear The Suit™ while working another job, if so inclined. That a person can wear it to sleep.

The awed silence in the room has come to an end. People snap photos and some record video. They type into tablets, laptops, and phones. I imagine the tweetstorm beginning to rage.

Greg says, "Now I want you to reach out and grab your neighbors' hands."

The audience responds in all seriousness, turning themselves into a set of paper dolls. They grew up with shit like this and aren't embarrassed. My sweaty palms meet other sweaty palms.

"Feel the connectivity," says Greg. "Feel that deep human frequency. Listen to it hum."

I TRY TO MOVE QUICKLY, but I'm caught in the flow of human traffic, people beelining for the bathroom, or better cell service in the lobby, or a cocktail bar on Carmine Street that was reviewed in last week's "Tables for Two." Wendy catches my eye and steps in my direction before being intercepted by a cheek-kissing acquaintance. Even from five yards away, I can see her cringe at the transfer of microbes to face. It takes all her strength not to wipe the mauve imprint with the sleeve of her sweater. I know because I know my wife.

When I reach the front row, she's able to escape the attempts of another aggressive schmoozer and pull me backstage. We land in a green room where bottles are popped, Greg's being toasted, and the *Rocky* theme plays from someone's phone, which has been placed in an ice bucket to amplify its sound. Lillian pours champagne into plastic flutes, spilling most on the floor. She winks as she hands me mine in lieu of a hello. I put the flute down and push past the handful of Communitiv.ly employees who mill about Greg. "It's like I'm a tiger," he says, "and the stage is my cage."

Wendy follows me into a de facto dressing area, floor messy with what must be Greg's rejected performance-wear: leather pants, fur blazer, knee-high biker boots. She gestures to the discards. "I had to convince him the Keith Richards look doesn't work when you're five-six and don't play guitar."

I think she expects me to laugh, that her coworker's clownish lack of self-awareness can unite us in snark as it has in the past. She looks nervous, like she sometimes gets with strangers: back stiff, chin to chest, voice trailing at sentence's end.

"The speech was something, though," she continues. "You must admit he's got presence. The audience ate from his hands."

She forms her palms into a bowl to illustrate what she's described.

"Reasonable mainstream," I say. "It's good. And that suit."

"You mean *The* Suit," says Wendy. "The Suit TM."

"Right. TM."

"It's brilliant, don't you think?"

I'm not sure what I think. It's been a long day. I know that The Suit™ may kill the UBI. It may end unemployment and eradicate the concept of personal space. It may be the decisive tool that turns millions of humans into consumerist cyborgs. It may cure cancers, diabetes, and ALS. It may take capitalism to its logical conclusion, the last stop on a journey that began when the first Egyptian sent silk up the Nile, and ends here, in this green room, as the weight of Greg's most recent bowel movement is AirDropped to the cloud. The reach of this product seems to be without limit, and whether this is a good thing—an even tradeoff for the complete annihilation of the ad-blocking software that protects our fragile, American souls—is better left for the artists of the future to decide.

All I know for certain is that, right now, I don't care. Maybe tomorrow, in the elucidating light of another sun-bleached morning, I will wake to the throb of my conscience. I will remember Ricky's body in the open casket, and I'll remember the fear on Donnell's face. I will recall Donnell's need for funds, and his even greater need for Ricky's SD bracelet. But here, in this moment, I'm looking at Wendy, and all I selfishly see is what the object on my wrist means for us: debts erased from the ledger, amends made to her dad, a chance to let the guilt and resentment rise like steam, leaving us stripped and clean; the way it opens our future like a long-clenched fist that has, without warning, softened its grip.

I say her name and touch her chin. I try to gently nudge it upward so her eyes meet mine. She shakes me off and steps back. I fall forward and try again to stroke her face, but she pushes me away. A hiss whistles through Wendy's teeth.

"Sorry," I say.

She lets out a breath, acknowledges her overreaction. She

removes a mirror from her purse and checks her reflection, moves a strand of hair behind her ear. She says, "I look like hell."

"You don't," I say.

In fact, she looks gorgeous, a subtle blush job hiding any remnants of bedbug warfare. Wendy's made-up face offers comforting wisdom: the past can't be erased, but it can be hidden until it's forgotten, buried beneath layers of powder and pigment.

"I'm sorry too," Wendy says. She means for overreacting, but also for more, it seems, from her refusal to meet my eyes or accept an embrace.

"I'm sorrier," I say back, and spread my arms to show the breadth of my remorse. "I fucked up. I know I fucked up. But I can fix it now."

I hold out my hand and show her the bracelet. She doesn't ask questions, but I sense she understands what it means. Maybe Lucas already explained. Wendy raises her chin so that our eyes align. She puts a fingernail at the nexus of her brows, drags it down across her nose and over her mouth.

"I fucked up," I say.

"I fucked Lucas," she says.

THE KIND OF DRINKING WE'RE doing doesn't warrant toasts or salutations or even the comforting clap of a sisterly hand across one's spine. Only the liquor will get rid of this feeling, and only after Rachel and I finish this bottle and I stumble to bed and go black.

Tom Breem's press conference plays on TV. He explains why he voted against the UBI. The Suit™, Breem thinks, provides a better solution to the unemployment problem. "An American solution," he says.

In the end, Breem wasn't the deciding vote. Six other Democrats switched from yea to nay. All cited The Suit™ as a mitigating factor. Beyond these walls, my colleagues surely celebrate; the result of the vote means our industry's saved. There will be no looting or riots tonight. Even the radicals seem strangely compliant. We've reached another inevitable point on the journey from status quo to status quo.

Soon we're burping, a chorus of escaped air. Rachel burps the alphabet. She burps the national anthem. We are burping and drinking and all I know is it's dark: this lightless room, the droneless sky.

WENDY

IT'S A BAD DAY FOR the beach, overcast with intermittent thunder. I like the cool wind off the water, clouds changing shape as they move across the sky. The Coast Guard used to store artillery here. The old fort is covered in graffiti. Condoms and bottles cover its sandy floor. It's the kind of place where they find bodies on cop shows. A man fumbles with his girlfriend's zipper and trips. There, in the dark, lies a decomposing corpse.

Despite the damp, the graffiti looks fresh: uranium greens and popping oranges outlined in silver. None of it is beautiful or artistically rendered, not like the subway trains of my Manhattan childhood. Today's spray-can artists shoot and run. They leave tags or simple logos, rudimentary marks of existence, poorly rendered self-promotional campaigns. No one takes the time to stencil belabored visions. This is art that captures the ephemeral moment; you can see, in the fluidity of the lines, the speed with which one gets from A to B. One thing I have now is time.

I spread the blanket and we sit, me on the blanket, Olivia suspended on the band of linen stretched between my knees. I've begun to dress like the women in the catalogues that arrive on my doorstep unsolicited. My colors are earth tones and muted blues. My fabrics drape loosely and flow. Beneath them, The Suit™ hugs my skin. Its aerating system lets the breeze inside.

I rock my daughter in the hammock of my skirt, attempting to match the ocean's laps, which swing in a kind of ideal cursive, both slack and exact. Olivia smiles. Spit pools at the corners of her mouth. Her eyes follow the path of a drone on the shoreline. Seagulls scatter.

The Suit™ measures my body's mechanisms: its waves and punctuations, the regulated movements of water and blood. This information bounces off satellites and towers. It swims invisibly through the air. Once the data leaves my body, then it's no longer mine, and, in a sense, I find that freeing, like a purge or a cleanse. What, after all, do these numbers mean? They are immaterial representations. I retain the fleshly stuff of life.

The beach's only other occupants are a couple of young men who wear bathing suits despite the sky's sunless state, and a female counterpart, fully clothed. I can't tell if any of them wear Suits™ beneath. Not everyone does, though it's much more common among the young.

The trio look like they're having fun. They drink canned margaritas and kick a semi-deflated soccer ball. The men bury each other in sand. When the ball becomes too deflated to kick, they take turns wearing it on their heads. Olivia likes their laughter. I like hers.

The trio reminds me of Michael and Ricky and me. Michael walking on his heels in hot sand to protect the tender balls of his feet. Ricky wearing my sun hat and doing Audrey Hepburn. I wanted to wrap them around each other and fit myself in the alcoves. I wanted to love Ricky because Michael loved him. I was a different person then, laid across those hours, half burnt, half in love.

The drone circles back and hovers just overhead. I'm used to surveillance. I like to imagine Lucas stationed at a monitor, observing his daughter's growth. He hasn't reached out. I'm not certain he knows she exists.

THE LAST TIME I SAW Michael in person was after Greg's keynote at DisruptNY. I watched his physical reaction when I told him: body falling under gravity's pull, a sharp increase in the speed of his breath. Michael fell to his knees and wrapped his arms around my calves. For a moment, he said nothing. Then he stood. He stepped away and paced, building speed as he circled the room, nearly tripping over Greg's scattered clothes.

A few seconds later, he came to a halt. He spoke in a modulated voice. He said that it—my betrayal—didn't matter. He understood why I'd done it. He was upset and he was mad, but he said he understood.

Michael kept insisting we could make it work. We were both in tears. I told him I was sorry, that I was so sorry. He asked if I still loved him and I said that I did. But, I said, love doesn't mean wanting to make things work. And I was tired of the effort. I was tired.

Michael's face resembled our daughter's in her minute of life, the look of desperation as she tried to clear the fluid from her lungs. They had the same almond eyes.

I'D LATER LEARN THAT MICHAEL left, the following day, for Montreal. He went looking for Broder. He returned, months later, bearded and alone.

I know about the beard because I saw him last week on the TV news, seated in a courtroom beside Donnell Sanders. Michael, it seems, has used his new fortune to retain, for Sanders, an elite defense team. To the courts, Michael has offered Ricky's SD bracelet as evidence of Sanders's innocence. For these altruistic deeds, the media has deemed him a crusader for justice. I imagine his new beard helps with this image.

But on the news, Michael looked downcast and bedraggled.

His eyes were bloodshot. His suit was unkempt. My guess is that he spends his nights lying sleepless, blaming himself for Broder's disappearance and his own failure to find him up north. My guess is that, despite the media's portrayal of Michael as Donnell Sanders's pasty white savior—a role he always fantasized he'd play—Michael knows that the prosecution will capitalize on Broder's absence. He knows that, unless the jury returns with a not-guilty verdict, no expensive legal team, or exonerating bracelet, or heartfelt testimony, will make up for Michael's initial mistake.

We're only one week into the trial, but a not-guilty verdict is already looking unlikely. The prosecution managed to pull the jury from Ricky's Tribeca neighborhood, meaning it's mostly made up of wealthy Caucasians. Three of the jurors work in finance. Two have personal ties to the police. Jay Devor will testify as a prosecution witness. And the prosecution claims that the gun Michael found contained Sanders's fingerprints. According to a piece I read in this morning's *Times*, accusations of police misconduct are incredibly difficult to prove. It has been reported that Sanders's attorneys have requested that their client plead out to a lesser charge—murder in the second degree.

SHORTLY AFTER THE SUIT™ LAUNCHED, a story surfaced, blaming me for fabricating Ricky's patronage of a nonexistent small-business grant and his support of GLAAD. Lillian wasn't mentioned in the article, nor was Communitiv.ly's Project Pinky campaign. In fact, nothing connecting Communitiv.ly to The Suit™ has surfaced. To distance the company from the scandal, Lillian let me go. My severance was more than fair. I've rented a little place here in the Rockaways. It doesn't feel like New York, so much as a small town filled with transplanted New Yorkers.

Michael sold our apartment, and has begun to pay off our various debts. He reimbursed my father for the money he lost in the crash, and I've been assured that our divorce settlement will leave me in an adequate financial state. I have no doubt that Lucas would provide if I were ever in need, though that's a position I don't plan to be in. I'm trying to live simply and to be self-sufficient. I'm a Type One employee; I don't wear a helmet. I want Olivia to see my eyes.

I don't think Michael knows about her yet. We communicate through lawyers. I don't know where he's currently living. The only friend I see is Penny from the vape bar. She offers to babysit, but I have nowhere to go that I can't bring Olivia. Instead, Penny and Sean take the train down and we walk along the water. Sean's a sweet kid. He's gentle with the baby. Sean and Penny sometimes dine with my father, Ellen, and me on Friday nights. We light the Shabbos candles, a new ritual that Ellen introduced. Sean knows all the blessings. He's not Jewish but has been to half a dozen bar mitzvahs.

I can't help thinking that Michael would do well as Olivia's father, that his parenting style would be energized and demonstrative and would complement my own. This is not something I would ever ask of Michael: to wet his head in the stream of my betrayal and suffer for Olivia's sake.

WIND SENDS SAND INTO OUR eyes. Olivia communicates her discomfort with a cry. I'm in love with her need. I feel useful. I lick my fingers and ever so gently wipe at the corners of her eyes. Her mouth forms an *O*. She makes a sound that is not prelingual so much as part of a distinct and communicative language. The sound is like, *Ga*. I unzip and free a breast from my customized breastfeeding model of The Suit™. The product can be customized for any number of conditions. This gives the consumer the illusion of control. I have no illusions.

The Suit™ notates the time and length of this feeding. When I zip back up, sensors in my built-in bra cup will measure the difference in the weight of my breast and use that data to assess the volume of milk I've dispensed, accurate to within an eighth of an ounce. What is done with this data, I can't be sure. Yesterday, I saw a piece online by someone whose Suit™ had detected a tumor. He'd had it removed before the cancer could spread.

The men to my left do their best to ignore me, but I catch them sneaking looks. My milk-filled breast is obscenely oversized. Olivia tooths down to make her claim. As if threatened, the female of the group stands from her towel and removes her jeans. She wears a bikini bottom beneath, the kind that ties on the sides, exposing her hips. She folds the jeans and lays them carefully in a tote bag, bending away from the men. She leaves her sweatshirt on. There is something of a tease in this ensemble, top half covered while her legs stand bare. Her legs are long and muscled. I imagine she's a runner, a former college athlete who does charity 10Ks twice a year. Or maybe a pole vaulter. I can picture her mid-vault, arcing over the bar. She walks toward the water. Her friends no longer look my way.

CIARAN IN THE BODEGA IS a bald, old Irishman with nose hairs long enough to be mistaken for a mustache. His grown children work the night shift. One, Timothy, goes to City College. A Type Two employee, he's saving to buy his girlfriend an engagement ring. The other, Ciaran Jr., is always in trouble: drugs, fights. He mocks his brother's helmet. Ciaran thinks he steals from the register. I don't doubt it; I've seen this son, a freckled lump of muscle. With me, Ciaran's style is somewhere between flirtation and paternal worry. The balance is right. I like listening to his stories, the local gossip. He knows everyone in the neighborhood, who they're screwing, what they owe the bank. I can't put faces to names but it doesn't matter. I find the smallness of life here refreshing, though maybe that's condescending. The store smells like cat litter.

"Wendy," Ciaran says. He was born in Galway, and still has the trace of an accent despite forty years in New York. This neighborhood used to be Irish, but Brooklyn's a free-for-all these days, a mad rush to beat the market.

"Large coffee, two cream," says Ciaran. I love the pride he takes in knowing my order. He often gives me small gifts: chocolates, hard candy, lollipops. I leave the gifts in a pile on my kitchen table. I kept the furniture that came with the apartment. Eventually I'll decorate. I don't plan to leave. I never eat the chocolates, but I like having them there.

I sit down on a high stool and hold Olivia in my lap. I drink the coffee as slowly as I can. I make a game of it, seeing how long I can pause between sips. I've traded my smartphone for an old-fashioned flip that doesn't have Wi-Fi. I feel more present this way, and the hours feel longer, which I like. Even at home on the laptop, I don't check my statistics. The knowledge that this freedom is a willful delusion doesn't make me feel any less free.

I eat a vegetable sandwich that includes the avocados Ciaran's begun to buy at my request. He sits next to me and makes faces at Olivia, who laughs. She's an easy audience. The skin on Ciaran's face is loose, as if he bought the wrong size shirt for his skull. He smells of cat shit. He tells me his wife always wanted a daughter. The ginger cat struts along the counter, one foot crossing over the other. It's unsanitary. I don't say anything. The cat likes Olivia and I sense the affection is mutual. I'm afraid of the cat, as I am of all animals. Olivia shows none of my fear.

"Look at her," says Ciaran. He points at the cat. "I took her to the vet for her yearly checkup, and the vet says that if Ginger were a human she might be a gymnast. Isn't that funny, a cat being a gymnast?"

I smile. Ginger sniffs around Olivia. Olivia laughs. Ciaran lets the cat lick an empty tin of tuna. He's gentle with the animal, stroking its fur in a way that reminds me of my mother brushing my hair before bed. Maybe the cat and I have ginger affinity. Sometimes I say Nina when I mean Olivia. She'll never know. I'm not sure to which *she* I refer.

THERE ARE PLENTY OF SEATS on the subway. That's one nice aspect of living this far out. I like to watch Olivia, imagine things from her perspective. I examine her features for signs of my own. People say she looks like me but I don't see it. I don't see Lucas either, though I'm always searching. Nina was my mother's name. Olivia's name belongs to no one. I imagine she's free of the burden of history, but each time we leave the insular paradise of our apartment I know this is not the case.

We switch at Fourteenth Street. The busker who's been here for decades is still singing the same Beatles songs over the same wrong chords and grinning. I find his smile upsetting: its width and consistency. I used to hate his voice, the way he reached for inaccessible notes. Now I think I'd miss him if he disappeared.

We wait a long time for a train. Someone's selling churros caked in powdered sugar. Olivia's face looks blotchy. I worry she's developing a rash. Two teenagers remind me of Ricky and Michael. They sit across from me on the train and I can't help staring. They're wearing shorts and their legs are hairless. They seem almost afraid of Olivia, as if looking might turn them back into babies themselves.

I DON'T GET OFF AT Fifty-Ninth. Something about the crowds outside Columbus Circle, the heat of exhaust pipes, manure from Central Park, people smoking outside the mall. Instead we ride up to Seventy-Second and walk south. There's a new storefront on West End, a bookstore. This is an interesting development. There hasn't been a nearby bookstore in years.

The new store was formerly a flower shop. I once went with my father to pick up roses for my mother. He bought her flowers every Friday. Only now I can't remember if the flowers we bought that day were for my mother or her grave.

The light inside the store is low. People must come here to hide. The store carries an impressive amount of small press books and poetry. I imagine it's a Columbia hangout, or maybe it's where writers come to browse after nearby sessions of psychoanalysis. I wonder if Michael still sees Dr. Becker. If so, he might be just down the block. He might walk into this store and see Olivia and me. This would happen in a movie. He wouldn't be mad. He'd tell me Olivia was beautiful, that I was beautiful.

It's a nice thing that this place exists. Bookstores are disappearing. Ever since they put Wi-Fi on subways, people read even less than they did before. But some people must; this store is testament with its posters advertising author events and its shelves of Staff Picks. The woman at the counter is reading Anne Sexton, studying the old sadness. It must seem ancient, absurdly unmedicated. She underlines in pencil.

I scan the fiction, not even looking for new novels. Instead I pull down books I own, or have previously owned. I often feel this urge to re-purchase, as if reading a new copy means I'll experience the book again for the first time.

The bookstore I'm in has a large children's section. I guess they must have to. People still buy books for kids as birthday gifts. A picture book on display is called *My Daddy Wears The Suit*™. Adult nonfiction has a number of titles on the subject as well. For or against, they're all cashing in.

A sign advertises weekday story time with a young guy who plays the French horn and has puppets. It would be nice to bring Olivia. She reaches for a stuffed monkey that sits in a basket with books about Curious George. The monkey and my daughter are the same size. I place the monkey in her stroller. Olivia rests her head on its chest.

I read aloud from a pop-up book about public transportation. So many of the books are New York–based. The store must traffic in tourists. Or maybe it's that children feel secure seeing familiar locations depicted in print, reassurance that the world is a solid and permanent place. I know Olivia doesn't understand what I'm saying, but it soothes me to read aloud, to trace my finger along the illustrations, wind the cranks and gears, push her fingers across the plush fabrics. As we're leaving, I skim the periodicals. I like the images on the covers of the style magazines, the fierce eyes of the models. These young women seem built for this world.

Olivia's hungry again and needs a change. I buy the Curious George book and an Edith Piaf postcard for Penny. Up close, I can see the clerk's tattoos. On her arm is a list of men's names. Each name has been crossed out. I relate to the sentiment. The crossing out can't erase the names, it can only obscure them. The names are still on her arm, reminders of moments in time and their obliteration. I imagine my own arm marked with *Michael*.

"What's her name?" asks the clerk.

"Olivia."

"A little blonde heartbreaker, huh?"

I say, "The hair is her father's."

MY FATHER ISN'T AT HIS apartment. He and Ellen drove to a farmer's market in Tarrytown this morning. They were supposed to be home by now. Maybe there's traffic. Tonight, I'll cook for the two of them with whatever they bring back. Lots of nice things are in season.

I've come around on Ellen. They seem happy. They're planning to buy a place in Brooklyn. I'll miss this old apartment. It's my main point of connection to my mother.

I open the windows and take off The Suit™. I've worked enough hours today. At first, I took care to hang the garment in the closet. Now I let it fall. I like to feel the air on my chest as Olivia feeds.

After, she quickly falls asleep. I cover myself with a light cotton blanket. The overhead fan circulates air. When my father and Ellen get home, we'll eat bread and olives at the kitchen table. They'll coo over Olivia and take pictures on their phones. Ellen will try to teach my father to post the pictures to Facebook for the hundredth time until he gets frustrated and she does it herself.

A soft sound comes from Olivia's mouth like the lowest setting on an air conditioner. Her ears wiggle. I hold a hand to her forehead. I hold a hand to my own.

On the floor sit the sealed boxes that contain my clothes and Michael's. There are ten boxes in all, a life in four square feet. Penny and I picked them up from storage last week. I haven't opened them yet, though I can't say why. I should bring this stuff to my own apartment. I should throw it all away.

There's a box cutter in my father's hardware drawer hiding

beneath Ziplocs filled with loose batteries and ancient screws and nails. The box cutter's handle is the orange of warning signs. I cut into the packing tape and brace for bedbug holocaust. I picture dozens of the insects crushed between skirts and T-shirts, more falling loose with each item removed.

Not so. Only my clothes are in the package, neatly folded. Michael's must be in another box. He shoved his in. I folded mine. I was preparing for this moment.

ACKNOWLEDGMENTS

THIS NOVEL'S VISION OF THE future was influenced by a many texts, most notably: *Rise of the Robots: Technology and the Threat of a Jobless Future* by Martin Ford; *Who Owns the Future?* by Jaron Lanier; *Eminem, Rap, Poetry, Race: Essays* edited by Scott Parker; *Whatever You Say I Am: The Life and Times of Eminem* by Anthony Bozza; *The Divide: American Injustice in the Age of the Wealth Gap* by Matt Taibbi; *Give People Money: How a Universal Basic Income Would End Poverty, Revolutionize Work, and Remake the World* by Annie Lowrey; and *Basic Income and How We Can Make It Happen* by Guy Standing.

I'm extraordinarily grateful to those whose editorial insights were integral to this book's completion. My agent, Erin Harris. My editor, Mark Doten. And my readers: Matthew Sharpe, Justin Taylor, and especially Robin Wasserman, who went above and beyond the call of duty.

"The Parentheses" first appeared, in slightly different form, in issue #1 of *Assignment Magazine*. Thanks to Benjamin Nugent for his astute suggestions and for coming up with the section's title.

Thanks to Aspen Words, the James Merrill Foundation, Arteles Creative Center, and everyone at Soho Press and Folio Literary Management.

Thanks to the Wilson and Rapp families for their unwavering support.

Thanks to my son, Julian Douglas Rapp Wilson, for the joy you've brought into my life.

This book is dedicated to my wife, Sarah Rapp, whose strength, patience, intelligence, and boundless love carried me through the long span of its creation.